Excalibur
The Second Horizon
Book 1

by

David F Shenton

Copyright Page & Legal Disclaimer

ISBN: 978-1-0673844-0-1

First Edition

Author's Note

This novel is a work of imagination. The scientific terms, technologies, and processes described within, such as *Adaptive Resonance Fields*, *Containment Units*, *Sensory Nodes*, and *Phase Detachment Protocol,* are fictional constructs created to serve the story.

References to real organizations, including NASA, are used solely for storytelling purposes. Their inclusion is fictional, and no endorsement or affiliation is intended.

The world you are about to enter blends real astrophysical principles with speculative invention. It is meant to inspire wonder, not to serve as a scientific manual.

Contents

Before Everything Changed

Recording sent to: Professor Roger G Fitzpatrick
William Jane University
Deep Space Communications
Estimated record time: 3 hours

She had just stepped into her university office when her assistant rushed in, breathless.

"Angela, I found something while clearing out your father's archives," he said, holding a printout. "It's an encrypted transmission addressed to him. The Deep Space Telescope Array reprocessed a batch of old data last night and flagged it as valid." He swallowed. "The timestamp says it arrived a month after he passed."

He hesitated, the page trembling slightly between his fingers. "And Angela... it didn't come from Earth."

She froze mid-step, her pulse stuttering. "That was over three years ago."

"Back then, we didn't have the tools to decode it. The message only resurfaced after the Array's new algorithms reprocessed the old data."

Angela's eyes settled on the photo of her father in his worn flight jacket, smiling beside that sun-bleached Nevada hangar. A familiar ache tightened in her chest.

A surge of urgency pushed her into motion.

Minutes later, a handful of trusted colleagues gathered in the dim briefing room. The overhead lights faded, and the wall displays flickered to life, washing their faces in a pale blue glow. No one spoke; anticipation hung thick in the air.

Angela opened her laptop. A quick check of her calendar showed nothing urgent. She hovered over the newly restored folder the DSTA had forwarded: *Legacy Comms*. Her fingers shook as she typed in her father's old password.

The playback began. She expected distortion, alien noise, the usual chaos of deep-space signals. Instead, a voice in perfect English, calm and deliberate. Her eyes widened. Her heart thudded. This wasn't random. This was the start of something.

***

"Hi there. My name is Stuart Thompson, and as wild as it sounds, I'm about to celebrate my birthday on this planet... and I say that without trying to be clever. You'll understand why soon enough because if you're seeing this, the story has already begun. What I'm about to share might stretch the bounds of disbelief. But stay with me... I'll walk you through it. I could tell this like a bright-eyed kid. But that version wouldn't do it justice. So, I'm borrowing the voice I had when it all made sense: the version of me that was grumpy, blunt, and unfiltered." They could hear Stuart chuckle in the background.

"Let me start at the beginning, because otherwise none of this will seem as simple as it once did."

For the past fifteen years, life had been quiet. I'd settled into a retirement home tucked away just outside a little town where folks knew each other's dogs by name, and where breakfast orders didn't need repeating. This was the kind of place where routine wrapped itself around you like a familiar blanket.

That morning felt like any other. I was in the lounge, locked in a tense chess match with Frank. He had me cornered with his queen and a pawn, and I was pretending not to notice. Frank was one of our livelier residents, the kind who grinned like he knew more than he let on. We jokingly called ourselves "inmates," half because of the locked doors and half because of the sameness that stitched our days together. Then again, those doors did a decent job of keeping a few of the more adventurous wanderers from taking off with the bingo cart.

Frank wore that trademark smirk like a second skin. Crooked and knowing, the kind that made you wonder what he'd just gotten away with. It was his tell, really.

Every time we played, that smirk would creep in just before he made a move. I never told him I'd figured it out. Letting him think he had the upper hand was part of the game. Why ruin the fun?

That battered silver flask of his made regular appearances too, tucked away under his jacket as if it were a covert operation. He thought it was a secret. It wasn't. The thing had more dents than a shopping cart in a windy parking lot, and it clinked every time he leaned back in his chair.

Classic Frank.

I remember one game night when he slid the flask over with a wink, as if it were treasure. The whiskey tasted like regret and bad decisions, but we laughed anyway. That was the point. Our games weren't about winning. They were about the banter, the borrowed time, and the kind of silence that felt like an inside joke. Frank's smirk and that flask were part of the scenery. Like the creaky chairs, the half-shuffled deck, and the way the night always ended too soon.

I remember hearing a door open beside me. I barely looked up until she spoke, Ann. She was in her late 30s, with kind eyes. She wore a subtle fragrance that reminded me of garden mornings and open windows. Her English accent had a softness that made bad news sound like bedtime stories.

"Stuart, would you mind coming with me to the director's office? There's something important he'd like to discuss."

I thought, "Crap, what now?" and pushed myself upright, hips groaning with every inch. My knee popped loudly enough to make Frank wince. I masked the wince before she could see it.

We walked down the hallway. Everything was just as always. The sterile hum of too-clean air, fluorescent lights buzzing like distant bees overhead. The sound of the linoleum as it clicked beneath our feet.

Ann didn't rush. She never did. Her steps were measured, as if she were counting them. Maybe she was. She had that kind of mind. It was quiet, precise, always two moves ahead. I'd say to her that she could run the whole damn place blindfolded. She'd just smile, as though she'd heard it a hundred times and knew it was true every single time.

I tried not to wonder, but of course, I did. Talks with the director weren't usually the kind that ended with cake and congratulations.

"Almost there," she said, as if we were heading to a picnic and not the director's office. That was Ann; she could make a summons sound like an invitation. If I had half her grace, I'd be a saint. But I don't. I'm just an old relic with a limp and a short fuse.

We reached the office; it always felt colder there, like authority came with a thermostat set to "intimidate." Ann opened the door, giving me a gentle nudge with her eyes.

Inside, everything looked surgically neat. The polished desk flowed into perfectly lined folders and shelves untouched by dust for years. A room that said, I run things here; as if the decor was part of his job title.

The director sat hunched behind his desk, swallowed by furniture that looked like it belonged to someone much taller, much more confident. I pegged him at maybe his early thirties, though the thinning hair and deep worry lines aged him up, as if time had worked him over harder than the years should allow. The poor bastard looked like he'd aged a decade trying to play boss. I've seen paperweights with more backbone.

His posture was rigid. Every movement seemed calculated, like his mind were juggling a dozen worst-case scenarios at once. Probably worried I'd say something "inappropriate." Hell, I might. Depends on how much crap he tries to feed me.

I never warmed up to the guy. He kept a polite distance, the sort that said, *I'll ask how you're doing, but I don't really want to hear the answer.*

The interactions felt scripted, as though we were nothing more than entries in his budget instead of people carrying histories, heartbreaks, and whole lives behind our eyes. I always figured he saw us veterans more as statistics than souls, proof of funding well spent. If I dropped dead tomorrow, he'd probably file it under "cost savings."

Ann guided me to the chair across from him, placing her hand gently on my shoulder before stepping back. I sat slowly, not because I was nervous. Hell no. These damn joints don't move like they used to.

He cleared his throat. "Mr. Thomson, thank you for coming."

I snorted. "Didn't exactly have a choice, did I?"

Ann gave me a soft glance. Not scolding, just that quiet reminder that she was still in the room. I respected her enough to dial it back a little.

I eyed the director, trying to make sense of his expression. He didn't look angry. Not exactly worried either. But there was something. The room went quiet. Heavy. That kind of silence doesn't just happen; it builds itself and grows roots. I didn't get a knot in my stomach; I'm not some green recruit waiting for orders. I've stared down flak cannons and bureaucrats alike. This was just another suit with a clipboard.

Still, I knew something was coming. And whatever it was... it wasn't good.

***

I need to pause and share something I've kept tucked away for a long time. My journey began on an airfield in England as a rookie pilot in World War II, back when the world was on fire and boys like me were tossed into cockpits with barely enough training to spell "altitude." I was young, dumb, and airborne. The training was hell. The tension was constant... and the noise? It lived in your bones. But somehow, in the heart of that storm, I stumbled upon something extraordinary... the simple, breathtaking freedom of flight.

Years later, serving in the Navy, I found myself once again carving through the skies, this time over Korea, and later the Falklands. Every mission carried risk, sometimes more than we let on. But that feeling never left me. That rare kind of peace that found you between radio chatter and the hunt for enemy silhouettes.

I used to steal moments, just seconds sometimes, where everything went quiet. No wars to fight, no politics, just the open sky and the steady hum of the engine. It was in those fleeting instants that I felt most alive.

It wasn't just flying; it was a kind of art, and at those heights, freedom felt like something I could touch.

***

"Anyway, before I drift too far into the past..."

My disconnect with the director wasn't just professional; it ran deeper, personal even. His weekly briefings were the worst part of the routine. Slow, syrupy monologues delivered like bedtime stories, as if we were children who couldn't handle plain facts.

I'd seen war. I'd buried friends. I'd waded through more red tape than most people could stomach in a lifetime. Apparently, I needed a babysitter. At least, that's how he made it sound, and it was beyond insulting. The way he talked, his careful words, just grated. It was as if he saw our minds as soft clay, fragile, impressionable, and assumed it was his role to shape our path. It was unbearable.

And me? I've never sugar-coated anything. I said what needed to be said, no matter who was listening. I made it clear I didn't think much of him or his clipboard kingdom. Maybe that rubbed him the wrong way. So what? I've earned the right to speak my mind, and I'll be damned if I start biting my tongue now.

That morning, though, he skipped the usual pleasantries. No fake smile. No, "How are you feeling today, Stuart?"

The director pressed his lips together, clearly deciding not to rise to the bait. "There's been a directive from head office. It concerns your placement."

"Placement," I repeated, dragging the word out like it tasted sour. "You mean they're shipping me off."

"It's not like that," he said, voice tight. "It's a transfer to a facility better suited to your needs."

"My needs?" I leaned forward, elbows on the desk. "You ever flown through flak so thick it looked like the sky was bleeding? Have you ever watched your wingman vanish in a puff of smoke and metal? No? Then don't talk to me about my needs."

Ann stepped in gently. "Stuart, maybe just hear him out."

I turned to her. "I'm listening, Ann. I just don't like fairy tales dressed up as policy."

The director slid the envelope across the desk. "It's all in here. Transports arranged. You leave in two days."

The envelope was thick. Too thick. I felt the weight before I even opened it and read it twice. Each word sat heavily the second time around. The tone wasn't angry or urgent; it was calm. Too calm. Like they'd rehearsed the phrasing to soften the blow. "No cause for alarm," they said. "For your benefit." That kind of language only pissed me off more.

Then I saw the seal at the bottom. The same insignia that used to mean honour, service, and pride. Now, it felt like a stamp of redirection, a symbol nudging me toward something unknown.

Truth? My first instinct? Tell them where to shove it. Loudly. But then... curiosity crept in. What was this place? A reward? A cage? Something in between? Didn't matter. They were footing the bill, and that meant I was going, whether I liked it or not.

Ann stepped a little closer, her voice barely above a whisper. "Stuart, I know this isn't easy. But maybe it's not all bad. You might find something good there."

For a second, the anger in me eased. "If you weren't the one saying that, I'd tell you to shove it too."

She smiled faintly. "I know."

And so, two days later, I stood at the entrance of the old home, suitcase in hand, and that damn letter tucked in the side pocket. The morning air smelled of fresh-cut grass. I turned to say goodbye.

Frank was there, grinning like he already knew something I didn't.

"Don't let 'em stick you with the decaf," he said, the same line he used every morning at breakfast.

He slipped his flask into my hand without a word. That gesture said more than speeches ever could.

Ann wrapped me in a hug that lingered longer than usual. She kissed my cheek gently, stepped back, and watched as I walked away.

I didn't know exactly what awaited me on the other side. But I knew I wasn't facing it alone. I didn't know what I was stepping into.

But I wasn't the only one. The letter said there'd be others. That was enough to keep me moving.

Even after everything with the director, I couldn't pretend the goodbye didn't sting. The people who stood by me made that place feel like more than just walls and schedules. It was home in ways I hadn't expected. Leaving them pulled at something deep inside.

I made my way down the steps for the last time. Each step felt weighted, not just with the luggage in my hand, but with years of laughter, routine, and quiet understanding. Every footfall echoed softly, like the past reaching up to remind me what I was walking away from.

The garden was quiet, brushed with morning light. I'd spent countless hours out there, losing track of time in old conversations and slow afternoons. My gaze drifted to the lounge windows, the ones that had framed so many changing seasons. It all felt alive with meaning, as if the place itself knew I was leaving.

The car arrived sleek, polished, rolling to the curb without a sound. Too formal for my taste, but fitting, I suppose. The driver climbed out, crisp uniform and all. He didn't speak, just gave a small nod and opened the door with the kind of calm you couldn't fake. My bags disappeared into the trunk like clockwork.

I stood there for another second. Just long enough to feel the pull of it all, the comfort of what I'm leaving behind, and the quiet ache of stepping into whatever comes next.

As the car pulled away, I glanced back. The home blurred in the sunlight, shrinking behind us. I lifted my hand. Not a wave, exactly. More like a small salute to everything I was leaving behind.

Inside, I was a mess of grief and hope, with just enough curiosity flickering to keep me from turning back. I wasn't sure what the next chapter would bring. But whatever it was, I was ready to meet it head-on.

***

"Have you ever contemplated what you might do if given the chance to relive your life? Would you choose the same path, make the same sacrifices, chase the same dreams? I've wrestled with that question more times than I can count, usually around 2 a.m., staring at the ceiling and wondering if I should've just opened that bakery."

"But now I find myself uniquely positioned to answer it. Because here's the kicker. I'm about to celebrate my 89th birthday and fight in a freaking space war. With a bunch of retirees around my age alongside aliens. Crazy, right? But somehow... I'm flying a damn spaceship."

Angela didn't say a word when the message paused. She just stared at the screen, trying to wrap her head around what she'd heard. He's fighting in a war, flying a spaceship with others just as old. It was so outlandish she almost waited for him to laugh and admit it was a joke. But the tone in his voice wasn't joking. And that was what unsettled her most. She found herself wondering how a man that age could do any of it, or how he was even still alive to say it.

Battle for Helia

While empires clashed and revolutions brewed across Earth in the mid-1800s, far beyond its reach, another reckoning stirred.
Across the galaxy, the Venorans faced a truth no history book would record. Most civilisations looked the other way, unwilling to be pulled into a war they didn't ask for. But few listened...

Personal account: Stuart Thomson – Venoran War Department

I should warn you: what follows isn't just history. It's drawn from transmissions received by the Venoran War Department and the last defenders of Helia; it becomes a story told in fragments... diplomacy, desperation, and the quiet defiance of a people who refused to vanish. These are not just a set of facts. It's a story of desperate calls for help. Of bold diplomacy and quiet resilience. Of a people staring down extinction and choosing to reach out across the stars, hoping someone, somewhere, would care.

***

"To understand what came next, we must return to the moment when Venor was still a myth. Centuries before, cloaked and silent, it stood at the galaxy's edge; unseen, untouched, exactly as its people intended."

Isolation wasn't fear; it was a choice. The Venorans were an ancient civilisation built on knowledge, explorers by nature, travelling the galaxy in search of discovery, not conquest. They had watched empires rise and collapse, always choosing silence over spectacle, distance over diplomacy. But silence never holds forever. A chance encounter shattered it. The Korrathi hadn't been searching for Venoran technology, or the Venorans themselves. Their fleets drifted through the outer systems like deep-water predators. They looked for the usual signs of life and advancement, hunting for energy surges, stray data streams, or the unmistakable heartbeat of progress. Venor gave them none.

For centuries, the Venorans had hidden their advancement behind ritual, myth, and silence. No broadcasts. No beacons. They integrated their technology into nature, making it indistinguishable from the terrain unless you knew where to look.

The Korrathi hadn't noticed Helia. Not at first.

Then came the anomaly a long-range Korrathi probe had intercepted a signal it was never meant to find, a gravitational signature far too precise to be natural. The anomaly changed everything. What began as a passive scan became a deliberate manoeuvre.

Deep beneath Venor's surface, the command centre stirred; monitors flaring to life, officers bracing for what they'd long feared.

Korrin leaned over the console. He spoke in a low voice. "Korrathi fleet is repositioning. They're not moving on. Their probe must have confirmed a detection. They're aligning with Helia."

Elta cursed under her breath. "They're afraid."

"Afraid of us?" Korrin was surprised.

"Of what we represent." She tapped the display, pulling up the old Venoran archive. A map of hidden outposts, cloaked research stations, and silent orbital arrays. "We have stayed quiet for too long. They thought we were primitive. Now they see the truth."

Korrin replied, voice tight with anger. "They'll purge us." He let the words hang heavy and final.

"They'll try," Elta said.

The Korrathi doctrine had no room for anomalies. No tolerance for civilisations that slipped past their filters.

The people of Venor had accomplished more than just surviving; they had evolved in secret. And now exposed, it stood as proof that the Korrathi weren't infallible.

Elta turned to Korrin. Her voice remained calm, but the room felt colder.

"Send the signal. All worlds. No more hiding."

Thrown into a conflict they never sought, the Venorans now battled to defend not only their homeland, but every colony, every distant outpost, every fragile thread of Venoran existence scattered throughout the galaxy. Venor had become the strategic nerve centre of the resistance.

As the galaxy shifted, so did Venor. Beneath its surface, the command centre became more than a bunker; it was the pulse of a scattered people. And at its heart stood Elta, not just a leader, but the quiet force holding the web together. It wasn't just a war room; it was the nerve centre of a defence network stretched across star systems.

This is where tactics came to life, where fleets shifted in real time, and where planetary shields were adjusted with precision. The colonised moons and terraformed worlds, each one vulnerable yet vital, looked to Venor for guidance and support.

Inside the command centre, the mood remained focused. Officers moved with quiet determination, watching holographic maps that hovered in the air, casting soft glows across tired faces. Red and amber alerts blinked steadily, each one a flare from a world under siege, each one a reminder that the fight was far from over.

Quadrant Leader Elta was at the heart of everything.

Elta didn't bark orders or pace the room. Her eyes swept across the displays, absorbing the chaos with a calm that didn't come from indifference; it came from experience. Years of it. The kind that teaches when to act, when to wait, and when to trust your gut, even when the numbers say otherwise.

"Vector shift on Axis-9," someone called out. "Two more cruisers are breaching the perimeter."

Elta didn't look up. "Redirect the outer sentries. Delay, don't engage."

"But if they push?"

"They won't," she insisted, voice low but certain. "Not yet."

Each order spun another thread in the fragile web holding the Venoran worlds together.

Venor wasn't under attack. Not yet, in the future, maybe. But every decision made in that command centre echoed across the Venoran homeworld.

Lieutenant Korrin adjusted his stance. "Families are evacuating from the southern ridge. Do we redirect the transports?"

Elta's gaze flicked from the casualty projections to the transport grid. "No. Keep the corridor open. If we close it now, we lose the ridge."

Korrin hesitated. "Understood."

She knew what was at stake. If Venor fell, other worlds would follow.

"Patch me through to Helia," Elta said, her voice steady. The words weren't a suggestion; they were orders, already rippling through the command centre. "We hold our position for now."

Across the Venoran worlds, from the icy ridges of Planet Teyra to the storm-wracked skies of the moon of Balon, their resistance stirred. Powerful energy weapons readied. Shield arrays hummed awake. A scattered people, united by necessity, braced themselves.

Inside the tactical command centre, the pressure hung thick in the air. It wrapped itself around every surface, every breath. Elta moved in slow, deliberate circles, boots whispering against the steel flooring. Her pacing wasn't idle; it was methodical and controlled. The only outlet for nerves she couldn't afford to voice.

Around her, holographic displays pulsed and shimmered. Enemy formations shifted, unfolding across space in jagged, synchronised waves. Heat signatures bloomed from around the Kurosian belt.

The Belt had always been the system's uneasy frontier, a vast, uneven arc of shattered moons and metallic debris drifting along Venor's outer orbit like a scar from some ancient collision. Its mineral-rich fields warped long-range scans, turning sensor sweeps into static-laced guesses, and every fleet entering the system had to emerge from FTL somewhere along its fractured length. It was both a shield and a threat. A natural choke point where ships could mask their approach behind drifting iron-heavy asteroids, and where danger always appeared first.

She paused at the console, fingers resting lightly on its edge, eyes scanning the feeds with a soldier's precision. No one spoke. They didn't need to. Her crew understood the silence, the weight of it, when even words felt too heavy to carry.

Then the signal hit. Sharp, urgent. Slicing through the room's static.

The voice was unmistakable; it was Administrator Lielon's from Helia.

"The Korrathi have landed," he said, breathless. "Assault teams are hitting weak points in our defence shield. Their warships are concentrating fire on a single sector. We've rerouted emergency power, but simulations give us five cycles. After that... we're exposed."

Elta's hands gripped the edge of the console, knuckles bone-white. Sweat traced a line down her temple, unnoticed. The data streaming across the monitors confirmed what his voice already carried... Helia was in trouble.

Static swallowed the transmission before he could finish.

Silence settled across the room like ash. Helia's message had been received.

"Quadrant Leader Elta, the Korrathi have deployed an interference field in orbit around the planet! They've shut down every outbound signal!"

The young officer's voice trembled with unease, but Elta remained still, calculating. She knew the enemy's strategy well... isolate, destabilise, and overrun.

Her mind raced. If Helia fell, the entire sector would be next. She turned sharply.

"Get me a tactical scan of the Korrathi fleet movements. Prepare countermeasures. Damn it," Elta muttered, slamming her fist on the desk. "We need a way to break that interference field. What's the status of their defence shield?"

"The Korrathi ground assault units have weakened the defence shield in critical sectors. They're becoming increasingly vulnerable to further attacks," the officer reported, urgency tightening his voice.

Elta's heart hammered as she fired off commands, her voice barely rising above the static and comms chatter. The air in the control room felt heavy, as another crack formed in their defence.

The Korrathi were moving fast.

A light-year away, the war wasn't theoretical; it was immediate, tactile. Alarms screamed, shields flickered, and Administrator Lielon fought to hold the line. Leaning over his console, his voice cut through the chaos. "Redirect power to sector three's shield generator, now! Get me real-time telemetry on the eastern approach. If there's even a flicker in that barrier, I want to know. This is no time to second-guess."

A young technician nodded, fingers flying across the interface. "Sir, we've lost primary support in the north quadrant. Rerouting backup capacitors, stand by."

Lielon didn't flinch. "Good. Keep it moving. I need that perimeter sealed."

Beyond the command centre, beneath the shimmering dome of Helia's planetary shield, Venoran soldiers braced themselves. Shockwaves rippled through the ground as Korrathi pulse weapons struck with mechanical precision, each blast sending jagged waves across the energy field. It flickered, stretched, held... but only just.

Every repelled strike came at a cost. The defences sagged, thinner and more brittle, like a wall patched too many times.

Lielon's shout tore through the noise, roughened by exhaustion and urgency. "Hold the line! Reinforce the western sector now!"

Outside, the air felt tight enough to snap. Each breath came out in thin clouds as the defenders pressed themselves low, eyes darting from shadow to shadow, waiting for whatever would break first. Silence or the enemy. The enemy pressed harder now, closer, louder, relentless.

The sky dimmed as Korrathi warships descended like vultures, casting long, predatory shadows that spread across Helia's buildings and landing fields.
Their numbers were staggering, an armada that made resistance feel like a whisper against a scream.

Back in the command centre, Lielon scanned the monitors at the unfolding chaos. His mind raced, assembling responses even as new problems surged across the screen. Officers called out positions, shield data, troop movements, all threads into a desperate strategy.

"Reroute additional power to the generators," he snapped. "Activate anti-ship systems immediately. We won't get another shot."

Outside, the Venoran fighters gave everything they had, and then more. Sweat soaked into scorched uniforms as they raced to reinforce the battered shield, hands moving on instinct while artillery lit the sky behind them. There was no pause, or relief, only the desperate push to hold the enemy back long enough to survive the next wave.

They hurled everything they had at the Korrathi, beams of energy lighting up the sky. For every Korrathi ship that fell, another moved in to take its place.

The air was thick with the stench of burnt metal and lubricant. Shockwaves hammered the ground, kicking up dirt in violent bursts.

The shield above flickered and gasped, its rhythm faltering like a dying heartbeat. Every blast chipped away at its stability. Its glow fading and flaring as the Korrathi weapons hammered the surface relentlessly.

Then came the voice. “Administrator Lielon, we’re losing power on the east side!”

Lielon didn’t hesitate. He leaned over the console, fingers moving across the controls like second nature. His voice cut through the surrounding chaos.

“Pull energy from the secondary generator; do it now!”

Above, the clouds churned. Shadows stretched long and slow across Helia’s rooftops; then the warship emerged. Massive and silent. Its hull parted the clouds as it moved through the sky with predatory ease. Cannons rotated, locking in slow, deliberate arcs toward the heart of the settlement.

For a single breath, everything on the battlefield seemed to stop. Everyone watching knew what came next. That ship wasn't just firepower; it was finality. If it got through, Helia wouldn’t stand a chance.

Lielon didn’t wait. His voice cracked through the comms like a whip. “All units, concentrate fire on that ship!”

The battlefield erupted into motion as Venoran turrets roared awake, firing rapid streams of energy at the massive warship overhead. Soldiers sprinted across the charred ground, weapons raised, scanning for even the smallest flaw in the Korrathi armor. Above them, fighter units sliced through the smoke-choked sky, releasing volley after volley into tight formations of enemy support craft.

The Korrathi ship never slowed. Its retaliation came instantly, sending blinding energy pulses slamming into the shield, each strike sending shockwaves rippling across the barrier's surface.

The ground trembled beneath Helia, deep, rolling vibrations that reached through concrete and bone. In the command centre, warning lights flared red, blinking in a relentless rhythm. Every display screamed the same message. That they were out of time.

Lielon stood frozen for a beat, the tension building in his body.

The shield, once a symbol of strength and certainty, now faltered before his eyes. Its glow, usually sharp and defiant, wavered. It pulsed erratically, flickering in and out.

Without looking up, he knew everyone in that room felt it too. What once protected Helia had become a question mark. For one breathless moment, it looked as if it would fail. The Venorans braced, knowing exactly what that meant, but they weren't finished.

In control rooms across the settlement, technicians threw themselves into the work. Sweaty palms slid across consoles as they rerouted power, fingers flying through emergency protocols. Shouts echoed, data spilled across screens, and through the chaos, a thread of focus held. Finally, a power surge.

Just before the breaking point, the shield stabilised. Its glow sharpened, humming back to life. It held.

Lielon let out a breath he hadn't realised he was holding. For now, they'd stopped the bleeding.

The shield held firm, yet the alarms sounded a persistent, urgent warning. The siege hadn't ended; it had only shifted into its next phase. Inside the command centre, Lielon stood rigid. On a nearby console, his gaze locked on the distorted readings crowding the screen.

A tense voice broke through the chaos.

"Administrator, we can break their interference signal using a counter-frequency with quantum resonance disruptors. We can reestablish contact with Venor."

Lielon's pulse quickened. "Move! Get them in place!" His voice cracked with urgency, every word tight with desperation.

Venoran engineers rushed forward, hauling the quantum disruptors into position along the perimeter. As each device powered up, a low vibration rolled through the air, spreading outward in soft, widening waves. The energy field collided with the Korrathi interference signal, stripping its strength bit by bit until finally the comms crackled to life.

Then, through the static, Elta's voice. Familiar. Grounding. "Administrator Lielon, we're through! What is your status?" Elta's words carried concern, but beneath them, an unmistakable resolve.

Lielon exhaled, the weight of survival pressing against his ribs. "Helia's defences are holding," he said, "but barely." His eyes flicked to the live battlefield feed flashing across the monitors. "Korrathi ground forces have established positions around our shield perimeter and are exploiting weak points with sustained, concentrated fire. Our defense teams are reinforcing at maximum speed."

He exhaled, the weight of the battle pressing down on him, suffocating with its relentless intensity.

"Their warships are targeting a single point on the shield; it's flickering. We have redirected all available power, but our simulations indicate we have only a few more cycles before integrity fails."

From Venor, Elta listened to the distant echoes of battle bleeding through the transmission. Machinery hummed, the distant tremors of explosions shaking the foundation of Helia itself.

At that moment, Lielon's report came through, edged with triumph. "We've countered their interference signal using quantum resonance disruptors."

Elta didn't hesitate. "Understood. Our defence fleet will be arriving soon. Hold your position and get ready for reinforcements."

Even as the order rang out, the Korrathi warship hammered the shield again and again, each impact dimming the barrier's glow. It wouldn't hold much longer. Time was slipping away.

In a surprise attack, a squadron of Venoran fighters launched, streaking through the battlefield, weaving between enemy fire with sharp precision. Their target: the Korrathi warship's weak points.

"Target lock confirmed," came the voice of the squadron leader over comms. "Engaging primary thruster junctions."

"Stagger formation," Elta's voice cut through the channel, calm and clipped. "No heroics. Hit and vanish."

The sky ignited as explosions rippled across the warship's hull. Metal groaned, systems faltered, and for the first time since the attack began, the Korrathi vessel shuddered.

Inside the command centre, the hum of machinery merged with the frantic chatter of officers relaying tactical updates. The dim glow of holo-displays bathed the room in an eerie blue, casting long shadows against the steel walls.

"Direct hits on the lower stabilisers," one officer called out. "They're losing altitude!"

The warship's advance faltered. Fire bloomed from its undercarriage, and its descent steepened, plummeting toward the mountain range outside the city.

The explosion lit up the sky in a flash of blinding white. A sonic roar cracking the air like thunder made flesh. The ground shuddered. Buildings shuddered. Troops halted where they stood, heads whipping upward, eyes widening as the shockwave washed over them like a breaking wave. For a single, suspended heartbeat, everything stopped.

Inside the Korrathi command vessel, the lead strategist didn't move. His gaze stayed fixed on the tactical display, jaw tightening as new data flashed across it.

"Helia's shield is failing. Continue pressure on the eastern flank. No deviation."

"They've downed one of ours," a subordinate muttered.

"Irrelevant. Their resistance is reactive. We are inevitable."

Inside the Helia command centre, Lielon's grip tightened on the console, watching the warship shudder, its structure buckling inward like a wounded animal.

"The Korrathi warship is falling," Korrin said.

A cheer erupted from one of the control crews; brief, raw, full of adrenaline.

Lielon allowed the smallest flicker of relief to crack through his expression.

"Confirm damage," he said calmly, his voice much steadier now. "I want eyes on that wreckage."

The squadron leader's fighter arced through the chaos, engines carving scorched ribbons across the sky. In the cockpit, his breathing was steady. "Target neutralised," he reported, voice steady. "Their secondary core is in meltdown. Structural integrity is failing." On every battlefield monitor, the tide began to turn.

Relentless fire twisted the Korrathi warship until its spine snapped with the sound of a mountain crumbling. The core gave a final, erratic throb before erupting into a violent flare, casting embers of hull plating into the deep silence of the void. Below, the battlefield exhaled; a brief, collective breath before the fury returned.

Inside the Korrathi ground command unit, a veteran officer watched the collapse unfold. "They fight like cornered beasts," he barked.

"Then we cage them," replied his second-in-command.

"No. We learn from them." Replied the veteran officer. "or we repeat this war with different names."

The Venoran forces continued to push forward with a ferocity that came not just from discipline, but from defiance. Boots stomped over scorched earth, through the remnants of earlier strikes. Turrets lit up the horizon. Ground squads moved in tight formation, their gunfire synchronised like second nature. Above them, fighters danced between wreckage and missile trails, each manoeuvre daring and precise.

A third Korrathi ship tried to regroup, limping through the chaos. Its hull blinked with systems dying; its confidence bled out through sparks and smoke. It wasn't a threat anymore; it was already a memory trying to hold shape.

In Helia's command centre, Lielon felt it. A shift. "We've got them!" His voice thundered through the comms. "All units, full barrage!"

The remaining Helia ships responded like a single entity. Engines roared. Missiles locked. Every shot was an answer to every moment Helia had been outgunned.

Monitors inside the command centre flared with data. Voices rose with urgency.

"Now's the time!" an officer shouted.

Lielon didn't blink. "Break their line."

The Venoran formation surged. Cracks opened across the Korrathi ranks; their confidence had finally shattered.

Inside the Korrathi command vessel, alarms pulsed. A synthetic voice echoed through the chamber. "Probability of collapse: 92%. Recommend withdrawal."

The strategist's jaw clenched. "Initiate slide retreat. Mark Helia for orbital cleansing with the full fleet in five cycles. No survivors."

Then, the shadows stretched across the battlefield as the Venoran warships broke from Slide Space. They weren't elegant or polished, just massive, steady shapes that meant survival. For the people on the ground, it wasn't awe or spectacle they felt first. It was a relief. Their ships had finally arrived.

The Venoran guns opened up the moment they cleared Slide Space. Their volleys were sharp and controlled, cutting clean lines through the Korrathi formation. The first shots shattered the lead ships' shields, forcing the Korrathi line to stagger and break apart. A second barrage followed... heavier, more deliberate, turning the sky into a wall of light and concussion. For those watching from below, the sudden precision felt unreal after so many hours of desperate, uneven fighting.

The Korrathi ships came apart slowly, almost unwillingly. Their cores dimmed, their frames sagged, and then they simply gave out. Systems failed, hulls buckled, and whole sections folded inward under their own weight. It looked less like a dramatic defeat and more like machines finally pushed past their limits. One by one, they came apart and fell away.

Helia was scorched. But still standing. Smoke curled from shattered rooftops. Bodies lay still among the wreckage.

The Venoran commanders gathered themselves, their breath ragged and bodies aching, their focus snapped back to the battlefield. The war wasn't done, not yet. The Korrathi ground forces were still pressing.

Lielon leaned into the console, voice sharp and steady. "Target their ground units. Don't let them breach the perimeter." His command cut through the comms like a lifeline, snapping every soldier back into motion.

Outside, war raged on. Flashes of blue and green lit up the field, not artful, not beautiful, but wild and violent, as if the sky itself were ripping apart.

Venoran troops pressed forward, their armour scuffed and scorched, their movements driven less by strength and more by pure determination. The Korrathi line began to falter, just slightly at first.

Then, all at once, formations buckled. Warriors stumbled, confused, splintering like glass under pressure.

"They're falling back!" someone yelled over the comms, breathless with disbelief, "retreating!"

What followed was a rush, a flood of Venoran fighters advancing, chasing down stragglers, locking down the battlefield as though they'd waited their whole lives for this exact moment. The Korrathi troops scrambled toward their landing craft, retreating into rising clouds of smoke and streaks of flame. In the sky, their vessels peeled away, engines flaring as they vanished into Slide Space, leaving behind the wreckage of defeat.

Inside Helia's command centre, no one cheered.

Lielon stood rigid, the tension still coiled inside him like wire. Victory felt brittle.

Then the speakers crackled.

The High Council's voice rolled through the room, firm, final. "We believe the Korrathi will return. While Helia braced for evacuation, Venor prepared for something else entirely. On Venor, the High Council had summoned their fleet captains. The Helia outpost must be destroyed. Leave nothing behind."

The words landed like a punch to the gut.

Lielon's hands curled around the console until his knuckles went white. Destroy everything? The gardens, the libraries, the places where laughter once echoed. All of it, scorched deliberately. And yet, he understood why.

The Korrathi couldn't be allowed a second chance, not here. Not with Helia. The cost of sentiment could be extinction.

Meanwhile, on Venor, the High Council had summoned their fleet captains. Inside the cavernous chamber, elders in ceremonial robes stood motionless around a glowing map of the galaxy. The room hummed with quiet tension... no debate, only contemplation.

War demanded decisions, but not all of them made peace with the soul.

Silence settled over the room, not out of surprise, but with the growing unease that gripped them all. Those gathered knew the elder's coming words weren't just going to be about strategy. They were at a turning point. He took another step forward, eyes scanning the faces before him. Captains. Historians. Survivors. Each one carried the scars from the last battle, some visible, some buried.

"We've survived," he said softly. "But survival alone won't carry us through what comes next." No one moved. "We will reach out for help," the elder continued. "To those who've watched from afar. To those who share our fears, even if they've never said it aloud. We'll offer what we've never offered before... our trust. We will seek alliances with other races to share certain technologies." Murmurs quickly spread around the room.

"To stand together," his voice gathering weight, "we must be willing to be known." The elder stepped back, allowing the silence to return, this time filled with resolve.

Among seasoned fleet captains, the idea carried weight. Sharing technology, once guarded like sacred relics, was more than diplomacy.

It was trust. Vulnerability. A signal that Venor was ready to stand shoulder-to-shoulder with others.

"We'll reach out," the elder continued. "Slide Space coordinates will be assigned. Planets with potential, strategic, yes, but more than that. Places where bonds might form, where alliances might take root." He paused. Not for effect, but out of respect, for what came next.

"Go there, speak to them. Not just with your titles, but with your honesty. Show them who we are. Show them why it matters."

Murmurs rolled through the chamber, not of dissent, but of quiet agreement. The silence that followed wasn't hesitation; it was resolve.

The captains nodded, the weight of centuries resting on their shoulders, and now, something heavier still. They had weathered too many battles, carried too many names in their memories, to ever consider stepping back now. Whatever waited beyond the next horizon, they would face it side by side, not as scattered commanders, but as one force, bound by everything they'd survived and everything they still refused to lose.

Return to Earth

Personal account: Gall

"It's been more than a century and a half since the High Council set this whole plan in motion, sending ships to every system we knew, hoping someone, somewhere, would finally respond. And after all this time, the war still hasn't ended. The mission hasn't changed either. It's kept going with the same purpose it started with, even though most of the galaxy has stopped paying attention."

"We were moving through a stretch of space so quiet it felt forgotten. No one expected anything out there; it was the kind of region you passed through without thinking. We were just getting ready for the trip back to Venor when it happened; a tiny flicker on the scanner. Weak, almost nothing. But it was there. And it was real. "

***

The echoes of the elders' plan continued to reverberate across the galaxy more than a century later. Reinforcements had been firmly established, though the formation of alliances with various races had been a painstakingly slow process. At the core of the Venoran Council's headquarters, a group of councillors gathered in a grand, dimly lit chamber.

Captain Gall entered the room, unsure why he had been called to the Council. His footsteps echoed lightly on the polished stone. The councillors had already assembled, standing in muted silence beneath the glow of flickering constellation maps, etched into every corner of the room, displaying centuries of history.

An elder stepped forward, his voice calm but carrying the weight of years. "Captain Gall," he said, meeting the captain's eyes, "I imagine you're wondering why we've pulled you from the front. You've seen the worst of it out there. The war isn't turning in our favour."

The chamber was quiet. Just the soft hum of tech beneath their feet and the distant echo of history pressed into the walls.

"Our supplies are thinning. Our recruits, young and untested, are slow to rise to the challenge. We've been sending ships, searching for allies from civilisations that might stand with us; some have returned with promise. But not enough."

He paused, not for drama, but to let the truth settle.

"That's why we're turning to you, and to the *Arcadia*. This next mission isn't about combat; it's about connection. Exploration. Highlighting a section of the screen, we need you to monitor this sector, find anyone who might help us survive what's ahead."

Gall didn't speak. He didn't need to. His eyes stayed fixed on the constellation map, tracing the faint glimmer of stars in the highlighted sector. Star systems illuminated across the screen.

The elder pointed to a marked region. "Our long deep-space reconnaissance drones have located a large water world within this system. It's been a million years since we passed through this region of space. We want to know what's become of the inhabitants of this world. If they've made it this far and really grown, maybe we can talk to each other, not as strangers, but as equals? There is a chance this could be the start of something."

His eyes returned to Gall, steady and hopeful. "We want you to find out."

Gall didn't shift or speak, but there was a quiet intensity in the way he stood. He absorbed every word, shoulders squared, not out of pride, but responsibility. His gaze stayed locked, calm but burning with a quiet fire. Though his hands rested at his sides, every so often his fingers twitched now and then, a subtle, involuntary readiness.

Across the chamber, the councillors exchanged glances that carried more weight than words. A few were hopeful, believing something good might finally emerge.

Three cycles later, *Arcadia* tore through the shimmering folds of space, emerging over the planet. A voice came over the comms. "Orbit stabilised."

Below the ocean world, vast and shimmering. Sunlight slid across endless waves, painting them in strokes of deep blue and gold. A scattering of islands broke the surface here and there, quiet and untouched, like punctuation in an unspoken sentence.

The crew held its breath as sensors swept across the planet and data poured in.

Life pulsed beneath the water, unmistakably evolved. Not just adapted, but born into the sea. The natives moved with a kind of poetry, their bodies shaped for speed and pressure.

Their cities drifted across the tides like constellations that had come loose from the sky. They glowed softly in hues of violet, sapphire, and jade, not from power cells, but from bioluminescent shellwork that lit the water from within.

There seemed to be no presence of steel or stone. Their world was woven from seaweed pressed and folded like fabric, reinforced with threads of glass-like silica drawn straight from the seabed. Living silica that breathed and shimmered.

These materials breathed with the water's rhythm, flexing gently with each passing current. Air travel was unnecessary here; the inhabitants moved as the sea moved, flowing from place to place in harmony with the waves. Agriculture thrived on the few landmasses, carefully cultivated and preserved. Every inch of soil mattered.

Aurelia, the ship's AI, activated with a soft hum, her voice balanced and calm.

"The inhabitants have developed a method of communication, yet surprisingly, they have not ventured into the realm of air transportation."

The planet held four vast cities, living structures anchored to deep thermal vents. Each city floated within shimmering bubble chambers, crafted from organic alloys that pulsed softly in rhythm with the tides.

"The world holds a population of one hundred million." Reported Aurelia. "But there is something quite alarming. The population numbers were slipping. Year after year, fewer births."

Gal responded, his words edged with concern. "Given the dwindling population, it's unlikely they'll meet the criteria we hoped for."

Gall stiffened, then slowly relaxed as he breathed through the frustration.

"Send word to Venor," he said, voice low but steady. "Let them know we've combed this sector and found no other civilisations at their level. We're heading home. But before we leave, dispatch a science unit. Their declining population... it needs answers. We owe it to them, and to ourselves."

The room fell into stillness, the kind that speaks louder than dialogue. Around the bridge, crew members exchanged glances, some wary, some thoughtful.

After two cycles with no word from the survey team, Gal gave the order, his voice low. "No promising results. We're heading back to Venor. Bring the survey team back."

The *Arcadia* slipped back into Slide Space for the return home, its hull catching streaks of ghost-light as it warped through volatile sectors. Each leap strained her bones, her systems groaning with effort. Unexpectedly, the warning lights bled from amber to crimson. Energy was low.

The ship slowly drifted to a halt in a dark patch of cosmos; no stars. Just quiet.

The Slide core began its recharge, silently counting down toward the next move. Shields remained at minimal capacity, weapon systems offline. They emerged from the darkness as a diffuse starlight signature, producing a negligible disturbance in the surrounding void.

The bridge dimmed to conserve power. A hush enveloped the space, broken only by the soft chime of systems recalibrating. Some crew members leaned into their stations.

Midway through the cycle, a console flared to life. The communications officer snapped to attention.

“Captain, I’ve picked up a peculiar signal,” she announced, her brow furrowed in concentration. “It’s close to our location. The signal is faint but steady. Our transponder is locking onto it.”

Captain Gall leaned forward, brow furrowed. “This sector’s meant to be uninhabited.”

“No known outposts. No traffic. No beacons,” the officer replied. “But something's there.”

The crew traded glances as low-frequency vibrations rippled through the ship, barely perceptible but undeniably real. Outside the viewports, nothing moved. No light. No shapes.

Aurelia shimmered into focus on the bridge, her holographic form flickering briefly before solidifying into a tangible presence. The crew quieted as she stepped forward, interrupting mid-conversation without apology, only urgency.

“I’ve found the source of the signal,” she said, her voice low and clear. “There’s an object at the point of origin. It’s broadcasting, but the signal’s been deteriorating for some time. The power source is almost depleted.”

Gall turned toward her, the edge in her voice catching his attention. His brow lifted slightly, not in alarm, but out of interest. Something about the unknown always pulled at him.

"Bring us closer," he said, stepping toward the console. "Let's see what we're dealing with."

The *Arcadia* adjusted course, drifting toward the coordinates. Silence took over the bridge, save for the steady hum of the ship and Aurelia's data stream scrolling across the display.

Then her voice returned, soft but charged. "It's a probe. Primitive, but intentional. Information-gathering. There's complexity here, maybe not in design, but in intention."

Her eyes flickered across the invisible data, reading patterns only she could see.

Gall didn't hesitate. "Get it aboard. Let's find out who built it."

The artefact was transferred gently into *Arcadia's* lab, treated as a relic instead of scrap. The scientists quickly gathered around, wide-eyed, curious, hands hovering before they touched anything.

One cycle later, Gall walked into the lab, sensing the change before a word was spoken. The researchers stood grouped around the probe, faces lit with quiet awe.

"Captain," called one researcher, breath catching, "we've made a breakthrough."

Gall stepped closer.

"The device is powered by a radiation source we can actually replicate, but there's more to it than that. It contains a disc with a mathematical notation and encoded coordinates, which we believe points directly back to its home."

Gall's gaze sharpened. "Someone sent this out, hoping to be found."

The scientist nodded. "Whoever built this, might be advanced enough to help us."

Gall's voice was firm, but there was a ripple of wonder lying beneath it. "Prep a team. Let's find their world."

Momentum surged through the *Arcadia's* crew. What began as a faint signal had evolved into a mission, and perhaps something greater.

"Restore its power," Gall said. "Return it to where it was found. Let it keep speaking, in case someone else is listening."

Hours later, the lead scientist approached Gall, energy in his step. "We've traced the origin," he said, opening a screen displaying a star map.

The sector glowed. A yellow star, with one liveable planet.

Gall leaned in, studying its profile as it flickered into view.

"How close?"

"One Slide. Maybe less."

The scientist smiled. "We've examined the disc's data; it contains audio and visual recordings from their home world, Earth. And, Captain, they look similar to us."

"This is good news. Send the location to the bridge; this will be our next stop."

***

At that very moment on Earth, a puzzled scientist in California stared at his screen at the Deep Space Telescope Array facility. The signals that had baffled him for days now began to align with something extraordinary. His eyes widened in disbelief as he realised the implications of the data being downloaded.

Today's transmission from the DSTA facility to NASA deviated from protocol. The report was flagged for immediate review.

[Voyager One, previously considered effectively non-functional after months of degraded and incoherent telemetry, has unexpectedly resumed stable communication.

A strong, clean signal was received without prior indication of recovery. The spacecraft is now transmitting continuous, high-volume data exceeding current processing capacity.]

It had been a week since the report about Voyager's extended life was sent to NASA. But today's report from the Deep Space Telescope Array was unlike anything ever recorded. A very excited scientist, James Hollins, a brilliant yet reserved scientist, broke his usual composure. His email, sent in the early hours, was written entirely in capital letters:

[WE HAVE BEEN CONTACTED.]

The words blared across the screen in all caps, but it was the quiet gasp that followed that froze the room.

James sprinted down the corridor toward the command centre, his pulse racing, breath short, adrenaline thundering behind his ribs. The doors hissed open, and the sight stopped him cold.

Everyone was crowded around the main display, their faces lit by the eerie glow of incoming data. Monitors beeped, status lights pulsed, and hushed voices threaded through the air. You could feel the tension, cutting the air. On the screen was a massive ship, suspended just beyond Neptune's orbit, casting a ghostly silhouette against the distant sunlight.

Dr Emily Carter turned from the console. Calm, always. But something in her eyes, something raw and uncertain, said this was different.

"James," she said, steady but low. "Is that really a ship?"

He didn't answer right away. His fingers shook as he gestured to the cascading signal patterns.

"It's not a flare," he said. "It's structured. Intentionally, and they're trying to talk to us."

From behind them came a quiet question "What do they want from us?"

James stared at the ship, its presence felt unreal. "No idea. But I think we're about to find out."

It was one of those rare moments from which stories emerge, when the sky subtly transforms and humanity holds its breath, aware that change is near.

Emily turned back to the console, her mind already sprinting. "If this is real," she said softly, "then it's the most important thing any of us will ever see."

James hesitated. "Oh, it's real." He swallowed, then added, "Maybe someone should call off the missile launches?" His voice broke slightly on the words.

Silence returned. A heavy kind.

The monitor flickered again, once, twice, then steadied.

Across its surface, elegant but alien script unfolded. Aurelia's system converted it into a simple message that stopped every breath in the room.

[*Greetings, people of Earth, we bring greetings from the Venoran people. We come in peace and wish to meet with you*].

The words hung there, heavy with the weight of what they meant. No one moved. No one even breathed. Then, as if the room suddenly remembered how to function, everything erupted at once. Scientists rushed back to their stations, voices tumbling over one another in a mix of excitement and disbelief.

Messages shot out across secure networks like flares in the dark, lighting up encrypted channels around the world. Governments, leaders, intelligence agencies... everyone was alerted. Meetings were called in the dead of night. Phones rang behind closed doors. Within days, a First Contact Committee existed, wrapped in secrecy. Their first unanimous decision was to keep this quiet, at least for now.

The committee drafted a response and sent it to the Venoran ship, asking it to move to the far side of Earth's moon, hidden, but close enough to watch.

Aboard the Venoran vessel *Arcadia*, Gall read the request with a single raised brow. The command deck glowed with soft, pulsing light that played across his calm, unreadable expression. His second-in-command stood at attention beside him, waiting for the order that would come next.

Gall's gaze drifted back to the display of Earth, a small blue jewel suspended against the endless blackness of space. "We will stop on the far side of Earth's moon as instructed," he said, his voice steady but tinged with curiosity. He leaned back in his command chair, tapping his fingers. "It's a strange request. These Earthlings are cautious, perhaps to a fault."

Around him, the bridge crew moved with focused urgency. The Arcadia, a gleaming giant, had moved free of its orbit around Neptune. With effortless grace, it angled toward the inner system, gliding past the outer planets. Starlight scattered across its hull in shifting colors, making the ship look alive as it cut through the dark with predatory precision.

Gall continued to think about the people of Earth. A civilisation on the brink of spacefaring, fragile yet brimming with potential. He hoped he could find the right way to show it, and make them feel comfortable with his approach.

A communications officer stepped up to Gall, curiosity bright in his eyes. He leaned forward without realizing it, as if the discovery itself had him in its grip. His hands moved in quick, expressive bursts as he spoke.

"I'm picking up transmissions from all over the planet," he said, excitement threading through his voice. On the monitor behind him, scattered broadcasts in dozens of languages flickered and overlapped, filling the bridge with a soft, chaotic hum of human sound. "Mostly news updates. They've developed sophisticated computer systems. This species is far more advanced than the last world we surveyed." He paused, hands falling still as he studied the data. "They're also beginning to build spacefaring vehicles. And their population... it's enormous. Much larger than we expected."

Gall didn't move. His arms stayed folded across his chest, his expression unreadable, but his eyes were fixed on the screen. The only sound in the room was the steady pulse of the control panels, beeping like a quiet heartbeat beneath the tension. Then, after a long moment, he gave a single, deliberate nod and spoke in a low, steady voice.

"Send a team down. I want to know more about them."

He turned and tapped his wrist, activating his communicator. "Patrasia, report to the command deck. Immediately."

The door to the command deck slid open. Patrasia entered, a woman in her middle years. Her white hair was long and loosely braided, a silvery sheen catching the low light as she moved. She was stunning. Her high cheekbones were striking, and there was a softness to her jawline that made her seem genuinely approachable and kind. But it was her eyes that held the most weight, glowing a deep and striking emerald. She wore a uniform similar to Gall's, though the blue-grey hue marked her elevated rank. People tended to pause around her, mid-thought, in mid-sentence, unsure whether she was simply listening or silently taking their measure.

Gall acknowledged her with a subtle tilt of his head. "We're sending a recon team to the surface," he said. "You'll lead it."

She met his gaze without hesitation, a hint of curiosity dancing in her otherwise composed expression. "Understood, Captain," she replied

Gall turned back to the screen, where Earth spun slowly in space, its colours vivid against the void. Somewhere down there was hope, which he intended to grasp.

Patrasia straightened, her stance crisp, eyes steady on Gall. "I'll be ready," she said simply.

Two planetary cycles later, they returned. The transport light faded, leaving Patrasia and her team standing on the deck, their faces tired, but steady. The command center hummed with a low, urgent energy as Gall waited for her to speak.

Dust clung to the creases of her uniform, a quiet reminder of whatever they'd just come through.

"What did you find?" Gall asked, his voice calm but edged with anticipation.

Patrasia stepped forward, voice firm and assured. "We touched down on multiple continents," she said, gesturing to the glowing sphere hovering behind her. "Their continents are divided into what they call nations. In the past century, they've seen dramatic advancements, science, technology, and even spacefaring capability."

She paused, her gaze narrowing. "But their history is littered with conflict. Wars. Internal divisions."

The hologram shifted, cycling through images of battlefields, peace agreements, and bursts of scientific progress, each one a snapshot of a species constantly pushing forward and tearing itself apart in equal measure.

Patrasia's words hung in the air like a soft ripple after impact. "After their last major war," she said, her tone measured, "several nations joined forces to sign a peace accord. Since then, they've built cooperative frame-works, systems meant to prevent conflict before it takes root."

Gall didn't answer right away. He sat still, fingers pressed together, clearly deep in thought. His gaze was intense while he thought it over. Then, slowly, he nodded. "And you believe they align with what we're looking for?"

A flicker of excitement stirred behind Patrasia's composed exterior. Her posture straightened just slightly. "Yes, Captain," she said. "Most communities demonstrate a genuine intent to collaborate. There are disagreements, and friction still exists... but the effort to resolve it peacefully seems real."

Gall leaned back in his chair, letting his gaze settle once more on the calm blue sphere turning slowly against the dark. For a few long seconds, no one spoke. It was pretty clear that from here on out, everything was going to be different.

He nodded slowly, eyes still on the display, processing Patrasia's assessment with the kind of quiet focus that said he was already thinking ten steps ahead. "Start figuring out the best way to approach them," he said. His tone was level, but the weight behind it didn't need emphasis. "Work out if a meeting's even possible."

He turned toward the glowing presence at the edge of the bridge. "Aurelia," he said, "before we go any further, I want to know everything. Their history. Their patterns. The way they think. Nothing overlooked."

Aurelia's voice answered with its usual calm clarity. "Understood, Captain. Initiating full-scale analysis."

The room dimmed slightly as the holographic interface bloomed into life, projecting centuries of Earth's history like short stories. The wars and the art, the way things fell apart and then how they built them back up again. It all played out like the memory of a planet trying to find itself. Gall stood in silence, taking it in. A species both fragile and fierce. Messy but brilliant.

He knew what came next would require more than data. It would require judgment.

By the next cycle, Aurelia's form reappeared, casting soft light across the command deck. The bridge fell silent. This wasn't just information. This was insight.

"To frame their timeline accurately," she said, voice steady, "we've aligned our analysis with their lifespan rhythms. The human lifespan is significantly shorter than the Venoran standard. This has shaped their evolution, both in pace and urgency."

Gall gave a slight nod, eyes narrowing thoughtfully.

"We've been here before," Aurelia continued. Her gaze met Gall's without hesitation. "Approximately two million Earth years. Our first base was on the fourth planet, but the atmospheric conditions turned hostile. We moved to Earth as its environment was more forgiving and showed more promise."

Murmurs stirred among the crew, quiet but tinged with awe. It wasn't just a mission anymore. It was a return.

Gall's eyes didn't leave Aurelia.

"Then maybe," he said softly, "we've been part of their story longer than they ever knew."

The holographic display shifted once more, casting a golden glow across the command deck. Earth appeared as it had long ago, untamed, windswept, and pulsing with possibility. Aurelia's voice dropped to a softer tone, threaded with something almost like wonder.

"In the beginning," she said, her gaze fixed on the swirling display, "nothing hinted at higher intelligence. Life was pleasant and abundant, but scattered and fragile. Of all the species we monitored, only one stood out, offering even the faintest hint of promise. Yet they were barely clinging on... haunted by harsh climates, dwindling resources, and the constant shadow of extinction."

Gall leaned forward slightly, his voice little more than a breath. "And?"

Aurelia paused, the silence hanging just long enough to feel heavy. "We knew evolution wouldn't be kind to them. Not in time. So, the directive came through. Intervention. We initiated a genetic modification program. Not to remake them, but to help them become what they were capable of."

The display shifted, revealing early humans stepping out of the wilderness, rough silhouettes moving through the raw beginnings of their world. Aurelia's expression changed, just a flicker, but there was unmistakable pride in her voice. "For a thousand Earth years, they grew into hunters, builders, and dreamers. Their curiosity was relentless. It became their engine, their flame."

She glanced toward Gall, eyes luminescent. "Eventually, the High Council shut down the operation. Said the experiment had run its course. The scientists withdrew. We left them behind... thriving."

Across the room, tension bristled. Aurelia's voice sharpened. "But Earth didn't stay isolated. Others found it. Not all had noble in-tent. The knowledge they introduced shifted the arc of human progress. Knowledge flowed fast, sometimes chaotically, most of the time unfiltered. And the humans, true to form, absorbed it all. They didn't just survive the disruption. They evolved through it."

Gall's body tensed. "So where do they stand now?"

With a final flicker, the display showed present-day Earth, a swirl of lights and cities stitched across continents like veins of fire.

"Though Earth is tucked away in an overlooked corner of the galaxy," Aurelia said, "its people have defied every projection. Their technological ascent is rapid... startling. Unlike anything we've seen among other species. They're no longer a forgotten experiment. They're something else entirely."

But the room itself felt quieter than before, focused on Aurelia's words.

Gall didn't move. "Then maybe they weren't just shaped by our presence," he murmured. "Maybe they became who they are... because we left."

Present time - Earth

It was Gall's tenth return to Earth, a number that should've dulled the experience into routine. But as the *Arcadia* slipped into orbit behind the moon, cloaked and invisible, he felt the old pull of purpose stir in his chest. From the command deck, he looked down at the planet's surface, where city lights flared like star clusters against the velvet of night. Familiar, but nothing about this mission felt familiar.

Earth's governments had embraced the Venorans with enthusiasm, shaking hands, signing accords, and speaking in poetic flourishes about unity and shared futures.

But though the crowds came in droves, the numbers thinned quickly. Most never met the strict Venoran criteria.

Gall still recalled the furrowed brows of Venoran instructors, their lesson plans slowly unravelling as they tried to mould undisciplined minds into order. The civilians, eager but unpredictable, didn't mesh easily with the precision of Venoran systems. Every session turned into a balancing act of patience and recalibration.

It wasn't sustainable.

During one of his visits, Gall had stood before the Earth Council, a quiet authority in the midst of rising frustration. The room had been still, thick with expectation.

Following several meetings, the Venorans and Earth's governments devised an alternative plan, which was to recruit ex-military veterans. Shaped by prior lives in service, these individuals carried with them discipline, resilience, and a remarkable capacity to adapt to the Venorans' military standards. It was a practical solution born out of necessity.

Gall could still picture the first group of veterans as they stepped aboard the *Arcadia*, faces etched with fatigue, eyes sharpened by something more than resolve. They didn't speak much, but their silence carried years of history, sacrifices too personal to put into words. And beneath all that weight, there was something else, a quiet spark of anticipation. Before arriving on the training world, the Venorans had reshaped their bodies in ways those veterans once believed impossible. Now, they stood ready.

In those first days, their wary glances and rigid postures had betrayed a restless struggle between curiosity and doubt. But as days turned into weeks, he watched them change. Their military instincts meshed effortlessly with Venoran techniques, and the program began to flourish.

Now, as Gall prepared for yet another meeting with Earth's leaders, his thoughts drifted back to that progress. The veterans hadn't just adapted; they'd shown creativity. Solving problems that even the Venorans hadn't anticipated.

With this final group aboard, Gall felt the shift; a quiet signal that the program was reaching its conclusion. Each new arrival brought less hesitation than the last, as though the world itself had begun to accept what was coming. This would be the last group.

A soft hiss broke the silence as the command deck doors slid open. An officer stepped in, spine straight, eyes sharp. "Captain Gall," she said crisply, "the Earth Council is ready to receive you."

Gall stood, his uniform catching the ambient glow of the console lights. "Thank you," he replied with a nod. "Has the final report been transmitted?"

“Yes, sir. Including their psychological assessments and integration metrics.”

Gall exhaled slowly, letting the weight of the moment settle across his shoulders. “They’re good people. Stubborn, but resilient. That counts for something.”

The officer hesitated. “Sir... is it true? This is the end of the selection program?”

Gall looked out through the viewport, where Earth loomed, blue and quiet, unaware of what decisions hung in orbit. “It is,” he said at last. “We’ve tested their limits, guided their first steps, waited through every uncertainty. Now it's time to see if humanity can help.”

She gave a nod of acknowledgement. “Best of luck down there, Captain.”

Gall headed towards the transport station and spoke into the panel. “This is Gall, beam me down to the council coordinates.”

A New Retirement Home

Day 1

Personal account: Stuart Thomson

"I had no clue that just a few days later, I'd be staring down at Earth from above. That idea wouldn't have made any real sense to me back then. It just felt like another Monday. But what was waiting for me... yeah, that was something else entirely. What I thought was a regular week turned out to be the beginning of a trip I still struggle to put into words. It changed the way I look at everything: space, time, and even myself. Funny how life does that. At the time, though, all of it was quietly tucked away beneath what seemed like just another routine start."

***

A few weeks before Gal's meeting with the Earth Council, Stuart Thompson, one of the last veterans, had just arrived at the airport. The limo ride had been smooth. My driver blurred the logistics together, navigating security and the bag drop until the tickets were in my hand and everything was accounted for. Making sure I didn't have to think about a thing. He even arranged a wheelchair escort, which, honestly, was a relief. By the time I settled into my seat, the pilot's voice crackled through the cabin speakers, calm and practiced.

"We're looking at a five-hour flight. Sit back, relax, and enjoy the ride."

I soon discovered that I wasn't going to be alone. I was joining a group of retired veterans, aged between 70 and 95, who had previously lived in retirement homes across North America, Ireland, and the UK. Overall, the flight was comfortable. We encountered a couple of bumpy sections at the beginning, but after that, I don't remember much of the trip, as I have a habit of falling asleep on plane journeys.

I was woken by the standard announcement coming over the speaker. "We will be landing soon."

The pilot's voice crackled over the intercom again. "Please fasten your safety belts. Thank you." I leaned toward the window, and that's when I saw it... an island unfolding beneath us like something out of a painting. It looked like an emerald floating in deep blue seas. The hills were covered in thick, wild greenery, and cliffs rose sharply along most of the shore like ancient guardians keeping watch.

There was just one opening in the rugged coastline, a wide beach glowing under the sun, gently sloping into the waves as if it were inviting us to step right in. It was there, tucked away near the water; this grand building, elegant and a little mysterious. It looked like a luxury resort dropped into the middle of nowhere... beautiful, but a little out of place.

As we got closer, the airport finally came into view. Just one small building and a lonely runway, carved straight into the jungle. It felt remote. Quiet. Like we were about to touch down in a forgotten corner of the world. The plane began its descent, bringing us closer to this unique and untouched corner of the world.

As the plane descended, the guy next to me couldn't resist sharing his thoughts, louder than necessary. "Bloody typical," he exclaimed, earning glances from a few nearby passengers.

"Take me from a spectacular home by the sea to an island in the middle of nowhere. I wouldn't be surprised if I end up buried in an unmarked grave under a coconut tree." His colourful remark drew a burst of laughter from someone seated behind us, adding a touch of levity to the moment.

The runway gave us a bit of a jolt, not dramatic, just one of those landings where everyone faintly grabbed their armrests. We coasted to a stop, and just as hands began to fumble for buckles, the pilot chimed in, voice playful and knowing.

"Thank you for flying Coconut Airways," he said. "Welcome to the beautiful island of Venor. We hope you enjoy your stay. Please gather your belongings and head over to the lounge."

It didn't take long before we were all huddled in what they called the airport lounge, though calling it a "lounge" might've been generous. The room was quiet. Empty. No other travellers. Just us, standing around, eyeing the jungle through tinted windows and wondering what exactly we'd signed up for. I was beginning to feel the weight of the silence when the loudspeaker crackled to life with an announcement.

"Will all guests of the Venor Retirement Home for Military Veterans please board the bus? Thank you." It was a strange announcement, as we were the only ones there.

We stepped outside and began to board the bus. A middle-aged couple managed the process, assisting with surprising efficiency. Despite their pale complexions, they exuded an understated strength as they hoisted suitcases and guided the veterans to their seats. I watched as a male attendant diligently secured a frail man in a wheelchair; nearby, two elderly men watched intently.

Just as he finished, a woman rose from the front of the bus, her presence commanding the attention of everyone aboard. "Good, now we are all aboard on behalf of the Venor Retirement Home. Welcome, everyone. We will be taking you to your new home, which is just under two hours from here, and we do hope you will be comfortable."

As soon as the bus pulled away from the airport, we hit a rough dirt road that cut straight through thick jungle. I leaned against the window, trying to get my bearings, but the landscape became a blur of green. I glanced back, expecting to see the airport still behind us. Nothing. Just flat land and thick foliage. We hadn't turned once, and yet the airport was gone, not obscured, just gone like it had been swallowed whole.

The ride got bumpier as we pushed deeper into the greenery. Vines and branches reached out and brushed along the windows, tapping gently as if they wanted to keep us there a little longer. Then, almost out of nowhere, we broke through. The jungle unfolded around us, not torn or trampled, but arranged, as though the path had always been waiting. Suddenly, we were in a clearing, flooded with light. It was so unexpected that I caught myself holding my breath.

The town looked unreal. Rows of buildings stood perfectly in line, their fresh coats of paint glowing under the afternoon sun.

From every lamppost, flowers spilled over in hanging baskets, swaying lazily with the breeze. Their pastel petals fluttered like soft little greetings. The whole place gave off the feeling that someone had arranged it all with love and care, but not in a cold, rigid way. It felt warm and lived-in, with its own quiet rhythm.

It had an odd charm to it, giving you English village countryside vibes, tucked right in the middle of nowhere, surrounded by wild jungle. The bus rolled down the main street, tyres humming over the pavement, before turning onto a winding driveway. And there it was, a grand old house at the end, stately but welcoming, with gardens so perfect they looked hand-combed. Every hedge was trimmed with precision, every flowerbed laid out with intent. It felt like we'd crossed into a whole other world.

The bus let out a soft hiss as it came to a stop, and for a moment, everything was quiet. Just the stillness, the air, and whatever waited behind that front door.

The bus doors hissed open; a woman across the aisle leaned toward the window as she said, "Is this... real? This place looks like something out of a storybook."

I gave a quiet nod, still absorbing the surreal contrast between jungle and manor. "Feels like we took a wrong turn and ended up in someone's dream."

The female attendants voice came over the bus speakers, "Your bags will be taken to your rooms; please exit the bus, you will be shown to your accommodations, where you can freshen up, and in one hour, return to the lobby where a guide will escort you."

As I stepped off the bus, I couldn't help but notice the man in the wheelchair being carefully escorted inside. He looked unwell, far too frail for what this journey required. I couldn't shake the thought that he belonged in a hospital, not here. It wasn't just the man's appearance that caught my attention; it was the two men walking in perfect sync on either side of him. Identical twins, unmistakably so, with sharp features and an unspoken, almost telepathic understanding between them. They each gripped a handle of the wheelchair as though their charge were a precious artefact requiring utmost care.

Entering the building, we climbed a short flight of stairs and were met with a striking sight. The lobby was spacious with unmistakable grandeur. The design immediately brought to mind a New Orleans mansion I had visited years ago, with its timeless elegance. Around the main floor, several doors led to other areas, but the true centrepiece of the room was the large chandelier hanging in the middle of the foyer. On either side of the space, two grand staircases spiralled gracefully to the next floor, completing the scene. I could've sworn I'd seen a photograph of this somewhere; the moment carried a strange sense of déjà vu.

As I walked into my room, I couldn't help but smile. It was beautiful, even better than I'd expected. The bed looked ridiculously comfortable, big and wrapped in crisp white sheets that made you want to dive right in and take a nap. In the corner was a small sitting area, nothing fancy, but warm and inviting in a way that made the whole space feel personal. Not just decorated for show.

The bathroom gleamed with minimalist elegance, bathed in a soft light that cast a hush over every surface. I stepped out onto the balcony, and that's when it hit me.

Below were perfectly trimmed gardens stretching out toward the beach, which just shimmered there in the distance, quiet and still. I stood there for a moment, taking it all in, feeling as if the noise of the world had faded into the background.

There was a nagging sensation at the edge of my thoughts. Something about the place felt... rehearsed, as if the tranquillity had been engineered, not earned. The air was still, the light too soft, the colours too vivid. It was the kind of perfection that made you wonder what it was hiding.

I stood there longer than I meant to, trying to shake the feeling. Eventually, the spell broke. We made our way back down to the lobby, footsteps echoing faintly in the stairwell, the hush of the place following us like a shadow.

The attendant was waiting, with a polite smile and the same relaxed posture, next to a pair of big glass doors. He didn't need to say anything. He just nodded, as though he'd known we were coming all along, and motioned for us to follow. The tranquillity of the place made it easy to forget where we'd just come from.

The room beyond was lively, filled with people engaged in various activities. Some were clustered around tables playing dominoes, others were deep in card games, and a few sat quietly absorbed in their books.

Don, the guy I'd sat next to on the plane, couldn't hold back his sarcasm.

"Wow, this place looks exciting. Going to love it here," he quipped with exaggerated enthusiasm.

I couldn't help but chuckle, leaning in to offer him some advice. "Maybe try using your inner voice for that kind of commentary," I said, amused.

Once everyone had gathered in the spacious room, a tall, distinguished-looking man stepped onto the platform near the windows. His white hair and smart suit gave him an air of authority. With a warm, welcoming smile, he opened his arms and began to address us, his tone inviting and reassuring. The atmosphere shifted, leaving me curious about what he had to say.

***

(The following content is based on the recorded accounts of multiple contributors.)

He stepped forward, his stature commanding without being over the top. His shoes made a soft, deliberate tap as he made his way to the centre of the room, and he paused for a second, scanning the crowd. His eyes had that mix of confidence and warmth, which suggested he'd done this a hundred times but still cared every single time.

He lifted his arms just a bit, as if he were inviting everyone in with the gesture. "Welcome." His voice slipped through the space, deep and velvety, reaching the back row without ever needing the mic's help. "Now that everyone's here, let's get started with some introductions. My name is Gall, and I'm proud to welcome you to the Venor Retirement Home for Military Veterans."

He moved around the platform slowly in front of us, not stiff or formal, as if he was taking his time to look at everyone. Their faces told the tale of long lives and the weight of stories hard-earned. A few were whispering to each other, but most just sat quietly, taking it all in. He raised his hand slightly, a gesture that both calmed and commanded attention.

"You weren't chosen by chance," he continued. "We visited hundreds of retirement homes across the continents, quietly searching for qualities long thought dormant. Courage, loyalty, and intuition. We looked past age and ailments. What we saw in you was the remnant of greatness, the spark that once ignited nations and led revolutions."

He stepped closer to someone in the front row, his voice steady. "You were commanders, medics, and warriors forged in fire and duty. And yet, even now, that call hasn't faded; the pulse in your veins, like history itself, is asking for one final campaign. You're not just here to live out your days. You're here to shape a new beginning."

Gall allowed a small, knowing smile to touch his lips before he continued, his voice steady yet inviting. "We asked each of you this question:"

If you had your life to live over again, how would you have changed it?

And just like that, the mood shifted. You could almost hear the gears turning in people's heads as they processed what Gall had said.

"What we offer isn't about finding a place to settle into retirement; it's an invitation to rediscover a new purpose, maybe even a second chance at something meaningful." Some of them leaned forward, eyes a bit more alive; others just sat back, staring at nothing in particular, lost in thought.

You could tell it struck a chord. That line (to rediscover a new purpose) hung in the air like a challenge and a promise all at once. There was something magnetic about the way he spoke, as if each person could already feel the weight of their potential being acknowledged and rekindled. This was no ordinary retirement home; it was a place that promised transformation, and Gall embodied that promise with every word and gesture.

Gall extended his arms, his demeanour calm and reassuring, as he addressed the group. "Rest assured, you are all in good hands here, and you will be well cared for during your stay," he began, his voice steady and warm. "Those changes we will discuss another day," he continued, drawing the attention of the audience. "Each of you is a retired military veteran or connected in some way with a unique background. Your service and experiences have shaped you in extraordinary ways, and here, we have a one-of-a-kind program designed to make your lives more meaningful."

Just as Gall finished his heartfelt spiel about hope and purpose, Don jumped in; he couldn't resist. He tossed out one of his trademark eye-roll zingers. "Yup, already been done, dominoes, and can't wait." Real sarcastic, sounding as if he were mocking the idea of all this deep talk. It got some chuckles from the surrounding folks, though. I thought I was a bit loose-lipped, but Don was on another level... the amusing level. Then he turned and looked straight at me, tapped his temple as if he was delivering comedy gold, totally cracking himself up.

Gall? Not even a flinch. This guy had the patience of a saint. He gave Don a calm, almost knowing smile, like he'd seen way worse interruptions, and just eased back into his speech with that smooth voice of his. Then he looked at us, each of us, like he was trying to connect, not just to give some rehearsed spiel.

Then came the hook. "In a couple of days, each of you will be offered something new," he said, with a glint of something unspoken behind his eyes. "A chance at something you probably thought was off the table at this point."

And man, you could hear a pin drop. Even the chandelier stopped humming for a second, I swear.

That's when someone in the crowd finally pushed back. "How do you even know about our experiences?" they asked, not angry, just kinda sceptical, like they needed proof this wasn't all smoke and mirrors.

Gall didn't miss a beat. He turned toward the voice, calm as ever. Gave a steady nod and said, "We've done our homework. You'd be surprised how much we know. Your stories shaped this whole thing." The way he said it? It landed. The tension just eased. People leaned back, letting it all sink in.

Gall stepped away from the microphone, like he knew he'd said enough. That was the end of the formal bit for now, but you could tell something had shifted in the room.

After Gall wrapped up his speech, nobody rushed off. We were told to take our time settling in and get to know each other if we wanted; no pressure. Staff circled around, friendly but low-key, ready to help out or answer questions. Not long after, one of them, neatly dressed in a charcoal-grey uniform, stepped forward with that calm, organised vibe and gave us the basics. She ran through what we needed to know, echoing the same welcoming tone Gall had set earlier.

Then, a voice echoed over the speakers. "Could I have your attention, please? Tomorrow's wake-up call will be at 7:30. Dining schedules are posted on the back of your doors." Some nodded, a few murmured their thanks, while others met the moment with a silent glance that said enough.

The room started to buzz after that. People broke off into small groups, trading stories, little laughs, and those first cautious introductions. Some folks dove right in, excited to chat, while others stayed back, quietly watching, still sizing things up. Bit by bit, the energy softened. You could feel things loosening up; people were starting to let their guard down.

As night crept in, the crowd thinned. A few at a time, people slipped away to their rooms, leaving behind the sound of fading laughter and the soft shuffle of footsteps echoing through the hallway.

Kayla had arrived with the others, one of the quieter members of the group, having recently left her retirement home. The move had come with mixed feelings of relief and uncertainty. She hadn't said much during the orientation, just polite nods and a smile when spoken to, but something in her eyes hinted at a lifetime's worth of stories she wasn't quite ready to share.

On the third morning, as a few of us gathered near the garden path, Kayla paused beside a hibiscus bush and said softly, almost to herself. "Funny how quiet can feel loud when you're not used to it."

Someone nearby smiled and asked, "Settling in alright?"

She nodded, eyes scanning the horizon.

"It's peaceful, yes." Then her focus softened, drifting into her own thoughts.

Later during lunch, as someone joked about the fruit being too perfect. Kayla raised an eyebrow and murmured, "Perfection's a funny thing. Makes you wonder what it's trying to distract you from."

That earned a few glances, but she just sipped her water and returned to her plate, unfazed.

A few days had passed as she watched the sun dip low and the sky turn molten; she clinked her beer bottle gently against the balcony railing and said to no one in particular.

"I spent forty years waiting for quiet. Now that I've got it, I'm not sure what to do with it." In the days that followed, Kayla fell into the rhythm of island life faster than she expected. Waking up to the whisper of waves and that salty-sweet mix of ocean air and garden flowers, yeah, it did something to her. The building itself felt like a retreat, elegant but not stiff. Just peaceful. Mornings were slow and easy. She wandered the gardens until a patch of shade called to her, where she'd sit and let the quiet stretch into something timeless.

Meals were relaxed, served with care in a sunlit dining hall where soft music played just low enough to blend into the background. A choice of fish, meat or poultry with tropical fruit, which seemed to show up with every meal. It was simple, but it felt good. As if the place itself was giving her room to breathe again. Evenings brought their own charm. Sunsets spilled liquid gold across the sea.

At seventy-seven, Kayla carried her years with grace. Her silver-grey hair was pinned in a practical bun as she settled into the balcony chair, sipping a cold beer and watching the world soften around her. It was a small rebellion against the tea-and-toast expectations that had followed her since her retirement home days. She watched as petals drifted lazily in the breeze; the air was tinged with a taste of salt and jasmine. It was in many ways a paradise.

And yet, beneath the warmth and serenity, a quiet unease clung to her. The place was beautiful; almost too beautiful, as if a postcard had been edited one time too many. But Kayla, with decades of pragmatism stitched into her bones, chose, for now, to let herself enjoy the illusion. After all, illusions had their uses. They bought time.

The next morning came gently. A soft chime and a warm intercom voice stirred the group. "Good morning, everyone. Breakfast is now being served in the dining area. Please make your way downstairs at your convenience."

Kayla took her time dressing, favouring linen for its ease. She stepped into the quiet procession heading toward breakfast, the dining room already alive with soft clinks and low murmurs. Tropical fruit: bright mango, papaya, and star-shaped slices of carambola greeted her plate like tiny celebrations.

Then came the second announcement, more formal. "Today, we will be conducting health checks to ensure everyone's well-being. After you've had breakfast, one of our team members will guide you to the clinic. Just follow their lead, and thank you for being so cooperative."

After breakfast, everyone made their way to the clinic. The clinic's entrance was sleek and polished, with clean lines and an almost futuristic air to it.

Stepping inside, Dave noticed the crisp scent of disinfectant that greeted him, mingling with the faint hum of machines. His gaze swept across the room, noting the surprising length of the space and the spotless rows of beds lining either side. He paused, taking in the peculiar sight that awaited him.

He'd expected the usual lineup of stethoscopes, IV poles and monitors. But each bed held something different: an arrangement of strange, unfamiliar equipment. Helmet-shaped devices hung suspended, connected to sleek laptops resting on nearby stands. Along the length of each bed was a large machine, its surface dotted with gauges strategically placed at intervals. The gleaming surfaces and intricate displays suggested advanced technology far beyond anything he'd seen before.

A nurse emerged from the corridor in a pressed white uniform, radiating calm. With a soft gesture, she invited Dave to move forward. As he passed the other beds, Dave watched the nurses instruct patients to lie down. The nurses gently slid small frames over the individuals, their soothing voices carrying words of reassurance.

"There's no need to be alarmed. These machines are simply scanning devices that allow us to gather readings from different points on your body," one of them explained.

Dave found himself fascinated and a little wary; his mind racing with questions about the purpose and capabilities of these machines. What kind of technology could this be, he wondered, that warranted such an elaborate setup? He'd always kept up with cutting-edge technology, but this was something else. Everything about the room felt off-kilter, futuristic in its precision, as if you were stepping into a clinic built for a world that hadn't arrived yet.

As he moved closer to his assigned bed, a voice from the front of the group broke the silence, cutting through the room's sense of intrigue. Dave turned his head slightly, curiosity flickering. It was the old doctor, the same one he'd spoken to the night before.

Parker Brooks, a tall man with a sturdy build that belied his 85 years, adjusted the collar of his crisp shirt as he stepped into the clinic. His sharp blue eyes scanned the room, taking in the gleaming surfaces, the peculiar helmet-like devices hanging over beds, and the quiet hum of advanced machinery. A former naval doctor, Parker had seen his fair share of medical facilities, but this one? This was different. The layout, the equipment, everything seemed foreign, almost unsettling.

He paused to get his bearings as, a man in a white coat approached him. Dr. Trill, by his badge, was middle-aged with a clean-shaven face and a calm demeanour. His movements were purposeful, almost rehearsed, as he carried a small laptop in one hand.

"This doesn't look like any clinic I've ever worked in," Parker remarked, his voice steady but tinged with curiosity.

Dr. Trill raised an eyebrow and asked, "Your name?"

"Dr. Parker Brooks," he replied. The words felt both natural and strange; after all, he hadn't actively practised medicine in years.

"Let me see..." Dr. Trill's fingers tapped his laptop screen, scanning through what appeared to be detailed records. "Ah, there we are," he said, his tone shifting to one of authority. "You're 85 years old, and following your retirement from the Navy, you lived in England for 10 years before returning to a small fishing village in Maine. Well, Dr. Brooks, you've been out of the Navy for 25 years now, and I assure you, many changes have been made in the medical field since your retirement."

Parker's eyes narrowed slightly, his lips pulling into a faint smirk. "Well, I guess so," he muttered, though quietly thinking. *Smart aleck.*

With a gesture toward the nearest bed, Dr. Trill encouraged him, "Give it a try; you won't be sorry."

Parker hesitated for a moment before walking toward the bed. As he moved through the room, his keen observational skills, honed through decades of medical practice and military service, couldn't ignore the nagging feeling tugging at the back of his mind. The staff, including Dr. Trill, seemed oddly similar to those he'd seen working at the home. Their appearances, their mannerisms, even the way they moved. It was as though they were cut from the same mould.

Something wasn't right, and Parker felt it settle in his chest like static. It was a sense, more than a thought, as if he were stepping into a room that looked familiar but hummed with something missing. The forest lacked any discernible scent; neither the musk of damp earth nor the aroma of foliage. Only silence remained. The airport had vanished from view almost instantly, swallowed by flat terrain that offered no explanation.

Also, the staff were polite and efficient, almost to a fault. But their eye contact lingered just a fraction too long, like scanning rather than acknowledging.

From the moment the plane had touched down, Parker had been noting fragments that didn't fit. The clinic was one of them. Too pristine, too quiet. Another tile in a mosaic he hadn't yet seen the full shape of. But the pieces were gathering, and he was paying attention.

Parker took his seat on the edge of the bed, his hands resting lightly on his knees as he glanced at the intricate setup of machines surrounding him. He recalled that in his younger days, he could make snap decisions and draw quick conclusions, relying on his instincts and experience. Now, though slower, his mind remained sharp. He made a quiet promise to himself that he'd figure out what was going on here soon enough. A spark of determination flickered in his eyes, steadying him for whatever lay ahead.

While the retirees lay on their beds, various instruments were connected to small, round metal plates fitted to parts of their bodies. A small apparatus was gently lowered onto their heads. Next, the nurse entered information about each of them onto her computer. The machine and headgear began to hum slightly with a gentle tone, not unpleasant, but quite relaxing. Gradually, the patients fell asleep.

One Life to Live... or Maybe Two

Day 3

Personal account: Dr. Parker Brooks

"Looking back, it's almost laughable; we spent weeks among them without the faintest clue that they were aliens. Friendly, yes, but aliens nonetheless. The pieces are finally falling into place, revealing a picture far more complex than we ever imagined. What else have we overlooked? What truths still lie beneath the surface, waiting to be uncovered?"

***

The alarm clocks rang sharply in each room, snapping the retirees out of sleep. Like clockwork, the announcement crackled from every speaker:

"Good morning, everyone. Please enjoy your breakfast. I suggest we all meet in the main hall at 11:00 am."

Dave Robinson groaned as he sat up, rubbing his temples. "Like being back on base," he muttered. "No sleep-ins, always meetings. I thought I retired for a reason." As the fog of sleep lifted, fragments of the previous day floated like puzzle pieces missing their edges.

Had an entire day slipped by? A missed breakfast was one thing. A missing day was entirely different. The unsettling thought clung to him as he dressed and headed to the breakfast room.

Eventually, the room settled down, and they took their seats.

"Ladies and gentlemen, there is nothing to be concerned about. This is a briefing regarding your physicals. I won't be going into details about the specifics of any one person and want to assure you there is no cause for alarm."

Dave abruptly stood up, his voice sharp with confusion. "Hold on, I was just at the clinic. The next thing I knew, I was back in bed, and it was the next day. What's going on here?"

Dr. Trill, a tall man with unnervingly perfect posture, stepped onto the stage and addressed the crowd with a practised smile.

"I trust you slept well?" he asked, his voice smooth as glass.

Dave opened his mouth to argue, but something in the doctor's gaze made him falter. He thought back; he had slept deeply. Too deeply.

"Well... yeah," he said reluctantly. The unease hadn't left. It had simply shifted shape.

Dr. Trill's smile widened in that easy, almost unsettling way of his. "Good, good. Those little vibrations you felt? That's just the system doing its job, using finely tuned sound waves to help your body relax. Most people drift off without even noticing. The younger ones try to fight it, but once you get a bit older..." He glanced around the room with a playful wink. "Well, naps start to feel like the highlight of the day, don't they?"

A ripple of half-hearted laughter spread through the crowd. Dave exhaled slowly, then sank back into his chair, the weight of uncertainty pressing on his shoulders.

Dr. Trill adjusted his glasses, and his voice shifted into a more practised tone, lecturing in a composed manner. "I want to thank you all for your cooperation. These tests were crucial. We've assessed everything, from your skeletal structure and blood composition to your major organs and cognitive processing."

From the back of the room, a voice piped up, cracking through the stillness. “Shouldn’t we be awake for that last part?”

Dr. Trill paused, tilting his head with measured amusement. “Not necessary. The headsets included earphones. You may have noticed a soft hum before drifting off? That sound initiates a controlled REM state. While your bodies rested, your minds remained fully active. It’s a specialised technique, exclusive to our facility. Some of you may even remember fragments from your conversations with us, woven into your dreams.” He let out a chuckle. “I have to say, you were all incredibly chatty.”

The earlier laughter faded, giving way to an uneasy silence. Dave’s fingers curled around the edge of his chair, knuckles pale. What had he said? What had the others revealed without knowing?

Dr. Trill’s polished exterior flickered, just briefly, then he continued without missing a beat. “In our final phase, we addressed minor ailments you've likely lived with for years. In a few cases, we also removed foreign objects that may have been causing discomfort.” His delivery was casual, as if he were announcing dental cleanings.

Whispers rose like smoke across the room. Dave’s heart thudded. His words slipped out, barely louder than a breath, like a breath trying to become speech. “Foreign objects? Did you put trackers in us?” he asked aloud, his tone tight with suspicion.

Dr. Trill met his gaze and smiled a little too easily. “No,” he said, chuckling. “Nothing like that. I assure you, everything done was for your benefit. You’re in capable hands. There’s no reason for concern.”

But concern was already there, growing in the silence that followed.

Dr. Brooks reached behind his neck and winced instinctively, and paused, realising there was no discomfort. His hand lingered on the spot, and his brows furrowed in surprise as he pressed the area more firmly. The ache that had burdened him for years had, quite inexplicably, ceased.

"All of you are suffering from age-related symptoms," Dr. Trill began, his voice steady but carrying a weight that made the room sit up and listen. His eyes moved briefly to Dr. Brooks, catching the unconscious way his hand drifted to his neck, fingers pressing lightly against skin, almost as if confirming something beneath it.

"Some of you," Dr. Trill said after a long, deliberate pause, "are suffering from a terminal condition that no one on this planet can cure."

The rest of the room seemed to let the words drift by, but one phrase snagged on Dave's nerves like a thorn. *This planet.* Something in the way Dr. Trill said it made Dave wonder, what if the cure wasn't here at all? What if it existed somewhere else entirely? The idea was absurd. He let out a short laugh, trying to shake it off.

"Everyone here is between the ages of seventy and ninety-six." He gestured toward the seated group, his voice shifting, changing to a more hopeful rhythm. "We can make your remaining years quite remarkable. We can address your health issues in ways that surpass conventional understanding."

A frail woman in a wheelchair wheeled herself forward slightly, her fingers trembling as they gripped the armrests. Her voice, though soft, was clear and deliberate, cutting cleanly through the whispers.

"Look at us," she began, her eyes scanning the room before settling back on Dr. Trill. "We are well past our prime. With no family left to rely on, we're on our own completely." Her watery gaze lingered a moment longer, the quiet strength in her words striking a chord. Without missing a beat, she follows up with, "So, I'd like to know, who's paying for this? And what do you get out of it?"

Gall stepped onto the platform with steady, unhurried confidence. The overhead lights caught the sharp lines of his tailored suit as he laced his fingers together. "I've been expecting these questions," he said, his voice calm and sure, carrying the ease of someone who'd rehearsed this moment more than once. He leaned slightly toward the crowd, as though letting them in on a secret.

"We understand how you feel," he continued, his tone smooth but tinged with a subtle undercurrent of urgency. "You've accepted the notion that there is nothing left for you to achieve. You believe that the chapters of your lives that mattered are already written, and now... you are mere observers." He paused, his eyes sweeping across the room, drawing their silent attention.

"Ok tell me..." His voice dipped, inviting rather than demanding, like a quiet tide pulling them in. "If you had the chance to step into something new..., would you?"

A faint smile tugged at his lips, not quite reaching his eyes. It lingered there, a quiet spark, a suggestion that his words carried more weight than mere curiosity. He looked at her as though he were holding a secret, something just beyond the horizon, waiting to be discovered.

She didn't answer but paused as she steadied herself. Her fingers gripped the arms of her wheelchair, knotted and pale against the cold steel. The silence stretched. Then she lifted her chin ever so slightly, the flicker of defiance glowing behind weary eyes.

"There's only one experience left for us to take on," she said. Her voice didn't waver; it cut through the moment, firm and final, like the closing of a door. But underneath it, something raw lingered. Not sadness exactly. More like certainty born from surviving too much. Her words hung heavy in the air, and for a moment, there was no sound but the faint murmur of agreement from the rest of the group.

Gall smiled faintly, lifting a hand as if to stop her train of thought. "May I ask your name?"

"Retired Air Force Lieutenant Colonel Paige Mitchelmore."

"Lieutenant, may I call you Paige from now on? Please hold that thought," he said smoothly. "I know where you are going, and the answer to your question is 'perhaps not,' as if he were reading her mind. Please allow me to continue," he urged, his tone both reassuring and insistent. "You will understand in time."

He straightened, his gaze sweeping over the assembled group, meeting their eyes one by one. Some held curiosity, others scepticism, and still others a wearied acceptance.

"For many years," he began again, his voice deepening with purpose, "we have been in contact with government agencies around the world." He paused for effect, letting the magnitude of his words sink in. "I'm going to share with you information that your military and governments have deemed 'Above Secret.'" The deliberate emphasis on the phrase "Above Secret" landed heavily, sending an almost imperceptible ripple of reaction through the retirees.

Gall's voice, rich and resonant, filled the room with a practised calm. "We hope," he said, each word measured, his tone steady but carrying the kind of weight that made people lean in. "That you'll take a moment... just a moment... to truly consider what lies ahead."

Silence followed. Not the usual kind. The kind that holds its breath.

His words seemed to linger in the air, pressing gently against every wall. A low rustle moved through the crowd, scepticism mingling with curiosity, but it fizzled quickly when another figure stepped forward.

The woman's presence alone seemed to quiet the room. Tall and poised, she had similar features to everyone else at the home. "My name is Patrasia," she said.

The way she stood, the lines of her frame silhouetted sharply against the soft light behind her, drew the eye without demanding it.

She paused as she reached the centre of the stage; the glow caught the angles of her face, tracing them with quiet precision. Her gaze moved over the room, not hurriedly, but deliberately. Little by little, the conversations gradually died away.

For a moment, she didn't speak. She stood there, her expression unreadable, the silence around her thick with anticipation. It was clear she wasn't stalling; she was choosing her words with purpose, letting the weight of the moment settle before anything else did. Then she spoke, her voice calm and even, which seemed to press down on the room itself.

"I'm going to be blunt with you," she said, her tone unwavering. "We are not of this world."

A single whisper broke the silence, low and incredulous. Don leaned toward Dave, his voice barely audible but charged with realisation. "I knew it," he muttered. "They're fricken aliens."

"My people," Patrasia continued, unfazed by their reactions, "explored the galaxy long before we discovered Earth. We first visited your world almost two million years ago."

A loud scrape broke the silence as Stuart shot to his feet, his chair screeching against the floor, resting his hands on the chair in front for support. "Is this some kind of joke you're playing on us?" His voice was frail, although his expression teetered between disbelief and anger.

Patrasia tilted her head, just a fraction, an instinctive gesture, as if weighing his doubt in the balance. Then, her voice broke the stillness.

"This isn't a joke," she said, calm but resolute, the sincerity in her voice steady, sincere, and just loud enough to echo faintly in the enclosed space. It wasn't loud; it didn't need to be. Her words carried.

She fixed her eyes on Stuart, and in that moment, they weren't speaking; they were daring each other to blink first. "I promise you, it's real," she added, and something in her gaze made him sit back, quieted not by fear, but by the weight of belief.

When she saw him settle, her voice softened. "Let me continue," she said gently. "What we're about to share... it will make things clearer."

She stepped forward, just a little, every movement deliberate, her silhouette etched in contrast to the low glow of the room. There was purpose in every step, like each one was part of what she had to say, even before the words came. Standing near the edge of the platform, she let her sharp, angular features come into full view.

"For instance," she said, her words carrying a pointed undertone, "you may have noticed subtle differences in appearance between the staff and yourselves." Her piercing gaze swept across the room, lingering on a few faces. Her unearthly grace, once merely peculiar, now distinctly alien, the realisation dawning in the wide eyes of her audience.

As her words settled over the crowd, a wave of unease rippled through the room.

From somewhere near the back, someone spoke just loud enough to catch a few ears, "I knew Doris had suspiciously perfect eyebrows... no way those things were human."

A few muffled chuckles broke the tension in the room.

"Our arrival on Earth was not merely a visit," Patrasia began, her voice unhurried with each word carefully chosen. "By chance, it was a rediscovery. The extensive records of this region of space had been obscured and forgotten over time."

She paused, letting the weight of her words settle over the room. When she spoke again, her tone had deepened; sombre.

"Aurelia, our ship's AI, wasn't actively searching for your world. Our first knowledge of Earth was... accidental. It came from a communication device you had built; we were unaware that we had stumbled upon a satellite of Earth." She let the sentence hang, her words inviting questions but offering no immediate answers.

The room remained still, suspended in a hush that felt more analytical than emotional. No one challenged her; there was nothing to dispute.

From the side of the room, Dr. Trill turned, his gaze meeting Dr. Brooks's with quiet intent. Something had shifted; not dramatically, but unmistakably.

"Dr. Brooks," he said softly. "Your initial observations about the clinic and equipment were accurate. I apologise for the fabricated story about advancements." His eyes darted briefly toward the group before meeting Brooks' hesitant gaze. "If anyone here chooses not to continue with our program, he or she may leave at any time. We will respect our previous commitment to address your medical conditions."

Sarah Kane spoke from her seat. "And you think our governments will let us go knowing what we now know."

He took a moment before acknowledging her statement. "If you had decided not to proceed, your memories would be wiped from the moment you left your retirement home and replaced with new ones. You will be assigned to other residences."

"Well, it's a good job I'm staying," she said with a smirk.

Dr. Brooks stiffened slightly, his hand instinctively pressing again at the previously aching spot on his neck. He didn't move to speak, but his lips parted as if he were on the brink of a revelation.

No one moved. The room held its breath. Dr. Trill's sharp eyes scanned the retirees, his practised smile unwavering as he leaned forward slightly, hands clasped in front of him.

"Thank you all for staying," he said, his tone smooth and calculated, as if he'd been certain of their decision from the start. "Now that we are all in agreement, I'd like to disclose something important.

Following your medical evaluations, we've identified several individuals in critical condition. For this reason, we are accelerating our program."

A faint murmur rippled through the group, only to be silenced when Patrasia returned.

"We call ourselves Venorans and have been embroiled in a long-standing conflict with the Korrathi race in our sector of the galaxy. Despite my race having superior technology, the Korrathi have the advantage of greater numbers and control over many planets. We have been seeking assistance from the leaders of your world to aid us in our struggle. For centuries, our people have been locked in this war that has been stalled for a long time. We have retreated from many of our homeworlds and now live in a few remaining systems. With the help of other races, including those from Earth, we have been able to push back against the Korrathi and take the fight to them. However, progress has been slow, and the constant state of war has left us weary and longing for peace."

"We have spent decades sharing our knowledge and technology, a small gesture of thanks for the kindness shown to us by Earth's people. Our presence here was kept secret, known only to your leaders." The lights are dimmed, and a 3D image appeared above their heads. A section of the Milky Way Galaxy is shown.

"This is the location of Earth and its solar system," she explained. Another area of the Milky Way lit up.

"And over here is the location of our star system." The image zooms in further, revealing six planets orbiting a red star.

"The second planet is our home, Venor. We are called Venorans," she concluded.

"From the very moment you arrived, you may or may not have noticed how quickly the airport disappeared from view while you were on the bus. The airport you landed at was an artificial structure we created to make you feel comfortable. Once it was no longer needed, we broke it down into its molecular components, blending in with the surrounding area."

Stuart leaned over to Don and remarked, "I knew it! I thought that was odd." A flicker of recognition passed over Parker's face. He smiled, just slightly. He'd noticed it too.

"How do you expect us to help you?" Paige's voice cut through the room, sharp and unyielding. She gestured around the group, her expression tinged with frustration. "Look around. You're sixty years too late." Her gaze rested firmly on Gall, daring him to refute her.

Gall remained composed, nodding slightly, as if expecting her reaction. "As we have already mentioned," he said, his tone measured. "We can repair your bodies at this facility."

Paige didn't back down. "And what about the age thing?" She countered, her voice steady but tinged with weariness. "I'm the oldest here at ninety-six. I don't expect to be around much longer."

Gall's faint, knowing smile returned. "Which is precisely why you have been chosen. Our intake is limited to those of advanced age with no living relatives."

The quiet statement settled over the room, its weight undeniable. Before anyone could respond, Dr. Trill rose from his seat, the subtle creak of the chair beneath him punctuating the moment.

"On board our ship," Dr. Trill began, his tone calm but clear, "are medical pods ready for each of you. You'll rest in stasis, connected to our medical system. We've already learned a great deal about your bodies, and we know exactly when each of you was at his or her physical best."

He paused, looking slowly around the room, making sure they were all with him.

"While we travel," he continued, "we'll reverse your biological age to match the peak of your physical and cognitive performance. Your bones, organs, and everything essential will be restored. You will be young and in the prime of your life."

The air shifted.

Trill's voice had just finished echoing through the chamber: *"You will be young again. In the prime of your life."*

For a moment, no one moved. They sat in stunned silence. Wheelchairs. Canes. Aged hands folded on their laps.

Then someone laughed. A short, startled burst. It came from the back; an old man with a voice like gravel. "You're serious... is this a con?" he said, half-choked, half-hopeful.

"I assure you this is real," Trill said.

A woman near the front blinked hard, her hand trembling as she reached for her own cheek. "I haven't seen my reflection without lines in forty years," she whispered.

The murmurs spread like wildfire.

"Young again?" "Like... before the surgeries?" "My knees. My lungs. My skin. All of it?"

A man stood slowly, his joints cracking. He looked down at his hands, then up at Trill. "I was twenty-three when I ran the Boston Marathon. I want that back."

From the other side of the room, Dave leaned back against the wall, arms crossed, a half-smile tugging at his lips. "You won't be running the marathon on Earth," he said, still smiling.

The room paused, then erupted. Some laughed, wild and unrestrained. Others wept quietly, overwhelmed. Some stared ahead, eyes glassy, as if trying to picture themselves without the weight of age.

One by one, they began to speak, not to Trill, but to each other.

"I'll dance again." "I'll swim without gasping." "I'll kiss someone and not feel fragile." "I'll be who I was, and more."

Slowly, they rose. Not as the elderly, but as a generation on the edge of rebirth.

They didn't cheer. They didn't shout.

And in that quiet, trembling moment, they looked at each other with something they hadn't felt in years. Wonder.

Dr. Trill lifted his hand. "I understand this is a lot to take in," he said. "And while we can't regrow missing limbs, we've developed replacements that feel real. They move with you. They look like you. They're almost indistinguishable."

He took a step forward, softening his voice. "Let's pause here. Think it over. We'll talk more tomorrow after breakfast, around eleven."

No one responded. Not quite sure what to say or how to react. Life as they knew it was changing. And there was no going back.

Past and Present

Personal account: Patrasia

"You're probably thinking, why delve into ancient history? Because where we are now only makes sense when we understand how we got here. This isn't just a backstory of the humans and Venoran meeting. It's a map of invisible threads, a glimpse at the forces that have been pulling us together for longer than we realised. Only by seeing the full picture can we start to understand what's coming."

***

The next day, the grand hall filled early. A low buzz of whispers drifted through the room, thick with anticipation. When Gall entered, the noise faded almost instantly as every face turned toward the platform.

"Good morning," he said, his voice carrying easily across the hall. "Today, I want to tell you more about who we are and why we need your help now more than ever."

He paused, letting his eyes move slowly over the faces before him, as if searching for a spark of understanding. "We have classified the people of Earth as one of the younger races, using our species as a benchmark. To put this into perspective, our civilisation was already exploring the galaxy while humanity was only just beginning to emerge from the forests."

A man near the front, his brow furrowed in thought, raised a hand.

"Ok why us?" he asked, his voice heavy with doubt. "Out of all the races in the galaxy, why do you think we can help?"

Gall turned to him. His expression, a blend of patience and quiet authority, softened as he met the man's gaze.

"Because, of all the worlds we've come across, Earth stands apart. You've endured, adapted, and pushed forward when everything told you to break. There's something extraordinary about that." His words hung in the air, heavy and still.

Gall inhaled deeply, his tone dipping lower, darker. "Our lifespan is significantly longer than yours; on average, we live up to 850 years. For more generations than anyone can remember," he said softly, "we've watched civilizations blaze into greatness, only to crumble back into dust. Through it all, we held fast to our law to observe, but never intervene."

The words settled like dust across the room. Someone shifted, the soft scrape of chair legs breaking the silence.

He lowered his gaze thoughtfully before continuing. "We've seen empires rise in the galaxy, then flicker and vanish. It was never easy to stand apart."

"We believed that remaining in the shadows was the best way to preserve peace. We feared that interference would lead to unintended consequences, igniting wars we could not predict or control. Isolation has be-come our greatest weakness."

His voice lifted with urgency. "We've always stood alone. But now, faced with a war we cannot contain, our numbers are not enough. We're nearing the edge. If we remain alone, we won't survive. Alone, we cannot hold out much longer."

The room was heavy with silence, Gall's words hanging in the air like storm clouds ready to burst. His piercing gaze swept over the audience once more, with a tangible intensity in his demeanour. The flicker of hesitation, the slight shifting of bodies, each reaction betrayed the mounting tension. "Many younger worlds," Gall continued, "are now looking to us for a solution, for hope. And you, the people of Earth, may hold the key to helping us drive back the Korrathi threat."

His tone sharpened. "I must also warn you, this war does not end with us. If the Korrathi win, your world may not escape. This is why we came to Earth for help. This isn't just about saving us. It's about protecting you."

The crowd stirred as whispers rippled through the room.

"For now," he continued, his voice low but firm, "Earth is safe. Its place on the outer edge of the galaxy has kept it hidden. Discovery might still be centuries away, perhaps a thousand years. But this great distance, great as it is, won't last forever." He paused, letting the significance of this revelation sink in.

His gaze swept across the room. "The Korrathi don't stop. Their reach grows every year. What seems far away now could be on your doorstep tomorrow."

The room tensed. Sarah stood up, her chair scraping the floor, her voice breaking the quiet.

"Who are the Korrathi?" she asked, eyes locked on Gall. "Why are they so dangerous?"

Heads turned. Gall met her gaze, his tone measured.

"They're ruthless," he said. "Relentless. Their fleets spread like a sickness through space, armed with technology stolen from every world they've crushed. But conquest isn't just their goal. They erase any culture showing even a hint of progress, viewing it as a threat."

Someone from the back spoke up. "Then why hide for so long?"

“We thought we were protecting ourselves,” Gall said. “For centuries, we cloaked our worlds, avoided contact, held to the hope that peace could last. But peace is no longer an option.”

The silence grew heavy. Gall stepped forward slightly.

“We first crossed paths with them five hundred Earth years ago. Their ships blotted out the stars. We retreated, praying they’d never find us. Eventually, they did.”

His voice deepened. “One of our outer worlds was attacked. We fought back. It wasn’t a choice; it was survival. That’s when they learned we existed. And now, they’re coming.”

His eyes swept across the assembly. “You must understand that their empire’s shadow draws closer with each day. If we fall, Earth will not remain hidden for long.”

He paused, letting the urgency of his words settle. “Our scouts have informed us that they anticipate the discovery of our homeworld within the coming year. We’ve spent lifetimes tucked away, out of sight from the rest of the galaxy, from empires that have left nothing but destroyed worlds. Now, we’re standing at the edge of the very thing we hoped to avoid... a war that could shatter the fragile peace we’ve spent generations protecting.”

Gall’s voice carried the weight of their plight as he addressed the gathered retirees. “Since they discovered our existence, the Korrathi have unleashed destruction on our outer worlds. They do not conquer with mercy. They annihilate.”

“For now,” he said, “the defence shield, an energy barrier that envelops each of our worlds, conceals us from their relentless scans. Those shields are merely a reprieve. The integrity of those shields are beginning to diminish with every passing cycle. That is why we turn to you.”

The hall was silent, save for the faint hum of distant machinery. Gall’s gaze swept over the crowd, his expression unwavering.

"We've had help from your governments, locating people who might be willing to stand with us. You, the people of Earth, are unlike any others we've encountered. Where our strength falters, yours shines. You see what others don't. You find new paths when none seem to exist. That's why we need you."

Sarah rose again, gripping the chair in front of her for support. Her prosthetic arm glinted faintly under the hall's dim lights.

"You say you're going to fix our bodies," she began, her voice tinged with scepticism. "But there aren't nearly enough of us here to fight your war."

Gall nodded solemnly, his response measured. "You are not the first group we have sent. Over the past ten years, many have taken the same path you are about to embark on. Today, thousands of your kind live and fight alongside us."

He took a step closer to the edge of the platform, his voice lowering. "I have recently received a communication from Venor that has changed everything. They've instructed us to halt recruitment here on Earth. We have closed the other Venor Retirement homes around the world; yours will be the final group we send. The situation has reached a critical stage; the Korrathi now have a spatial estimate of our home world's location."

Gasps rippled through the room, but Gall pressed on. "As a result, we are advancing the program. It will take several months to travel to our star system in Slide Space. While in stasis, your bodies will undergo full regeneration, and any injuries will be repaired, getting you back to full strength. Meanwhile, essential knowledge and skills will be gently transferred into your minds."

He stopped, his voice softening as he regarded the recruits. "I will not force you into this fight. Now that you understand our situation, if anyone wishes to return home, please raise your hand."

The silence hung heavy until a gruff voice cut through it. "Sir," then the sound of a chair being moved back, Don stood up.

"Here's how I see it," he said, sweeping a hard look around the room. "My time on Earth is almost done. And some of us won't even make it to next year." Then he pointed towards the Venorans behind him. "They're offering us more time. A second shot, and I'm taking it. I've got nothing left to lose... and everything to gain."

He dropped back into his seat, daring anyone to challenge him. One handclap cracked through the silence... then another as everyone joined in.

"Thank you for those words. I will ask again, does anyone wish to return home?" His eyes moved slowly across the room, waiting. When no hands rose, his expression softened, a flicker of hope breaking through his otherwise stoic demeanour.

"You honour us," he said quietly, his voice thick with emotion. "Now, let us stand together against the darkness."

Patrasia rose to her feet, her movements deliberate as she faced the assembly. The dim light of the hall caught the intricate patterns on her robes, causing them to shimmer as she moved. Her voice carried an air of quiet authority as she spoke.

"I want to share something extraordinary we discovered about your race," she began, her eyes narrowing with intensity. "While searching our ancient records of your solar system, we uncovered an astonishing truth. 1.5 million years ago, one of our research teams visited Earth."

The crowd shifted uneasily, murmurs rippling around the room. Patrasia continued, "They studied the gene structure of Earth's native people and were shocked to find striking similarities to our own. Your race held the potential to unlock mysteries that even we, an advanced civilisation, could barely comprehend."

She paused, letting the weight of her revelation sink in. "At that time, your ancestors were struggling to survive in a harsh and unforgiving world. One of our scientists, defying the laws of our people, did something unimaginable. Seeing potential that was unparalleled in the galaxy, the scientist modified the genes of your ancestors, adding a catalyst for adaptability and learning. What we did not foresee was how this single action would spark a journey that transformed your people from a struggling species to one with boundless potential."

Gasps filled the room, and Patrasia's voice softened, tinged with regret. "For a thousand years, our scientists secretly studied your ancestors, watching as small groups began to show signs of advancement."

Patrasia's voice carried an air of measured fascination as she addressed the crowd. "What moved our scientists more than anything was your resilience. When we first witnessed your race, you had only just emerged from the safety of the forests. Hunting and gathering, facing each new day as a test of endurance. Nature wasn't kind. Predators were lurking, the climate was unforgiving, and basic survival was a challenge."

For a moment, her gaze became distant, her voice shaded with awe. "In just a couple of generations, something unexpected happened. You didn't just survive; you adapted, and communities emerged. Your shorter lifespans didn't hold you back; they became the rhythm of change. Every generation passed down something precious: hard-earned wisdom, sharpened thinking."

Her expression darkened, shadowed by memories. "In time," she said, her voice low, "our leaders learned what the scientists had done. They had broken a sacred law that we held above all else. No interference. They demanded that the research team return home immediately. And just like that, the connection between our worlds was severed. You were left behind, to piece together a future from the remnants we left you."

Patrasia's gaze swept solemnly across the assembly, her voice now tinged with eagerness as she continued. "We eventually returned five thousand years later. What greeted us defied expectations. Your species had spread across the continents, erecting cities of staggering ambition. Yet amid this brilliance, we saw the scars of countless conflicts, wars fought against rival tribes, nations, and ideologies."

"And so, we left your world again, leaving behind only the echoes of our influence. Your ability to adapt and ingenuity; these are the legacy of that forbidden act. And now, in this pivotal moment, it may be the very thing that saves us, and why we came to Earth."

"Our recent arrival on your planet was purely accidental. We had slowed our ship to recharge our Slide Drive engines when we picked up a faint signal from one of your satellites. From the disk we found onboard, we were able to locate Earth."

There was quiet admiration in her eyes, unspoken but unmistakable. "What we found upon arrival completely surprised us. The transformation your world has undergone... was astonishing. Since the last time we set foot here, the growth we've seen defies logic. Where most civilisations crawl through centuries of change, you've raced forward. This wasn't gradual progress. It was a leap. You've built and uncovered truths that civilisations far older still wrestle to comprehend. Now, you are crafting vessels that one day could pierce the void." She let her words sink in.

"You've reshaped mountains, charted the stars, and coaxed order from the raw noise of existence. What you've done is not just progress; it's transformation."

There was a softness in her voice, the kind that only comes with genuine respect. "What we saw wasn't just progress; it was proof. Proof of your creativity, your grit, and an unshakable will to survive."

Patrasia's voice dipped, steady but edged with memory.

"Our recent first contact with Earth didn't unfold the way we'd hoped. Before we could even speak with your leaders, one of our scout ships, just quietly studying your atmosphere, was fired upon. We neutralised the threat quickly, but the damage was done."

She glanced across the room, her eyes scanning the faces turned toward her. "The reaction across your communication networks confirmed what we feared: we hadn't gone unnoticed. And with that, we knew we couldn't afford silence. Any delay could spark conflict. We had to act fast to open a channel, to start a dialogue, to stop fear from defining the story between us."

She straightened slightly, her final words falling like dust over old history.

"And the rest," Patrasia said softly, "you already know."

The hum of conversation faded as Dr. Trill's voice rose with calm authority, cutting cleanly through the noise. "If anyone is near someone named George Hollins," he said, looking around the room, "please let us know."

A rough voice called out from the back. "He's here. We brought him."

All eyes turned, curious and alert, as three figures emerged from the shadows. George Hollins looked fragile, hunched in his wheelchair, shrinking under the weight of sudden attention, a quiet echo of the man he used to be. On either side of him stood the twins. They didn't speak, but their presence said enough: still, sharp-eyed, steady. The years had weathered them, but their strength was intact.

They didn't need words. One glance between them was enough. Hands tightened on the wheelchair's handles. They moved together, guiding George forward with quiet precision. Protective, yes, but more than that. They were guarding him like something the world had forgotten, something valuable.

Dr. Trill gave a short nod, his face unreadable but clearly taking everything in.

"Thank you," he said. "An orderly will be with you shortly."

One twin touched the other's arm, a silent signal. Something had shifted. Whatever this moment meant, it wasn't routine. George's arrival had stirred something deeper, and the twins seemed to sense it.

They stepped back again, not leaving the space but blending into it. Still watchful. Still waiting. You couldn't miss them, even if you tried.

Gall stood up and addressed the group, his tone reassuring as he continued. "Tomorrow morning, we will begin transferring you to our ship. You are welcome to bring any belongings with you. I know some of you may be expecting a ship to descend to pick you up, but that will not be necessary."

Pausing for a moment, he allowed the anticipation in the room to build before delivering the next piece of information. "Some of you may have heard about teleportation in your science journals," Gall began, his voice steady but warm. "Well, it's no longer just theory. We've made it real."

Smiling as he looked around the room. "We're going to use it to transport each of you directly to our ship, the *Arcadia*. It's completely safe, and while you might feel a little tingle, it won't be uncomfortable. One moment you'll be here in your room... and the next, you'll be standing onboard."

Gall's eyes moved slowly across the room, meeting each veteran's gaze with quiet intent. No one flinched. They'd heard plenty in their time; this was just one more truth to carry. Then, the silence began to shift. A ripple of low voices stirred, not frantic, but thoughtful; part wonder, part restless energy; as the weight of what they'd just heard settled in. “And now the fun begins,” he said, though the words were more for himself than anyone else.

First Day in Space

Personal account: David Robinson

"Something is different today... the town, the building, vanishing before our eyes, as if reality itself were unravelling. And now, we're leaving. Not just for another city, another country, but for space. A journey beyond anything we ever imagined."

***

Donald Northey noticed something peculiar as he gazed out the window; most of the buildings were missing. The road that led them there was now a jungle pathway. Curiosity got the better of him. He stepped into the hallway and looked out the window toward where the clinic once stood; it too was now replaced by jungle. The hallway echoed with footsteps. Don caught the orderly by the arm as he passed. "Where are all the buildings?" he asked, eyes searching for answers.

The orderly explained that the town and its buildings were constructed using integrated atoms, which are manipulated to create the structures.

"We are currently closing all non-essential areas," he continued, "and once we leave the planet, the remaining buildings will disappear, leaving no trace of their existence. The area will return to the jungle." With that, the orderly continued down the hall.

The audio system activated, instructing all the veterans to remain in their designated quarters while transport arrangements to the ship were initiated. As requested by the governments of Earth, the Venoran ship activated its cloaking shield to prevent any further detection by Earth's detection equipment. Don felt a mix of excitement and apprehension. The reality of their situation was sinking in. He returned to his room, his mind racing with thoughts of the journey ahead.

The door clicked shut behind him. His intercom activated with a faint crackle, and a poised, tranquil voice resonated through the room. "My name is Aurelia, and I'm the ship's AI. We are ready to welcome you aboard. This will only take a few seconds."

Don inhaled deeply, bracing himself, as a subtle tingling sensation crept over his skin as the transport process began. Then, just like that, he was no longer outside his room. He had materialised inside the ship, surrounded by fellow veterans. The room was large and glowed with a gentle ambient light.

A quiet hum of advanced machinery filled the room, then a figure stepped forward. It was Gall, "Welcome aboard," greeting them with a warm smile. "You are now part of a mission that will not only protect your planet but also help our struggle against the Korrathi. Together, we will ensure the safety of both our worlds."

As Paige materialised, breathing in slowly, she muttered under her breath, "Well, that wasn't too bad."

Later, after all the veterans had settled in, they met in the meeting room and were briefed on their roles and the training they would undergo. They were told that the journey to the training planet Zeph 3 would take one Earth month. During this period, they would enter stasis, undergo physical regeneration, and receive skill augmentations to align with those of the Venorans.

Dave entered his living quarters, which, despite being reminiscent of their retirement home with its couch, lounge chairs, small kitchen area, bathroom, and bed, had one notable difference: a large stasis chamber in the corner of the room. Overall, quite comfortable.

After a quick study of the pod, he remarked, “Suppose I'm going to get to know you pretty soon.”

A familiar voice crackles over the intercom, interrupting the quiet of the ship's interior. “Attention all veterans, in one hour, you will be taken on a comprehensive tour of our vessel.”

Later, Aurelia's friendly voice spoke over the intercom, inviting them to step outside their rooms to meet her and that she would be their guide. Within a few minutes, a female hologram appeared on a hovering platform, introducing herself as Aurelia. The veterans were surprised at what they saw; the AI appeared lifelike, resembling a Venoran. Her holographic body was tall and slender, with a smooth metallic sheen that reflected the ambient light, giving her an almost ethereal glow. Her features, the same as the Venorans', were finely sculpted, with high cheekbones, a straight nose, and piercing eyes.

She warmly greeted each veteran and encouraged them to take a seat, explaining that she would be leading them on a tour of the ship. Aurelia describes her other duties, which include being programmed with all the scientific knowledge of the Venorans. Additionally, she can provide support for any function on board the ship.

The group had just passed an open door just as an orderly was exiting. Standing on either side of the door were the twins. They looked more relaxed than on the first day we saw them.

They exchanged no words, but a glance from George was enough to command their next steps. Were they his bodyguards, caretakers, or something else entirely? The air around them felt heavy, purposeful.

For a fleeting moment, one of the twins locked eyes with me, his face betraying a flicker of recognition.

As George passed, his eyes glanced over to the group as if he were assessing them. A few noticed and smiled at him in acknowledgement. He had been taken out of the meeting hall on the first day, and this was the first time that anybody had seen him since. The twins, looking even more relaxed, joined the group.

"Who is he, and where are they taking him?" a curious voice asked.

Aurelia explained, "His name is George Hollins. He's being transferred to the medical centre, and we can only hope he arrives in time. He's suffering from a degenerative brain condition that's begun shutting down his body. This man is vital to our program; he once possessed a brilliant tactical mind."

She paused before continuing, "We deviated from our original plan to keep you on Earth a little longer, easing you into the details while treating him there. The general's condition has declined more rapidly than anticipated. We had no choice but to accelerate the timeline. If we lose him, it will be a serious setback to everything we've built."

The twins remained silent, watching intently as the orderly continued pushing the wheelchair down the hallway, stopping at the transfer station at the end of the hall. He pressed a button, and they vanished.

Aurelia's voice came through clearly. "You will be travelling aboard a Galaxy-class vessel named *Arcadia*. To your left is the transfer station; it shows your current position and allows movement to other areas of the ship."

"Aurelia, how big is the *Arcadia*?" someone asked.

"The *Arcadia* has 10 levels and is as wide as one of your football fields. The vessel comprises living accommodations, recreational facilities, dining halls, a scientific laboratory, a historical library, a medical centre, engineering operations, the primary control deck, navigational systems, and shuttle deployment bays."

"How many crew members does the *Arcadia* have?" enquired Don.

"Currently, we have 265. I should also point out that the number in your group is 90, which the *Arcadia* can easily accommodate."

The tour continued for a couple of hours; finally, Aurelia announced, "I understand this has been an exhausting day, and some of you may want to retire early, but first, we will proceed to the mess hall." Once inside, Aurelia gestured to the walls, where small compartments glowed with images of food and drink. She calmly explained how to access each one. "Just name or describe any food or drink item. These will be assembled to feel and taste like the original; additionally, all essential nutrients have been included. Direct your voice to the opening and make your request. This is where my tour ends." With that, she turned and exited the room.

Paige had been seated at the table, her wheelchair positioned neatly, as if she had been waiting for some time. When a woman approached and gestured toward the empty seat across from her, Paige smiled at her. "Sure, go ahead."

The woman, likely in her mid-80s, was about 5 feet 4 inches and moved with the steady caution of someone familiar with the toll of old age. She sat down with a warm smile and extended her hand. "Hi, I'm Sarah Kane."

"Paige Mitchelmore," she said, extending her hand for a handshake. As their hands briefly met, Paige's eyes lingered on Sarah's other arm, noticing the way it rested stiffly against her side. Sarah caught the glance and gave a knowing chuckle, speaking before Paige could ask.

"Oh, that? I lost it when a grenade went off beside me," Sarah clarified matter-of-factly, her voice edged with a mixture of acceptance and old frustrations. She flexed the fingers of her prosthetic arm, giving a quick, almost dismissive shrug. "They fitted me with this replacement soon after, as I wasn't fit for the field; then stuck me in an office job. I hated every second of it." She leaned back in her chair, her expression softening into something closer to nostalgia. "When I hit 50, I said that was it and took early retirement. My husband and I moved to Florida after that. We never had kids; it never seemed like the right time. Eventually, we drifted apart and divorced, but we always stayed on good terms. I heard he passed away a few years back."

Sarah's gaze grew distant for a moment before she shook her head lightly, pulling herself back to the present. She finished with a quiet laugh, her expression relaxing. "That's my story. What's yours, Paige? I overheard you in the hall saying you're 96; that's a good age," remarked Sarah. She also noticed that Paige appeared very frail; she could tell age was catching up as she hunched over the table.

Paige's voice was deliberate, her words measured as though each one carried the weight of the years she had seen. "Thanks, but I think I only have a year or two left. It would be nice if I could make it to 100." She managed a wry smile, glancing down at the chair she had grown too familiar with. "These last few years haven't been kind. I've been stuck in this thing, barely able to get around. Relying on it has taken the joy out of living."

Her gaze softened, her thoughts drifting to a life long gone. "I was married to an incredible man. He was so patient with me, even when my work kept me away. I focused so much on my career that I never stopped to think about having children. It's my greatest regret; if I could go back, I would change so much." Her voice faltered, but she pressed on, her fingers gripping the armrest tightly. "Now all I have left to look forward to is... well, and the call from above." Then, almost imperceptibly, a spark lit up her expression. "Although," she added, with a glimmer of excitement breaking through the heaviness. "From what Gall shared with us yesterday, maybe that call can be delayed. Maybe there's a chance for a new start after all."

Sarah leaned forward, curiosity flickering in her eyes. "What did you do before you retired?"

Paige hesitated, her lips pressing into a tight line. "Sorry," she finally said, her voice tinged with the faintest note of apology. "I can't divulge."

"Oh, come on!" laughed Sarah, throwing up her hands. "You're 96. We're on a spaceship with aliens, for crying out loud. Can it really get more secret than this?"

Paige sighed, a reluctant grin tugging at her mouth. "Good point," she admitted. Her tone shifted; "This is almost like a confession," she said. "I worked at Area 51. I led a team that reverse-engineered a couple of spaceships." Her grin turned into a chuckle. "And now I finally know where those ships came from. We studied every component of those crafts, every feature. We even wrote reports about what they could do. Believe me," she said, sweeping her hand toward their surroundings, "none of them came close to this ship. And yes," she added with a knowing laugh, "everything you heard about Roswell? All true."

Sarah was surprised at Paige's revelation: "Dang, spaceships... I knew it, would have loved to have been there."

Later, Aurelia materialised in the common area, her presence commanding attention as she gestured for the veterans to rise.

"We will be leaving your solar system in 24 hours," she announced, her voice calm and steady. "Get a good night's sleep. I will wake you in eight hours."

The group exchanged glances, a mixture of exhaustion and anticipation passing between them. Aurelia's piercing gaze lingered momentarily before she departed.

When the allotted hours had passed, Aurelia's voice crackled over the comms in each of their rooms.

"Greetings. Treatment protocols commence today, targeting skeletal integrity, circulatory health, and organ function. Proceed to the designated transfer stations and initiate relocation by requesting 'hospital.'"

Dave hesitated only a moment in his room before stepping toward the station. He leaned close, speaking clearly, "Hospital."

With a hum and a shimmer of light, the world around him blurred. His stomach lurched as he stumbled forward, catching his breath just as the scene stabilised. A sterile, pristine medical bay greeted him, its walls aglow with a faint blue light. Standing next to a sleek metallic bed was a Venoran doctor.

"Greetings, Dave," the doctor said warmly, inclining his head. "I trust the transport wasn't too much of a shock. One of your predecessors called it a 'rush.'"

Dave raised an eyebrow, still shaking off the disorientation. "A warning would've been nice, you know. And ditto for when we were beamed up from Earth."

The doctor chuckled, motioning toward the bed. "Please, lie down."

Dave complied, his eyes tracing the futuristic equipment as the Venoran pulled a translucent screen from thin air. The doctor's sharp, intelligent eyes scanned the data rapidly.

"Let's see," he began. "Eighty-four years old, an engineering scientist with multiple doctorates. You joined the military, took combat training, and excelled in special task force assignments. Later, your academic career flourished before retirement; that's quite an impressive résumé, Dave."

Dave swallowed hard, unsure how to respond.

The Venoran's tone softened as he continued, "You've endured quite a bit of lung damage leading to a breathing issue, arthritis in your knees and fingers. But no worries, I'm connecting you to the central computer now. This head harness will stimulate the cognitive areas of your brain. These enhancements will progress while you're in the stasis chamber back in your room."

As the Venoran fitted the sleek device to Dave's head, he said reassuringly, "This will be a short day for you after the treatment."

Sleep claimed Dave swiftly. Through the soft haze of the hospital light, faces and forms flickered into view, moving with intent as they filled the beds and began their treatments.

The quiet ambience of the room was broken by Aurelia's voice, crackling softly over the comms: "Dave, time to wake up."

Slowly, Dave brushed away the remnants of slumber, still entangled in conversation with the Doctor in his mind, when a flash of realisation struck him; he was back in the familiar confines of his room.

He blinked himself awake, his body instinctively stretching with an ease he hadn't felt in decades. He lay still for a moment, marvelling at the absence of the familiar aches in his knees and fingers. For the first time in years, he took a deep breath, filling his lungs effortlessly. The sensation was almost disorienting; he had forgotten what it felt like to breathe without pain.

He swung his legs over the side of the bed, his bare feet touching the cool floor. His movements were fluid, free from the stiffness that had once plagued him. A cautious smile crept across his face.

"I'd forgotten what it was like with no pain," he murmured, flexing his fingers. They moved freely; no creaks, no resistance. For a moment, he just stared at them, as if they belonged to someone else. The memory of a constant ache lingered like a shadow, already fading.

"How long have I been asleep?" Dave asked, stretching and shaking off the grogginess.

Aurelia's voice crackled over the comm. "Six hours and thirty-seven minutes. The mess hall is open. You may go there now."

"Thank you," he responded as he rose to his feet, his voice tinged with both gratitude and wonder. The gravity was less than that of Earth's, and the sensation of his body being weightless was exhilarating, almost unreal. Dave took a steadying breath, relishing how natural it felt. He quickly left his room and headed down the hallway. The sensation of moving so smoothly, without any discomfort, felt oddly unfamiliar. The air felt crisp as he moved toward the transfer station, his strides brisk and unimpeded.

Arriving at the device, he made his request for the mess hall.

Instantly, a shimmering light enveloped him. When it faded, he found himself standing in a bustling dining area. The vivid hum of activity, the clinking of trays, and the symphony of voices hit him all at once. He paused at the doorway for a moment, letting it all sink in, the smell of warm food drifting through the air. Then the sounds of laughter from his fellow travellers as they mingled around the room. *Wow, this is great,* he thought with a faint grin, moving toward the source of the enticing aromas. He stepped up and asked for a Hawaiian pizza. The smell hit instantly: bubbling cheese, sweet pineapple, a wave of comfort he hadn't realised he missed. His stomach growled in anticipation.

The hall hummed with chatter and laughter, the kind that comes easily when everyone's been through the same fire. It wasn't just noise; it was comfort. Familiar. Like home, if home had steel chairs and linoleum floors.

Scanning the room, he spotted a nearby table already occupied by another veteran. The man was hunched slightly over his plate, fork in hand, lost in thought, or maybe just enjoying the quiet.

He wandered over, his pizza in hand. He nodded toward the man's plate, curiosity getting the better of him. "Hey, what'd you get?" he asked, his voice easy, a smile tugging at his lips.

"It tastes like chicken, and the chips are fantastic," the veteran replied with a grin, his eyes twinkling with mischief as he gestured toward Dave's pizza adorned with golden pineapple. "Are you Canadian?"

"No, but I lived there for a while and got addicted to it," he chuckled, extending his hand. "I'm Dave Robinson. I used to be an engineering specialist of sorts. And you?"

"Donald Northey, but just call me Don. I was a weapons specialist."

"Oh yes, you were the one with no inner dialogue the first day we arrived, very amusing," Dave recalled with a smirk.

Don nodded, laughter bubbling up from his chest. "That's what they say," he replied, his voice rich with humour, the hallway filled with the warmth of shared experiences and newfound friendships.

The Journey Begins

Personal account: General George Hollins.

"The next 24 hours blurred into a rhythm of medical checks and quiet introductions. Between weird blood pressure straps and retinal scans, they traded names, shared smirks, and gradually mapped out the constellation of personalities aboard. Just as Gall had hinted, nearly everyone had ties to the military, either forged in service or through family legacy. There was Sarah Kane, who once worked security on a lunar outpost that officially didn't exist. Dave Robinson, who had been calibrating climate systems on Mars-adjacent habitats."

"Now, with the ice broken and the silence no longer necessary, stories spilled out in quiet corners and over ration-bar coffee. The weight of secrecy, once etched into their posture, began to lift. For some, this was the first time they could speak openly about what they'd done and who they'd been."

***

A soft hum filled the room as Aurelia materialised, her holographic form flickering momentarily before solidifying. "Welcome," she said, her voice calm yet authoritative. "For the next portion of your journey, we will be travelling to Zeph 3, the Venoran training facility designed to prepare you in the use of various equipment and defence tactics.

After completion, we will continue to our home planet, Venor." As her image faded, the ambient lighting shifted, casting the walls in a faint silver glow.

Gall's voice cut through the room, steady and warm. "We are about to leave lunar orbit and exit your solar system. This is your opportunity to witness a sight few have seen. Please direct your gaze to the outer hull."

With a low mechanical groan, a section of the ship's wall slid open, not outward, but into transparency. The room fell silent. Outside, the vastness of space stretched endlessly, filled with brilliant stars. The moon loomed large, filling their entire view, then slowly, it drifted from view. The Earth started to shrink, appearing as a pale blue marble in space.

The tension that had gripped them since leaving lunar orbit finally began to ease. Their shoulders dropped; breathing became easier. That stress of the moment started to melt into something quieter. Something like wonder.

Mars had already slipped past, rust-red and distant, like a memory you didn't know you missed. Then came Jupiter, massive and swirling, its storms rolling slow and deep. Saturn followed, its rings catching the light like something holy. Someone gasped. Someone else reached out, palm pressed to the hull, half expecting to feel the shimmer of it.

The *Arcadia* moved like it belonged out here, gliding past the giants of the solar system. Every moment etched itself into memory.

Paige was still, her face half-lit by the violet glow of starlight. Her hands, once clenched tight around the armrests, now rested gently in her lap. They were still damp, not from fear anymore, but from the sheer immensity of what she'd just witnessed. Years of simulations and drills had never prepared her for this: the stars weren't data points or navigational anchors. They were ancient. Alive! Watching.

Behind them, Earth had shrunk to a blue dot. Paige felt something tug inside her; not fear, but something deeper. Recognition. That little orb had held her entire life. Every version of herself. Every mistake. Every hope. And now, here she was, floating free of it all.

She glanced sideways. The others were whispering, pointing, wide-eyed. But Paige stayed quiet, watching as Uranus drifted past like a pale ghost. The hull caught her reflection: strange, elevated, alone. And yet, somehow, this was exactly where she was meant to be. This wasn't just a trip through space. It was a step away from who she'd been, and toward whoever she was becoming.

Inside the *Arcadia*, the atmosphere was thick with tension, not from dread, but from anticipation of their next discovery. Their hands tightened around their armrests, fingers white-knuckled. Others clung to the seats as if bracing for turbulence. No one spoke; they could not take their eyes away as galaxies curled like brushstrokes on an ink-black canvas. It was both beautiful and terrifying.

Aurelia's voice broke the silence. "All systems are stable." Her tone held the serenity of someone, or something, that had seen this all before.

The captain's voice echoed over the comms. "Prepare for the next phase of our mission."

A ripple of unease moved through the passengers. The ship lurched, a faint shift in momentum that still managed to stir their stomachs. Next, the acceleration. Not chaotic or jarring, but powerful, controlled.

Strange Signal

Personal account: Dr. Parker Brooks

"Everything was happening so fast as we readied ourselves to enter the stasis chambers. Seven days ago, the Venorans shattered our understanding of reality. Two days ago, we abandoned Earth, leaving behind everything familiar. And today, the unknown calls to us. A signal. Faint, distant, yet undeniable. The Arcadia has intercepted something at the edge of the solar system. It shouldn't be there. It shouldn't exist. And yet, it does. A signal; someone, or something, is reaching out?"

***

The *Arcadia* moved silently through the solar system, with stars shifting outside like distant beacons in the void. All seemed routine as the vessel approached the outer edges until an abrupt jolt shuddered through the ship. The low hum of the engines faltered, and the *Arcadia* slowed dramatically, breaking the steady rhythm of its journey.

Gall's voice crackled through the communication system. "We will not be engaging the Slide Drive just yet. We've picked up a strange signal emanating from the Kuiper Belt, at the fringe of your solar system."

Almost instantly, the ship's shields activated, their energy shimmering as they absorbed the impact of asteroids in the dense, floating field. Larger objects thudded against the shields, harmlessly deflected as Pluto's shadow began to rise in the distance. The *Arcadia* continued its pursuit, narrowing the signal's origin to the farthest reaches of the Kuiper Belt.

"The signal originates from a large asteroid, about half the size of Earth's moon," Aurelia reported with precision.

With the asteroid expanding in their viewport, the *Arcadia* initiated a full-spectrum surface analysis. Gradually, the search honed in on the source: a structure hidden within the asteroid's rocky terrain.

Gall furrowed his brow, his tone inquisitive as he addressed Aurelia. "Aurelia, why haven't we detected this signal before?"

Aurelia's holographic form glowed faintly in the centre of the command room, her features serene, but her words anything but. "The signal operates on an extremely narrow beam," she began, her voice calm and analytical, each syllable gliding into the silence. "It's aligned to a single focal point across the galaxy to extend its range. Without precise alignment, the signal would not reach its destination."

A ripple of unease moved through the room. Crew members leaned forward, eyes narrowing, as if hoping to decipher the implications before Aurelia spoke them aloud.

"These asteroids," she continued, "take millions of years to complete their orbits, which explains why the signal wasn't detected earlier." Behind her, a soft pulse of data traced orbital paths, decay patterns, and fragments of lost time. "The signal originates near a mountain range. There's a structure down there showing significant damage. If anyone had been there..." Her tone didn't change, but the room seemed to tighten around her words. "They were likely killed when the damage occurred. I've also detected a directional beacon. It's still active, but the alignment is damaged."

The room descended into complete silence. Heads turned toward the screen, where the image of the asteroid rotated slowly in space like a wounded sentinel.

Patrasia stepped forward, squinting through the haze of the projection. Her voice was barely above a whisper. "Those buildings are ancient. It looks like they've been here for a very long time."

The silence snapped as a chime sounded, followed by Gall's voice over the comms. "We have detected a structure on the surface with a signal emanating from it. We'll be sending a team to investigate." The announcement hung like a challenge in the air.

"Patrasia and Dr. Trill," Gall continued, "meet me in the transfer room, with suits on."

Patrasia nodded and turned toward the corridor, her boots echoing against the metallic floor. Dr. Trill followed, silent, his eyes fixed on the monitor that still displayed the jagged silhouette of the structure. Whatever awaited them down there would have been waiting a very long time.

In the transfer room, anticipation hung thick in the air as the crew prepared themselves. Gall stood with Patrasia and Dr. Trill, the two technicians at their side, silent but focused. He lifted the communicator, his words crisp and final. "Initiate transfer to the surface."

Seconds later, they found themselves on a platform affixed to the side of the building. They could feel the uneven ground beneath their boots. The surrounding area was a mix of fractured slabs and scattered debris from the ruined outpost. No sound accompanied their movements. The walls rose around them, fractured and jagged, the remains of a forgotten time. Their edges looked brittle enough to crumble with a single touch.

Dust hung in the air, drifting through the narrow beams of their flashlights like fine debris caught in a slow current. The silence was heavy, broken only by the distant groan of metal shifting under the team's weight. Parts of the shattered building crunched underfoot. The sound, though muted inside their suits, still felt unnaturally loud in the stillness.

A technician reached out instinctively, brushing a gloved hand against the wall beside him. His fingers traced the deep cracks etched into the surface.

A faint tremor shivered through the ground, soft but unmistakable. Dust broke free from the fractured ceiling, drifting down as the structure sent a quiet warning through the floor beneath them.

Gall's voice broke through the radio with a sense of urgency. "Stay alert. This place could collapse at any second."

"There's a doorway over there," Patrasia pointed out, her voice betraying a hint of nervous excitement.

Making their way through the doorway, they entered a corridor, where they eventually found themselves in a circular chamber. Its walls scorched and its floor littered with the wreckage of long-dead technology, a grim picture of whatever catastrophe had struck. Around the room were burned-out panels, shattered consoles, and twisted metal scattered like bones.

Dust coated everything, muffling the sound of their footsteps as they moved cautiously through the room. Gall tapped his communicator. "Aurelia, Scan the building." The AI hologram materialised. "Yes, Gall?"

Moments later, Aurelia replies, "Massive explosions on all floors occurred following an asteroid impact. The building has two additional levels below us, containing 100 life support chambers. The signal we picked up is coming from one chamber," Aurelia said, her voice tinged with intrigue. "It's still active."

The landing party felt a mixture of unease and curiosity as Aurelia led them deeper into the ruins. They approached a doorway buried under rubble and together managed to clear all the debris. Each movement had been slow and deliberate, muscles straining against the weight of the broken structures.

Finally, they cleared enough space to slip through the entrance. Inside, rows of life-support chambers waited in silence, their surfaces buried under thick dust. The silence inside was haunting as they inspected each pod; the scene they uncovered was devastating, long-dead aliens frozen in their final moments. Many had been crushed beneath collapsed beams, while others had suffocated when their chambers cracked open, their life-sustaining atmospheres bleeding away into the void.

Eventually, they made their way to the source of the signal. A solitary chamber buried beneath layers of ancient wreckage. Dr. Trill touched the chamber and felt a low hum coming from within, steady and rhythmic. The chamber glowed faintly with a bluish light, its alien systems still stubbornly alive despite the surrounding devastation.

Dust coated the thick viewing pane like frost. As they gently cleared it away, a shape began to emerge from the haze. Conversations faded.

There inside the capsule, lay a tall and slender alien woman, her skin an opalescent sheen under the dim lighting, her features delicate and serene. Long tendrils of hair floated gently in suspension, as if time itself refused to touch her. Though clearly preserved in a life-support system, she looked more like a sleeping oracle than a remnant of catastrophe. Her presence alone defied the ruins outside.

Gall broke the silence, his voice a mix of astonishment and disbelief. “I’m surprised she’s still alive, with all the devastation near her.”

Aurelia’s hologram flickered beside them, her tone clinical yet revealing. “The alloy material above her chamber is exceptionally durable. It deflected falling debris and shielded her from harm.”

Dr. Trill's voice rose, driven by urgency. "We need to get her out of there. She's survived for so long in this capsule; if the reawakening process succeeds, she could hold vital knowledge about this place, about her people."

Gall turned to the control panel, his hands moving with precision. "The systems are ancient, but I think I can override the lock and remove the capsule from its station," he said softly, his focus unshaken.

While Gall worked, Patrasia's gaze wandered, drawn to the walls. Symbols were etched deeply into the surface, worn but legible. Her fingers moved slowly over the markings, their patterns etched like whispers into the surface. A spark of intrigue lit her eyes.

"These symbols," she murmured, her voice heavy with curiosity. "They look like a form of language. If we can decipher them, we might learn more about who these people were."

"It's done," announced Gall, as the lock released and the capsule moved slightly in its station as zero gravity took over.

"Aurelia, analyse the life support and verify the compatibility with *Arcadia's* environment."

"Our environment is suitable; you will need to attach a portable energy supply."

In a short while, they were ready to proceed. "Beam the life support chamber to the hospital room and connect it to our energy system immediately," Doctor Trill instructed, his voice steady with urgency.

Gall's voice came through their communicators. "We have completed our mission here. Return to the ship."

Doctor Trill made his way directly to the hospital. He approached the chamber that housed the alien survivor. Anxious to get started. "Aurelia," he commanded, his voice firm, "perform a thorough scan of the occupant. Evaluate any risk of contamination to the crew, the subject's health, and immediate environmental needs."

Aurelia responded without delay, her tone as ever calm. "The female occupant is in optimal condition. Our environmental parameters are fully compatible."

Aurelia had summoned the veterans to the conference room, its clean lines and soft lighting offered a sense of order and focus.

Gall stood before them, his face etched with fatigue and something darker: uncertainty. "You've heard the basics," he began, his voice low but taut. "An ancient structure. Life-support chambers. One survivor."

He let the silence linger, his eyes sweeping the room. "But what you haven't heard is that the signal we traced is active. And it's not random. It's targeted."

A murmur rippled through the group. One veteran leaned forward, his voice sharp. "Targeted? Toward what?"

"Towards a distant sector of the galaxy. We're not sure what's there; our scans show nothing. But the signal keeps transmitting, as if it's reaching for something, or someone."

Aurelia's hologram flickered to life beside him, her tone clinical but edged with urgency. "Analysis confirms a repeating pattern. Coordinates. Possibly instructions. My assessment of the pattern suggests that the destination point may no longer exist. Further analysis is underway."

Patrasia stepped forward, her voice hushed. "And the survivor? Could she be the key?"

Gall nodded slowly. "Absolutely. If we can revive her, we may learn who she was, what her people were doing on that asteroid, and why they left behind a signal, that's still calling out across the stars." Returning his attention to the retirees, "While you are in your pods, we will address the survivor's needs and make every effort to establish communication with her."

Several hours later, Gall's voice rang through the ship's comms. "We are about to leave the solar system. All crew members, please return to your stations."

The announcement drifted through the ship, calm and unobtrusive. On the main viewing deck, the veteran crew remained still, their eyes fixed on the unfolding spectacle outside. Space stretched out in every direction, vast, silent, and impossibly beautiful. Ancient stars shimmered across the void.

The *Arcadia* began to pick up speed as the stars outside started to shift. Slowly at first, then all at once, they stretched into dazzling streaks of light, twisting and trailing like ribbons caught in a solar wind. The galaxy didn't just move; it seemed to blur, folding into itself in a breathtaking display of motion.

No one spoke as they bathed in the glow of the shifting stars.

The comms crackled, to the sound of Gall's voice. "We hope you enjoyed the first part of your journey."

A soft mechanical hum followed as the viewing windows slowly dimmed and slid shut, drawing the curtain on the celestial performance.

After a short pause, Gall spoke again. "The slide drive is about to engage. The next phase of our journey will take us to Zeph 3. All veteran crew members, please return to your quarters and enter the stasis chambers. Once you're inside, the regeneration cycle will kick in automatically."

The announcement faded into the soft hum of the ship. In one of the quieter corridors, Dr. Brooks slowed down. Just ahead, he spotted Don standing beside his chamber, unmoving.

Parker moved slightly, his footsteps light. "Are you alright?" he asked.

Don didn't look up right away. "Yeah. Just taking a moment," he said with a faint smile.

By that time, Parker had crossed the hallway to join him. Don glanced up, his expression torn between humour and unease.

"What's up, Doc?" he quipped, though his voice betrayed a hint of nervousness. Parker leaned casually against the doorway, his tone calm but probing. "Are you ready for the next leg of our journey?"

Don hesitated, his gaze shifting to the chamber before him. "Honestly, I've been wondering if we'll even wake up. What if something goes wrong?" His words hung in the air, the unspoken fears they both shared lingering between them.

"Well, I'm particularly looking forward to waking up," he replied, a wry smile on his face as he tapped his temple. "If I had stayed on Earth, I wouldn't have been around much longer, thanks to a brain tumour that had been growing up here. But don't worry about not waking up. Honestly, all of us here are near the end of our lives anyway. And drop the 'Doc'; just Parker will do."

His eyes lit up as he shifted the conversation. "We're going to be okay," he said, his excitement spilling over. "I've been reviewing their medical database, and it's astonishing! I mean, they've shared everything with me: every neuron, every gene, every intricate part of human biology. Don, they even allowed me to run simulations of how they're planning to regenerate us. Let me tell you, they are light-years ahead of us. Whatever you can think of, they've already invented it."

Parker leaned closer, his voice brimming with enthusiasm. "And the best part? We're not losing anything while we're in regeneration. All of our memories, every detail of our past lives, will be perfectly preserved. They know how to isolate and protect our memories during the process."

Before Don could respond, a Venoran doctor approached, their calm yet authoritative tone cutting through the moment. "Please return to your stasis chamber. We need to begin the process simultaneously for everyone."

Parker nodded from the doorway, offering Don an encouraging smile before turning and heading back to his room. Don settled down in his chamber, shifting restlessly as he tried to find a comfortable position. The hallway was silent as Parker entered his chamber. He lowered himself into the cushioned harness, the cool material cradling his head. After a few moments of fidgeting, he finally settled in.

The rest of the group had already taken their places in stasis. Across the hallway, a soft click of metal echoed through the chamber as the cover slid shut, locking Parker inside. A cool mist began to drift in, curling gently around him. He let out a slow exhale, watching it fade into the air. A low-frequency hum pulsed through the chamber, easing him into sleep as his vision dimmed.

The same ritual played out in other areas of the ship; one by one, they drifted into sleep. The last thing they felt was the faint vibration beneath them before everything slipped away, and the long sleep began.

Solara

Personal account: Gall

"Today, while exiting the Sol system, we found a survivor sealed inside a stasis chamber, her pulse dormant beneath layers of dust and forgotten history. The chamber was hidden within a ruined outpost, a place where time itself had stood guard. But she is no ordinary survivor; she is someone who has lived through a chapter of Earth's history."

***

Immediately upon Slide Drive activation, *Arcadia's* shields shimmered protectively around the ship, enabling the crew to leave their stations. Doctor Trill returned to his patient, still sealed within her stasis chamber. He summoned an orderly and studied the vessel closely. Intricate carvings adorned the sides, converging at a small, enigmatic button.

"I assume this activates the door," he said cautiously, and pressed it. "She's lucky. Her activation cycle failed. Had it opened on time, she would have passed on a millennium before we discovered this station."

A metallic click echoed as the release mechanism activated, cracking open one half of the chamber door. Dr. Trill reached inside, tracing a pathway along the inner wall until he paused at an indentation. Instinctively, he pressed it.

The chamber hummed to life. Fluids surged into the woman's wrists. Her chest jerked as she drew in a sharp breath, then slowly sank into a steadier rhythm. Consciousness crept back in small waves. She could feel cold air brush against her skin. Disjointed sounds flickered through her awareness, a language she couldn't place. She could hear muffled voices speaking with a quiet urgency, the low hum of machines that seemed to breathe with the room.

Her pulse quickened. Thoughts scrambled to form meaning. Light pierced her senses as she peeled open her eyes, met by the unfamiliar face of an alien male hovering above her. A jolt of panic surged. Her mouth opened, but no sound escaped, only silent terror.

Then, gently, the figure raised a hand. A single finger pressed against his lips. No words, just a calm, quiet plea for her to stay still. His composed presence seemed to anchor her. Fighting exhaustion, she exhaled and slipped into a light, uneasy sleep. The life-support lines disconnected one by one, and with a soft hiss, the remaining door segments swung open.

Time passed. Then, gradually, at what might have been dawn or dusk, her senses began to stir. Her eyelids fluttered once more as her gaze swept across the unfamiliar room. Disorientation clung to her like fog. Confusion flickered in her eyes. Her lips moved faintly, searching for words that wouldn't come.

Dr. Trill met her with a warm, reassuring smile. His voice softened to a whisper, so as not to startle her. "Relax," he murmured. "You're safe now. We're here to help." His calming presence seemed to cut through the fog.

Carefully, almost tenderly, the team moved around her. Hands guided her with gentle precision, lifting her from the chamber as though she might shatter. They settled her on a nearby bed, the sterile chill of the room softening in their presence.

Even at her most vulnerable, she still held a kind of quiet presence. Taller than most of the women on the ship, she moved with an easy confidence. Her dark skin caught the light with a warm gold beneath it, and her hair fell softly to her shoulders, framing her face without effort.

She wore a suit designed with a purpose. Loose where it needed to be, yet tailored enough to follow her movements with ease. Around her waist, a sturdy belt anchored a collection of well-worn pouches, each marked with subtle details of what each contained. There was nothing frivolous in her look. Every piece had its reason. Nothing she wore asked for admiration. Each piece demanded functionality, designed with precision, not approval.

But it was her eyes that drew everything inward. Pale blue, softly glowing, and filled with stories.

She remained motionless, her breathing faint and rhythmic. Voices murmured somewhere beyond the walls, barely audible. Gentle tremors beneath her body kept time with the moment, reminding her she was still here.

Her vision began to sharpen. Shapes took form. Edges found meaning. But clarity didn't bring comfort, only confusion. The room was unfamiliar, as were the faces. Something was off. Something had changed. This wasn't where she'd gone to sleep.

Two figures stood nearby, watching. Strangers. As she tried to move, panic surged. She couldn't make herself move. Her body was numb, impossibly heavy, everything around her, alien. Her mind clawed for answers, but they scattered like leaves in a storm.

Dr. Trill offered a reassuring smile and laid a hand on her shoulder, guiding her to remain still. She trembled, tried to speak, and failed. He gestured gently for her to relax.

He looked over to the orderly. "Call Patrasia and ask her to come to the hospital."

Moments later, Patrasia arrived. Her warm presence eased the tension. "How is our latest patient?" she said softly.

"I think you should work with her for a while," said Trill.

Patrasia stepped forward and crouched beside the woman, her eyes settling into the same line of sight. She offered a soft smile, met only by the flicker of confusion in the woman's eyes.

The woman raised a hand toward her wrist, fingers sluggish and unresponsive. Frustration flashed across her face.

Patrasia noticed and pressed the button herself. A hush fell over the room as the woman's voice crackled to life, faint and trembling yet unmistakably clear. "Who are you... where am I?" Her voice wavered between confusion and fear.

Patrasia moved closer. "I'm Patrasia," she said, with a soft and reassuring tone. "You're aboard the Venoran Galaxy ship, *Arcadia*. We're headed to Zeph 3. The crew is a blend of Venorans and Earthlings. We detected your signal while leaving this solar system."

The woman blinked, processing. Her brows drew together, and emotion welled in her eyes. "Where are the rest of my people?" she enquired in a shaken tone.

Patrasia's voice softened. "You were the only survivor," she said. "The others perished long ago."

Before she could stop them, her eyes filled with tears. "My name is Solara," she said. "I had been waiting for the ship that was to take me home." Her voice trembled, caught between memory and longing.

She looked past the room, gaze drifting somewhere unreachable, back to that lonely outpost at the edge of the solar system. It was there that she was to board a mineral freighter bound for her homeworld. That sense of finally going home, of closing a long and tiring chapter, had felt almost within reach. "The trip went smoothly right up until we arrived at the outpost," she said, her voice unsteady.

"Then the asteroids came. The impact was devastating."

Not one. Not a cluster. A wave, silent, fast, and deliberate, as if the void itself had chosen to erase them. The station's defence grid was activated too late. The railguns fired, but the targeting systems lagged. The shielding buckled under the first strike. By the third, the outer ring was gone.

The words hung in the air like static. "Alarms went off around the station." She remembered the panic spreading through the station, quiet at first, then growing, as people scrambled for safety with uncertainty pressing in. People scrambled for escape pods that weren't designed for mass exodus. The impact was devastating. Then came explosions around the station. The lights failed, and structures were falling around me. All that was left were the stasis chambers. I had no way of knowing it would become a tomb.

"I was unaware... unaware of the destruction unfolding while I slept. It used to feel alive; now it's nothing but silence." Her glowing eyes shone with pain. "But the distress call; we sent one. My people should've received it."

"We don't know why you weren't rescued," Patrasia said. "But we'll try to find answers. For now, rest. I'll return soon."

Later, Patrasia gently updated her. "Judging by the decay of the buildings," she said carefully, "you've been in stasis for a very long time. It's likely that everyone you once knew is gone."

Solara lay back, grief pooling in her chest. Staring at the ceiling, thinking about those she'd lost.

Memories of her mate surfaced. His steady understanding of her need to reconnect with her origins had always grounded her. He had stayed behind on the third planet, quietly running the operation.

Now, as her eyelids fluttered closed and sleep began to pull her under, her mind wandered, not to the sterile room around her, but to a world she'd never set foot in. She could see it so clearly, shaped from the stories her parents had once spoken to her in the dark. Lush skies, quiet hills, the silver seas, a home that had lived only in her imagination.

And in that fading moment, she saw them. Waiting. As if no time had passed at all. Hope, faint and fragile, followed her into dreams.

When the next cycle came, Patrasia returned to the hospital to check on Solara. She was surprised to find Doctor Trill in the fitness room, standing beside a treadmill where Solara walked briskly.

"Doctor Trill, what are you doing?" she called, her voice a mix of disbelief and irritation.

"Our patient is responding remarkably well," he replied with evident satisfaction.

Patrasia's tone soft. "Solara, you need to slow down and let your strength return naturally."

Solara nodded, pressing a button to reduce the treadmill's speed. She stepped off, moving with careful precision, and followed Patrasia's gesture to a nearby table. Patrasia settled into the chair across from her, notepad resting lightly in her hands. Her voice was soft, almost coaxing. "I want to understand you better," she said. "Why were you on that asteroid? Where did you come from?"

Solara took a moment before speaking. She met Patrasia's eyes, calm and thoughtful, the kind that had seen far more than she let on. It felt as if she were sifting through old memories, brushing the dust off stories long buried. Only to her; they were recent.

"My name is Solara," she said at last. Her voice was steady, touched with a hint of quiet pride. "I was a communications officer. That star system has been in our hands for generations. My job was to coordinate transmissions between our mining colonies and our homeworld, *Anunn*. Our people have been working in that solar system for generations; it's part of who we are."

There was a subtle shift in her expression as curiosity crept in. "You mentioned 'Earthlings' who are they?" Patrasia tilted her head, a flicker of a smile playing at her lips. "They're the indigenous people of the third planet in that system."

Solara froze. Her brows lifted, disbelief spilling across her face. "That's not possible," she said, half smiling. Her voice rose in disbelief. "They were labourers in our mines. Primitive. Tribal. There's no way they could've evolved." The words lingered between them, sharp in the silence.

Patrasia's tone remained even, unwavering. "Solara, maybe I can help fill in the blanks. Our studies of Earth stretch back more than a million years, from the earliest migrations out of the forests to the open plains."

She paused, her eyes steady. "Long before your people discovered Earth, our kind had been protecting the inhabitants. When Earth's population stood on the brink of collapse, ecological disaster, and famine, we stepped in. We guided their progress. But once they recovered, we withdrew. We let them find their own way."

Her voice softened. "And in our absence, they changed." Patrasia's gaze softened. "We also witnessed your race's arrival and the influence it brought. You posed no threat, so we didn't interfere."

She leaned forward. "Your stasis chamber tracked stellar movements. Using those records and cross-referencing star charts from Anunn, we calculated how long you've slept. You've been in stasis for approximately 4,000 Earth years."

Solara's breath caught. Her eyes widened, shimmering as reality collided with disbelief. She reached up with trembling fingers, brushing hair from her face. So much time had passed, it was unfathomable, echoed inside her.

"The people here call their planet Earth," Patrasia continued. "We call them Earthlings. On our planet, they're also known as Terrans. They're young compared to us, but in the last 4,000 years, their progress has been astounding. They no longer live in tribes. They live in sprawling cities with billions of people." Solara's lips parted as a faint whisper slipped out. Disbelief, and a quiet sense of wonder tangled through her thoughts as she tried to grasp the future she'd missed. Her expression carried grief, but beneath it flickered a small, steady determination.

"Earthlings are quick learners," Patrasia said, a hint of admiration softening her voice. "For centuries, while your people walked among them, they watched quietly, curiously. They studied how you shaped stone for shelter, how you coaxed life from barren soil. Your people didn't just leave behind structures and tools; you left them a blueprint."

She let the thought settle before continuing.

"When the Anunn withdrew from Earth, the Terrans didn't collapse without their overseers. Freed from the constraints of the mining colonies, they drifted across continents, carrying fragments of the knowledge they had absorbed, knowledge never meant for them, yet planted all the same. At first, they copied your methods step by step, building as they had been shown, cultivating land with the techniques you introduced."

Her tone shifted as she recalled more details.

"But once your people were gone, nothing held them to those early patterns. That was when the real change began. They made their own choices. They wove Anunn teachings into their instincts. Mud huts rose into structures. Simple crops grew into systems of trade. What your people gave them wasn't a method; it was a spark."

Patrasia glanced at Solara, gauging her reaction.

"To you, this history is recent, but to the crew of the Arcadia, it belongs to antiquity. Four thousand years have passed since the Anunn last set foot on Earth. Long enough for myth to replace memory. Long enough for Terrans to rise into a civilization your people would never have imagined possible."

“Others visited Earth,” Patrasia continued. “Some came to mine its minerals, carving deep wounds into the crust before vanishing into the stars. Others hovered in orbit, silent observers of humanity’s rise and fall. Most left the planet untouched, leaving the people of Earth to evolve at their own chaotic rhythm.”

She spoke of the Martian skyline, where the red dust shimmered under twin moons. “According to the preserved accounts, it was during the establishment of the first observation post on Mars that a significant transmission was detected. Initially, the signal appeared only as a faint distortion, a narrow filament of sound concealed beneath multiple layers of encrypted hostility. Subsequent decoding revealed its true nature. A fleet was advancing toward Earth’s star system, its purpose explicitly identified in the recovered data: the conquest of Earth.”

Solara’s breath caught, her eyes wide with alarm.

“We mobilised a defence armada for Earth,” Patrasia said, her voice now edged with steel. “The battle that followed stretched across the solar system, from the icy rings of Saturn to the shadowed craters of Luna. Starfire lit the void. Debris rained across planetary atmospheres. It was a war Earth was never meant to see.”

She paused, letting the silence settle.

“In the final battle for Earth, we destroyed their command ships. This turned the tide swiftly in our favour. With no remaining command ships, their fleet quickly collapsed. In the end, they surrendered. We allowed the few remaining ships to leave Earth's solar system.”

Patrasia’s gaze darkened with memory. “A few Earthlings witnessed the conflict; unable to comprehend what they had seen, they recorded it as a divine war. Over time, those depictions became myth; to some, it was an awakening, an inspiration. To others, they were warnings.”

"In the centuries that followed, they developed mathematics and science. They learnt to reverse-engineer ships that had crashed on Earth. Now, they're approaching space travel."

Solara furrowed her brow. "Why are they on your crew?"

"We are fighting for our survival," Patrasia said, her tone grave. "We're strong, but we're isolated... and we are few. Our greatest threat is a race called the Korrathi. They number in the millions, and their only purpose is to dominate the galaxy."

She drew a slow breath before continuing. "That was when we reached out to Earth's leaders. We laid out our plan with details of the threat we faced, the resources we lacked, and the ways they could stand with us. After hearing us out, they granted permission to contact their elder fighters."

"Elder fighters?" Solara echoed.

Patrasia nodded. "Yes, military veterans who with our technology," Patrasia said gently. "We rejuvenate them; restore what time has taken and offer them another life. In the end, the choice to stand with us is theirs alone."

Solara sat quietly, the weight of it all sinking in. "I have a lot to learn," she murmured, eyes searching the air between them.

"We'd like you to stay," Patrasia said. "Our crew could use someone like you." Solara hesitated, stretching the moment as she considered. Then she gave a small, steady nod. "Yes... yes, I'll join you."

A soft smile touched Patrasia's lips. "Welcome aboard. While the Earthlings remain in stasis, you'll be able to study our situation and learn about Earth's people."

Rejuvenation

Week 6

Personal account: Paige Mitchelmore

"So much has happened to us. We're not just travelling across the stars; we're being remade. Time has worn us down, but now, against all odds, we are being rejuvenated. The impossible is unfolding before us, and somehow, we are at the heart of it. What lies ahead is unknown, but one thing is certain: we are no longer who we once were."

***

Six weeks after leaving Earth's solar system, Doctor Trill and Gall were having a conversation.

"My monitors have shown that the humans are ready and can now be removed from stasis. The regeneration process has been completed; all surgeries have been successful. Education has reached the desired level."

The ship began to slow down, and the blur of stars gradually became clearer.

"Keep the *Arcadia* at sublight until we are closer. It will take an extra day, but it will give the humans a chance to get adjusted to their new bodies," said Gall, smiling.

The stasis chambers opened one by one, and gradually, the veterans opened their eyes. The comms crackled in each of their rooms as Aurelia's voice broke the silence.

“Greetings, we are close to our destination. Please head to your cleansing stations and refresh yourselves. You will find your uniform in the wall closet. When you are ready, please proceed to the main meeting room on level four.”

Stuart climbed out of his stasis chamber, bracing himself against the side table.

Legs wobbly, be careful, he thought to himself until his body adjusted. After a few moments, he headed for the shower, letting the warm water steady him. Once finished, he walked over to the closet to retrieve his uniform. As he walked past the mirror, out of the corner of his eye, he caught a glimpse of his body and took a step back for another look.

“Bloody hell, they weren’t kidding,” he exclaimed. His grey hair, which had thinly covered his head, was replaced by thick brown hair. His potbelly was a thing of the past. His body was now toned, and he could stand up straight again.

Flexing his muscles in the mirror, “Oh yeah, baby,” as he continued posing. The aged lines and skin blemishes had vanished; he looked like he was in his late 20s. He dressed in the uniform provided and walked over to the mirror for another look. Cocked his finger as if he were pointing a gun at the mirror, smiling, he headed out to meet the others.

Sarah opened her eyes and stretched her arms, and climbed out of the chamber while holding onto it for a couple of seconds for balance. She moved her long hair out of her eyes. Looking at a lock of hair in her hand, she immediately shouted,

“No grey,” she gasped, bolting to the mirror.

Her reflection stopped her cold. The steel strands that had framed her face were gone, replaced by rich auburn waves that shimmered beneath the lights, just as they had decades ago. She leaned in, fingers grazing her cheek. Smooth. Unlined. Every crease and furrow erased. Her mouth parted in disbelief, revealing bright, flawless teeth that clicked lightly as she tested them.

A stunned laugh escaped her lips as she twirled once, hair lifting with her motion, her body light and fluid in a way it hadn't felt for years.

She stopped. Both arms rose together, fluid as breath. Her right was no longer metal, but something softer, unreal. She flexed her arm while curling each finger like a pianist waking from a dream. No scars. No seams. Just skin, smooth and silent. She stared at the arm in awe, turning her wrist over again, testing the motion like a violinist reacquainting herself with forgotten grace.

After a quick shower, she slipped into the uniform with practised ease, running her fingers through her hair one last time, and ran out the door, faster and freer than she'd moved in years.

Don blinked against the soft overhead glow, disoriented but alert. He eased his body into a sitting position. No stiffness, no pain, and he swung his legs over the edge of the chamber. The smooth movement caught him off guard. Hadn't he felt like a rusted hinge before going under?

Curious and unsettled, he crossed to the cleansing station, bare feet padding against the cool floor. The mirror's reflection stopped him short.

His brows climbed. The man staring back wasn't the one who had entered the chamber. This one had tight skin, clear eyes, and a full head of hair. He leaned in, opened his mouth, and tugged at one of his teeth with the pad of his finger.

"Wow," he murmured, a grin creeping across his face. "Those suckers are real."

Across the hallway, Parker emerged from the chamber and immediately picked up his medical scanner. Excitedly, he ran it across his head; the tumour was gone. Looking in the mirror, he flicked his hair at his reflection. "After all these years, nice to see you again."

Don and Parker left their rooms at the same time, their expressions a mix of curiosity and excitement.

"This is like meeting someone for the first time," Don remarked.

"And on top of that, we are both feeling great," Parker added jokingly as they made their way to the meeting room.

Aurelia observed the reactions of the Earth crew with interest. "The rejuvenation process appears to be successful," she relates to Gall.

There was already a large group of men and women in the meeting room, most having trouble making out who was who.

When the twins entered, their identical appearances instantly drew the group's attention. It was as if the room itself paused to take in their striking symmetry, their sharp features, and composed demeanour. The silence lingered until one voice, warm and inviting, broke through, effortlessly easing the tension.

The moment the twins entered, conversation faltered, and chairs subtly shifted. Heads turned. Eyes locked. Their mirrored features, sharp jawlines, matching suits, their identical strides casting an almost surreal stillness across the room. It wasn't just resemblance; it was precision. A photograph that has come to life.

The silence lingered until one of them stepped forward, voice smooth and warm enough to stir the room back to motion.

"Hello, everyone. I know you've all had questions; we've felt them too," he said with an easy smile that softened the room's edges. "I'm Christian, Chris if you prefer, and this is my brother, Owen."

Owen stepped closer, drink in hand, posture relaxed but purposeful. The slight lift at the corner of his mouth carried an easy; unforced confidence, his gaze drifting over the group with quiet curiosity. "We've been with George a long time," Chris continued. "When George was reassigned to the retirement home, he asked us to come with him. Looking around at all of you now, sure glad we did."

Owen nodded, his voice even and respectful. "We're grateful to be here. And finally, meet all of you. George often spoke highly of his team. He was truly honoured that you accepted the Venoran request."

A beat passed. Kayla leaned forward, one elbow resting on the table as she met their gaze directly. "What's the connection between you and the general?"

Chris turned toward her, his smile revealing a quiet sincerity. "We've stood beside him for years, through split-second decisions, quiet victories, and losses that taught us more than textbooks ever could. He trusted us. And we learned that loyalty isn't earned lightly. That's why we're here now."

Owen's smile curved wider, his stance softening. "We might've looked a little sharp walking in wearing suits, serious faces, but don't let that fool you. We're not here as soldiers. We're here as friends. Ask us anything. About us. About George. Or whatever else you're wondering."

Shoulders eased across the room. The air felt a little less taut, a little more open. Though their entrance had stirred a quiet tension, the twins now carried it away with disarming sincerity.

With mechanical precision, the overhead lights flickered once. A figure stepped into view.

"Greetings, everyone," Gall said evenly, his voice cutting through the relaxed hum. "The enhancements to your bodies have been completed."

Chris exhales, "This is amazing; are there further treatments to be made?"

"No, all treatments have been completed. Things to note: your neurological, skeletal, as well as blood and organ surgeries have been completed, and all are permanent. In addition, your life spans have been doubled due to these corrections."

The excited group began to talk among themselves, absorbing the moment with wide-eyed wonder. Gall raised his voice slightly to be heard above the rising chatter.

"Can I have your attention?" Gall's voice cut through the room. "Let me introduce you to General George Hollins." He paused, letting the name settle.

"Some of you may not have met him before. The elderly man in the wheelchair, flanked by the twins? That was George. We stole him away on the first day."

A ripple of recognition moved through the crowd.

"He'll be overseeing all units. From now on, each team leader will report directly to him."

George stepped forward. He was tall, broad-shouldered, nearly matching the twins in height. The wheelchair was gone; forgotten like a discarded chapter. In his place was a man reborn: muscular, agile, composed. His jaw was defined, his cheekbones sharp, and his steel-grey eyes scanned the room with quiet authority. They held the weight of experience, but none of its wear.

He didn't speak. He didn't need to. His presence did the talking.

George moved forward to address everyone, carefully placing the beer he was holding on the table.

"As this meeting is informal, I'd like to begin by saying... wow. I'm just as stunned as the rest of you to be standing here with a second chance at life. Like many of you, I was nearing the end. On top of that, I was battling cancer, and my body was slowly shutting down. If I hadn't moved into the retirement home when I did, I likely wouldn't be here today."

He took a short pause before speaking again. "While in stasis, we were all educated far beyond what we knew in our past lives. Yes, I know the Venorans had ulterior motives. We have lost nothing but gained, hell of a lot more. For each of us, time was almost up."

"Today, we start a new life with a purpose again. This is our chance to give back. I have read all of your profiles and have assigned each of you a suitable designation. Review the wrist communicators for instructions. Your training will start in the morning. Meet me in the main loading bay; from there, we will be transported to the planet below. For the rest of the shift, you kids enjoy yourselves."

"We have another new crew member, who has been waiting patiently to meet you." George leaves the room, and seconds later, he returns with Solara, introducing her to everyone in the room.

The reaction to seeing the alien woman for the first time was a mix of awe and apprehension. Very different from the Venorans' appearance. As she stepped into the room, her tall, imposing figure commanded immediate attention. She stood taller than most, carrying herself with a blend of elegance and understated strength. Under the lights, her dark skin glowed with a golden warmth that turned heads and held gazes. Conversation halted. Crew members glanced at one another, uncertain of what her arrival might mean.

Her black hair fell to her shoulders, framing a face that was hard to forget, especially those blue eyes, faintly glowing, sharp and unblinking. But it wasn't just her appearance that held their attention. It was the way she moved, the intelligence in her eyes, the quiet confidence in how she stood. She didn't need to raise her voice or make a show of strength; her presence alone did the talking.

Her voice was steady and clear as she recounted what had happened before entering into stasis. Whatever apprehension lingered among the crew began to dissolve, replaced by a growing respect and curiosity for the formidable ally who now stood among them.

George smiled as he picked up his beer from the table, cleared his throat and shouted, “Cheers.” He moved through the room, striking up conversations with his new team members.

Don and Dave were catching up on past events. Dave laughed. “Do you remember the first couple of days after we first met? I remember some of your quips and thinking that you had no control over your inner thoughts. I tell you, Don, some of those lines were hilarious, though.”

Don turned to Dave, a confident smirk playing on his lips. “I can control them now,” he said, his voice steady. He glanced around the room, his eyes scanning the crowd. “Have you been looking around? There are quite a few lookers in the room.” He nodded subtly towards a tall blonde. “See the tall blonde over there? Her name is Paige.” He shifted his gaze to another part of the room, his expression softening slightly. “And over there is the one I spoke to earlier. She told me her name was Kayla.”

“And remember, a few weeks ago, all we wanted to do was take a nap after meeting everyone in the group for the first time,” recalled Dave.

From behind them, they heard someone speak in a low voice. “And here we are, 80-year-olds checking out the babes,” Parker said, smiling. “And that Solara is a bit of a looker, too.”

Sarah was standing and laughing with the rest of the group when a tall woman with short blond hair walked up to her and asked, “Sarah?”

Sarah turned to see who was speaking. “Yes,” she answered.

The woman smiled. “It’s me, Paige.” Standing before her was a striking woman, somewhere in her late twenties. “Sarah, I can hardly believe the transformation!” Paige exclaimed, her voice filled with awe. "It's unbelievable! I can walk again!" She stepped back. I measured myself earlier. "I'm 5 feet 8," she said with pride. "It's been years since I stood this tall." Paige flexed her fingers, a wide smile lighting up her face. "My fingers used to be stiff and painful from arthritis," she said while moving her hands gracefully through the air. "But look, no pain at all!" She ran her palms over her thighs, feeling the strength beneath the fabric. "My legs feel and look as they did in my youth."

"Oh yes, they certainly do," Parker said as he strolled past, a playful glint in his eye.

Paige's cheeks flushed crimson at the sound of his voice. Sarah caught her subtle reaction, a soft chuckle slipping out as she added, "We are back in action!"

Something in Sarah's movements caught Paige off guard. "Wow," she said softly, her eyes tracing the motion. "Your arm... it's different." With an infectious burst of excitement, Sarah replied, "I've grown a new one! I have all the usual sensitivities; it's as though nothing ever went wrong." With a sudden movement, she bent down and lifted the nearest table effortlessly to shoulder height, holding it there for a moment before gently setting it down. "I believe I can lift a lot more. Call me the Bionic Woman!"

Paige let out a laugh, her eyes sparkling with amusement. "Note to self. Never challenge Sarah to an arm-wrestling match," she said, grinning while giving her a playful nudge. The moment lingered in shared laughter, easy and warm.

Across from her, Sarah scanned the room, a mischievous glint in her eye. "Have you seen the lineup? It's a total hottie central," she said, raising an eyebrow.

Their laughter spilled out; it was the kind of moment that made everything feel lighter.

Meanwhile, the general moved among his crew, a drink steady in his hand, though his thoughts were anything but. He watched the room closely, listening to the laughter and easy conversation. Bonds were forming between people who would soon depend on each other in ways they hadn't yet imagined. Every smile, every shared joke, a crew slowly becoming a family.

He thought about the different backgrounds and the skills each person brought.

Lieutenant Stuart Thomson stood out. Sharp instincts, steady hands, and the kind of grit that only came from years in the cockpit.

Sergeant Sarah Kane moved with quiet confidence. Her posture was steady, her steps deliberate, but there was something else, too. A drive. A need to prove something, maybe to herself more than anyone else.

Paige Mitchelmore: quick-witted, adaptable, and razor-sharp. She had a knack for dissecting problems and spinning up solutions before most had even finished asking the question.

Together, they weren't just preparing for a mission. They were stepping into the unknown, armed with trust, talent, and the beginnings of something that felt a lot like family.

He took a slow sip, letting the heat from the drink ease into his chest. The path ahead was anything but simple; danger hung in the air. But beneath all that, something steady rose in him. Confidence. Not the loud kind, but the kind that comes from knowing the people around you have your back. This crew wasn't just a group of professionals; they were his people. If they stuck together, they could handle whatever came next. He made a quiet vow to himself: keep that trust alive. It was the one thing that could carry them through.

George leaned on the railing, eyes drifting across the room. His mind wandered through the choices he'd made, the weight of each one pressing on his shoulders. Every call he made mattered, not just for the mission, but for the lives tied to it. He saw them now, scattered across the deck, talking, working, waiting. Each face reminded him why he couldn't afford to slip. They were counting on him. And he wasn't about to let them down. A sense of purpose welled up inside him. This was his crew. His mission. And he was ready to lead, not for glory, but for the ones who couldn't fight for themselves.

Owen and Chris finally reached him near the edge of the command deck, the hum of voices around them like distant static. The twins exchanged a look, grins creeping across their faces, eyes gleaming with mischief.

Then, without warning, Owen slapped a hand on George's back. The sound cracked through the air, bouncing off the metal walls.

Jolted, he was pulled from his thoughts. He turned slowly, his gaze sharpened but amused.

Owen chuckled, rubbing the back of his neck. "George, you practically twisted our arms to get us here. But from what I'm seeing, you've got things locked down. Starting to think you don't need us watching your six anymore."

Chris shifted his weight, his tone playfully sceptical. "This crew looks sharp. This mission, it's got a pulse to it. You sure we're not walking into something deeper than we're ready for?"

George's eyes narrowed, not with suspicion, but with thought. He straightened, setting his beer down on the table beside him with deliberate care. He looked over to the twins, letting the silence settle just enough as they leaned in ever so slightly.

"Boys," he said, voice calm but edged with gravel, "this mission stopped being about me the moment all of them signed on." He gestured across the room where veterans chatted, techs checked readouts, while recruits listened closely, each one a variable in the vast equation ahead.

"I asked you here because you know what it means to have someone's back when things go sideways. Not because I needed you for protection, but because they will."

His gaze met their eyes. The weight behind his words wasn't a burden; it was trust.

A grin crept across his face, half serious, half a challenge. "Buckle up," he said. "Is it dangerous? Hell yes. But what worries me isn't just the mission. It's whether you two can keep up."

The twins exchanged a look, brows raised, grins widening as if they'd just been handed a dare.

Chris reached for his drink. "Then I guess we'd better prove you right."

The general lifted his glass in return, the lines around his eyes softening. "Bottoms up."

Their glasses met with a clink, as if sealing something unspoken. No ranks. No protocol. Just three friends; seasoned, sharpened, ready, as the hum of the ship continued beneath their feet.

Zeph 3 Arrival

Personal account: Kayla Shaw

"Well, we landed on the training planet today. Honestly, it was wild, like one second, I'm on Earth, with its familiar skies and smells, and the next I was standing on alien ground under a sun that didn't feel quite right. The whole thing was so fast, my brain hadn't even caught up yet. The energy here... it's something else. We're young, we're strong, and we're ready. You can feel it in your chest with every heartbeat. It's like we're on the edge of something big."

***

The *Arcadia* disengaged the Slide Drive, slowing to sublight with a deep, resonant hum that vibrated through the deck plates. The shift wasn't violent, but it was enough to make a few of us brace instinctively. The kind of reflex you don't lose, even after rejuvenation. Outside the viewports, space stretched endlessly, distant suns blinking like watchful eyes in the dark.

Aurelia's voice cut through the silence with practised precision. "Attention all personnel. Prepare for arrival at Zeph 3." Her tone wasn't loud, but it carried. It rippled through the ship like a change in gravitational pull.

We all gathered around the viewports; as Zeph 3 emerged, there was no hiding our awe. Forests of impossible blue and green sprawled across its surface, beneath the gaze of its crimson star. Light streamed through the alien atmosphere, casting halos across the sprawling canopy below. Oceans shimmered with a hypnotic lustre, their surfaces blue with speckles of white as unseen tides pulled on them. Rivers flowed through jagged mountains that rose to the sky, their peaks etched in shadows against the distant glow of the sun.

No one spoke. There was only silence and wonder.

"Aurelia, tell us more about the planet," Kayla said, unable to tear her eyes from the unfolding alien tapestry.

"The planet Zeph 3," Aurelia replied, her voice unhurried. "Twice Earth's size. Twin moons that move in synchronicity along the star's rotation. The planet's fast axial spin compresses the day into fourteen hours, with sharp temperature shifts. Temperate climate when light, frigid in the shadows. Your climate suits will adapt automatically, but stay alert. The air is breathable, which means full surface recon is viable." Her words hung like sparks within the cabin's confines.

The intercom crackled to life again, low and deliberate. "Orbital entry in progress," came the unmistakable voice of the general. Authority echoed with each syllable. "Earth teams, prepare for descent. Assemble in the transport bay. We beam to the surface in one hour."

Crew members exchanged quick, knowing glances before scattering through the hallways, the clatter of gear, murmurs of readiness, and the hum of anticipation trailing behind them.

Arcadia adjusted its orbital systems, stabilising with a graceful shift that felt almost ceremonial.

Trainees hurried toward the transport bay, their boots beating like drums against the polished metal floor. The general stood tall and cantered, his silhouette framed by blinking guidance lights and the quiet roar of readiness.

In a burst of light and a whisper of charged energy, the transport sequence initiated. One by one, teams blinked out of existence, carried across the vacuum and reborn on alien soil.

Parker was stunned when his boots hit the ground, which felt soft, damp, and eerily warm. His eyes flared with wonder. “First alien planet I’ve ever set foot on!” he burst out, his awe raw and infectious.

The ground team had been holding its breath right along with him. The tension of descent, the silence of touchdown, the shared anticipation of being part of history. And, of course, the small matter of the unofficial bet they’d made during the flight: whoever spoke first after landing would trigger the team’s pre-agreed response.

So, when Parker blurted out his line, the release was instant.

“Hell yeah!” they shouted in perfect unison, the kind of timing that only comes from a group who had absolutely rehearsed this in the cargo bay. Their voices rose into the alien sky.

Parker grinned broadly, his chest heaving with excitement. “Quite amusing,” he muttered with a chuckle, his gaze already fixed on a towering hangar nestled among a forest of iridescent blue-leafed trees.

The planet's crimson star bathed the rugged mountains in a warm glow, casting long shadows that danced across the terrain. The flora below teemed with life, erupting in a vibrant spectrum of colour. Hues unlike anything found on Earth rippled through the landscape: violet fronds with luminescent leaves, each shimmering as if dusted with glitter. High above, large-winged creatures cut through the air in graceful pursuit of their smaller prey.

Something screeched in the distance, a sound too deep, too resonant to be harmless.

The group stood entranced, their gazes shifting from the alien skies to the ground below. In front of them, a tall figure walked towards them, emerging from the misted horizon, with deliberate grace. His features were unmistakably Venoran, angular, almost sculpted, with iridescent eyes that glowed faintly in the fading light. Despite his commanding presence, there was an air of warmth about him that invited trust.

"Greetings," he began, his melodic voice harmonising perfectly with the surroundings. "I am Drowen." With an elegant sweep of his arm, he gestured toward the breathtaking landscape and the large flying creatures. "Watch for the larger ones. They are... opportunistic hunters. For your own safety, stay near the hangar if you want to avoid trouble."

Just as he finished speaking, a sharp, guttural screech tore through the treeline. Something big.

A shadow swept across the ground, fast, jagged, unmistakably predatory. Branches snapped somewhere beyond the ridge, followed by a heavy thud that made the soil tremble beneath their boots.

Parker stiffened. "Holy mother of Murphy, what the hell was that!"

Drowen didn't look up. "A Skryth."

As if summoned by the name, the creature banked into view, a dark shape slicing across the crimson sky. Its wings were broad and multi-jointed, folding tight as it dipped, then snapping open with a thunderous beat that sent dust swirling around their boots. The membranes shimmered faintly in the alien light, giving the beast a flicker-like glow as it circled.

Its body was lean and angular, built for speed, as its matte hide drank in the sunlight rather than reflecting it. A long, whip-like tail streamed behind, slicing through the air with each turn. Four faintly glowing eyes scanned the ground, two forward, two set wider, giving it a predatory sweep of vision that made every trainee feel exposed.

Another screech ripped from its narrow jaw, the sound vibrating through the soil like a warning.

Drowen lifted a hand, calm but firm. "Hold your ground. Do not run. Running triggers pursuit."

A second shadow streaked overhead, wings beating with a low, thunderous pulse. The creature banked sharply, circling back toward their position.

For a moment, everyone froze.

Then, just as the Skryth dipped lower, a piercing whistle erupted from Drowen's wrist device. A burst of ultrasonic sound rippled through the air, invisible but powerful.

The creature shrieked, veering off violently. Leaves spiraled down in its wake as it retreated toward the distant mountains.

Silence returned in a slow, uneasy wave.

Parker exhaled shakily. "Opportunistic hunters? You could've led with *that*."

Drowen's iridescent eyes flicked toward him. "I did."

He lowered his wrist device, expression unchanged. "They rarely attack groups this large. But they test boundaries. Think of this as your first lesson. I will be guiding you through our training facility," he began, his voice crisp but low. "Rapid preparation is essential. You've landed on an alien planet, so let me ask: what is the most critical thing to check before touchdown?"

Silence.

Don's voice broke through, sharp and unapologetically playful.

"What are the women like?" he drawled, grinning as though daring a response.

Laughter rippled through the crew like static discharge: quick, nervous, and borderline loud. Relief flashed across a few faces, briefly defusing the tension. Even Drowen's lips twitched, a micro-expression barely born before his features reset. Composed once again, he offered no reply.

"Guess he's a robot," Don muttered, his smirk lingering just long enough to be noticed.

Drowen's gaze swept calmly over the terrain. The jungle beyond shimmered strangely in the planet's odd twilight, leaves rustling without wind.

He raised a hand, elegant and deliberate. "The environment," he began, voice shifting into the tempo of command, "is your first concern. Check the air; is it breathable? The planet's gravity and the air pressure."

His tone settled into quiet authority, a melody wrapped in warning. "Without these conditions, your body becomes your enemy."

He stepped forward, gliding more than walking, and tapped the stud on his suit. "The technology you wear adapts to Earth's conditions, but only if you engage it." His words felt heavier now, the weight of survival pressing into each syllable.

Trainees hesitated, then one by one, their fingers moved. The air filled with a soft hiss, followed by the slick unfolding of helmets. A shimmer of translucent alloy wrapped around each head, sealing them in safety with the smooth grace of well-rehearsed engineering.

Wide eyes peered through visors. No one spoke.

"Touch the stud again, and your helmet will retract. But do not grow careless."

The glow of Zeph 3's sun caught their visors, casting angular reflections like firelight against steel. The gravity pressed harder now, a subtle drag in each motion. A few shifted uneasily, noticing the weight of their limbs.

Drowen watched them with the patience of someone who had seen this many times before.

"This is one of the few planets in this sector we've surveyed that possesses gravity stronger than Earth's," he said. "Without your suits, you'd be exhausted within minutes."

The trainees gathered in a loose semicircle, boots pressing into the unfamiliar soil. The sunlight was dancing across the curved surfaces of their helmets. The building had a steady hum that blended with the rustle of leaves from strange plants swaying gently in the breeze. The air was breathable, but it left a metallic tang on your tongue, like licking a rusted pipe.

With each step they took, their boots sank slightly into the springy ground. Drowen, remaining composed, commanded their attention. "Behind me stands the training facility," he began, gesturing with a precise motion toward the gleaming complex. The interconnected domes shone brilliantly in the sunlight, their curves reflecting shifting hues of crimson and gold, as though alive.

"This facility was built at the request of the first Earth trainees who realised they couldn't survive without it," he said, eyes scanning the architecture with quiet pride. "They learned the hard way that preparation wasn't optional; it was the difference between adapting and disappearing."

The trainees listened, quietly but focused. Around them, the strange landscape hummed with life as fast-moving creatures zipped through the clouds, their voices fading in and out against the breeze, while glowing plants swayed gently as if breathing.

Drowen gave them a once-over. "This facility is not here to make things easy for you. We put you into real-world scenarios, situations we've encountered, and ones you're likely to face yourself."

A distant roar rolled across the landscape; low and guttural, this was too close. Several trainees turned sharply.

Drowen didn't flinch. "In five weeks of intense training, you will come out stronger, sharper, and ready."

Some exchanged glances, a smile crossing their faces as they accepted the challenge.

"Tough? Definitely. Impossible? Maybe. But you are here for a reason, and hesitation isn't an option."

"We had avoided conflict with the Korrathi for years, shielding our worlds from their reach. That worked until they found us. From that time, Earth and our allies have helped us fight back. We've learned from every battle, fine-tuning our approach, making sure our training always stays one step ahead."

Air hissed around the massive metal doors before they began to slide open with an almost eerie silence, inviting the teams into the dimly lit interior. What surprised them first was the sheer enormity of the hangar. And then they saw it: towering before them was an imposing Korrathi battleship, its battered exterior hinting at the ferocity of past conflicts.

"This vessel was salvaged after sustaining considerable damage from a carefully placed explosive mine, created by one of our earlier teams to defend an outpost." For a few of you, your mission will be to delve deeply into the mysteries of the Korrathi and their technology, housed within this ship.

The trainees approached a large doorway, which overlooked a sprawling docking bay. This was a first for them. Filling the entire bay was a diverse collection of spaceships standing in carefully arranged rows. Each model had distinct engineering designs. They continued the tour and began to move downward. The walls shimmered to life with holographic projections displaying intricate schematics of Korrathi technology and refined tactical strategies.

When they reached the next level, Drowen continued his voice steady.

"This sector houses advanced flight simulators and weapon control systems, designed to mirror the exact specifications of those onboard our fleet. Several crafts are displayed here for hands-on familiarisation. At the forefront is one of our Galaxy-class explorers.

These ships have the most powerful engines in our fleet, capable of sustaining a crew of 500."

A smirk tugged at the corner of Sarah's mouth as she quipped, "It's a bloody flying saucer, just like those rumoured to be in Area 51."

Drowen, unaffected by the comment, gestured toward another vessel, seamlessly continuing the tour. "That sizable craft is our battle cruiser. It operates effectively with a crew of 80, affectionately referred to as a 'B Cruiser' by previous trainees. This ship is outfitted with multiple tactical weapons, two hangar bays, and a shield deflector that enhances its defensive capabilities. The B Cruiser carries a squadron of combat fighters."

Stuart raised his hand, concern etched across his face. "How does our fleet stack up against the Korrathi?"

Drowen's expression darkened. "Honestly? They've got the advantage in numbers. When the war broke out, we were overwhelmed. Our losses mounted quickly, too fast to count. But with help from your people and others like you, we've managed to push back. The training has made a real difference. Our casualties have dropped, and we've slowed their advance."

He paused, then added, "We've outfitted all our planets with defence shields. For the moment, they've held strong, sparing us from more danger. But recent surveillance suggests the Korrathi are preparing another strike, this time targeting our outer worlds. Once your training wraps up, we'll head back to our home world. There, we'll need to regroup and plan our next move."

Training - New Tools, New Rules

Week 12

Personal account: Stuart Thompson

"On the surface of a distant planet, we train once more. A lifetime ago, we had endured similar trials, pushing our bodies and minds to their limits. But this time, it is different. This training, devised by humans on a world far from Earth, is unlike anything we've known before. The methods are new; the stakes are higher, and the planet itself seems to challenge us at every turn. Halfway through the training, everything changed, and all hell broke loose. All around the complex, alarms shrieked, signalling an alien intruder alert. Somehow, it had slipped past the Arcadia; this was not a training session."

***

The general made his way to the front of the group, his presence magnetic, drawing every eye without a word. He paused, his sharp gaze scanning the faces before him. With a voice that cut through the ambient hum of the facility, he began.

"Listen up." He shifted his weight slightly, easing into a relaxed stance. One hand rested on the back of a nearby chair, the other gesturing gently, as if inviting the group into the conversation rather than commanding it. There was a quiet steadiness in his posture, the kind that came from years of guiding people through challenges, not barking orders at them.

"Each of you has been assigned to specialised training programs designed to sharpen your skills. You'll be cross-trained in multiple disciplines. We can't afford weak links. If one goes down, someone else can step up. No exceptions." He paced slowly, letting the weight of his words settle.

"This should be familiar territory. You've all been exposed to Venoran tech during stasis. Now it's time to prove you can use it."

He paused for a moment. "Now, I'd like you all to look at the devices on your wrists. These devices can be used as a communicator, a universal translator, or a terrain scanner that shows all obstacles and distances around you. The scanner also displays living objects within its range, blue for the good guys and red for everyone else."

Excitement spread through the group, a ripple of energy they could hardly suppress. Paige, engrossed in the communicator's controls, let her curiosity slip into words. "Cool," she muttered, unaware she had spoken aloud.

"Please review your training programs and attend the assigned training areas."

Stuart joined others already at the controls of various flight simulators in the room.

"You should also note that the controls of each flight simulator will change depending on the ship's configuration. Take the Korrathi Battle Cruiser for instance; its fighter controls will be difficult to use. The Korrathi hands are different; they have four long fingers and are somewhat wider than yours; you will have to adjust to handle those controls."

Don and Sarah entered the weapons training area, followed by the rest of the group.

"Weapon specialists, your training will cover operating these weapons, taking them apart, and reassembling each type laid out before you."

The room was filled with various weapons, from traditional firearms to advanced energy weapons, each meticulously organised on racks and tables. "You will also get acquainted with those on board the ship."

Paige walked up beside Sarah and, in a questioning tone, asked, "So you and Don are working together?"

Sarah turned and gave Paige a playful poke to shut her up in case Don might overhear anything. Paige glanced back at Sarah, her eyes twinkling with a knowing look, before she slipped back into her group. The moment was brief, but it added a flicker of warmth to the otherwise intense training session, like a secret shared in passing. Something about the way Sarah and Don had interacted earlier had caught Paige's attention, and now her curiosity was quietly buzzing.

Next up were the engineers.

The lead Venoran engineer stepped forward, his voice sharp with urgency. "Everyone here will learn the science behind the starship, and how it flies."

The engineers were led to a separate zone, a sleek, glass-walled chamber humming with energy. Inside, they got their first glimpse of the starship's beating heart: propulsion systems pulsing with alien tech, glowing energy cores suspended in magnetic fields, and navigation controls that responded to thought as much as touch.

Paige and her group were guided back to the trio of ships waiting in the docking bay.

At the edge of the landing bay, Drowen raised a hand, halting the group in front of the vessels. "You're here to understand how these ships work, from their armour plating to their weapons systems," he said.

He led them through the corridors and observation decks of each vessel. Pausing to examine the reinforced hulls, energy shields, and the sleek weapon arrays that lined each ship's exterior.

"You will be given hands-on experience with the ship's controls and systems, learning how to manage power distribution, target acquisition, and defensive manoeuvres," he explained.

At the next entrance, the group stepped into a medical facility, where the chief medical officer was waiting to receive them. She wore a crisp, tailored uniform. Her posture was upright, exuding quiet authority, but there was a warmth in her demeanour that made her instantly approachable.

With a motion of her arm, she turned and led them along a corridor. The soft hum of machinery filled the air, and the glow of sophisticated equipment cast subtle reflections on the polished surfaces.

"Take your time to explore the equipment," she said. "Utilise the computer stations and review the records detailing our regeneration process and critical medical procedures."

Drowen approached the general. "If I may, General, please come with me." He led him to a large room filled with monitors surrounding a central chair. "This is a simulation of the brain; all our ships are equipped with one of these."

They walked over to the central chair. "Please have a seat. From this chair, you'll have direct access to all personnel and be able to monitor their status in real time. You can communicate with individuals or address the entire fleet simultaneously. The primary monitor provides a comprehensive view of an entire solar system, your ships, and any opposing threats. Beyond tactical operations, it also serves astronomical functions, displaying distances between star systems and neighbouring galaxies. Gall has also informed me that you may include yourself in any of the other training sessions."

“Noted!” responded the general.

It had been 20 cycles, and the training had been progressing well in all areas. Each team had been making remarkable progress in its required programs. But this day was different; alarms blared around the building, and the room's lights flickered. The general instinctively reached for the controls. “What's happening?” he demanded.

Drowen's expression turned serious. “We have an intruder alert. This is not a drill. General, you need to take command from here.”

As new reports flooded his desk, the general sifted through the data with practised precision, already calculating his next move.

He tapped the control panel, bringing up the live feed of the hangar and its surrounding corridors. The system responded instantly with a red glow highlighting the intruder.

“Patch me into the hangar feed,” he barked, stepping closer to the console. The screen shifted, revealing a chaotic scene of blaster fire lighting up the shadows. His voice cut across the room with crisp, commanding force. “All personnel, we have an intruder alert. Prepare to mobilise.” He turned to Drowen without missing a beat. “Status update. Now.”

His command echoed through the chamber, setting the defence operation into motion.

Drowen worked quickly at the console, eyes darting across the screen as he tracked the intruder’s movements. “General,” he said, his voice tense, “the intruder is heading for the main hangar bay.” The general didn’t hesitate. “Send in the security teams. We can’t let them reach the ships.”

Paige and her squad moved towards the intruders' location. Moments earlier, they'd been deep into their training session when the alarm blared. The ship jolted, causing them to lose their balance. Paige caught herself against the wall, heart pounding, and scanned her team. Everyone was upright; they had no time to waste.

"You heard him. Let's move!" she barked, leading the sprint toward the hangar bay.

Dr. Brooks' voice came over the comms. "Medical bay ready."

She could hear the general's voice on her wrist monitor. "Paige, location?"

"Close," she replied, checking the display. "We're nearly at the hangar bay." Her monitor lit up the intruder's location. Blaster fire cracked through the corridor, fast and close.

Paige raised her fist. "Down," she said, low and firm.

The team dropped behind a stack of crates, crouching in the haze. Smoke curled through the air. The hum of energy weapons echoed around them.

"Visual?" she asked, her voice tight.

"Negative," one of them said. "Too much interference."

They scanned the chaos ahead, assessing the situation before making their move. Whoever was out there wasn't just skilled; they were fast.

The twins had the intruder cornered, their weapons blazing as bursts of fire ricocheted through the room. Amid the chaos, Chris spun toward Owen, his voice cutting through the noise. "Owen, do you have a plan?"

Owen's brow tightened. His mind raced. He steadied himself, voice low but firm. "We flank him. I'll lay down cover fire and have two assault teams move in. Chris, take your squad left. Paige, lead yours to the right. We catch him off guard, we end this."

Plasma fire erupted from all sides, adrenaline flooding the intruder's system. Every escape route was collapsing under the coordinated assault. The twins kept him boxed in, their energy blasts deflecting off structures around him. He scanned the room, desperate for a crack in their formation.

His training screamed at him to keep moving, to avoid being pinned. But they were too precise. Too fast. Too damn good. Paige's blaster fire was sharp and unyielding, forcing him to pivot toward the doorway. Just as he moved, her teammates reacted, cutting off his escape.

He shifted his stance. If he was going down, he wasn't going down without a fight. He prepared to strike just as another attack came from the opposite side. Chris's team swept in with practised precision, a wave of movement closing in on his location, tightening the net. His breathing was heavy. They had anticipated his every move.

Then came Paige's voice, firm, unwavering. "Drop your weapon!" Her blaster was locked onto him, aimed directly at his chest.

His grip tightened around his weapon, his mind racing through the possibilities. Surrender? Fight? He could feel the room shrinking, his options dissolving one by one. He had never been cornered or outmatched.

And for the first time, he realised, he wasn't getting out of this.

The intruder stood motionless, his towering frame a stark contrast against the cold, sterile glow of the chamber's light. His grey skin, mottled with splashes of black, blended seamlessly into the shadows, more like living camouflage than mere pigmentation.

Four arms hung at the ready, each gripping a weapon built for one purpose... destruction. Energy blades sharp enough to cut through steel hummed with a deadly blue glow. The rifle in his upper hand pulsed with restrained fury, its barrel hot, twitching with every subtle movement of his fingers. A plasma staff vibrated softly, unstable energy surging through its core. The jagged combat spike in his lower grip gleamed with dried remnants of past battles: close, brutal, unforgiving.

He didn't move; his actions remained controlled and unreadable. The tension in the room was suffocating, thick with the promise of violence. One wrong move, and it would all come crashing down.

The weight of inevitability pressed on him, just enough to make his broad shoulders sag. Not defeat, just recognition. His glowing green eyes, once fierce with defiance, dimmed slightly. Not from fear. From understanding he'd been outmanoeuvred.

His anger didn't subside. His arms stayed raised, weapons gripped tight. His muscles were locked, not to strike, but to keep the fury from spilling out. Rage simmered just beneath the surface, barely held in check. The sharp lines of his face, once carved with defiance, had settled into something colder. Still. Calculating. For a moment, he didn't move. His mind raced through every possibility, every risk, every slim chance of escape. None of them held.

He let out a slow breath. Controlled. Final.

His fingers loosened. One by one, the weapons slipped from his hands, hitting the floor with a hollow clatter that echoed through the silence.

The sound echoed through the chamber, final and undeniable.

He realised his position was lost. Even in surrender, the alien's presence drew every eye, not like a vanquished foe, but like a predator behind glass, waiting for the moment the lock failed. The room held its breath, the silence heavy with the sense that this wasn't the end of his defiance.

"Good work, everyone," Owen said, exhaling with relief. "Let's get him back to the general."

They moved quickly through the corridors toward the command centre. The general's voice was heard on the communicator. "All personnel, stand down. Threat neutralised." The red alert faded from the monitors, replaced by a soft blue glow. Tension drained from the trainees' shoulders as they returned to their stations.

The general stepped forward, his boots scuffing against the steel floor. He turned to Drowen, his eyes sharp with restrained pride. “Looks like your training simulations weren’t just theory after all.”

Drowen gave a rare smile, brief, flickering like a candle in the wind. “They held up under pressure. But this was just a sample, not a victory lap. We stay sharp, always.”

The general nodded, his expression sobering. “Agreed, we all need to be ready for whatever comes next.”

The intruder, now cuffed and unreadable behind his alien features, was led down the corridor toward the holding cell.

The harsh lighting cast jagged shadows on the walls when the interrogation room was activated. Inside, the air felt thick, charged. The intruder’s posture was relaxed, almost casual, but his eyes moved with purpose; alert, analytical, still calculating his next move.

The general leaned forward as if studying him. His voice dropped to a low growl. “Where is your ship? How many of you are there?”

The alien’s lips curled into something between a smirk and a sneer. His words twisted into riddles, each laced with quiet menace, suggesting catastrophe without ever naming it. “You’re recycling the same tired warnings we’ve heard before,” Drowen said, his voice cold.

The intruder sneered. “All you have are raw recruits. You might as well surrender. My commander already knows.”

A quiet smile passed between the general and the others. Drowen stepped forward. “If I may, General?” The general nodded.

Drowen spoke, his voice steady. “These recruits have spent their lives training and fighting. That’s something your commander will never understand.”

If the alien was capable of surprise, it showed then, in a flicker across its face.

A heavy silence settled over the room. The alien said nothing more. Time dragged. An hour passed. The general’s patience was wearing thin. With a curt nod, he signalled the security team to escalate.

Just as the guards moved in, the intruder's eyes narrowed. With a subtle motion, he pressed two elongated nails together, activating a hidden device buried beneath his skin.

Before anyone could react, the device emitted a high-pitched sound. The crew watched as the intruder convulsed and collapsed onto the floor. The device had released a lethal dose of a fast-acting toxin, ensuring that the intruder would not be able to reveal any information.

There was silence in the room as the gravity of the moment pressed down on everyone. The general cracked his knuckles, frustration and anger evident on his face.

"Find out who sent him and what he was doing here," he said, his voice filled with determination. "Additionally, we need to be more vigilant than ever to protect this base and mission."

"Drowen, what do we know of this creature?"

"We have seen these creatures before. They are mercenaries working for the Korrathi. The Korrathi use them to scout planets for potential threats. Their goal is to gather intelligence on planets showing signs of advanced technology and report back to the Korrathi command central."

Two weeks after the alien intrusion, a crisp announcement cut through the facility. "This is Hollins. I want everyone to complete what they are currently working on and report to the central hangar in one hour." A mix of curiosity and apprehension spread through the group as they awaited his arrival.

The heavy door swung open as he entered, his sharp gaze scanning the room. "Today, we are going to try something new."

Paige felt the weight of scrutiny as he approached her, his expression challenging.

"OK, Paige, let's see how good you are at hand-to-hand fighting." Frustration bubbled up inside her, and she faced her limitations head-on. "But I don't know how?" she confessed, her voice trembling slightly with anxiety.

Without warning, he lunged toward her, but something primal took over. Instinct kicked in as she ducked, gripping his wrist tightly. In one swift motion, she swept her leg beneath him, sending him crashing to the ground with a thud.

Disbelief hung in the air as he hit the ground.

"How did I do that?" she exclaimed, her voice half in shock, half exhilarated.

The general, lying flat on his back, couldn't hide the hint of admiration that glinted in his eyes. "Instinct," he said, voice low but steady. "You reacted without thinking. That's good. While you were in stasis, many skills were integrated, self-defence being one."

Paige's eyes widened in realisation.

"You can release me now."

"Sorry, General," she said with an infectious smile, as she looked around at her teammates, who appeared equally astonished.

He stood up, flexing his wrist, and looked across the floor at the teams. Then he turned back to Paige, a smirk playing on his lips. "Glad you never had a knife handy," he joked, lightening the mood.

The twins lingered close, unable to suppress their smiles. He noticed a grin tugging at the sides of their mouths. "Don't get cocky," he said with a laugh. "I could still drop you both before breakfast."

He turned and addressed the room. "What Paige was able to do applies to all of you," he said, tone booming. "Stasis didn't just update you on the war; it trained you. Combat protocols, tactical reasoning, threat analysis. It's all in there."

He stepped forward, scanning each face.

"You may not remember the drills, but your bodies will. When the time comes, trust your instincts. That's what it's there for. I want groups of four to confront one person in the centre. When you hear the buzzer, switch positions; each of you will take his or her turn in the spotlight. No one is going to miss out on the fun." His voice suddenly erupted with energy. "Go get them!"

The training session unfolded with fierce intensity, as each participant had to defend themselves against attackers from all angles. Hours slipped by in a blur of flying fists, sharp kicks, and quick pivots. Sweat poured down faces, every muscle screamed, and each breath felt like a battle. Just as exhaustion began to settle in, the general's voice cut through the chaos.

"Alright, everyone, that's enough!"

They halted their sessions, each breathing heavily, their limbs trembling from the effort. Everyone except one group.

At the centre of the room, Kayla was still moving, her movements fluid. She spun, ducked, and struck with precision. One kick sent an opponent crashing to the ground. Another followed, swift and clean. Her eyes burned with focus. Her body was a blur of motion. Luckily, before the start of the session, everyone had been fitted with suits that dissipated the blows.

The general's gun fired into the air, a sharp crack that silenced the chaos. "Enough, Kayla! Session is over!" he barked, his tone firm. "You've made a mess of your teammates. Learn to control yourself, especially when sparring against the good guys."

With the training finally wrapped up, he let out a breath and cracked a soft smile. "Alright, that's enough for today. Head back to the *Arcadia*, get Doc to patch you up, and for the love of all things decent, take a shower. You guys stink."

The trainees chuckled, some groaning as they gathered their gear. His tone shifted slightly to a serious one. "Tomorrow, we are going to switch things up, so make sure you're ready." The promise of something new hung in the air, sparking curiosity and a few nervous glances.

The following day, the group were transported to the planet's surface. Drowen stood waiting, arms crossed, his presence commanding without a word.

"Follow me," he said, turning on his heel and leading them through the cavernous hangar while activating the open switch. As the massive rear doors slid open, the trainees were met with the sight of a towering structure that dominated the horizon. Its surface shimmered beneath the alien sun.

The doors opened, and he led them inside. Their footsteps echoed before being swallowed by the vast space. The walls stretched high above them, disappearing into shadow, while the floor was etched with faint grid lines, with lights that lit up beneath their boots.

Drowen motioned for the group to gather in the centre. He took a couple of steps up to the raised platform that contained a sleek console. Its exterior pulsed with diagnostic lights and hovering holo-readouts. He tapped a few commands, then pressed a button, and suddenly, the floor beneath them seemed to vanish. A rush of weightlessness hit, and startled shouts echoed as trainees grabbed at each other, trying to stay upright.

Drowen chuckled. "Today, we're practising zero-gravity manoeuvring."

He adjusted the console, slowly easing the anti-gravity field until they drifted gently back to the ground.

Drowen motioned to the rows of suits lining the wall. "These are built for today's exercises," he said. "Your suits have thrusters on the arms and legs to help you move around. You'll want to get the hang of them, especially if you ever end up outside the ship, drifting in open space."

He distributed weapons; their weight unfamiliar yet powerful in the trainees' hands.

"When I reactivate the anti-gravity, objects will start to careen through the air. Your challenge is to neutralise as many as you can. Beware of the larger obstacles; colliding with one will be quite uncomfortable."

He emphasised the instruction, and a hint of mischief danced in his eyes. "We'll break the day into two four-hour sessions, with a break in between."

As the first session commenced, chaos erupted. The trainees zipped around the chamber as if they were caught in a game of zero-gravity pinball. Some slammed into walls or equipment, while others, still figuring out how to control their suit thrusters, collided mid-air as they tried to hit the spinning targets.

By the end of the first session, Drowen gathered the group and reviewed their performance statistics. "Group proficiency is sitting at forty percent," he said, scanning the data. "Some of you are way behind."

There were a few groans, but no one argued. They knew it hadn't gone smoothly.

As the day went on, they were getting the hang of it; their movements became more controlled, and collisions less frequent. By the time the session wrapped up, their accuracy and coordination had improved noticeably.

"I'll see you all again tomorrow," Drowen said with a nod, his tone more encouraging than before.

That night, the hospital wing buzzed with activity as trainees nursed their bruises and injuries. Doc stood beside Don, scanning the deep bruising with practised ease.

Chuckling, he said, "This training is great. I'm getting plenty of practice thanks to you guys."

"You should've been in there," Don replied, his voice tinged with exhaustion.

Doc grinned. "Not part of my duties," he said, his tone light.

With a smooth motion, he ran a specialised medical tool over Don's bruises. Almost instantly, the discolouration faded, and his muscles relaxed as the healing process began.

"There, you're all set."

Don sat up, running his fingers over his once-bruised skin. Satisfied, he flashed a quick smile. "Catch you later, Doc," and left the room, ready for whatever came next.

The following day, the gravity chamber pulsed with energy as the trainees pushed themselves harder than ever. Sweat formed in tiny droplets floating around them. Their movements were smoother, more synchronised.

Kayla shouted over to Dave, who was floating nearby. "Hey! Can you float a bit farther away? I didn't sign up for a sweat shower. You're misting me like I'm part of your backyard irrigation system."

"How do you even know it's mine?" he chuckled while flipping over in the zero gravity. He placed his hands at his sides and pushed off the wall, gliding toward a more open area.

In the chamber now, there was no fumbling, no hesitation, only precision. The hum of the targeting modules created an eerie harmony with their controlled breathing.

Drowen stood at the edge of the chamber wall, observing with quiet satisfaction. When the last drill concluded, he clapped once, the sound muffled in the chamber's artificial atmosphere.

"That," he declared, "was teamwork in its finest form."

The group gathered, catching their breath, exchanging nods of appreciation. Some wiped their foreheads, their visors fogging up momentarily, while others examined the wear on their suits, battle scars of simulated combat.

Drowen's gaze swept over them, landing on each face with unwavering intensity. Then he spoke, "The progress you've made today, tells me you're ready."

A murmur of agreement rippled through the team, but it was Dr. Brooks' voice, calm yet firm, that silenced them. He stepped forward, datapad in hand, scanning the results.

"We have one final evaluation before you move to the next phase. Rest now, because tomorrow, guess what, we push harder," he said with a chuckle.

Then, a wry grin spread across Drowen's face. "You heard the order. Rest while you can. Oh, and don't get too cosy. Take this time to recuperate before the next round of training until Dr. Brooks gives us the green light."

As the trainees exited, some murmured about the challenge ahead, and others simply basked in the moment. They had stepped beyond their limits, and tomorrow, they would do it again.

Korrathi Attack

Personal account: Sarah Kane

"Funny how quickly things unravel. Yesterday, we were floating around in zero gravity, acting like a bunch of raw recruits. Today, we're fighting for survival. Somehow, the mercenaries got a message through to the Korrathi. And now, they're coming."

***

Gall stood on the bridge of the *Arcadia*, high above the planet's surface. The control panels blinked quietly around him, as the low hum of the ship's systems filled the air. Everything was running smoothly until a voice broke the calm.

"Sir," a senior officer called out, urgency cutting through his usual composed tone. "We've detected an anomaly on the space grid. It appeared just moments ago."

Gall turned, eyes narrowing. The officer pointed to a glowing panel displaying a map of nearby space. Two flickering signals pulsed on the screen, unfamiliar, fast-moving.

"Can you confirm their course?"

"I ran their current trajectory," the officer replied as he scanned his console. "They're heading straight for us."

Gall didn't hesitate. "Launch a long-range drone. I want data on those objects now."

Within seconds, the drone shot from the *Arcadia's* launch bay, slicing through the void on an intercept path. As it neared the target, streams of data began pouring in.

"The drone has identified Korrathi life forms," the officer reported, voice tight. "They are long-range discovery ships. Heavily armoured. Equipped with laser cannons." Without missing a beat. "Sir... they've just destroyed the drone."

Gall's expression tensed, lips pressed into a thin line. "There must have been another mercenary shadowing the one we apprehended, an accomplice we missed." He paused, recalling the interrogation. "The Commander, that's who he mentioned. He must have already sent his report to him."

Gall scanned the incoming report, his eyes flicking across the details. Korrathi Discovery Ships were dangerous enough, but their sudden appearance and the swift destruction of the drone meant the Korrathi knew they were here. And they weren't coming to talk.

His mind raced, calculating the implications.

"Aurelia, notify crew members to prepare for immediate action. Enemy spacecraft detected. Activate the shields on the training ships."

After receiving the communication from Aurelia, the general immediately alerted all the teams to begin setting up a defence around the hangar.

He quickly reached out to Paige, his voice steady but laced with urgency. "Can we get the ship's shields up and running?"

"The best we can do is activate two of them, but we'll need the engineering teams over here for those," Paige responded.

"Dave, do you copy?" the general called out. Dave, who was already aware of Paige's request, replied, "On my way."

The general's eyes narrowed as he processed Paige's response. His mind raced, calculating the implications of the Korrathi ship's vulnerability. Without missing a beat, "Paige, what ship has no shields?" His voice cut through the tension like a knife.

"The Korrathi," she replied, her voice steady with a hint of urgency.

"All units, prepare for immediate engagement. We will be targeting the Korrathi ship's weak points. Activate our defensive measures and have the laser cannons on standby." His next orders were precise and rapid-fire.

"All teams go immediately to the Venoran training ships and activate shields." Don and Sarah head to the Korrathi Battle Cruiser and check its weapons capabilities. "Paige, can you stretch the shield to cover the Korrathi ship?"

Knowing that every second counted, the general's mind ran through various strategies.

Paige's heart raced as she processed the situation. "I need a few minutes," she said, her voice steady but laced with urgency. "We are unable to use any of the weapons on the Venoran training ships while we have the shields up."

The discovery of the Korrathi ship's arrival in orbit over Zeph 3 sent a wave of tension through the crew.

On the ground Dave had arrived with the additional shield generators, Paige felt a glimmer of hope. She quickly linked the Venoran shields to the main control centre.

"General, the coverage of the Korrathi ship will not last long," she warned.

His reply came instantly. "Understood." Almost immediately he called Sarah and Don from his communicator, requesting a status update on their weapons.

Sarah's response was immediate: "We have 24 torpedoes, and only one laser turret is working."

He leaned in, eyes steady. "Here's how we play it. Let the Korrathi take the first shots; those will more than likely take out most of our roof coverage. Paige, on my signal, drop the shield on the Korrathi ship. I'm banking on their first instinct being restraint and not firing on their ship."

A Korrathi ship swept in from the nearby mountains, skimming the treetops as it bore down on the settlement and unleashed a barrage from its cannons. As the Korrathi ship began its assault, General Hollin's voice echoed through the communication channels.

"Shields up," he ordered. The first barrage of fire from the Korrathi ship tore through the roof and walls, exposing the training ships. On its second run, the Korrathi targeted the Venoran training ships, firing its laser cannons, which dissipated on impact.

The general watched the battlefield unfold exactly as planned. "Good, the Korrathi are directing fire at the Venoran ships, as I hoped. Now, Paige, drop the shields around the Korrathi ship and open fire." Paige's hands moved swiftly over the controls.

Don's voice crackled over the comms. "Aim for the engines; the body is too well protected."

The crew's coordinated efforts were productive. Immediately, the rear of the Korrathi ship received a couple of direct hits to one of its engines. A large explosion could be seen at the rear of the ship, with smoke trailing behind. Severely damaged, it began to gain altitude to escape the planet. Another explosion sent the ship crashing to the ground.

Sarah's eyes widened as she processed the sudden shift in the remaining ship's strategy. Her heart pounded, but she maintained a calm exterior. They were going after the *Arcadia.*

"General, this is Sarah. The second ship has broken off its ground attack; it appears to have located the *Arcadia.*"

His mind raced through the possible implications. The Arcadias' defence was critical, and its safety was paramount. He knew they had to act swiftly to protect it.

"Send a communication to Gall, and have him take the *Arcadia* out of orbit, keep it cloaked and in contact."

"We are going to board the second ship." He declared, his voice cutting through the tension like a blade. His thoughts were a whirlwind of strategies and contingencies. He trusted Gall's ability to handle the situation, but the stakes had never been higher. Every second mattered, and he was determined to keep the *Arcadia* protected.

The general was briefing the twins and two other marines when Kayla came running, her face set with determination. "Sir, I have checked *Arcadia's* database on the Korrathi," Kayla said, her voice tinged with a mix of urgency and determination. She extended her wrist and projected an image above her communicator. "You'll easily recognise one when you see it."

The image showed a Korrathi, upright like a man. Its body was covered with fur, patchy black and brown, that blended seamlessly into the forested environment of its home world. Its arms were long and corded with muscle, hanging low like coiled springs. The four fingers on each hand moved with chilling precision, built to grip, to crush, to wield a weapon, to end a life.

But it was the face that lingered in the mind. If you could call it a face. The nose stretched unnaturally from brow to lip, giving it a look that was both alien and disturbingly familiar. It wasn't just a tool, a sensor, tuned to threats most species couldn't even perceive. And those eyes. Yellow, slitted, unblinking. Made for darkness. Made for hunting.

The general studied the image, his expression unreadable. But inside, gears turned fast. This wasn't just another enemy. This was a predator. With a tone of urgency in his voice, he turned to his team.

"We know what we're dealing with. Let's move."

Kayla felt her pulse quicken. She trusted him, but the Korrathi image had carved itself into her nerves. There was no room for hesitation.

Owen and Chris were already geared up, exchanging a silent nod. No bravado, just readiness. Years of training had forged them into something solid, something reliable.

The general's mind stayed locked on the mission. No distractions. No doubts. Time was the enemy, and he had no intention of losing.

The image of the Korrathi served as a stark reminder of the challenge ahead, but it also fuelled their resolve to protect the *Arcadia* and its crew.

He tightened his grip on the container of explosives while handing Kayla a gun with his other hand. "Kayla, here is your weapon," he said, his voice steady and calm. He tapped his communicator. "Gall, I want you to beam us directly onto the Korrathi ship."

They were inside almost before they realised it. The humid air hung heavy around them, moist against their skin. Dim lights flickered overhead, which made the place feel like twilight back on Earth. He paused, just for a moment, his eyes scanning, every sense sharpened.

On the command bridge, Korrathi officers hunched over their consoles, eyes locked on scanning equipment. They moved with precision, sweeping sector after sector in search of the *Arcadia*. Outside, the Discovery ship had dispatched scout ships to locate the *Arcadia*. They flew in perfect formation, sensors tuned to pick up even the faintest trace of the *Arcadia's* energy trail. It was a net, and slipping through it was getting harder by the minute.

The Venoran crew knew the clock was ticking. Every second they kept the Korrathi distracted bought the general's team a little more time.

He broke the silence. "We need to take this ship out before they find the *Arcadia*. Move fast."

Kayla's eyes darted down the corridor, her voice low. "General, I think they know we're here." She held up her scanner. "We've got a large group closing in."

Owen and Chris tightened their grips on their weapons, exchanging a glance that said everything. No fear. Just focus.

The general waved his hand, pointing towards the twins. Indicating that they positioned themselves on either side of the doorway behind large containers, while the other two marines climbed a ladder to an access walkway above the group. The general and Kayla moved to the centre of the room, positioning themselves behind a large station.

The Korrathi moved swiftly along the corridor, their footsteps pounding against the cold metal floor, each echo a grim warning. Kayla's pulse quickened as she stared at the flickering display.

"There are seven of them now," she murmured, voice taut with urgency.

The air shifted. The hiss of the door opening was barely perceptible before chaos erupted. The Korrathi surged in, dark figures cutting through the dim light. Then came the sharp, unforgiving crack of gunfire. Three Korrathi crumpled instantly, their bodies folding to the ground in eerie silence. The remaining four dove for cover, their weapons spitting fire in retaliation.

Chris was already moving, a shadow weaving through the carnage. He slipped behind a Korrathi with the practised grace of years spent in the field. The blade flashed once, quick, clean, final. A muffled gasp. A body slumping.

Kayla didn't hesitate. Her fingers flew across her tablet, activating a magnetised grenade they had attached to a console. The explosion was sharp and controlled, sending a Korrathi sideways into the wall. Another hid behind a support column. For a fraction of a second, he hesitated, a fatal mistake.

Owen was already there. His rifle swung upward, the butt of the weapon crunching into bone with brutal force. The enemy staggered, dazed, but not for long. A precise shot finished what the impact had started.

Silence flooded the corridor, thick and suffocating.

They exhaled as one, an instinctual release, though none dared relax. Kayla's eyes darted to her monitor, her breath sharp and uneven. "One is missing," she called out.

A single Korrathi had vanished into the shadows. And they all knew he wouldn't run for cover. He would run for reinforcements.

Hollens' mind was quickly assessing various tactics. "Need to move fast; they will have reported our location," he added, opening the container of explosives he had been carrying. His thoughts were focused, knowing that every second counted. "Position these around anything that looks like it will cause maximum damage," the general instructed as he passed out the explosives. "Pair up. Kayla, you're with me. Let's meet back here in 20 minutes. Okay, move out."

Each team split off quickly, moving through the ship with purpose. Owen crouched beside a fallen Korrathi, its body twisted unnaturally. He slid a grenade beneath it, pulling the tripwire just enough so the creature's weight kept it from triggering, at least for now. His movements were precise; one mistake, and it could all go sideways.

Kayla and the general advanced slowly down a narrow corridor. The soft shuffle of their boots against the metal floor echoed faintly in the silence. The air was heavy, the lighting dim, just enough to cast flickering shadows that made everything feel off-kilter.

They approached a spacious compartment that resembled a storage bay. The overhead lights cast a pale light across the room. Machinery lined the walls, strange and unfamiliar. Another section held shelves stacked with vacuum-sealed food packs, stored alongside large containers, ready for distribution.

A low boom rolled through the corridors, echoing from the direction where they'd left the body. Chris took a backward glance down the corridor. “Hopefully, it took a few more out,” he muttered.

Kayla scanned the space ahead of them, her grip tightening on her weapon. Nearby, there were several racks filled with bulky containers; prying one open, Hollens called out, “Bingo! We have a weapons container; these might come in handy,” he declared, his voice filled with a sense of triumph.

Kayla opened a second to see rows of round objects held in a cushioning material.

“General, I think these look like explosives of some sort.” Kayla slid the explosive into a container and set the timer for 25 minutes.

Without a sound, they quietly exited the room, moving slowly along the corridor. The silence was shattered as the doors on either side burst open, catching them completely off guard.

Korrathi had been waiting for them, jabbing their weapons into the general and Kayla’s ribs. With no time to react, the Korrathi ordered them to put down their weapons.

Kayla set her weapon down with deliberate calm. In the next instant, she whipped her leg around, sweeping the closest one's legs out from under him. She moved with cold efficiency. One blow to the neck, and it was over; no struggle, no sound. The general countered by running full-on into the group, catching them off balance. He quickly drew his knife, plunging it into a Korrathi. He grabbed its weapon and fired off a shot at the second while Kayla finished off the last one.

"I think I saw an image of an engineering room on the wall panel over there," Kayla said, her voice steady despite the adrenaline coursing through her veins.

They quickly located the engineering room and entered, moving silently behind two attendants. In perfect sync, they drove the butts of their weapons into the Korrathi skulls with brutal precision. The creatures crumpled instantly, unconscious before they hit the ground. Moving quickly, they placed explosives around the room.

"Kayla, that's it, we're out of time," his voice tight with urgency. "We need to regroup."

They turned back, moving fast through the corridor. The sound of pounding footsteps echoed behind them, growing louder. Just as they reached a nearby room, the other two teams burst in under a hail of gunfire. One marine stumbled through the doorway, clutching his arm, blood seeping between his fingers.

Without missing a beat, Kayla and the general dropped into position and opened fire, forcing the Korrathi to duck behind cover. The twins slid across the floor into a protected corner, weapons already raised. "Without hesitation, they fired back. The room exploded in a storm of energy blasts as searing light, and deafening pulses, recoiled off every surface."

Through the crackle of gunfire and shouted commands, a voice cut through, unnatural and jarring. A Korrathi, speaking through a wrist-mounted translator, addressed them in broken English.

"You fight, but you will fail."

The words hung in the air, chilling and deliberate. It wasn't just a threat; it was a promise.

"Terrans, yes, we know of you; it's no use hiding. You have nowhere left to run. Comply, or you'll be jettisoned into open space."

Our repairs are complete, and we have additional ships joining us very soon. We will take what we need from your training facility and destroy the ship that brought you here."

General Hollens checked his watch, motioning to the others to get ready, and called, "Gall, transport now!" Just as they left, they heard several large explosions echoing along the corridors.

Upon their arrival aboard the *Arcadia*, Aurelia greeted them with an update. "We have successfully transported all personnel from the ground," she informed.

Gall entered the room, displaying a demeanour of satisfaction. "General, your team executed its tasks with exceptional skill. The Korrathi vessel has been neutralised, and the remaining ship has sustained significant damage, rendering it inoperable for an extended period. We are making preparations to depart from orbit; however, we must eliminate the training facility to prevent the Korrathi from acquiring any intelligence."

The *Arcadia's* cannons activated, and moments later, the training facility was destroyed, leaving a crater where it once stood. The wounded Marine was taken to the hospital.

Kayla hung back and walked over to the general. "Why did you pick me?"

He turned and looked at her. "I knew you could handle the situation after seeing you in combat training down on the planet. I noticed how quickly you anticipated every move your opponent made. I am also aware of certain details about you that are not publicly documented, such as the fact that your time at Area 51 is a cover story. I know that the agency had been placing you in high-pressure situations, and you handled those quite effectively. There is no need for you to pretend anymore; we all have new roles to fulfil."

Aurelia's voice crackled through the comms, sharp and urgent. "There was a third Korrathi ship trailing the others and had just emerged from hyperspace. They are boarding the *Arcadia*."

The Korrathi were moving quickly through areas of the ship and had managed to capture most of the crew, moving them to the storage hangers. Solara and Paige were among the first group captured, along with most of the Venorans.

The general, Sarah, Doc, Kayla, Dave, and the twins quickly retreated to one of the outer hull inspection compartments. The general's eyes were sharp with urgency. "We need weapons! What do you have, Dave?"

Dave grimaced, patting his pockets. "Got a trusty pocketknife."

Doc, with a tinge of concern, added, "All I have is a flashlight."

Sarah, with a worried expression, remarked, "It doesn't look good."

"Sarah, your new arm isn't just a replacement; its strength is a weapon," said the general. She was so accustomed to using it as a regular arm she had forgotten how it granted her superhuman strength, allowing her to lift heavy objects effortlessly and deliver powerful blows in combat.

Owen spoke quietly. "Sir, the weapons lockers aren't marked. They won't know their exact location. If we can reach one of those transfer stations, we should be able to jump directly to the weapons locker floor."

In a low whisper, the general explained what Doc needed to do. "Keep the flashlight handy. Remember, they're not used to bright lights. When the moment comes, blast them with the full beam." Doc nodded, understanding the plan.

The group left the compartment and quietly moved along the hallway. The sound of approaching voices made them freeze. They quickly darted behind a large door, keeping it slightly open. They could see two Korrathi methodically opening doors and checking each room.

Dave signalled back to the group by flashing his knife and pointing to Doc's flashlight. Doc nodded in acknowledgement. As the two Korrathi approached the door, Dave and Doc quietly backed away, positioning themselves strategically.

The moment the Korrathi pushed the door open, Doc shone the flashlight directly into the eyes of the nearest Korrathi, blinding it. In an instant, Dave leapt at the other Korrathi, plunging his knife into its side, while muffling its mouth to prevent any sound from escaping.

Simultaneously, the rest of the team sprang into action. The blinded Korrathi stumbled, disoriented by the sudden brightness. Doc used the opportunity to slam the flashlight into its head, while Sarah stepped in with precision and snapped its neck effortlessly.

The general grabbed a Korrathi body while speaking to the others. “Pull them inside and grab their weapons. Next stop, the weapons room.”

With quick, silent movements, they dragged the Korrathi into the room, relieved them of their weapons, and prepared to make their next move.

At the other end of the ship, Solara and Paige, along with 3 Venoran crew members, were being held in a storage locker with guards outside.

Solara spoke in a quiet voice to the group. “We are in luck; over there, that’s my stasis chamber.”

Paige shot her a look. “Your stasis chamber?”

“My suit is stored inside,” she quickly explained, her voice urgent but steady. When we first set foot on your planet, your people mistook us for gods, unaware that the suits we wore granted abilities far beyond your understanding.”

"On my world, we relied on anti-gravity suits whenever we stepped outside our ship. They amplified our strength for mining to nearly ten times that of humans, and the suits also increased our height, making us far more imposing to the local inhabitants. Because we worked in hazardous environments, especially asteroid fields, our suits have reinforced armour for impact protection."

Solara moved with deliberate calm as she opened a hidden compartment, careful not to make a sound. She pulled the folded suit out and placed her hand on the breastplate. Immediately, the suit expanded, revealing a humanoid figure around 8 feet tall. Solara pressed the breastplate again, causing the rear to separate and open. She stepped into the suit, which formed around her shape, encasing her in armour.

Standing in the center of the room, now fully encased in armor, Solara instructed everyone to move to either side of the door to avoid any shots from the Korrathi. With her large, gloved hands, she banged on the door. The guards opened it, and their eyes widened in surprise at the sight of the giant figure before them.

Solara swung her arm, her fist connecting with the head of one Korrathi and continuing its path into the head of the second, sending both crashing into the corridor wall, where they lay motionless. Picking up the fallen Korrathi weapons, they moved down the hallway.

The group stayed close behind Solara, sweeping from one storage bay to the next, ambushing guards and freeing the captives inside.

"We need to get to the bridge and locate the others," said Gall, his voice filled with urgency.

They made swift progress, with Solara leading the way. neutralizing every Korrathi they encountered on the route. The Korrathi, seeing the imposing figure approaching, directed most of their energy blasts at her. Her suit absorbed each blast effortlessly, allowing the team to return fire with precision.

They arrived at a transfer station and were instantly transported to the bridge, accompanied by their giant friend, opening fire on the Korrathi standing over the consoles.

With the bridge back under their control, the crew acted instantly. Weapons surged to full power. The *Arcadia* thundered awake, hurling a storm of energy fire into the last Korrathi ship. Metal screamed, as the hull peeled back like scorched paper. Under the relentless barrage, the vessel twisted, ruptured, and blew apart in violent bursts, reducing it to burning debris drifting through the void.

Paige moved to the monitors, scanning for crew locations. A few guards and bridge officers stayed behind to hold the command deck, while the rest split off to free the remaining crew.

Elsewhere on the ship, the general's team had just cleared the outer hull and reached the weapons lockers. They began loading up quickly, checking gear and ammo.

"Now it's our turn to hunt," Sarah said, her voice steady, eyes sharp.

Pushing forward, they ran into scattered Korrathi search teams. The encounters were brief, quick bursts of gunfire, with no hesitation. But when they reached engineering, the tone shifted. The Korrathi were ready this time.

Suddenly, weapon fire erupted around them.

"We need to get behind them," the general commanded.

Dave and the two Marines circled the outer edges of the room while the general's team provided covering fire, creating a distraction. Dave's group had managed to get behind the Korrathi. One of the Marines had a flash grenade and hurled it into the centre of the enemy's defensive position, temporarily blinding them. Seizing the moment, the team moved in swiftly, securing the Korrathi fighters.

"Move out and search the rest of the ship. Locate any crew members," ordered the general.

They quickly found some of the Korrathi who had barricaded themselves in the medical quarters. Chris threw a grenade into the midst of the Korrathi fighters. Stunned, they were swiftly overpowered. The rest of the teams moved through the ship, finishing off the remaining Korrathi. When the general's team arrived on the bridge, they were surprised by the sight of the towering figure standing before them. Instinctively, they raised their weapons, ready to face this new threat, their hearts pounding in their chests.

Paige came around from behind the giant figure. "Hold your fire."

With caution, they lowered their weapons. The giant's back split open, and from within stepped Solara, intact, composed, and startlingly real. The husk of her outfit loomed behind her, empty. The fighters applauded as Solara stepped forward, and she gave them a puzzled look, unsure what to make of the Terrans' reaction.

Aurelia came online, her voice calm and clear. "Gall, all Korrathi have been rounded up. What should we do with them?"

Gall thought for a moment before responding. "Well, there's an empty planet below; beam them down. Aurelia, before we leave, run a diagnostic on the ship." Moments later, the AI responded. "The *Arcadia* is functioning efficiently."

"Then I think we had better leave," Gall said with a sigh of relief.

The general turned to Solara, admiration and curiosity in his eyes. "Solara, you were a surprise. I'd love to hear about your life, and I'm sure the others would too."

Solara nodded, showing a faint smile on her lips. "I'll be happy to share my story."

The *Arcadia* engaged the Slide Drive engines, leaving the battle scene behind. The tension on the ship eased now that the Korrathi issue had been resolved, and the ship was secure. Their next stop would be Venor.

Black Hole

Week 18

Personal account: Donald Northey

"The final jump to Venor was supposed to be routine, one last manoeuvre before reaching our destination. But in an instant, everything unravelled. Our ship's in bad shape. We're not flying; we're stuck in the gravitational grip of a black hole."

***

The *Arcadia* groaned under the pressure, its hull trembling as though something enormous had seized it. Alarms erupted, slicing through the quiet as the ship was violently yanked out of Slide Drive and thrown into chaos.

Something had hit them. Something powerful.

Just moments before, everything had been calm. The *Arcadia* was moving through space, systems humming in quiet harmony, preparing for the final jump to Venor. The crew was relaxed; they'd been through this drill countless times.

Then, without warning, the calm shattered. Aurelia's voice came through the comms, smooth and composed.

"We're ready to begin our last jump to Venor. Take your positions."

Crew members moved with quiet efficiency. Some strapped into their stations, others wrapped up conversations over half-eaten meals in the common areas. Two days into the mission, the rhythm of deep-space travel had settled in.

Then everything changed.

A brutal jolt tore through the ship as it came to an abrupt halt. Bodies and loose objects flew across the room. Alarms wailed, drowning out shouts and confusion as the *Arcadia* veered off course, its trajectory shattered.

"What the hell was that?" someone yelled from engineering.

"Brace! Brace!" shouted Don as the *Arcadia* rolled violently.

It felt like an impact, but there was nothing. No warning. No enemy. Just the sickening sense that something massive and unseen had struck with terrifying force.

The Venorans didn't hesitate. Their instincts took over, honed by years of training. They moved fast, with purpose. Most were already strapped in, locked to their stations, riding out the chaos they'd rehearsed a thousand times.

But not everyone had that kind of luck. Restraints snapped under the sudden force, sending bodies hurtling across the deck. Some slammed into walls, others into consoles. Now the crew was scrambling, bruised, bleeding, and disoriented, grabbing for handrails with trembling hands, trying to make sense of what had just happened.

"Engineering, this is Gall. Run a full system check. Prioritise propulsion and life support."

"Slide Drive's offline. Structural integrity holding at 72%. We're rerouting power to stabilise life support," came a panicked reply.

There was chaos around the ship. Alarms blared. Shouts overlapped.

Moments before, the ship had been serene; everything was running efficiently. Now it was gripped by an unknown force, and no one knew what had struck them.

Gall raised his communicator, his voice clipped. “Solara, find out what happened.”

Without hesitation, Solara initiated a scan of the surrounding space. Moments later, she turned to face Gall, her voice steady despite the storm raging inside her.

“I’m picking up a strong gravitational anomaly. There’s a small black hole, and it's close.”

Down in engineering, Dave was already staring at the same readings. He didn’t sound surprised when he spoke, only troubled.

“I see it. But this doesn’t make sense.” His eyes narrowed as he pulled up deeper diagnostics. “A black hole that small shouldn’t be stable. It should’ve evaporated long ago. For it to still exist and exert this kind of pull, something must be stabilizing it. Feeding it. Containing it.”

“Black holes don’t behave like this on their own.” He hesitated, the implication settling in. “But... something has.”

A look passed between the Venoran crew, seasoned spacefarers who knew the signs all too well, as the realisation settled in. A black hole meant imminent danger. The ship’s structural integrity could fail, and if the Arcadia was caught in its pull, everyone aboard would be lost with it.

Aurelia materialised beside Gall, her expression unreadable. “I’ve completed a deeper analysis. The black hole’s gravitational pull is weak overall. Fortunately, our momentum carried us to the very edge of its event horizon, the least dangerous region. But it was still strong enough to disrupt the Slide Drive's momentum.” Her tone remained calm. “Initiating a ship-wide systems check.”

A sudden burst of static crackled through the comms, followed by Dave’s voice, rattled by the violent jolt engineering had taken.

“Bridge, I saw the anomaly, but what the hell caused us to come out of Slide Drive so suddenly? Half my systems just redlined.”

Gall quickly explained what had happened on their end: the sudden wrench out of Slide Drive, the near-miss with the event horizon, the ship's momentary loss of control.

Dave exhaled, the sound tight. "All right... that tracks. But we've got a bigger problem." He pulled up the engine diagnostics. "The gravitational shear knocked the slide engines out of alignment. They're offline and they'll stay that way for a while." His tone hardened. "This is going to take every engineering team working together. Until then, the Arcadia isn't going anywhere."

The atmosphere on the bridge was tense while maintenance crews worked stabilise the systems. A few officers let out quiet breaths when Aurelia confirmed there was no immediate threat.

Gall felt some of the tension ease from his own chest at her words. "We need to stay focused," he said, keeping his voice steady. But the strain in his eyes betrayed him; he was holding it together by will alone.

Throughout the ship, reports of injuries continued to come in. The hospital ward was filling up quickly. Faces told the story: pain, exhaustion, and the kind of weariness that settles deep in the bones.

Gall stood at the threshold, scanning the wounded. The sight hit him hard as he forced himself to stay composed, even as the weight of responsibility pressed down.

The bridge crew fell silent. The hum of the machinery seemed to swell in the absence of voices, filling the room with the uneasy calm before a storm. Even the consoles' blinking lights felt slower, as if the ship itself were holding its breath.

The general's voice cut through the stillness, steady but sharpened by urgency. "Gall, why didn't the ship steer clear of the black hole?"

Heads turned toward him, not out of curiosity, but under the weight of the question hanging in the air.

Gall stiffened. He drew a slow breath, trying to steady the rush of thoughts clawing at his composure. “It came out of nowhere,” he said, tension threading through every word. “Our navigation systems didn’t stand a chance. The sensors missed it completely.”

Aurelia’s voice broke the silence. “Gall, your analysis was correct. The navigation system was functioning at optimal efficiency prior to encountering the black hole. As for the *Arcadia*, there is considerable damage throughout the ship; teams are working on the repairs.”

Frustration flickered across General Hollen's face. “We need to guarantee this doesn’t happen again. Our crew’s lives depend on it.”

Gall acknowledged the general's comment, his voice steady but shadowed with unease. “Normally, we can detect black holes. Arcadia’s Slide Drive is programmed to identify gravitational anomalies, recalibrating its trajectory in real time without pilot input. But this one,” he paused, the words snagging in his throat like static. “Its signature was distorted, as if it were folded inside out. We didn’t see it because it didn’t behave like any singularity we’ve ever charted.”

A hush fell over the room. The hum of the engines pressed against their ears, louder now, almost intrusive. Monitors blinked in a quiet rhythm. Someone shifted in their seat. The creak of a boot against metal echoed through the room.

Gall’s voice broke through the silence. “This wasn’t just a navigational failure. It was something else. Something we’ve never seen before.”

A warning chime pulsed from the console. The ship shuddered, subtly but unmistakably. Gall turned sharply toward the display, eyes narrowing.

“We’re not drifting,” he said. “We’re slowly being pulled. Our engines are offline, and we are unable to stop the gravitational pull.”

Ideas anyone? Asked the General.

At that moment, Dave joined the conversation. “I think I may have something that might work. We can create a focused kinetic pulse using compressed plasma from the emergency tanks. But for it to work, we need something to push against. We can’t use the black hole; it’s too unstable and would absorb the energy.”

Solara turned from the console, her eyes narrowing. “Then we need mass. Something solid enough to resist the pulse and reflect the force toward us. A nearby asteroid, a derelict hull, anything with enough inertia.”

She had been monitoring the black hole. Yes, it was small, and yet it was powerful enough to cause significant damage. But something caught his attention on the navigation screen. “There,” pointing to the screen, “there’s a planet orbiting the black hole, unaffected by its pull. We need to get a team down there to find out why it’s seemingly immune to the black hole's gravitational pull.”

Reports of the anomaly had been streaming in, fragmented and urgent. Solara remained at her station, her gaze locked on the fluctuating data. “The black hole is small,” she murmured, her hands moving between different screens on the console. “I suspect it’s been adrift in intergalactic space for eons. Out here, where stars are sparse and matter is thin, it’s had nothing to feed on. No accretion. No growth. Slowly and silently drifting through the dark, like a predator starved by the emptiness itself.”

A hush fell over the command deck as they absorbed everything they had seen and heard.

Aurelia’s voice cut through the silence, smooth but edged with urgency. “I’ve completed my analysis of the anomaly,” she announced. “What sets it apart from other black holes is that it’s artificial. Someone created it.”

Gasps rippled through the crew. The general leaned forward, eyes narrowing. “Artificial? Are you saying this was engineered?”

"Correct, it lacks the usual gravitational signatures and radiation patterns of a natural singularity. It's stable in ways that defy known physics."

Solara's brow furrowed. "Then whoever made it understands forces we've barely begun to grasp."

The deck fell silent again, the weight of the revelation settling over them.

Gall stood frozen at the viewport, his eyes locked on the impossible sight before him. His voice, when it came, was barely above a whisper. "This isn't right." His fingers curled against the glass, as if he could will the planet to reveal its secrets. "It should be gone. Torn apart. Consumed. But it's just... there. Untouched. Like the abyss didn't even notice it."

He exhaled sharply. His gaze moved to the flickering shield, pulsing, shifting, reacting. "And that shield was no accident. No natural phenomenon. Someone or something built it. But why?"

"Were they protecting the planet?" Gall mused, his mind racing. "Or keeping something inside?" His throat tightened. "If that shield is stopping it from being pulled in, we need to adapt that shield technology to the Arcadia."

Aurelia completed her scan of the anomaly. "It has a lifespan significantly shorter than the black holes we've charted. Based on my calculations, it was created between two and three million years ago. Given its current rate of evaporation, it may only last another million years."

Page's voice was heard over the comms. "I don't want to be a buzzkill, but unless we repair the Slide engines, it's going to add a considerable amount of time to the journey, about 1500 years to be exact, using the fusion engines. By then, it would be too late to help anyone."

Gall felt the weight of the situation pressing down on him. The crew's lives depended on their ability to repair the ship and understand the anomaly of the black hole. The warning lights strobed red across the console, casting jagged shadows on his face. He tapped his communicator and opened the connection to central comms. “Attention repair units, I need all spare technicians in engineering immediately,” he said, each syllable sharp with urgency. “We must concentrate on the Slide Drive.”

Dave's voice crackled over the comms. “We are ready to fire a kinetic pulse toward the planet. I need the ship oriented to align the pulse emitter towards the planet.”

Outside, the planet loomed, silent, shrouded in electromagnetic interference, and eerily still.

The navigation officer adjusted the settings on his console. “Thrusters engaged.”

The *Arcadia* groaned under the strain, its enormous hull shifting as the thrusters fired in sharp, controlled bursts. The gravitational pull clawed at the ship, trying to drag it off course. The navigation officer's eyes were fixed on the alignment display as it inched toward stability.

“*Arcadia* is aligned,” confirmed the officer.

Dave didn't hesitate. He initiated the firing sequence, his fingers moving across the console. “Directing power to the emergency plasma tanks. Charging emitter.”

The lights dimmed momentarily as power was rerouted. A low hum built in the core of the ship, vibrating through the decks.

“Firing pulse emitter... Now!”

A shudder rippled through the ship. The kinetic pulse surged through space toward the planet's surface. The ship lurched briefly.

The officer's voice came through again, strained. “We need more. It's not enough.”

Dave gritted his teeth. “Firing secondary pulse... Now!”

The second blast was stronger; more violent. The *Arcadia* was flung outward, torn free of the black hole's grip in a single violent jolt. Alarms blared, but then, silence.

The officer turned to his console, eyes scanning the readouts as *Arcadia's* systems steadied. He exhaled sharply. "Stabilisers locked. Hull integrity is normal. We're back in operational space."

A sigh of relief rippled through the ship as they heard the navigator's report.

"Well-done, Dave," the general said, stepping onto the command deck with a rare smile. "Keep the plasma tanks charged. We may need them again."

Dave nodded, but his expression remained grim. "We might need them sooner than you think," he said. "This orbit isn't sustainable. *Arcadia* hasn't settled into a permanent trajectory; we're still at risk of being pulled back in."

The general turned towards the viewing screen, watching the planet's surface shimmer with strange, shifting patterns. "Then let's see what secrets it's been keeping. It's time to find out what this planet is hiding from us."

Last Days of Relentus Prime

Personal account: General George Hollins

"It's been over five months since we left Earth, and it's finally hitting us. This isn't just an adventure anymore. Now it's survival. We've been through hell out here. Things I never thought we'd face. And now, there's something even more terrifying ahead. There's a black hole. It's just there, waiting. Everyone's doing what they can, working nonstop on the Slide Drive, hoping it'll fire up in time. It's the only shot we've got to break free before we're gone. With the Arcadia temporarily freed from the grip of the black hole, we must now turn our attention to the planet and uncover whatever secrets it holds."

***

Gall and General Hollins were discussing the repair status and the black hole problem. "Putting it in Earth terms, it's a gamble," he said. "But it's the only one we've got. Repairs will take time. We might as well use it."

Gall nodded. "We will prep the teams."

Within the hour, the crew had been mobilised. The hum of activity filled the corridors, boots brushing against metal, voices echoing with urgency. In the command centre, Hollins' voice echoed through the comms, flat and urgent. "All investigation teams. Meeting room two. Immediately."

The room filled quickly as engineers, scientists, and recon specialists gathered inside. Hollins stood at the front, holding his hand monitor, eyes scanning the room.

“By now, you’ve all heard about the dormant black hole,” he began. “But what’s more interesting is that a planet is locked in orbit around it. Our scans show man-made structures. That’s your mission.”

A murmur rippled through the crowd. One of the recon officers leaned forward. “Structures? Out here? That’s impossible.”

The general answered back, “So is a planet surviving this close to a black hole?”

Hollins continued, his voice firm. “There’s no atmosphere. No signs of life. It’s dark, very dark. Take full lighting kits. We believe the planet suffered a catastrophic event that stripped away a third of its mass. Whatever did that... it wasn’t natural.”

Sarah raised her hand. “Could it have been a weapon?”

Hollins didn’t flinch. “Possibly. We can’t say for certain. What we can say, because the data won’t let it go, is that it’s not where it was.” A faint smile crossed his lips.

“Something moved the blackhole taking the planet with it. Now it’s drifting through the void, and it's vast, more than fifty light-years wide. And the Venorans? They’ve got nothing on artificial black holes.”

He stepped forward, his voice lowering as he added, “Activate your suit monitors. We’ll be watching everything you see. If there’s anything down there, anything that can help us, we need to find it. Dismissed.”

Later, Alpha 1 and Alpha 2 teams gathered in the landing bay; Stuart walked over to the group, who were already standing near the shuttles.

“I’m your pilot, and for today’s excursion, if you look over to your left, you will see a group of ships; we are going to take the large one.” Once everyone was buckled up, “Shuttle’s ready to go,” Stuart said, his voice crackling through the comms to the operations room. The landing bay doors slid open, and the shuttle lifted smoothly, its hull humming with power. Slowly, the shuttle glided into the void, its thrusters pulsing with a dim amber flare.

"Alright," Stuart murmured as he adjusted the controls. "Let's see what's down there. The general is particularly interested in the large city beneath us."

A broken planet loomed ahead, like an eerie shadow drifting through the void, its stillness broken only by the occasional pulse of dim starlight.

As the planet loomed into view, he reached out instinctively and brought the holographic map to life, its glowing contours flickering across the cabin. The outline of damaged buildings, fractured infrastructure, and remnants of civilisation opened up on the map.

Adjusting the display, he zoomed in. "Based on these scans, there are several areas of interest that could hold significant information or artefacts."

As the shuttle descended, the darkness swallowed the terrain in a silence so profound it felt almost spectral.

Leaning forward, he flicked on the shuttle's lights. The beams cut through the dark in a sudden burst, revealing the surface below. A cold, barren landscape stretched out beneath them. The faint glimmers of starlight were the only backdrop to the planet, which appeared to have been shattered and left to freeze.

Near the base of a rugged mountain range, clusters of abandoned villages clung to the rock. The remains of the villages leaned against the mountains, as if they'd been standing guard for centuries.

Stuart's fingers gripped the controls as his eyes fixed on the shifting terrain, alert, expectant, bracing for what might emerge from the horizon. The shuttle eased lower, skimming the jagged peaks before slipping into the valley. The engines murmured beneath them, a quiet hum that felt almost respectful in the stillness.

"The city should be just ahead," his voice sounded steady and confident.

Then it came into view. Faint shapes began to emerge at first, rising slowly from the shadows like memories surfacing. Ruins, broken and silent, stretched across the valley floor. Stuart leaned forward, squinting through the dust blown up as the ship passed overhead. No one spoke. They just watched, the weight of what they were seeing settling in. Crumbling towers and collapsed buildings lined the horizon. The city clung to itself like a memory refusing to fade, barely holding itself together. They circled slowly as the shuttle drifted above the ancient metropolis. Most of it was buried in shadow, silent and forgotten. Searching for a clearing, Stuart activated the full array of observation lights, their glow casting sharp relief against the fractured terrain.

"Ah, there we go."

The shuttle settled into what appeared to have been a park at one time, its landing struts pressing into the dust-coated ground.

The city stood before them, waiting.

"Suit up, everyone. Let's go take a ride." He hit a control on the console as he pushed out of his seat, shutting down the engines. "You'll find two transport vehicles inside. Once you're in the main compartment of the shuttle, it'll pressurize and you can take your helmets off."

From inside the shuttle, Stuart lowered the environmental force field inside the docking bay. The rear of the shuttle opened, allowing the transport vehicles to depart.

The ship's lights cut through the haze, lighting up the dust that still floated from the shuttle's touchdown. Their face shields gradually adjusted to the planet's darkness, allowing them to see the outlines of buildings. A few of which were still standing, reaching high into the sky, while others were in various states of decay.

Above them, the gravitational distortion of the black hole bent the surrounding light, creating an eerie but mesmerising glow. The event horizon remained ominously dark, an abyss beyond which nothing could escape. But the accretion disk surrounding it blazed with intense radiation, illuminating the void with a strange and haunting beauty. Surprisingly, illuminating the surface of the planet with a faint light.

Stuart activated the team's internal communication: "Guys, if you need me, call me right away."

Alpha 1 and Alpha 2 took off in different directions to explore the city, their vehicles gliding over the firm surface, feeling like a vast, ancient highway.

With each turn of the wheels, dust, untouched for millions of years, lifted into the air, forming soft, swirling clouds that drifted lazily around the vehicle. The headlights sliced through the darkness, casting a beam across a landscape that seemed to stretch on forever, silent and endless.

Alpha 1 came to a stop outside a square building. They entered through a wide archway. As they walked, the ground beneath their boots felt hard, resisting every step. Dust puffed up with each movement, then settled again, as if reluctant to be disturbed.

For the Earth crew, walking without air and relying on breathers was deeply unsettling. The silence was total: no breeze, no rustling, just the crunch of their footsteps and the low hum of their life support systems.

Their suits shielded them from the planet's harsh conditions, but they could still feel the strange texture of the ground through their boots, a mix of jagged rock and fine powder, with patches so smooth they felt almost like glass. Combined with the sensation of near-weightlessness, every step felt slow.

“This place gives me the creeps,” Kayla murmured, her voice barely crackling through the comms.

“This place is ancient,” someone else said, eyes sweeping across the lifeless terrain. “Whatever happened here, they took everything with them.”

Slowly, they passed through the stagnant haze, where dust clung to every surface like memory. The place hadn’t been disturbed in millions of years, and each step felt like a quiet violation of something sacred. Eventually, they discovered the remains of a building that was barely holding together.

“I think this is far enough, said Chris. We can set the lights up here.” As each light was switched on, its beam cut through the dark, illuminating strange symbols carved deep into the stone. Bit by bit, the outline of a city long forgotten began to reveal itself.

Inside, the building opened into a vast chamber. The ceiling arched high above them in a perfect dome. As their lights climbed upward, tiny tiles embedded in the surface began to glow; faint points of light formed a map of the stars. A few glowed brighter than the rest, as if they were meant to mark something that once mattered.

The interior spaces were organised around a central hub, with corridors radiating out like spokes on a wheel.

“These aren’t just decorations,” Aurelia’s voice came through their helmets, sharp and thoughtful. “They might be part of a system... maybe energy, or a method they used to communicate.” The idea remained a puzzle waiting to be solved.

“If this place was trying to say something,” Stuart muttered over the comms, “who was it talking to?”

Each hallway branched off into different chambers, some housing strange, crystal-like machines that gave off a soft hum when touched, as if they were still alive, still waiting.

“Careful,” Chris said, his voice low. “They react to contact; could be harmless, then again, it could set off some kind of chain reaction.”

In one of the larger rooms, the team stumbled upon a ring of towering pillars, each etched with symbols no one could decipher. They stood in a perfect circle around a raised platform. At its centre was a large, translucent orb hovering just above the surface.

A voice crackled over the comms. “Could be a communication device, or maybe just an ornament.”

The room itself was a blend of opposites: smooth, flowing curves that met sharp, deliberate angles. It felt both natural and engineered, like its builders had mastered the balance between technology and the world around them. Even with signs of age and damage, the structure held firm, proof of a civilisation that knew how to build things to last. Arch-shaped doorways led off in different directions.

“Splitting up might be faster,” she said, half to herself.

“No,” Stuart replied quickly. “Stay together; I need you looking out for each other, just being cautious.”

The room greeted them with rows of open racks, some positioned beneath the window with shelves that mirrored those along the walls. It felt like a store, or something that once was. Outside, in the main square, was a central stone with artwork or symbols along its sides.

Kayla ran her fingers along the artwork, trying to get an understanding of what it depicted. “These aren’t just decorative,” she murmured. “They’re telling a story, I think. It could be a language.”

At that moment, a female hologram appeared.

“Whoa!” Kayla jumped back in surprise.

Her skin was green. Her head appeared slightly longer than that of a human, with braided red hair flowing to her waist. The rest of her body was distinctly humanoid, which intrigued Kayla. She hadn’t meant to stare, but her eyes lingered anyway. There was something about the alien, something unexpectedly graceful. Not just in the symmetry of her features, but in the way she held herself, quiet and composed.

“There’s something elegant about her,” Kayla replied.

“Elegant?” Chris chuckled. “You’re admiring the alien?”

Kayla smirked. “For an extraterrestrial being, she’s striking. I can just imagine one of our guys trying to flirt with her, given the chance.” A smile crept across Kayla's face as she envisioned such an encounter.

Kayla’s heart thudded in her chest as the hologram turned toward her. The hologram's gaze was sharp and unblinking. It felt like it was looking straight through her. Then it spoke, with words she couldn’t make out. The hologram's voice echoed in the stillness of the room. A chill crept down her spine. Her bright blue eyes never wavered, tracking her every movement as if she were studying her. The hologram raised a hand and pointed at different structures scattered around the chamber. As her hand aligned with the image, it flickered to life in the air.

The first room reminded Kayla of a shop, sort of. It had the same quiet order, shelves neatly arranged, and everything on them seemed bizarre.

“Alien food?” Chris asked, peering over her shoulder. “Looks like something out of a fever dream.” One item shimmered like molten glass. Another twisted as if it was trying to escape its container.

“Some of these look edible,” Kayla said, uncertain. “Others, not so much,” making her stomach knot just looking at them; too bright, too alive. She took a cautious step forward, eyes scanning the shelves. “It’s like walking through someone else’s idea of comfort, and realising you didn’t belong.”

The walls were cluttered with spaghetti-like coils, vats of quivering gel, and shapes that glimmered as if they were still taking in air. She hesitated, unsure whether to be curious or cautious.

The next room was something else entirely.

All sizes of creatures filled the space, some towering, others barely knee-high. One had limbs that bent in impossible directions, while another were wrapped in scales. A few had skin that glowed softly, pulsing in rhythm with some internal beat.

Kayla's breath caught. "They're beautiful," she said softly.

"Beautiful?" Chris echoed. "I'd say unsettling."

"Both," Kayla replied. "Like walking through a dream."

She reached for her communicator and tapped it. The soft chime echoed through the chamber, sounding far too loud in the room. Her fingers lingered on the device, as if it might anchor her to something familiar. Her voice was calm and steady. "I think this was a meeting place for alien races," she said, speaking to her team back on the ship. "I can make out at least six different types."

Static crackled briefly before a reply came through. "Copy that, Kayla," said General Hollins. "We can see them from your suit monitor."

Chris moved around the room, his eyes moving from one flickering image to the next. The aliens in this room were different from the others. One had bioluminescent skin, glowing like a jellyfish in the dark. Another covered in scales, almost reptilian. "I'm seeing creatures with multiple limbs, some with elongated heads, and one looks almost plant-like."

The hologram continued to point, its gestures deliberate, as if guiding Kayla through a story only it could tell. She swallowed hard, thinking she saw the hologram's bright blue eyes looking at her.

She could feel goosebumps on her skin as she shuddered, repeating her earlier comment. "This place really gives me the creeps." Kayla turned away from the hologram to avoid its stare and entered an adjacent room. "I don't think this is just a store," speaking quietly. "It feels like they were trying to communicate. Maybe even collaborate."

Near the edge of the city, Alpha 2 was nearing an area that looked as if the ground had been torn apart. From their vantage point, they encountered a mesmerising sight: a steady beam of light connecting the black hole to the planet.

Dave had his eyes fixed on the monitors as he spoke to the general. "I can't make out which direction the beam is flowing. Can your monitors determine the direction?"

The general's voice crackled through the communicator. "Yes, it appears to be coming from that tall, pinnacle-shaped building just ahead," the voice crackled through the comms. "Keep me posted."

"Will do." Dave gave a small nod, even though no one could see it. As they drew closer, their lights swept across the massive structure. Carved on the surface were alien symbols and intricate designs.

Solara lowered her gaze, drawn to one of the carvings. Brushing it gently with her gloved fingers, as if afraid to disturb whatever story it was trying to tell.

"Someone cared about this," she said softly. "It meant something."

Inside, their beams cut through the dimness, revealing a vast chamber that stretched farther than expected. In the centre of the chamber stood a stone pedestal, its surface etched with more symbols, some familiar, others completely foreign. Strange panels lined its edges, untouched by time.

Solara and Dave exchanged glances. No words, just a shared understanding. This wasn't like the meeting hall Kayla had found. It felt more like a crossroads, a place where knowledge had once been shared.

Moving deeper, their flashlights swept across the walls. Dust hung in the air, catching the light like glitter. Then one of the beams landed on a towering stone pillar at the chamber's heart. Its surface was rough, worn down for more than a millennium. Stepping closer, Dave ran his hand along the grooves.

“Whatever this was,” he said quietly, “it mattered.” Solara touched the pillar. “The stories it could tell if only someone could listen,” she said.

Dave pressed the intercom, his voice breaking the silence. “Solara, what do you make of this?”

She walked around the pillar, cautious but curious. Dave was pointing towards a square glass object protruding from the stone. As her hand touched the glass object, a soft glow began to spread across its surface. The light grew brighter, pulsing with energy.

Dave took a step back. “Uh... that’s new.”

As a hologram appeared.

But it wasn’t the familiar green female figure Kayla had seen before.

This time, the projection revealed a creature with lizard-like features, standing on thick, powerful legs. It wore a brightly coloured overshirt with intricate designs around its edges. Its body was broad and muscular. The arms were equally robust, ending in hands that were unlike anything Solara had seen. Three long, sturdy fingers and a thumb-like appendage positioned at the back, almost like a tool designed for precision.

Dave let out a low whistle. “That’s not someone you’d want to arm wrestle.”

The creature positioned its hands in a way that suggested it was attempting to communicate with whoever was observing the hologram. The creature emitted a series of vocal sounds as it pointed skyward toward a brilliant beam shooting into the heavens, a pillar of energy that seemed to connect the earth to the stars.

The creature then shifted its attention to the ground, indicating with purpose the square blocks that sprawled out before them, which extended endlessly into the murky distance. Dave followed the creature's gaze to the floor, puzzling over the blocks. While no longer glowing, they still held an air of mystery and allure.

Solara's voice came over the comms. “I have heard this language before, but not from these creatures. It's a common language used by many races to communicate with each other, and I believe I can decipher it.”

Dave raised an eyebrow. “You're saying this thing is speaking a second language?”

“Something like that,” Solara replied. “Give me a moment. I think it's trying to tell us where to go.”

The hologram's gestures grew more deliberate, its eyes locking onto Solara as if urging her to understand.

Dave glanced at the others. “Well, I hope it's not telling us to run,” he said with a chuckle.

“General, this is Stuart. I'm on board the shuttle with Parker. We're getting a slow, faint pulse coming from beneath us and moving away from the city. Do you have it on your scanners?”

“We're unable to detect anything from up here,” he added, frustration evident in his tone. “The interference from the black hole is scrambling our sensors. I think it's worth a closer look. Let's get more boots on the ground.”

Parker let out a deep sigh, stretching his arms overhead. “Finally. I was starting to feel like a piece of furniture, just sitting here.” His relief was evident, action was better than waiting.

The general's voice crackled through the comms. “Alpha 2, how long until we get a full report?”

Solara responded, her tone brisk but measured. “We're moving forward. There's nothing substantial in this building, so we are moving on. There's another intact structure just ahead, which could be operational. We're heading towards it now.”

A short while later, Solara's voice returned with urgency. "General, we've reached the building. It appears to be a technology centre of some kind. There are consoles everywhere. What's strange is that they still have power. Dave has managed to activate a few of them, and they're displaying a planetary grid, lines radiating outward from a central point." She paused, absorbing the implications. "That central point it's not out there. It's right here, in front of you; inside the machine you're using."

The significance of her words hung in the air. The entire planet was connected, monitored, and structured with a precision beyond anything they had expected.

A short distance beyond the city, Stuart and Parker reached the final ridge. Below them, the land fell away into a vast, hidden valley; an immense basin ringed by jagged peaks that rose like the shattered teeth of some long-dead leviathan. He stopped the transporter to scan ahead. It wasn't the surrounding mountain range that made him pause; it was what lay within.

The valley floor was impossibly flat, unnaturally smooth, as if something had razored away every trace of nature's hand. No rocks, not even soil, disrupted its glass-like expanse that stretched out before him, far too smooth to be the work of nature. As they descended into the valley basin, it wasn't long before something unexpected emerged from the gloom.

Jagged seams of earth had been pushed upward and split apart in ways that didn't seem natural, like something had been trying to force its way through. Deep cracks ran across the terrain, and the soil felt tight, as though it had been holding back pressure for a long time and finally gave way.

Parker knelt beside one of the twisted ridges, dragging his fingers slowly across the broken surface. "General," he said, while simultaneously glancing up at Stuart, "Looks like the land was peeled back. Something tried to break through."

His voice carried a mix of awe and unease. The deformation wasn't random; it radiated outward, as if shaped by an unseen force still lingering beneath.

Parker pressed his palm to the ground, his fingertips brushing a vein of exposed material glinting faintly in the dirt. "Feels metallic," he murmured, his fingertips still pressed to the fractured earth. He looked toward the ridge, eyes narrowing. "Sweep the lights across the valley. If something pushed up from below, we might not be alone out here."

The beams cut through the dark, slicing across twisted terrain and broken soil. Dust swirled in the air, catching the light, like ash suspended in water. Then the scanners hit something flat, immense, and unmistakably unnatural.

From the valley floor, half-buried beneath layers of sediment and time, massive hangar doors came into view. The matte surfaces bore the wear of decades, yet the structure remained intact, untouched by decay.

They radiated containment, not simply of mass, but of intent. Whatever lay behind them had been buried with purpose.

He tilted his head back in Stuart's direction. His voice came low, laced with mischief. With a grin curling at his lips. "I wonder what's behind door number one."

They approached the building and headed towards a narrow gap in the wall, just wide enough to squeeze through. Paker flicked on his flashlight and swept the beam inside. The moment the light hit the interior, they stopped in their tracks.

It was huge. Not just big, it was immense. Darkness swallowed the room. The ceiling was lost in shadows, and the walls were barely clinging to form before fading like phantoms. On the inside, their footsteps didn't echo; the structure swallowed them. It didn't feel like a building anymore; more like a tomb, or maybe a monument to something ancient and forgotten. Dust coated everything, layers of it, pressed into every surface, every shadow.

In the centre of the room, a wide walkway sloped downward, disappearing into the depths. Along its edges, faint symbols glowed, casting a soft, silvery light across the floor.

"I think the path is somehow telling us to go this way," Stuart said, as the beam from their lights disappeared into the distance. They stood for a moment, caught between awe and unease.

Parker glanced at the structure overhead, then turned to Stuart. "This place doesn't look too stable," he said, keeping his voice low. "Let's take it slow. I'd rather not get buried under a thousand tons of alien architecture."

Proceeding slowly, they followed the hallway's winding path. With each turn, the air grew heavier, carrying the quiet sense that they were moving far below the structure's upper levels. Eventually, the passage opened into what resembled a vast cavern. The blackness was suffocating; beyond the reach of their lights, the world simply fell away. A few steps inside, Parker's beam caught a panel on the wall fitted with four levers. Curious, he reached for one, and the panel flickered to life.

"For fuck's sake, Doc," shouted Stuart, "what about being cautious?"

"Sorry, I couldn't resist," then looked towards Stuart and nodded his head in the direction of the levers.

"Okay, to check out the other levers." Stuart shrugged his shoulders in passive agreement.

"Great," Parker muttered, his voice edged with anticipation. One by one, he flipped the levers in reverse, each motion triggering a faint hum beneath their feet.

Section by section of the chamber lit up. Artificial lighting flooded the complex, revealing the towering walls of a structure buried deep beneath the surface.

Dust swirled in the sudden illumination, disturbed by their footsteps as they stepped forward, their eyes adjusting to the brilliance.

The final lever engaged with a snap, revealing the outline of something big. Even as they backed away, they still could not take in its full scale as it emerged from the shadows. Yet, even as they stood back, they still could not take in its sheer size; its form remained obscured, its identity uncertain.

They paced along the side of the structure, tracing its contours, then it hit them... it was a spaceship.

"Okay, that's officially gigantic," Stuart said, half-laughing.

He spoke quickly into the communicator, reporting back to the General, "We've discovered what seems to be a complete spaceship. My guess is they were in a hurry to launch, and something went wrong."

"We've been monitoring your video feed," the General replied. "Pick up the other teams and return to the ship. We need to review everything you've found."

"Yes, General," Stuart responded without hesitation.

Both Alpha teams returned to the *Arcadia*, then just as they exited the landing bay, each of their communicators activated.

"This is Hollins. All landing teams meet me and Gall in meeting room one."

Everyone gathered in the room, and the teams went over the exciting discoveries.

"You guys have done a great job. The details of your findings have been uploaded to Aurelia's database."

A few days later, Dave and Solara sat down with Gall and the General to go over what they'd found. The translations revealed something extraordinary: the planet known as Relentus Prime was once home to a reptilian species that thrived on exploration and intergalactic trade. Gall's precise scans, combined with his deep analysis of ancient structures and the team's painstaking translations, led to a jaw-dropping revelation. The planet had been drifting through space for at least a million Earth years. Maybe even longer.

Its people were long gone, swallowed by time. All that remained was a shattered planet, the remnants of a civilisation that had once pulsed with life.

And yet, one mystery still lingered. We could not find any records of the planet's original location within the Milky Way.

Speculation led them beyond their home galaxy to the distant fringes of a neighbouring galaxy. Had it once orbited a star at the outer edge? Had it belonged to another civilisation that has been erased from history? The questions lingered, unanswered, tantalising.

Solara shared an exciting development, revealing that she had successfully translated one of the languages spoken by a race her people had encountered. Additionally, Dave had managed to establish a connection between the knowledge centre found on the planet and *Arcadia's* central brain.

Aurelia materialises. "I have uploaded Solara's translations. There is a large amount of information regarding Planet Engines and the black hole. They also disclose how an experiment went wrong."

The general nodded thoughtfully. "We need to get a better understanding. Let's reconvene at 09:00 hours. Aurelia, gather all the data we have so far."

At 0900 hours the next cycle, the Alpha teams entered the meeting room, where the General was speaking with Gall.

He turned as they arrived. "Take a seat, everyone. The scientists aboard the *Arcadia* have uncovered a considerable amount about the planet."

Trill addressed the room. "The inhabitants of Relentus Prime left this hologram to tell the story of their final days. Solara has provided a translation."

He activated his wrist monitor, and a hologram of the reptilian creature they had seen on the planet appeared. "As you can see, it's pointing at the energy beam coming from the black hole, explaining how the blocks received the energy."

He eagerly begins to describe the latest findings. "We've never encountered an artificial black hole until now. According to the data I've received, it appears the experiment went awry."

Trill activated the hologram, and light spilled into the chamber like fragments of memory.

The hologram's voice shimmered, ancient and resonant, recounting the twilight years of Relentus Prime.

It spoke of a people who bent the laws of creation, forging a black hole to power their world and engines large enough to move a planet through the stars. It was more than a story; it was a spectacle, a chronicle of a civilization that turned its planet into a starship.

Their sun was dying. To escape its final destruction, they built planetary engines around their world, propelling it toward a distant star system. The black hole, terrifying as it was, became their salvation, an endless source of energy drawn through siphons and power stations. What had once been a cosmic threat became their greatest asset.

"It's unclear why they chose to relocate the entire planet rather than settle a new one," Aurelia interrupted.

Kayla tapped the table lightly. “It’s hard to imagine that a civilization that vanished millions of years ago was more advanced than any today.”

Trill leaned forward. “The hologram depicts how they locked their planet into orbit around the black hole, harnessing its limitless energy.”

Dave’s voice broke in, excitement in his tone. “I know how they did it. The chamber generated micro black holes in equilibrium, each confined within containment units to prevent uncontrolled growth.”

The general’s eyes narrowed. “Then how is the planet not affected?”

Dave faltered. “I haven’t figured that out yet.”

The hologram continued, the projection shifting to show tremors rippling through the planet as the engines roared to life. The world lurched, just enough to pull itself clear of the event horizon. For the moment, disaster was held at bay. But the black hole kept growing, its pull tightening around the planet. Shields buckled under the strain, the crust began to fracture, and volcanic systems tore open under the pressure. The machines resisted, but the planet itself became the casualty.

Gall stepped closer to the console, his voice cutting through the narration. “Aurelia, run a comparative analysis. I want to know how they reinforced the shield, and whether we can replicate it.”

Aurelia’s eyes flickered as streams of data scrolled across the holographic interface. “Processing.” Moments later, she displayed figures of technicians installing reinforced sensory nodes along the shield’s framework. Her voice steadied. “The reinforcement wasn’t just structural. They layered the shield with adaptive resonance fields, while the reinforcement nodes were recalibrated in real time to counter gravitational fluctuations. It wasn’t a static barrier; it was alive, constantly adjusting to stress. That's how they kept the system stable for millions of years."

Gall folded his arms. "So, they anticipated the black hole's growth?"

Aurelia responded. "Exactly. Their engineers designed the shield to evolve. The nodes weren't just anchors; they were sensors, feeding back into a central matrix that redistributed energy where the strain was greatest. If we could replicate even a fraction of this adaptive shielding, we might stabilize our own systems against similar anomalies. But the energy requirements are staggering. They had the black hole itself as a power source; we don't."

Gall exhaled slowly. "Then the question isn't whether it can be done. It's whether we can survive long enough to find a way."

The hologram flickered, its reptilian figure gazing out as if across time. "I was programmed to preserve their story," it whispered. "Not just the facts, but the choices they made."

The chamber fell silent. The hologram's final words lingered like an echo from the abyss. Trill's gaze swept the room, his voice low and deliberate: "Dormant or not, the black hole still radiates. And if it wakes again, it won't be their story we're watching; it will be ours."

For a short while, silence settled over the room. No one spoke. No one moved. The team had just witnessed the final chapter of a civilisation, a story not just of science and failure, but of heartbreak, resilience, and the unbearable cost of survival.

Aurelia appeared. "From the data I have gathered, they evacuated the entire population successfully."

Trill turned to the group. "We came searching for scientific data, something that might help us. But what we found was far more than that. We found their legacy. And I believe that somewhere, far beyond the reach of the black hole, the descendants of Relentus live beneath a new sun."

A moment of silence hung in the air, heavy with awe and uncertainty. Gall broke it, his tone grounded and firm. "We need to return to the situation we're facing. We're still orbiting the black hole. If it starts pulling again, we won't have planetary engines to push us out."

Trill nodded. "Agreed. We need a shield, one that can hold against gravitational distortion and energy surges. Something akin to the one crafted by the people of Relentus."

"Analysis complete. Based on the hologram's account of shield development and the data I've extracted from the planet's archives. I was able to cross-reference the shield architecture from Relentus Prime with our current systems. Their containment design relied on a layered energy field with three concentric rings, each tuned to a different frequency of gravitational distortion."

She projected a holographic model above the central table. The rings shimmered, rotating slowly around the planet, each one pulsing in a
distinct rhythm.

"The outer ring absorbed ambient gravitational waves," she explained. "The middle ring redistributed the force across the planetary surface. The inner ring acted as a stabiliser, locking the planet's orbit in place."

Trill leaned in. "Can we replicate it?"

Aurelia nodded. "Not entirely. But we can adapt the principles. I've already begun modifying the *Arcadia's* deflector grid to mimic the frequency modulation. It won't hold forever, but it will buy us time."

Dave studied the model. "What about the energy source? We don't have planetary reactors."

Aurelia's eyes flickered. "We don't need them. The siphon arrays we installed are drawing energy directly from the black hole's accretion disk. It's unstable, but sufficient for short-term shielding."

She projected another schematic, this time showing a lattice of energy sensory nodes forming a shell around the *Arcadia*, each one pulsing in sync with the ship's core reactor.

"These nodes," she continued, "will generate a counter-gravitational field. Not strong enough to repel the black hole entirely, but enough to stabilise our orbit and prevent drift."

Kayla frowned. "Won't that drain our power reserves?"

"Normally, yes," Aurelia replied. "But we're not using our own energy. We'll be siphoning from the black hole, just like Relentus has. We'll install siphon arrays on the outer hull. They'll draw ambient energy from the accretion disk and feed it directly into the shield system. It's risky, but it's the only way."

Gall crossed his arms. "And the risk?"

Aurelia didn't hesitate. "If the modulation fails, the shield could collapse inward. The gravitational feedback would tear the ship apart."

Dave leaned forward. "We don't have a planetary crust to anchor the shield. We'll need to create a dynamic field, one that moves with the ship and adjusts in real time."

Gall added, "We'll also need to recalibrate the ship's inertial dampeners. The gravitational fluctuations near the event horizon could tear us apart if we're not perfectly balanced."

Dave nodded. "I've got the dampeners. But we'll need to test the shield before we get any closer."

Aurelia's voice softened. "We have one chance. If the shield fails, we won't get another."

The crew worked through the night. Engineers crawled through maintenance shafts, installing siphon conduits and reinforcement nodes. Aurilia ran simulations, each one more brutal than the last. Failure meant collapse. Success meant survival.

Finally, the shield was ready.

Gall stood at the command console, eyes locked on the swirling mass of the black hole outside the viewport. "Activate the shield."

A low hum settled into the *Arcadia's* frame, deep and steady. A faint glow spread across the hull as the energy nodes synced with the gravitational waves outside. Slowly, the holographic rings came online, wrapping the ship in a shimmering shell that drifted and pulsed like distant auroras.

Telemetry streamed across the monitors, graphs steady, numbers holding. Our orbit is stable. The black hole's pull had all but vanished.

"We've bought ourselves some breathing room," the General said, his voice thick with relief. He stepped forward, eyes sweeping the command deck. Around him, the crew leaned back in their seats, as the tension in the room finally starting to ease.

He placed a hand on the railing, the faint hum of the shield resonating beneath his fingertips. "We're not out of danger," he continued, "but we've bought ourselves breathing room. That's more than we had an hour ago."

Outside the viewport, the black hole loomed, still vast, still hungry, but held at bay by the shimmering shell of *Arcadia's* new defence. The ship floated in its fragile orbit, a speck of defiance against the cosmic abyss.

The General turned to Trill and Gall. "Let's make this time count. Whatever Relentus left behind, we will find it. And we make sure this ship is ready for whatever comes next."

A quiet murmur of agreement passed through the crew. The battle for survival wasn't over. But for now, they had a chance. And that was enough.

The Relic

Personal account: Stuart Thomson

"You can't make this up. After everything... the chaos on Zeph 3, the black hole and the near-destruction of the Arcadia, we've uncovered something beyond belief. A spaceship. Not just any vessel, but one of colossal proportions, buried beneath the planet's surface, hidden for who knows how long."

***

The repairs to the Arcadia are going well. Systems were beginning to stabilise; now our focus has shifted. The ship on the planet is ancient, a relic, and its design is unlike anything recorded. Its scale is overwhelming; the smooth, unbroken hull disappearing past the edge of our floodlights. Whatever built this... it's far beyond Venoran tech. We are hoping to discover its secrets. And more importantly, who left it here?

Following the report about the final days on the planet, General Hollins made a ship-wide announcement about Stuart and Doc's discovery of a construction dock housing a large, and what looked like a complete spaceship.

The video footage of the ship was broadcasted throughout the *Arcadia*.

"Approaching the ship's location, you'll notice it's partially buried with only the upper half visible above the planet's surface. The hatch to the construction dock appears to have malfunctioned, leaving parts of the ship exposed above ground. Remarkably, the ship is well-preserved despite the passage of time."

Addressing the group, Gall stated, "It seems that the repairs to the *Arcadia* will take some time. During this period, I believe it would be a good opportunity for us to explore the ship."

The general thought for a second. "Sounds good to me. Let's get some investigative teams down there and have them start mapping the ship. This ship's hull is in remarkable condition, with no damage except for a couple of scratches. I want to see if we can get it off the planet. If it won't fly, maybe we can strip it for parts."

A ripple of excitement moved through the crew. A fresh mission was taking shape, and the thought of diving deeper into the planet's secrets had everyone on edge, in a good way. And if they were lucky, the tech they uncovered might just give them the edge they needed to keep going.

At the start of the next cycle, Gall led the initial crew down to the construction dock. The ship was enormous; its sleek frame and strange alloy glinting in the cold, muted light of the hangar. It looked like it had been built by minds far ahead of their time. The ground crew broke off into smaller units, each with a job: checking the frame for stress points, poking around the engines, and mapping the layout inside.

The Venorans had already locked down the area with a shimmering force field that wrapped around the dock like a bubble. The air inside was clean and cool, maintained by the quiet hum of the pumping stations. Machinery ran in the background, steady, unobtrusive, keeping everything breathable for whoever came through next.

Sarah and Paige were practically vibrating with excitement as they suited up. This was their first descent to the construction dock, and it showed. Their eyes were wide, taking in every detail with the kind of awe that only comes from stepping into something completely unfamiliar.

A gigantic dock stretched out before them, alive with motion. Crews hustled between towering structures, voices sharp and focused as they relayed updates through their comms.

"Let's split up and check things out," Paige said, her voice buzzing with energy. She was already moving, drawn toward the massive ship towering in front of her. She slowed, eyes tracing its outline. "This thing is huge," she murmured, half to herself.

The ship's surface caught the dock lights, scattering reflections at shifting angles. Paige reached out, brushing her fingertips against the smooth metal. Its design was sleek, almost spectral, beautiful in a way that felt deliberate, but with something hidden beneath the surface.

A wave from Sarah caught her attention. "Paige! Over here, I think this is an entry point!"

Paige hurried over, her gaze landing on a strange symbol etched into the hull: a hand with three long fingers. Sarah moved closer; intrigued, she pressed her own hand against it. To her surprise, warmth pulsed beneath her palm. Then, with a soft hiss, the hatch slid open.

Darkness greeted them from inside, deep, untouched, as if the ship had been waiting for this moment.

"We're in," Sarah said, her voice trembling with excitement.

Paige entered, her heart thudding with a mix of excitement and unease. Inside, the atmosphere pressed in, untouched and ancient. As more teams arrived, their boots rang out against the metal floor, the sound bouncing through the empty corridors.

"Man, it's pitch black in here," Don said, squinting as he joined Kayla. They switched on their flashlights, narrow beams slicing through the shadows as they moved deeper into the ship.

Over the next hour, crews hauled in portable lights, setting them up one by one. A warm glow gradually filled the space, revealing the ship's interior. As each team arrived, they shared the same reaction of astonishment at how well preserved the ship was. For a ship this old, it looked almost untouched.

Doc and Stuart wandered into a cavernous chamber that could only be the engine room. Stuart stopped in his tracks, looking up. "Doc, this is the biggest engine room I've ever seen," he said, his voice bouncing off the walls.

The space stretched upward, at least four, maybe five stories high. As they walked toward the centre, they noticed they were standing on a glass-like floor. Shining their lights downward, they illuminated the ships' engines beneath them.

"Guess those are the main engines. What do you think, Doc?" Stuart asked, his eyes darting from one massive piece of machinery to another.

Doc stepped closer, squinting at the towering structures. "Looks like it," he said, running a hand along a conduit. "These systems probably power the entire ship. The layout's consistent with high-output fusion drives."

Stuart whistled low. "I was thinking the same. But man, the scale of this thing... it's unreal."

Doc chuckled. "You say that now. Wait until we find the reactor core."

Stuart grinned. "You're hoping it's still working, aren't you?"

"Wouldn't mind seeing it light up," Doc admitted. "But let's not get ahead of ourselves."

Just then, a loud clang echoed from the far end of the chamber. Both men turned sharply.

"Did you hear that?" Stuart asked instinctively, reaching for his flashlight.

"Yeah," Doc said, already moving toward the sound. "Could be structural settling... or someone else poking around."

Meanwhile, on the other side of the ship, Paige and Sarah stepped into a wide, domed room. Rows of consoles and display panels lined the walls, silent and dark.

"This has to be the bridge," Paige said, her voice low with awe.

Sarah nodded, brushing dust off one of the consoles. "Everything's intact. It's like the crew just stepped out."

Paige leaned in, studying the interface. "No power, but the layout's familiar. If we can reroute energy from the core, we might be able to bring this place back online."

Sarah smiled, already scanning the room for access points. "Let's see what this ship still remembers." They placed lights around the room, revealing the hull's sweeping curve that had remained untouched, possibly for millions of years.

At the centre of the bridge stood what appeared to be a command seat, flanked by clusters of small consoles on either side. A short distance in front of them was a large window with several monitors around its outer edge. The seats were made of a strange, resilient material that had not deteriorated over time. The walls were lined with mysterious devices and instruments, their purposes yet unknown. Through the hull windows, they caught glimpses of the construction bay, a space so vast it felt more like a cavern than a dock. From the main observation deck, the full scale came into view: the bay stretched out endlessly, far larger than anything they'd imagined. Far below, the floor blurred into shadow, where the faintest movements betrayed the presence of engineers at work.

"Sarah, this ship must be enormous."

"They definitely didn't cut corners when they built this place," Paige said, her voice full of admiration. "This bridge feels... comfortable, like it was meant to be lived in."

Paige turned slowly, her boots echoing softly against the polished floor. The bridge was breathtaking; all around were sweeping curves of alloy and glass, consoles arranged with elegant precision, and a panoramic view that stretched all around. Everything, from the layout to the materials, spoke of a civilisation that didn't just build for utility; they built with pride.

"Whoever designed this," she murmured, "they weren't just engineers. They were artists."

Sarah stepped up beside her, running her fingers along the edge of a console. "It's like they wanted whoever stood here to feel something. Not just command a ship, but understand it."

Paige nodded, still absorbing the scale of it all.

A few cycles later, Stuart and Doc had found the engine room. Stuart glanced at his handheld monitor, tapping through layers of data. A faint pulse flickered across the screen.

"Doc," he called out, "that signal we tracked the other day; it's not coming from this chamber. It's deeper. Below the ship."

Doc looked up from the panel he'd been inspecting. "Below? As in subdeck?"

Stuart nodded. "No below the ship. We've logged everything we can here. I think it's time for us to go outside again."

Doc straightened, slinging his toolkit over his shoulder. "Let's gear up. If that pulse is still active, something down there's alive, or at least operational."

Outside, near the base of the ship, Solara crouched beside a row of consoles, her scanner humming softly. Dave stood nearby, watching as she examined the crystal plates arranged beneath each station; hundreds of them, etched with intricate symbols.

"These aren't just decorative," Solara said, her eyes locked on the data streaming across her tablet. "They're operational plates. Each one contains the full specs and instructions for the component it's paired with."

Dave leaned in. "Like a blueprint encoded in crystal?"

"Exactly," she replied. "It looks like they were mid-installation when they aborted completing the ship. The ship was never finished."

Not far from their location, Stuart and Doc had tracked the mysterious pulse to a room near the ship's stern. Entering cautiously, they found a large schematic of the vessel displayed on the wall, and at various intervals were rooms. From each room, lines stretched across the schematic, converging at a wall-mounted panel.

Intrigued, Stuart slipped out of the room, the low murmur of the teams fading behind him as he crossed the hangar floor. He moved toward the ship's hull, drawn to a wall-mounted panel he hadn't noticed before. His eyes caught sight of it just above a platform strewn with thick cables. He reached out and touched it. Immediately, the panel slid inward, revealing a network of connection points hidden within.

Stuart called Doc over. "I think all the lines on the drawing lead right here; these must be the connection points for the entire ship," he said excitedly, gesturing toward the wall panel. "Each cable has a different fitting. That makes things easier."

After they had made all the connections, they stood back, waiting with bated breath. But nothing happened. Frustrated, they returned to the wall chart to re-examine the drawing, hoping to find a clue.

Doc returned to the room where they first saw the drawing. He studied the intricate details, running his fingers along the paths of the power

conduits.

"Do you see something?" Stuart asked, his voice tinged with curiosity.

"Think so," Doc replied, studying the massive wall-sized drawing. "I'm pretty good at reading plans. This feels like looking at a map of the human nervous system, just trying to figure out exactly where those cables lead. These specs are nothing like anything I have seen before, and this drawing covers the entire wall." His tone was one of determination as he tried to make sense of the complex schematics.

Doc's eyes lit up as he pointed his flashlight. "Got it! I found where those cables are headed, it's that room over there!" he called out, unable to hide his excitement as he directed the beam toward it.

They entered the room, which displayed a different image on the wall of a console with letters beside individual levers. Looking around, Doc located the same console, which had several controls in two rows running across it.

"Stand back," Doc announces cautiously, just as Stuart walks into the room to see Doc pulling the levers down.

The lights on the ship's wall map illuminated. Inside the ship, the lighting came on in all areas, and consoles and screens began to spring to life, startling a few crew members around the ship.

Everyone's communicator activates as Stuart makes an announcement. "All good guys? Doc just found the on switch."

Paige walked into a room just as all the lights came on. "At last, now we can see clearly," she said.

Looking around the room, she noticed a wall panel that had come to life, displaying a map of the ship. She walked over to the panel and moved her finger along the map.

"Here we are in the bridge area, Sarah. Take a look at this. There's a lot more to this ship than we thought. Below us, you've got living quarters, loading bays, and hangars for various ships. Each bay has its own symbol. If those symbols are numbers, there could be hundreds of them down there. The elevators in the hallways connect to every section."

Paige and Sarah continued their survey of the room, moving from one console to another while entering notes about their findings into their laptops. After a few hours, they reported back to the general onboard the *Arcadia*.

"General, it's Paige. I'm on the bridge with Sarah. Initially, we believed this was an evacuation ship due to its capacity to carry a large portion of the population. However, we've discovered that this ship also has attack capabilities. I have translated a partial list of its supplies, and it is carrying a significant arsenal of weapons. I'm now thinking its primary purpose was as a warship."

"That's great news," said the General over the communicator. "Continue to analyse the bridge equipment and figure out how it might work. I'm going to come down soon for a walkabout to understand the ship's layout."

Don and Kayla stepped into one of the newly discovered elevators and descended to the lower floors. The passageway at the rear of the ship suddenly illuminated. "Lights are online, finally makes poking around this place a lot smoother," Kayla remarked, her eyes scanning the intricate designs on the walls.

"These loading bays are packed with equipment," Don observed, moving his flashlight around the room. "Looks like they were preparing for lift-off and packed everything they would need for a long journey."

"Don, the hangar bays are just below us. We should check those out," Kayla suggested. She felt the excitement building within her with each discovery.

They took the elevator down to a gigantic bay, their lights revealing rows of smaller ships lined along the walls in hangars that looked as if they stretched into infinity. Larger ships were neatly arranged around power points on the floor of the landing bay.

Kayla tapped her communicator and added, “Don, Paige just informed the General that this ship has attack capabilities. I’m guessing the smaller ones over there are fighter ships, while these larger ones are likely transporters.”

Gall and the General beamed down to the construction bay. Pausing at the entrance, staring up at the massive hull of the ship. “Damn,” the General said, whistling low. “This one is a beauty.”

Gall nodded, eyes scanning the sleek lines and faded insignias. “Better shape than I expected. Ground crews weren’t exaggerating.”

The moment they entered, the atmosphere changed; the air felt cool and sterile.

Running his hand along the inner bulkhead, Gall noticed the faint oscillation beneath the alloy surface... steady, rhythmic, almost like a heartbeat. The material wasn’t standard composite; it felt denser, smoother, with a low-frequency hum that suggested active energy routing just beneath the skin.

“This isn’t just structural,” he muttered, eyes narrowing. “There’s a live conduit network embedded in the walls. Power distribution, maybe even data flow.”

The general glanced over. “Still operational after all this time?”

Gall nodded slowly. “Not just operational, optimised. Whoever built this, they engineered systems we haven’t even theorised yet.”

The General chuckled. “Makes you wonder what else they left behind. Secrets don’t stay buried forever.”

On the bridge, Sarah was looking at a glowing panel. “Paige, check this out. I think it’s some kind of navigation interface.”

Paige leaned in, brushing dust off the surface. “Looks like it’s still active. That’s not just residual power. This thing’s alive.”

Meanwhile, in the hangar bay, Gall pointed to a row of smaller ships lined up with surgical precision, sleek, angular, and built for speed.

“They could be fighter ships,” he said, stepping closer. “Fast, maybe even interstellar. The hull plating is composite, lightweight, but reinforced. Probably designed for deep-range recon.”

The general crouched beside one, running his hand along the underside. “Designs tight. No wasted space.” He tapped a panel near the cockpit, and it hissed open, revealing a compact interior. The controls were minimal: just a few touch-sensitive surfaces, a manual throttle, and what looked like a neural interface port tucked beneath the console.

Gall leaned in. “Dual-mode control system. Manual for precision, but capable of syncing with the pilot for faster response. That’s high-end tech.”

The General nodded. “Means they could fly it like a fighter or wear it like a second skin.”

Gall moved to the rear of the craft, inspecting the propulsion system. “The drive assembly… it’s not standard ion or fusion. It’s something else. Maybe something we haven’t even named yet.”

The general stood up, brushing dust off his gloves. “Judging by the mix of ships, they weren’t just planning for one kind of mission. They were covering all their bases.”

Back on the bridge, Paige hesitated for a moment in front of the console, eyes scanning the unfamiliar symbols. “These controls aren’t standard,” she murmured. “But the layout’s familiar… sort of.”

Sarah raised an eyebrow. “You’ve seen something like this before?”

“Not exactly,” she said, fingers hovering over the panel. “But systems tend to follow patterns. Power, navigation, and comms; they all usually sit in the same spots. You only have to feel it out.” Her fingers hovered over the console, hesitant at first. Then, with growing certainty, she tapped a few buttons. Lights flickered to life across the interface. “There we go,” she murmured, a small smile tugging at her lips. “It’s like learning a new language. You start with the basics and guess the rest.”

A low hum filled the room as a holographic map flickered to life. “Whoa,” Sarah breathed. “That’s a star chart. And those markers... they’re not from any system I recognise.”

Throughout the ship, ground crew moved steadily, cataloguing everything from the symbols etched into the walls, the strange machinery to the subtle way the corridors seemed to shift as they walked. Every discovery added to the mystery. And none of them could shake the feeling that the ship was watching.

They moved through the corridors, checking in with the research teams scattered throughout. Everyone had something to share: new findings, strange symbols, systems that were still partially active. There was work to be done, and every discovery raised more questions than answers. Eventually, they reached the bridge just as Solara arrived to help Paige understand how the ship operated. “Sir, Sarah has just left to check out the status of the newly discovered weapons department,” Paige reported, glancing down at her tablet.

The general looked up from the console he’d been inspecting. “Good. What do you have so far?”

Paige didn’t hesitate. “The ship’s condition is remarkable; it’s like it rolled off the line yesterday. Most of the bridge controls just need minor adjustments to fit our hands. I’ve already spoken with engineering. They say it’s doable.”

He nodded, encouraging her to continue.

“We’ve also got a language barrier,” she added. “All the monitor data is still in the original script. Solara is working on converting each system to English. It’s slow, but she’s making progress.”

The general folded his arms, listening intently.

Paige kept going, her voice steady but carrying the weight of everything they’d uncovered. “Bottom line, we need to figure out how to actually use this thing. You've got access to weapons, navigation, comms, life support, shields, pilot controls, and star maps. It even has systems that monitor the ship's structural health. This isn't just a ship; it's a fortress. A damn masterpiece."

She paused, letting that settle in the air. Then her tone shifted, a faint grin tugging at the corner of her mouth.

"You know," she said, half-laughing, "back home I used to dream about owning a car with all the bells and whistles. Fully loaded, top of the line. But this?" she gestured around the control room. "This makes that look like a toy. We're standing inside the most advanced ride in the galaxy."

She leaned against the console, her expression turning serious again. "But power without mastery is nothing. If we can make this thing flyable, you'll need a crew that knows it inside and out."

The general nodded slowly, letting her words sink in. "You're right," he said. "This isn't just a mission; it's a commitment. We're not just learning how to fly it. We're learning how to earn it."

Paige gave a small nod. "Exactly. And we've only scratched the surface."

He gazed around the command centre, the hum of advanced technology pulsating beneath their feet. The weight of history and destiny pressed against him, settling deeper with every passing second.

Gall turns to the general. "We can supplement any areas in which you do not have a crew member available for the position. Paige, you and Solara do what you need to do and make things work."

The general called Dave on his communicator. "Meet me in engineering and bring Kayla. We are going to need her here too."

Upon entering the engineering room, the general surveyed it with practised precision. "Wow! Look at this place. I can't get over how everything is still in pristine condition."

"Yes, remarkable," said Gall.

Kayla had just come from the landing bays and met Dave outside Engineering.

"Sure, glad those elevators are working," Dave said as the door swooshed open. "Would've been a long hike from the other end of the ship."

The general turned to him first. "I want you to check out the engine systems. See if you can get them working again?" Dave gave a quick nod, already scanning the room. "I'll take a look. If there's power, I'll find it."

Then the general turned to Kayla. "Kayla, please log everything you see. I want a complete inventory."

"Got it," she replied, pulling out her tablet. "I'll start with the control panels and work my way through the storage units."

Without another word, they split off, Dave heading towards the engine controls, Kayla moving along the wall, eyes sharp, fingers already tapping notes.

Gall, looking towards the General, offered some assistance. "I can spare a couple of my technicians to assist in this area."

"Good, let's proceed," the General replied.

The general called Stuart over the communicator. "Stuart, let's meet up in the hangar bay. I'm also going to bring one of Gall's pilots."

As everyone arrived, they took a moment to look around, taking deep breaths at the impressive sight of all the ships. The hangar was massive, filled with various types of craft.

Gall turned to the other Venoran standing beside him and introduced him. "I believe you have already met this pilot." Stuart walked over to greet him; it was Drowen, whom they had all met on the first day on the training planet.

"Oh yes, our tour guide," Stuart said with a smile.

Drowen answered back, "And I remember you."

Stuart spoke first. "This is not just a place to park shuttles. There are several squadrons of various types of craft here, General."

The general looked at them. "I have asked you two to be here because we need to know how these things fly, and what their capabilities are. If you need any other crews down here, contact me."

Stuart and Drowen began to inspect the hangar, noting the different types of ships and their configurations.

Meanwhile, in engineering, Dave and his team started examining the engine systems while Kayla meticulously logged each piece of equipment and its status. The General and Gall discussed the potential uses of the ships and how they could integrate them into their fleet. Dave crouched down next to the main engine, examining the intricate network of tubes and circuits. He ran diagnostics, taking notes on his tablet.

"The engine systems are complex, but I think I can get them running with a bit of work," he reported.

Engineering teams had been working on the ship around the clock, and information about the ship was growing. There were also many living quarters; Doc had discovered a fully equipped medical centre and laboratory, which he was pretty excited about.

At the end of one shift, Dave called the general. "We have something to show you."

"On my way, will be with you shortly." The general stepped into the engineering room and heard a voice from above. Dave, half-leaning over a railing, called out, "Just a sec!"

Dave came down a flight of stairs and walked over to the general. Excitedly, he lifted his hands into the air and twirled around, arms outstretched as he gestured with pride.

"All the equipment you see around us is a control centre. From here, you could fly the ship. It's a backup to the bridge should something happen up there. The translations they are doing on the bridge are automatically being updated here."

Dave walked to the centre of the room, stopping before a wide glass floor panel. Beneath it, the mechanical heart of the ship pulsed with
energy.

Unaware of how quickly he was speaking, Dave launched into his findings with growing excitement. "As power began to trickle in, the engines came online," he said, breathless. "Though we're still expecting a major boost once they reach full charge."

He extended a hand, gesturing below them. "And there are the engines," he continued, his voice steady but brimming with anticipation. "There are three. You have the standard Sublight engine, the Warp Drive, and then... this."

His fingers hovered above the console, eyes locked on the third mechanism, enigmatic, silent, and unlike anything they'd seen before.

"This one is entirely new to us, and we're still working out how to make it function. Based on their logs, it's called a Dimensional Shift engine, or D-shift for short. It sounds impressive, but we've barely scratched the surface of what it actually does." He exhaled slowly, letting the words sink in. Excitedly, Dave adds, "This isn't just any ship... it's the second of its kind. They had already tested a prototype, much smaller, crewed only by a handful of scientists and engineers. Their sole mission was to test the Dimensional Shift engine."

"But the moment it entered D-Space, all contact was lost. It simply vanished. Gone without a trace. Thankfully, the builders were meticulous, obsessive even, about documentation. Their logs end abruptly the instant the D-shift engine engages. And now, we're here to pick up where they left off. To solve the mystery, they left behind. After the disappearance of the prototype, several critical upgrades were implemented. The most important update was the integration of a Quantum-brane manipulator, the heart of the D-shift engine. This device allows the ship to harmonise its vibrational frequency with elusive higher-dimensional membranes, a feat once thought impossible. The builders' logs delve into wild levels of detail. There's information on Phase Detachment and Quantum Tunnelling metrics. Theres a whole wall of equations that look like they were scrawled by a physicist having a religious experience."

Dave let out a low whistle, then smiled, half in admiration, half in disbelief. "Someone really went all in on this. I won't bore you with the techno-babble just yet. Once we've decoded every layer and confirmed the systems are stable, you'll get the full report."

He turned back to the group, his expression both exhilarated and cautious.

"The D-shift opens a singularity and pushes the ship out of our dimension to a point just beyond what we'd call reality. If it works," she said, eyes on the console, "we could cross impossible distances in an instant and skip normal space travel entirely."

The general didn't answer right away. He watched the readouts flicker, as data continued to roll past like a silent warning.

"I'm guessing there's a catch," he muttered.

Kayla stepped closer, her brow tight. "There is," she said. "It didn't work. And I think I know why."

She drew a slow breath. "I found a note from the chief engineer. The prototype was seconds from takeoff when a massive earthquake hit somewhere near the port. The quake didn't start the launch, but it threw the calibration out of alignment. The ship shifted just enough that the D-shift engine kicked in before the systems were fully stable."

The room went quiet.

Dave frowned, "So the quake knocked everything off balance?"

"Pretty much," Kayla said. "It disrupted all pre-launch calibration."

The general's eyes narrowed. "And the first prototype?"

"Gone," she said softly. "But not destroyed. The logs suggest it went somewhere else. They were supposed to clear the planet, hit warp, and then engage the D-Space engine. But with the calibration off, the engine locked onto the wrong membrane. Instead of slipping into the intended layer, it punched through a chaotic fold."

A technician at the back of the room raised his hand hesitantly. "Uh... somewhere else, like... another dimension?"

Kayla nodded. "Possibly. But without the right coordinates, it's like tossing a message into a black hole and hoping someone reads it."

"And this ship?" the General probed.

Kayla sighed, frustration flickering across her face. "Theoretically, the engine requires momentum near light speed before engagement. But that's not the real issue."

She glanced at the console, then back at the general and Dave. "One of the energy transfer stations was severed. That cut off the power surge needed to launch. The result? Just a faint trickle of energy. Enough to start the sequence, but nowhere near enough to complete it."

A heavy silence settled over them. The builders had dangled the promise of revolutionary travel just out of reach.

"So, you're telling me," the General said, letting the words sink in, "they were right there. They had it all figured out: instant travel, jumping between dimensions, stuff that shouldn't even be possible. The ship was ready; the tech was actually working. But then the ground shook, the power cut out, and the whole dream just went up in smoke."

Dave stepped forward, his voice calm and deliberate. A spark lit his eyes, a mix of awe and reverence for the machine they'd built. "This ship," he began, gesturing toward the massive structure surrounding them, "was still a prototype. The D-shift engine was entirely experimental. Other than the previous prototype, nothing like this had ever been built."

He let his gaze sweep across the room, ensuring the weight of his words landed. "It was larger than anything in their fleet, monumental in scale, and not just for its size. It had a dual purpose. The engines were originally designed for a warship, and this vessel was meant to be the proving ground for their newest technology."

The general thought for a moment. "That explains the partially open doors. The ship had only nudged them. Okay, after all that, can it be repaired?"

Kayla hesitated. "What if we reroute through the auxiliary grid? It's not designed for that kind of load, but..."

Dave cut in, his tone sharp but not unkind. "We'd fry half the ship before the engine even blinked."

Kayla nodded. "Then we need a stable surge. Something clean, something controlled. Or we risk tearing the ship apart before it ever leaves the planet."

The general exhaled slowly, eyes scanning the room. "Then we find another way. Because if this engine really works, we're not just talking about travel. We're talking about rewriting reality itself."

He paused, letting the thought linger before continuing, his voice quieter. "And as we know, the inhabitants of this planet didn't just master spaceflight. They discovered a way to harness the energy of a black hole."

His eyes flicked toward the looming celestial anomaly above. "They built one, right there, suspended above us, to power their entire planet. A marvel of engineering, yet also a mystery."

Harnessing a black hole, a force capable of swallowing stars, was beyond anything they had imagined possible. Now, they stood examining the remnants of a civilisation that had achieved the unimaginable.

Dave exhaled, shifting his stance. "The question now is whether we can finish what they started. Whether we can unlock the secrets of this ship, of this technology, and take a step beyond what we once thought was possible."

The general walked to the centre of the room and looked down at the chamber below.

Dave pointed and explained, "That reactor chamber has an atmosphere capable of generating a black hole, which can only expand to the size of its containment chamber."

"Wait... there's another one," the General murmured, gesturing toward the one above the planet. "Funny how they always show up where we least expect them." He turned slowly. "Inside the ship, you say?"

"Ah, thought you might be a bit concerned," Dave replied. "The builders installed several safeguards. Along with the containment chamber, they constructed the reactor with a series of magnetic containment fields, plus backup systems, to ensure the black hole remains stable and doesn't consume the ship."

Returning to the task of powering up the vessel, he continued: "What they needed was the energy generated from the black hole above to kick-start the ship's systems. But one of the energy transfer stations failed, significantly reducing the supply. That left them with insufficient power to initiate engine start-up. Essentially, fix the station, you fix the ship."

Power had also been cut to the overhead hangar doors, which had closed onto the ship during lift-off. Their only solution was to engage the Trans-Dimensional engine. But as the engine activated, the ship began to phase, just as the power failed. They had no choice but to abort.

The result: a partially phased vessel, frozen mid-transition, with sections protruding through the hangar doors. They couldn't clear the entrance in time. And with the imminent collapse of all planetary power systems, they evacuated.

This ship had been designed to escort all evacuation craft through space to their final destination. And that was where the Chief Engineer's report ended.

Dave leaned against the console, eyes distant, as if tracing the stars themselves. "I haven't figured out exactly how long ago this happened, but it must be over a million years. I gave up trying to determine their destination once I realised the scale of time involved."

"The history of this planet was preserved by two things: first, it's located in a vast void in space, low risk of impact. Second, proximity alone should've doomed it. The gravitational pull of the black hole should've swallowed it whole."

"It was blind luck that we passed through the outer fringes. Any closer, and we'd have been goners. The black hole may have caused problems, but it had its good side. We were lucky to find it when we did. We're not sure how much longer it'll last. This discovery will keep scientists busy for a long time. And who knows what other revelations we might uncover."

Gall looked over to the general. "I'll send some of my technicians to the damaged transfer station. Hopefully, we'll be able to make the necessary repairs."

The General nodded. "I'll have crews cleaning up topside. We could use the *Arcadia's* tractor beam to move the larger debris from the hangar doors."

Suddenly, Aurelia's voice activated from Gall's communicator, her tone efficient and calm. "I will make the arrangements for the tractor beam to be activated."

"Thank you, Aurelia," Gall replied.

Just then, Paige's voice came over the General's communicator. "General, we have been training a crew to operate the ship and have covered most of the systems on the bridge. We should have round-the-clock crews fully trained very soon."

The general smiled, which was a rare sight. "Thanks for the update."

Back in the launch bay, Stuart and Drowen were moving between the ships, checking each one in turn. A second team from the Arcadia had arrived and was already digging into the equipment scattered throughout the hangar.

The general and Gall headed down to the bay to get an update on the ships stored there.

Stuart was giving their report to the general. "General, these ships are new, loaded, and ready to go. The ones we are calling fighters have two seats, plus they have quite a few weapons onboard, and they can also generate a force field. The larger ships are transporters capable of carrying a crew of about 100, and there is still room to carry additional equipment should you need it. The controls seem simple to use now that we have the translation database making all the necessary language conversions."

The general nodded, absorbing the information. Then he stepped forward, his voice steady and pragmatic. "If we are unable to make this ship flyable, we can at least take a couple of those ships onboard the *Arcadia* and reverse engineer them."

"We've also received feedback from *Arcadia's* investigative team. They found a ship-repair area in here, along with cables running to each vessel. Those cables aren't just tethers; they're energy fuel lines. Ever since we connected the external power feed, a small trickle of energy has been charging every ship in the bay. We believe this vessel has its own internal power-distribution system, and once she's fully activated, these ships could be charged in a matter of minutes."

The general sent Stuart and Dave to inspect the damaged receiving station, hoping it could still be salvaged. A short while later, the two of them suited up and headed for the shuttle bay.

"I've been dying to try one of these," Stuart said as they walked toward one of the alien shuttles, its power cells almost fully charged.

"Strap in, Dave."

The alien shuttle hovered for a brief moment, its sleek form swaying gently from side to side as Stuart wrestled with the controls, determined to regain steady flight. With a triumphant surge, they soared out of the gap formed by the partially open hangar doors, the alien landscape unfolding below them.

"Well, that was easier than I expected," Stuart remarked, with a mix of relief in his voice. It wasn't long before they located the station. The ship's headlights cut through the dark, sweeping across jagged ground like searchlights on a prison wall. As the ship's lights reached the edge of the receiving station, everything changed. The ground was cracked and unstable, a chaotic mess of broken earth and twisted metal. It was clear now: whatever had happened here was far worse than they'd anticipated. Gall's technicians had already arrived and were busy cleaning the site.

Dave didn't look up. His eyes stayed glued to the monitor as the data poured in. "Stu..." he said quietly. "It's worse than we thought. The station's gone, collapsed into a massive sinkhole. Looks like an earthquake hit the area hard. When it went down, it severed its link to the energy source."

The shuttle touched down with a soft thud, and Stuart directed the high-powered headlights to encompass the hole and its treacherous surroundings.

Dave suited up and emerged from the ship to find thick dust still floating around the shuttle's landing.

From the comfort of the ship, Stuart called out, “How are we going to reposition that back in line with the inlet and outlet ports? It’s nearly 50 feet down, and the crater must span almost 200 feet across!”

“I’ll head down and check the connections,” Dave said, squinting over the edge of the crater as the dust began to settle. “We need to make sure this station’s still able to draw power.”

He scanned the wreckage below, eyes narrowing as he spotted the faint glint of energy lines half-buried under twisted metal and dust.

“Stu,” he called out, waving to him, “come take a look at this, right here along the crater wall.

Stuart arrived, looking at the crater, “What is it?”

“You see those transfer lines? We need to check for breaks or burnouts before we try rerouting anything.”

“I think this station might be salvageable.”

Sturt reflected on the challenging task ahead. “I'm on it.”

With the help of Gall's technicians, they managed to get most of the repairs completed. Now all they needed was a bit of external assistance.

Dave opened his communicator. “*Arcadia*, we require support down here. The station needs to be lifted out of the hole and realigned with the energy source, which is directly over where I’m standing.”

Gall’s composed voice came through in response, steady and reassuring. “We can use the tractor beam. Stand clear.”

A glowing beam of light materialised from above, bathing the area. Enveloping the station with a graceful yet powerful motion, lifting it high from the abyss and placing it firmly on solid ground.

“Great! I’m sending you a parts list. I think we can fix it.” His voice was calm but edged with anticipation.

As soon as they received the parts in their hands, Dave and Stu got to work. They worked fast, hands steady as they reconnected the inlet and outlet ports, muscle memory guiding each motion. When the last seal clicked into place, Dave stepped back, batting the dust off his gloves. Grabbing the lever beside the control panel, he pulled it down with a grunt. A deep metallic thud echoed through the chamber as the locks engaged.

"Let's hope this does the trick," he muttered, just as the sound of mechanical locks echoed through the chamber. The lever clicked into place, and a low hum began to build, vibrating through the floor, sending a faint pulse rippling through the station.

Dave tapped his comm. "General, we've got power flowing from this end. We're heading back to the ship to see what's changed," he said, urgency rising in his voice.

From a gantry high above the alien craft, Don watched the cleanup unfold. He took a slow breath, steadying himself as the full scale of the ship came into view. It was massive; from his position, he could barely make out its total size. The *Arcadia*, impressive in its own right, looked like a toy in comparison. You could fit it inside the alien vessel several times over.

"If they can get this thing running," Don murmured, half to himself, "it's got a straight shot to liftoff." His voice carried a mix of wonder and cautious optimism.

On the planet, Stuart and Dave were making their way back to the bridge. Just as they stepped inside, Paige's voice rang out over the intercom.

"Attention, everyone. We're about to power up. Standby."

Her words echoed through the corridors, and the crew instinctively paused, eyes turning toward the nearest console or display. The moment had arrived, and no one wanted to miss it.

Paige took a deep breath and moved the bars to the top of her display. "Powering up...now!" She watched intently as the power range increased, gradually rising until it reached full capacity. The life support system blinked into action, showing that it was fully operational. The control panel before her lit up, showing all four power station indicators.

The general tilted his head toward Stuart. "Take her up," his voice betraying his eagerness.

Stuart climbed into the pilot's seat, his eyes bright with anticipation. "I've been waiting for this," he said under his breath, fingertips brushing the controls as if he'd been operating the ship for years. The ship gave a low shudder as ancient systems stirred, metal groaning, lights flickering to life. It was waking up.

"Initiating the stabilisers," Stuart announced.

The ship gave a shudder at first, causing the crew to grab onto their stations. Moments later, it levelled out.

"That's better," General Hollins commented, a hint of relief in his voice. "The slant was annoying."

Paige scanned the readings. "The engines will need a jump start to get them fully charged. I'm going to redirect an additional 50% from the power matrix."

General Hollins' voice resonated through the ship's communication system. "We are going to test the ship; attention to all external engineers, disconnect power lines and clear the area. All personnel onboard, prepare for flight and take necessary safety precautions."

Above, the hangar doors shuddered, their rusted joints groaning after an eternity of silence. Metal scraped against metal in a long, aching cry, and clouds of dust spilled downward. Slowly, the opening widened, revealing the ship to the vast emptiness above.

The ship stirred.

It was like watching a giant wake from a dream. A low vibration rolled through its frame, shaking loose centuries of stillness. Dust drifted off in lazy spirals as the engines came alive, first a whisper, then a rising growl.

Looking out the nearest viewport, Dave watched from his seat as the ship began to lift, slow and steady, as though it was remembering how to move.

The surface of the planet slipped away, shrinking as the ship climbed until it became nothing more than a shrinking sphere. A hush moved through the crew before the first breathless cheer broke out. After everything they had uncovered, every secret and impossible revelation, they were finally seeing the ship in its element. They had brought her back from the edge of time, and now she was showing them what she truly was.

"Bring us alongside the *Arcadia*," General Hollins said, his voice firm but warm, a smile tugging at the corners of his mouth.

The *Arcadia* drifted silently in the void as its crew clustered at the observation panels. The alien vessel emerged from the darkness... vast, elegant, and unlike anything they'd ever imagined. It filled every viewport, a monolithic silhouette that swallowed the horizon.

At the fore, a sleek bridge jutted forward like the prow of a cathedral, commanding and deliberate. The midsection stretched endlessly, layered with decks that shimmered faintly, hinting at forgotten technologies, cryptic architecture, and secrets buried in time. It dwarfed the *Arcadia*, a leviathan built for purposes no human had yet conceived.

Along the hull, turret bays bristled like dormant sentinels. At the rear, twin landing bays yawned open, flanked by additional turrets poised to repel any threat. The vessel was not just a marvel. It was ready.

Four vertical emitters lay flush with the ship's surface: silent, inert, and waiting. At a command, they would rise with precision, each one capable of unleashing a concentrated beam of devastating energy.

Gall called the engineering team onboard the *Arcadia*. "How are the repairs coming along?"

"Just energising the slide engines. We will be ready by the end of this shift," reported his chief engineer.

"General, we should test this ship," Solara urged, eyes bright with anticipation.

"My thoughts exactly," General Hollins replied. "Chart the nearest galaxy. Take us there, maximum warp."

Without hesitation, Stuart initiated the warp bubble. The ship lurched forward, not violently, but like a giant holding its breath, and in a blink, they were piercing the void far faster than the *Arcadia* ever had.

Sarah called out the warp speed, "Warp 5... 7... 9."

"General," Stuart reported, "even at this speed, we won't reach another galaxy in our lifetime."

Dave met the general's gaze, steady, unflinching. "The D-shift is online."

They exchanged a look between them and almost immediately, "Engage the D-shift," Hollins ordered.

"Activating Phase Detachment... entering Quantum Tunnelling now," Stuart announced.

A singularity opened ahead of the ship. *Excalibur* slipped into a surreal stillness, coasting soundlessly as if the surrounding universe had vanished. Space itself bent away. Stars blurred into ribbons as the ship navigated through the fabric of space-time, sidestepping debris with automated precision.

"Approaching the outer shell of the target galaxy," Stuart confirmed.

"Disengage D-shift," said the General.

"Slowing... exiting tunnelling phase... re-entering warp," Stuart called out.

Moments later, reality shimmered back into form. Sarah monitored the instruments, eyes wide. “Warp 9... 7... 5... steady at Warp 2. Wow, that was a rush.”

Dave stood at the viewport, awestruck by the swirling cosmic sea. “Do you realise we can cross galaxies in the blink of an eye... and still be home for dinner?” He said, with a grin tugging at his lips.

The bridge went silent as they fully became aware of what they had just accomplished. After system-wide checks, Paige gave the all-clear.

“The hull’s intact. No damage reported, sir.”

“Good,” Hollins said, straightening in his chair. “Stuart, take us home.”

The ship vibrated through the hull. Lights along the corridor flickered, then steadied as the ship surged forward. The singularity opened as space warped around it... stars stretched into luminous threads, the void bending like liquid glass. With a final pulse, the D-shift drive was engaged, and the vessel vanished into the slipstream, leaving behind only a ripple in the dark.

Gall stepped alongside the general. “You’ve done a great job adapting to the controls. Everything is running smoothly.”

“Well, you can thank Paige and her team for that,” General Hollins replied, nodding in appreciation.

Moments later, the hum of the D-shift drive began to fade. “Reducing warp speed,” Stuart called out. Gradually, the ship slowed as it neared the planet and came to a stop a short distance from *Arcadia*.

“Sarah and Don, have you got a handle on the weapons?” said the General.

“We have all the weapons charged; we just need to test them,” answered Don.

“There's a debris field following the planet. We could use that,” announced Solara, her eyes scanning the monitors.

“Okay, let's go clean it up,” the General replied, a determined look on his face.

“Looking forward to this,” said Don, his voice steady with anticipation. From the side of the hull, four vertical emitters emerged like ancient monoliths. In an instant, each fired a concentrated energy beam, converging midair in a blinding pulse. The resulting particle stream twisted like a whip through space, vaporising everything it touched. The turrets along the midsection directed plasma energy pulses into space, melting bits of rock to dust. At the rear, laser cannons fired round orbs of energy that exploded upon contact, disintegrating objects in their path.

The general noticed the satisfied grins on Solara's and Stuart's faces. “Okay, you two, you can stop grinning. Playtime is over,” he said with a smirk.

From the bridge, the general addressed the entire crew. “You have all done well to get this ship working. Now, let's have some fun. I think we should give this ship a name. I want everyone to enter a name for the ship and place it in this box. We will vote on the names entered. Gall, Paige, Solara, Drowen, and I will be the judges.”

A few hours later, the General announced, “We have a name. First off, we are not going to use the *Enterprise*.” This brought a few laughs from the group, and Chris muttered to himself, “Damn it.”

“I name this ship the *Excalibur*. Well-done, Dave,” the General declared.

Dave smiled and nodded in acknowledgement. “I was just at the window looking at the stars, and when *Excalibur* just popped into my head from a book. Probably because I was reading about King Arthur.”

Laughing, Sarah said, “Okay, get over it, Sir Dave.”

Paige looked across at Sarah, gave her a knowing wink, and caught Sarah blushing. Paige leaned over to Sarah's ear and whispered something, causing them both to giggle.

Aurelia came online just as Gall returned to the *Arcadia*. "Gall, we have received a communication from Venor. They noted that we are long overdue. I have informed them of the status of the *Arcadia*, and they are inquiring about the repairs and how long before completion."

"Aurelia, contact engineering and update me on their progress," Gall instructed. Moments later, Aurelia responded, "Slide engines are back online, but there's a problem with the bubble. It will not generate around the ship. Without a bubble, the ship will be crushed when we reach slide speed. It will take us a considerable amount of time travelling at low warp speed to arrive home."

"Aurelia, let them know of our situation and give them an estimate of how long it will take for our return," Gall ordered.

Gall addressed the crews of both ships, his voice steady over the comms. "We'll have to abandon the *Arcadia* and return aboard the *Excalibur*. Preparations are underway to transfer all personnel and equipment."

But during the next shift, Paige contacted General Hollins. "I think we might be able to bring the *Arcadia* with us," she said. "I need to speak with Dave first."

"Alright," the General replied. "Look into it. We leave at the end of the next shift."

An hour later, Paige stepped into the General's quarters, datapad in hand. "We're confident we can make it work. The *Excalibur's* landing bay is significantly larger than the *Arcadia*. There's more than enough room."

She paused, then added with a faint smirk, "Getting it through the doors might be tight, but it's doable."

"Excellent," Hollins said, a note of satisfaction in his voice. "Notify Gall. Tell him to guide the *Arcadia* in."

The *Arcadia* began its slow, deliberate approach toward *Excalibur's* hangar bay. Inside the control room, tension hung in the air; no one spoke unless necessary.

"We're aligned," the pilot said, fingers gliding over the console with practiced ease.

"Barely," Dave muttered, eyes locked on the external monitors. The other ship loomed close, its hull just meters away. One wrong move and they'd be scraping metal.

The *Arcadia* crept forward, casting long shadows across the hangar floor. Its outer hull hovered dangerously close to the bay doors.

"Slow it down," Paige said sharply, watching the readouts. "You're drifting left; you need to compensate."

The pilot adjusted course, sweat beading on his forehead. "Thrusters at minimum. Any softer and we'll stall."

A loud creak echoed through the chamber as the starboard wing brushed the edge of the bay. Sparks flew. "We're scraping!" someone shouted.

"Hold steady!" Dave barked. "We're almost through."

The *Arcadia* inched forward. The grinding noise faded, replaced by a taut silence.

That was close, too close. Way too close. Dave thought.

His pulse hammered in his ears. His eyes tracked every flicker on the monitor, every shadow sliding across the hangar floor.

One wrong twitch and we're tearing metal. Come on... come on...

He didn't look away. Couldn't. The ship was clearing the final edge, the tension in the room coiled so tight it felt like the air itself might snap.

Almost there. Just breathe. No... don't breathe. Not yet.

The grinding stopped. Silence.

Dave felt it... pressure releasing, breath exhaled in unison. The ship was in. *We made it. Damn.*

"General, we're in," Dave announced.

"*Arcadia*, log the entry sequence," the pilot said, glancing at the console. "We'll need it when it's time to exit."

General Hollins's voice came through both ships. "Prepare to bring the warp engines online."

Stuart locked in the coordinates and eased the *Excalibur* into warp. The ship surged forward. Sarah, announced the increments: "Warp 5... Warp 6... Warp 8 and holding."

As the drive engaged, a gentle vibration coursed through the hull. For a moment, the motion resembled the rear wheels of a powerful car spinning before gripping the pavement. Everyone aboard felt time stretch. Their movements slowed, caught in the distortion.

Stuart reached for the control panel and pressed a button. Time snapped back to normal.

"Sorry about that, everyone," he said. "Forgot to engage the time filtration. I'll set it to auto from now on."

Then he noticed the clocks. "General... look at the time."

The clocks were racing forward. For over an hour, they continued to accelerate. Gradually slowing until the readings stabilized.

"Can anyone tell me what just happened?" Hollins asked.

Paige stepped forward. "I believe we've just caught up to normal time. Based on my calculations, we were trapped in a time dilation field, likely caused by the black hole. We've been out of phase with the rest of the universe for three months. To us, it felt like a few weeks."

She glanced at the others. "We were lucky. A larger black hole would've slowed time even more. We could've been out of sync for years."

Solara's voice cut in. "Venor is calling."

"Patch it through," Gall said.

After delivering his report on the *Excalibur's* recovery, Gall received grim news.

He stood at the centre of the bridge, scanning the latest updates. "Looks like things changed while we were out of contact," he said, voice calm but edged with concern.

He gestured to the tactical display. Red indicators pulsed across Venor's surface.

"The Korrathi hit the planetary shields hard. They've breached several zones, enough to get fighters into the atmosphere."

He paused, letting the weight settle over the crew. The room was quiet, except for the hum of the ship's systems.

"They're not probing anymore," he said quietly. "This is a full breach."

"So far, Venor and its allies have intercepted and destroyed all enemy craft that have made it through the breach," he continued. "But long-range scans show more Korrathi ships en route."

Gall's expression darkened as he relayed the latest transmission.

The crew gathered around the central console. The message was coded, urgent, and grim. No one spoke. They didn't need to.

"There's hope the situation will stabilise before we arrive," Gall said, eyes flicking across the message. "But it's tenuous. If the defences fail, Earth-based teams are ordered to avoid Venor entirely."

A heavy silence followed.

General Hollins stepped forward. "We're not abandoning Venor."

He let the words hang, then continued. "I know the directive. I know the risks. But we didn't come this far to watch from orbit while a world burns. If things deteriorate, we'll adapt. We'll assist. We'll stand with them."

He turned to the crew. "No more tests on the *Excalibur*. Everyone to his or her station. Solara, enter the coordinates for Venor."

Solara nodded, fingers already moving.

The general's voice softened. "Venor isn't just a name on a chart. It's a promise. And I intend to keep it."

"Even at this speed, we won't reach Venor for weeks," Paige noted.

"Engage the D-shift," Hollins ordered.

Stuart activated the drive. The vibration vanished as the ship slipped out of warp and into D-Space.

For hours, the *Excalibur* glided through the void. There was no sense of motion, only lights streaming past the windows, colors fading into the dark behind them.

Aurelia broke the silence. "Approaching the Venor system."

Stuart eased the ship's speed. A ripple of turbulent energy cascaded through space. A low hum built, subtle at first, then rising into a bone-deep vibration that pulsed through the hull.

Excalibur pressed against the fabric of space like a tidal surge. Then, with a burst of light, it tore free from D-Space, a brilliant fracture across the black sky.

On the Korrathi command vessel, alarms chirped. Scanner arrays pulsed. A spike lit up on the tactical grid.

"There's a large space distortion," an officer said urgently. "Something's coming through."

"Sir, it's appearing at the edge of the Venoran system."

The commander leaned in, watching space twist unnaturally, as if reality itself were peeling back.

"It's a ship," he breathed. "Larger than three of our motherships combined."

He stepped forward, breath catching. The air felt heavier, charged. He gripped the console, talons sinking into the reinforced fabric.

"Report," he barked, though his voice trembled.

“The vessel... it just warped into local space. Energy readings are off the scale. We have no record of anything this size.”

“Notify the fleet,” the commander said. “Let them know it’s here.”

Battle for Venor

Personal account: Sarah Kane

"It didn't look good. Our long-range scanners painted a grim picture of Korrathi ships swarming the planet like a dark tide. Atmospheric sensors flagged the massive pressure spikes of Korrathi ships breaching the shield, their supersonic wakes likely shattering every window for miles. Civilian transports appeared as desperate, flickering icons on scanners, streaking upward in escape attempts; some blipped out of existence while others cleared the atmosphere. We were the last hope."

***

A hole in space opened as *Excalibur* decreased slide speed and slowed to sublight. "Outer fringes of the Venoran system," Stuart reported, his hands moving over the controls with the kind of casual precision that came from years in the seat. *Excalibur* eased out of D-Space in a seamless glide, announcing its arrival in its own quiet way.

A quiet settled over the bridge, the kind that comes when everyone knows things are about to get serious. Hollins noticed it in the way people sat a little straighter and stopped fidgeting. Even the usual background hum felt muted, like the ship was waiting with them.

"Sarah, what do our long-range sensors show?" asked the general.

She focused intently on her display, the crimson sun of Venor looming ominously before them, casting an eerie glow across the bridge. With a touch, the large screen flickered to life, revealing a chaotic swarm of vessels circling the planet like predatory birds of prey.

The scale of the mess hit them immediately. Venor was barely holding together. Burned-out hulls drifted in orbit, defence lines flickered in and out, and the whole system looked strained to its limit. Hollins let out a slow breath, taking in just how bad it was.

"Opening the tactical display, sir," she replied, her voice crisp as she activated the interface.

The screen displayed a comprehensive list of all ships detected in the vicinity, each entry accompanied by detailed descriptions, including ship dimensions, crew capacity, armament specifications, and species affiliations. As she relayed her findings to the general, she continued scrolling until her display abruptly flagged a new development, prompting her to pause.

"Sir, I'm detecting a secondary Korrathi fleet. They will arrive in approximately one hour. Analysis reveals significant numbers of ships with various configurations. Currently, the Venorans have 90 fighters and 20 battleships at their disposal."

Stuart's voice cut in. "General, five Korrathi battleships are attempting to breach the atmosphere. The Venoran planetary defence shields are holding, for now."

"Let's see what *Excalibur* can do." His gaze swept the tactical display; clusters of Venoran defence units lit up in blue, Korrathi formations pressing in red. The odds were shifting, and not in their favour. He felt it in the silence between updates, in the weight behind each flicker of movement on the screen.

Excalibur was built for moments like this. Advanced systems, overwhelming weapons; she was their best shot at turning the tide.

As the colossal spacecraft moved towards the planet Venor, it was confronted by two sleek Venoran ships, darting through space like predators on the hunt. Without a moment's pause, both vessels unleashed a hail of energy blasts, their weapons illuminating the dark void with fierce, vivid bursts of light. Their blasts pounded against *Excalibur's* fortified hull, dissipating harmlessly against its shields.

"Hold your fire!" a commanding voice filled the channel. This is Captain Gall of the Venoran ship, the *Arcadia*. "I have the new Earth team with me!"

The assault halted abruptly. Silence pressed on, then the comm link flickered to life. A man's face filled *Excalibur's* main display. His beard was coarse, just beginning to show flecks of grey, framing a face marked more by experience than age. His skin was taut, his features sharp, blue eyes fixed and unblinking, with unsettling clarity.

He held the silence like a seasoned negotiator, calm and deliberate. There was no bravado, no threat, just a quiet confidence, as if he'd already run the calculations and knew exactly how this would unfold.

"This is Captain James Dunne," he announced, his strong Irish brogue resonating with warmth and authority. "Please accept our sincerest apologies for the misunderstanding. I trust your impressive vessel sustained no damage. We've got a couple of Canadians here, bless their hearts, who are a tad too eager on the trigger. You can understand our hasty reaction. We were not informed of your expected arrival."

General Hollins leaned forward, steady and composed. "Apologies accepted," replied the General, his demeanour steady amidst the tension. "We have just been in contact with Venor, and our scanners have accounted for all vessels in the vicinity."

Captain Dunne offered a wry smile. "Ah, you can imagine the state we are in; we've had quite a bit of action lately. You appeared as just another alien ship among the chaos. And to whom do I have the distinct pleasure of speaking?"

"This is General George Hollins of the *Excalibur*," he introduced himself. "We also have the *Arcadia* and its crew. What is your status?"

"It's grand to make your acquaintance," Dunne responded, though the enormity of the situation was evident in his eyes. "As ye can see, we find ourselves in a bit of a pickle. The planet's shields are faltering in several areas, necessitating urgent repairs to the shield generators. We have already lost a few ships in the fray. I do hope you might lend us a hand in this predicament," the captain implored, his voice a mix of hope and urgency.

The general exchanged a glance with his tactical officers before offering a resolute response. "Captain," the General replied the *Excalibur* was built to be the center of attention. Let's see what damage we can cause. Besides, we have been itching to try this ship out."

Captain Dunne arched an eyebrow. "Doesn't look like anything the Venorans have. Where exactly did you pick this beast up?"

The general allowed himself a small smirk. "I'll explain later. For now, let's see what damage we can cause."

"Gall, you'd better move your ship clear," Hollins warned. "*Excalibur's* going to be in the thick of it. I reckon we'll be drawing plenty of attention."

The *Arcadia* slipped out of *Excalibur's* hangar bay with practised ease, far more gracefully than during its tense arrival. Its engines hummed low as it angled toward Venor, positioning itself just beyond the perimeter of the defence fleet. Its mission was clear: intercept any Korrathi fighters that managed to break through.

"All stations, prepare to engage," the General commanded, his tone leaving no room for hesitation. "Tactical teams target Korrathi vessels attempting to breach the atmosphere. Fire at will."

The *Excalibur* didn't just move; it skipped through space, vanishing and reappearing only a few kilometres from the enemy formations. Venoran forces now moved to flank their new ally, while Korrathi warships regrouped, uncertain but preparing to attack the unexpected fortress in their midst.

Meanwhile, Lieutenant Stacey Morgan, one of the Canadian-Venoran pilots who had participated in the initial strike on the *Excalibur*, watched the massive vessel in motion with narrowed eyes, not out of doubt, but sheer astonishment.

"Dunne, are we absolutely certain they're with us?" she asked, still tracking *Excalibur* on her screen. "You saw the size of that thing. That's beyond anything Earth's ever built."

Dunne nodded, his tone steady. "I know we need all the help we can get; besides, they're human."

Stacey exchanged a glance with her squadmate. "Liam, are you online?"

"Yeah," Liam replied, his voice tinged with awe. "We just fired on that thing a minute ago... and now it's about to save our asses."

Stacey exhaled, her grip tightening on the controls. "Let's make sure we earn it."

On the bridge of the *Excalibur*, General Hollins eyed the tactical display. "Stacey and Liam, I need you to intercept those enemy bombers."

Stacey hesitated for half a beat, then saw Dunn's approval flash across her comms. She nodded, voice clear and confident.

"Copy that, *Excalibur*. Engaging now."

The Venoran ships banked hard, engines flaring as they dove into the fight. Their hulls caught the glare of weapons fire, slicing through space with sharp, deliberate movements. Stacey and Liam dropped into formation mid-flight, their fighters syncing with the Venoran squadron like muscle memory.

"Targeting grid locked," Liam muttered, fingers flying across his console. "We've got incoming... three, maybe four squadrons breaking left."

Stacey's HUD lit up with red markers. Her pulse thudded in her chest, but her voice stayed calm. "Copy. Let's clear a lane."

The Venoran pilots moved with brutal efficiency. Pushing through Korrathi formations, scattering enemy fighters in bursts of plasma and flame. The comms buzzed with clipped orders, static, and the occasional shout of warning or victory.

Stacey rolled her fighter, locking onto a Korrathi interceptor. Her HUD blinked red, then green. "*Excalibur* just cleared a lane. Let's make sure we earn it. Tail the big girl and pour it on!"

"Fox three," she said, releasing a missile. The enemy ship vanished in a flash of white light.

Liam's voice came through, breathless. "That's two down. You good?"

"Still flying," Stacey replied, scanning the chaos ahead. "Let's make sure they don't reach the fleet."

The tide of the battle was beginning to shift. The alliance of Venoran, Terran, and now *Excalibur* was throwing the Korrathi ranks into disarray.

Aboard the *Excalibur*, the crew moved like clockwork. Orders snapped through the comms, hands flew across consoles, and the ship's systems surged to life. Energy beams and plasma pulses tore into the void, each shot precise, each impact devastating.

Energy flared across the Korrathi flagship's forward viewscreen as *Excalibur's* barrage intensified, each blast painting the bridge in violent pulses of white and blue. Officers scrambled at their stations, claws tapping frantically against overheating consoles.

"That fire pattern, it's coming from every vector!" the sensor officer shouted, the hair on his neck standing up.

Another impact rattled the deck, sending a tremor through the command dais. “Shields can’t compensate, Commander!” the helm officer growled.

Commander Vorthak leaned forward, eyes narrowing at the sight of *Excalibur* cutting through the void like a living weapon. “No Venoran ship has that much power.” A fresh volley slammed into them, and the bridge lights flickered.

“Commander... they’re targeting us again!” the gunnery chief warned. Vorthak’s jaw tightened, the muscles along his neck rigid with defiance he no longer fully felt. “We hold,” he said, forcing the words out. “The rest of the fleet is on its way.”

The barrage didn’t let up. Within moments, the Korrathi assault on Venor began to crumble under the sheer force of *Excalibur’s* firepower.

General Hollins stood silent, eyes locked on the tactical display. He didn’t speak. He didn’t need to. The hum of *Excalibur’s* systems said it all.

Excalibur surged forward, cutting a path through the chaos as it placed itself directly in the path of the Korrathi fleet, its massive form dwarfing even their largest ships. For the first time, the Korrathi saw it up close... the sheer scale of its weaponry was impossible to ignore.

A ripple of hesitation passed through their ranks.

Then, the shift came. Their weapons locked onto *Excalibur*. The battle was about to begin.

“Incoming enemy fighters!” Sarah called out.

The tactical display lit up, red blips swarming toward them as *Excalibur* was engulfed in a barrage of Korrathi fire. The shields flared, absorbing the hits, casting the battlefield in a haze of light and distortion.

“Lock on targets and fire,” Hollins ordered.

Excalibur's cannons roared, unleashing a storm of laser fire. Don activated the fusion lance. Four vertical emitters extended from the hull, each pulsing with raw energy. A moment later, they fired, merging into a single particle beam that tore through the Korrathi fighters, shredding them mid-flight.

"General, there's a larger formation inbound," Solara reported, eyes fixed on the tactical display.

Excalibur pressed forward, unfazed by the carnage. Fighters that came too close were vaporised against its shields. Plasma cannons fired in rhythmic bursts, carving through enemy lines.

"We've got some coming in from the rear!" Stuart shouted.

"I see them," Sarah replied, cool and focused. She activated the rear laser cannons. Blazing spheres of energy erupted from each turret, vapourising them instantly.

The few remaining Korrathi fighters broke off, retreating to their main battle group. Others continued their assault on Venor.

"Sarah, open a channel to the Korrathi fleet," Hollins said, his voice calm but firm.

"Channel open," she replied, fingers moving across the console.

"This is the Terran ship *Excalibur*," Hollins announced. "If you continue attacking Venor, we will inflict far greater damage on the rest of your fleet."

Silence.

No response from the Korrathi.

As *Excalibur* moved into the heart of battle, its fighters launched in perfect formation, sleek vessels cutting through the void like razors of light. "Stuart, dispatch a squadron of fighters," General Hollins ordered. "Sarah, coordinate with the Venoran pilots for the joint operation."

For the Venoran pilots, Stacey and Liam, the shift was abrupt. Minutes earlier, they'd opened fire on *Excalibur*, mistaking the Terran warship for a threat. Now, they were flying in formation with their fleet, trusting the very vessel they'd targeted to help turn the tide against the Korrathi offensive. "This is insane," Liam said over comms as he locked onto a Korrathi interceptor. "We tried to blast these guys out of the sky five minutes ago."

"Focus, Carter," Stacey snapped, her ship banking hard to dodge incoming fire. "They're here to save Venor. We don't have time for debates."

The dogfights intensified as the Venoran and *Excalibur* squadrons clashed with the Korrathi forces. Stacey quickly noticed a startling difference; while Venoran ships had to rely on agility and precision to evade enemy fire, *Excalibur's* fighters tore through battle with near invulnerability. Their armour plating repelled plasma blasts like rain against steel.

Nearby, Kayla, one of *Excalibur's* pilots, grinned as she dodged a barrage, watching the enemy fire bounce harmlessly off her hull. "Will you look at that? Not a scratch!" she shouted, exhilarated.

Stacey cursed under her breath. "We're not that lucky. If a blast hits us, we're done."

"Then let's not get hit," Liam responded, boosting his thrusters as he weaved through enemy fire.

Despite their technological disadvantage with *Excalibur's* fighters, the Venoran pilots relied on years of experience, fighting with unmatched precision. Stacey and Liam took point, cutting through the enemy ranks with expert manoeuvres, eliminating Korrathi bombers before they could breach Venor's shields.

From the bridge, General Hollins observed the battlefield. "Don, focus the particle beam on the Korrathi carriers hanging back."

The energy surge was immediate, a catastrophic arc of destruction that ripped through four enemy carriers in seconds.

As *Excalibur* unleashed its first barrage against the Korrathi fleet, Stacey, Liam, and Captain Dunne watched in stunned silence. Plasma pulses roared through the void, obliterating enemy fighters in waves of searing destruction. The ship's particle beams fired next, a catastrophic arc of energy that sliced through Korrathi carriers like paper, reducing them to scattered debris.

"Ah, bejesus," Dunne muttered, his sharp blue eyes widening. "I knew she looked powerful, but that... that's a different beast entirely."

Stacey barely had time to process what she was seeing. She had spent years in combat, flying against overwhelming odds with nothing but skill to rely on. Now, here was this massive Terran warship casually tearing through the enemy with firepower unlike anything she had ever witnessed.

"Carter, did you see that?" she called over comms.

"Yeah," Liam replied, weaving through the chaos in his fighter. "That power is something else."

Stacey and Liam fell into formation with *Excalibur's* fighters, working alongside them as Venoran and Terran forces began systematically dismantling the Korrathi fleet.

Dunne, still watching from the *Arcadia*, let out a low whistle. "Sweet saints above, General, remind me never to cross you."

From the command deck, Hollins watched the destruction unfold. A flicker of satisfaction crossed his face; a brief, restrained smirk. With a chuckle, he replied, "Good job we are on the same side then."

The battle was far from over, but for the first time, the Venoran pilots felt something unfamiliar: a fighting chance.

As more Venoran and *Excalibur* fighters synchronised their attacks, the Korrathi fleet faltered. Victory was now within reach.

"General, more Korrathi ships are coming out of Slide Space," Solara reported, her eyes widening as new blips appeared on the tactical display.

With the arrival of new reinforcements bolstering their ranks, the Korrathi quickly countered. More carriers and battlecruisers began to materialise, each deploying a fresh wave of fighters to join the fray. This time, the Korrathi changed their tactics, staggering their locations and strategically hiding among the debris. As the Venoran ships approached, they were ambushed by Korrathi fighters lying in wait.

From their defensive positions, the Korrathi ships opened fire on the Venoran ships, inflicting significant damage. As the battle intensified, *Excalibur's* crew knew they had to adapt quickly to the evolving situation. This was their first real battle, but despite the fear and uncertainty, they drew strength from one another, determined to protect Venor.

Suddenly, alarms blared, a deep, resonating warning that sent a chill through the bridge.

"Sir, we're detecting an anomaly!" Sarah's voice crackled with urgency. "Massive energy surge from the planet's surface!"

The battlefield ignited.

A blinding column of pure energy erupted from Venor, lancing through space like a sword forged by the cosmos itself. It struck the Korrathi battleships with unimaginable force, sending shockwaves that rippled through their formations. Ships spiralled, their systems overloaded, their formations breaking apart as chaos overtook them.

"What in blazes was that?" The general demanded, his shock tempered only by instinct.

Sarah's fingers flew over the controls, analysing the incoming data. "We have a message from Venor," her voice steadied as she relayed the information. "It appears the Venorans have activated an ancient defence mechanism called the Guardian. It's generating a powerful energy field, disrupting the Korrathi ships."

Gall's eyes widened. "I thought it was just a legend. If we can control that power, we might have a chance." His voice was thick with awe, but urgency pushed him forward. "General, the Guardian is an ancient weapon of my ancestors, which will buy us time, but we must act quickly to repel the Korrathi forces while it recharges."

The general nodded, his mind racing. "Inform all units to maintain their positions. We need to capitalise on this opening. We end this now."

Gall took a sharp breath before speaking; his words rushed but steady. "The Guardian was built in secret by the greatest minds. Thousands of years ago, we were a thriving civilisation, but we faced relentless threats from hostile alien species. To protect Venor, our ancestors constructed a defence unlike anything seen before."

His voice deepened as he continued. "The Guardian generates a colossal energy field, strong enough to disable entire fleets. It is powered by a rare element found deep within Venor's core, making it nearly impossible to replicate. My people embedded it within the planet's crust, its existence concealed for millennia."

The general didn't let him finish. His eyes burned with determination as he snapped out a command. "All ships, focus fire on the Korrathi battleships. Let's drive them back!"

Energy rippled through the bridge. The general's body tensed, as he leaned forward, gripping the edge of the console. He could feel the tide had shifted; now was the time to push.

With renewed vigour, the *Excalibur* and Venoran fleets launched a coordinated assault. The battle began to turn as the Korrathi ships struggled against the unexpected power of the Guardian.

As the Korrathi fleet struggled to regain its composure, the combined forces of the *Excalibur* and Venoran fighters pressed their advantage. *Excalibur's* turrets continued to unleash devastating plasma pulses, while Venoran ships executed precise strikes against the now disorganised Korrathi fighters.

Stuart, monitoring the rear sensors, shouted over the background noise of the battle. “More enemy fighters incoming! They’re attempting to regroup.”

The general's resolve hardened. “Sarah, coordinate with the Venoran command. We need to launch a counteroffensive while we have the upper hand.”

Sarah relayed the orders, her fingers flying over the controls. “Understood, General. The Venoran command is mobilising its reserve fighters to join our assault.”

The *Excalibur* and Venoran forces surged forward, their combined firepower overwhelming the Korrathi ranks. Fighter squadrons wove through the battlefield, exploiting gaps in the enemy’s defences created by the planetary weapon’s devastating strike. As the battle raged on, *Excalibur* and her crew knew this was their moment to break the enemy's advance.

“General,” said Dave, “just throwing this out there. Can we use the D-shift to flank the Korrathi carriers?”

The general frowned, his brow furrowing deeply as he considered the suggestion. He crossed his arms, his mind racing through the tactical implications and potential risks. His fingers tapped against a bicep in a rhythmic, thoughtful pattern.

“We don’t have the space to build the necessary speed for the manoeuvre,” he replied, his voice tinged with frustration.

Paige interrupts. She leans forward, her eyes alight with determination and excitement. “We can make room, though. If we use the warp drive and head to the Venoran sun, we can slingshot *Excalibur* around and back toward Venor. This would give us enough momentum to engage the D-shift.”

Her words came out in a rush, and she pointed to the tactical display with a sense of urgency. Solara, standing beside her, nodded in agreement, her fingers flying over the console as she programmed the course.

"Let's do it, Stuart and Sarah; get ready to fire once we materialise," said the General.

Excalibur turned, and immediately Galls' voice crackled over the comms, "Where are you going?"

"Trying something out, engage the warp engines." The general replied, his voice calm.

The ship entered warp, then everything became a blur as they sped along the coordinates Paige had entered. *Excalibur* arced around the sun, gathering momentum, disappearing as the Trans-Dimensional engine engaged. Moments later, they materialised behind the Korrathi. The particle beams began to take apart the Korrathi carriers, leaving a wide path through their fleet. The Korrathi fighters, caught off guard, appeared to be flying all over the place, seemingly with no direction. *Excalibur* positioned itself between the Venor fighters and Korrathi.

"Let's try again. Open a channel to the Korrathi," ordered the General.

"I do not like to repeat myself; unless you leave this area of space, you will be facing the destruction of your fleet, said the General."

The message hung in the air, the threat clear and unmistakable. *Excalibur's* manoeuvre and decisive attack had shown the Korrathi the strength and determination of their opponents. Now, it was up to the Korrathi fleet to decide its next move.

The combined strength of the Venoran forces and Excalibur's crew hit the Korrathi fleet like a tide they never saw coming. Formations buckled. Command channels filled with static and panic.

What had begun as a confident assault dissolved into scattered, frantic maneuvers as the realization set in... they were outmatched, and badly.

With no orders left to give and no ground left to hold, the surviving Korrathi ships broke away in silence, their drives flaring as they slipped into Slide Space and vanished from the battlefield.

The general issued a general broadcast to the crew, "I think we can all agree they accepted our terms, and that both the flight and weapons tests were a success." There was a quiet thread of satisfaction in his voice.

Cheers erupted around the bridge as the crew celebrated their hard-earned victory. Their bodies relaxed, the tension of battle finally easing as they revelled in their success. They exchanged relieved smiles and congratulatory pats on the back, their camaraderie strengthened by the challenges they had overcome together.

Under the noise, the usual post-battle fatigue crept in. A few crew members leaned back in their chairs, letting the adrenaline drain. Others kept their eyes on the tactical display a moment longer, watching the last Korrathi signals disappear just to be sure. Hollins let a breath, feeling the pressure ease off his shoulders bit by bit.

The General turned toward Dave, Paige, and Solara. "That was a good call, great strategy you guys."

"I think we all need a stiff drink after that," Sarah said, a wry smile on her face.

Solara looked puzzled. "A stiff drink?" She questioned, her brow furrowing in confusion.

Dave leaned over to her and said with a chuckle, "I'll explain later."

After everyone had taken a break, it was back to work as usual. The atmosphere on the bridge had shifted from tense to more relaxed.

Outside the glass, the orbit was a mess of metal and memory. Rescue craft picked their way through the shattered remains of ships, their spotlights cutting through the dark, while the planetary shields pulsed with a weak, uneven rhythm. This wasn't a clean win... not by a long shot. Hollins watched a piece of debris drift past, took a slow, steadying breath, and turned back to the bridge. The war wasn't over yet.

"Solara, have the ship's systems checked for any damage; we received a lot of hits."

"Yes, sir."

Dave's voice crackled over the comms. "General, look out the window at the ship's hull."

The general walked over to the window, his curiosity piqued. He observed small robots flying around the ship's hull, diligently inspecting and repairing any damage that had occurred. "What are those?" he asked, his brow furrowing in surprise.

"That's our external repair crew. When the systems check was activated, an automated command was sent to them, and they popped out of various sections of the hull to check for damage and make any repairs," Dave explained, a hint of pride in his voice.

The general responded with a smile, "This ship certainly has everything."

Solara turned from her console, her expression shifting as she addressed the general. "Sir, we've received a communication from Gall. He's calling from Venor."

General Hollins straightened, a flicker of anticipation crossing his features as he opened the channel.

"Our command central extends an invitation to everyone aboard *Excalibur*. We want to discuss what the future holds for your crew. The citizens of Venor are eagerly awaiting your arrival. They want to meet you in person to see the faces of those who fought beside them."

The general let his gaze sweep across the bridge as his crew listened. This war had demanded everything from them: tireless vigilance and the weight of the unknown pressing down. Now, at last, a moment of respite.

He exhaled slowly before replying. "Give us two hours to clean up, Gall, and we'll join you. These old-timers have been on constant alert for over a year; consider this a well-earned furlough."

A ripple of relief moved through the bridge. After months of tension and uncertainty, the prospect of stepping onto solid ground, onto Venor itself, was almost surreal. Meeting the people and seeing the planet they had fought to protect felt like the first step toward something more than survival.

Conversations across the command deck turned lighter, tinged with cautious excitement as preparations began. The weight of the battle still hung in the air, but the mood had shifted; they weren't just looking toward the next jump. They were looking toward the end of the war itself.

Shore Leave on Venor

Personal account: Sarah Kane

"Finally, a few days of relaxation. After everything we have gone through with the Venorans, the firefights, the evacuations, the nights we stayed awake because the scanners wouldn't stop blinking, it almost doesn't feel real. The ground under our boots isn't metal anymore. It's earth. Their earth. Soon, battle plans for the next stage of the war will be drawn. But right now... right now I'm letting myself enjoy this."

***

The crew materialised in a golden shimmer, the transporter beam fading, revealing the Command Central building, where a massive gathering of Venorans stood waiting.

At the forefront stood a face they knew well... Patrasia, the one who had been with them from the very beginning. With a warm, steady smile, she stepped forward and greeted the newcomers. "On behalf of everyone here on Venor, welcome. We are honoured to have you with us."

It was clear that they saw the arrival of the *Excalibur* crew as a pivotal moment for their future.

The crew exchanged glances, their excitement unmistakable. Everything they had endured, from first contact with an alien civilisation to the shock of being given a second life and the discoveries they made on their journey to Venor, had shaped them in ways none of them could have imagined. It had been an adventure unlike anything they had ever known.

Sarah caught her breath, scanning the faces before her, noting the flickers of hope and curiosity dancing in the Venoran eyes.

Patrasia continued, her voice carrying a tone of genuine warmth.

"We will be holding the meeting in the building behind you, but first, you have a couple of hours to wander the city. Please take this time to rest and explore."

Above them, they could see what were once pristine buildings that now bore the scars of the fierce battle that had raged above. Skyscrapers, which had once reached proudly towards the sky, now had gaping holes and scorched facades. Streets were littered with debris from collapsed buildings and shattered glass. The air was thick with the smell of smoke and the faint hum of emergency sirens.

Despite the damage, the Venorans were already hard at work, determined to rebuild. Teams of engineers and medics moved swiftly through the streets, tending to the wounded and assessing structural damage. They saw Venoran civilians providing aid to those in need. Worker bots moved from building to building, repairing structures. They could see buildings being completed before their eyes, just as the retirement home had been built.

At the heart of the central plaza, a massive statue stood partially destroyed, its once-flawless form fractured, yet still undeniably regal. A symbol of Venoran unity, it had weathered the worst, and like the people it stood for, it refused to fall. And then, there was The Guardian.

Its presence lingered. Not just as a weapon, but as a protector. The energy field it had left behind shimmered faintly, twisting in the air like a whisper of power. It had crippled the Korrathi fleet, saved lives, preserved the very heart of Venor, and even now, its residual force hummed beneath their feet, as if the planet itself refused to let go of its shield.

Crimson light fell from the red sun, washing the city in a glow that was both eerie and breathtaking.

Sarah was walking with Kayla and a group of engineers, taking in the lighter gravity and the surreal glow of Venor's red sun. "With everything happening so fast from the moment we entered the Venoran system, we never got to see their world properly," she murmured.

"I never considered the effect their red sun would have on everything," she added, her tone reverent as she watched the light ripple across the city. Around them, alien species mingled with a large contingent of humans, all moving through the recovering streets.

Just then, Don drifted past, placing a hand on Sarah's shoulder as he floated by with a wide grin. "I feel like I'm gliding," he said, half laughing. "Solara had told us that Venorans class Earth as a heavy-gravity planet, but I didn't really get it until now. The moment our boots hit the ground, everything felt lighter, our breathing a little easier," he said.

He was already half-floating beside them, grinning like he'd just discovered a new superpower. Sarah looked up at him with a smile and said, "The gravity is lighter here than on Earth; you need to turn on your gravity suit."

"Not for a while, I can cover more of the city like this," said Don, laughing.

Seeing him enjoying himself, Sarah switched off her gravity suit and joined Don on his walk around the city. The sensation of the lighter gravity was immediately noticeable. Each step felt springier, and they were able to glide effortlessly over the ground.

Sarah felt an exhilarating sense of freedom as she moved through the city. The reduced gravitational pull made every step feel buoyant, as if she were walking on a cushioned surface. Her muscles loosened, her body light and agile. The novelty of it all brought a smile to her face, and she couldn't help but laugh.

The cityscape of Venor was unlike anything they had seen before. The architecture was a blend of sleek, futuristic design and organic shapes, with buildings that seemed to flow and pulse with a life of their own. Street vendors were setting up among the chaos of damaged buildings, selling exotic foods and trinkets, while holographic signs advertised various goods in an array of alien languages.

A low hum filled the air, from many types of machinery. Drones hovered as alien species mingled, each contributing to the slow, deliberate healing of the city. The glow from the red sun shimmered across the landscape, giving the city a surreal and almost dreamlike quality.

As the General, Dave, Paige, and Solara strolled through the city, they noticed Sarah and Don walking towards them.

The general's face lit up with a genuine smile as he saw Sarah and Don. He had rarely seen his crew so relaxed and happy since leaving Earth. The sight of them enjoying themselves brought a sense of relief to him. "Looks like you two are having fun," he remarked warmly.

Dave chuckled, noting the spring in Sarah and Don's steps. "I see you've discovered the joys of lighter gravity," he said, grinning. He observed the team's high spirits with a faint smile, the camaraderie settling over him like warmth after a long, cold stretch.

Paige's eyes twinkled with amusement as she observed the scene. "You guys look like kids on a playground," she teased, her tone light and playful. It was refreshing to see everyone's morale lifted after the intense battles they had faced.

Solara tilted her head slightly, a curious expression on her face. She had always been fascinated by new experiences, and seeing her crew members adapt to the new environment intrigued her. "How does it feel to walk without the gravity suits?" She asked, genuinely interested.

Sarah laughed, her eyes sparkling with excitement. "It's amazing! Everything feels so light and effortless. It's like we're floating on air," she replied, her enthusiasm infectious.

Don nodded in agreement, a broad smile on his face. "I haven't felt this relaxed in ages. It's a nice change from the constant tension we've been under," he added, his voice filled with contentment.

For a brief moment, amidst the ongoing conflict, they found solace and joy in the simple act of exploring this new world. It was a reminder of what they were fighting for... a chance to preserve a way of life for many races.

Later that day, the *Excalibur* crew met with the council members. During the meeting, participants discussed the Korrathi occupation of multiple planets and emphasised the urgent need for our support in reclaiming them.

The leader of the Venoran council stood before them, his expression etched with the weight of countless battles, sacrifices, and desperate hope. His voice, steady but brimming with restrained intensity, filled the room.

"For many cycles, we have strategised and mobilised resources to build a formidable defence fleet," he began, his piercing gaze sweeping across the assembled crew. Every word felt deliberate, measured, woven with both the exhaustion of war and the resolve to end it.

"It's important to note that for two of Earth's centuries, we have refrained from initiating any attacks on the Korrathi homeworlds, focusing instead on safeguarding our own planets."

There was an undercurrent of unspoken suffering in his tone, a silent acknowledgement of battles fought not just with weapons, but with the will to endure.

"With your help, we can leverage the formidable capabilities of *Excalibur* to liberate our captured planets from Korrathi control."

A beat of silence settled over the room, an almost tangible shift in the air. The *Excalibur* crew exchanged glances, knowing that this mission would alter the balance of power across the sector forever.

"We will launch attacks against their strongholds and resource hubs. Not to annihilate the Korrathi, but to ensure they never attack again."

The tension wound itself through the room like a coiled spring, pressing against every soul in its path. There was no cheering, no immediate response, only an understanding that what had just been spoken was a declaration of intent, of war, of a battle that would define generations to come.

Elsewhere on Venor, the *Excalibur* crew stood beneath a darkening sky, watching the wounded planet stir with faint signs of renewal.

Excalibur hadn't come out of the battle unscathed; that much was clear. It had taken a few solid hits, enough to leave some sections under real strain, but most of the damage was just scrapes, scorch marks, and dents. Compared to the Venoran ships that limped away with fractured hulls and failing systems, Excalibur had gotten off lightly. Their vessels were hurting in ways that would take weeks to mend, while *Excalibur's* wounds were mostly skin-deep.

Venor's cities also bore the relentless pace of reconstruction. Many buildings now stood tall once more, their structures nearly flawless, as if time had reset itself, but the scars remained in ways only those who had lived through the battle would truly see. The city plaza, once battered, now gleamed, its polished exterior masking the horrors that had unfolded there.

After five cycles, the moment arrived... *Excalibur* was ready.

Preparations for the liberation of the Venoran worlds had begun. Fleets to be mobilised in 10 cycles, and for the first time in centuries, the tide was about to turn.

Exploring Dimensional Space

Personal account: Donald Northey

"Well, Dave's done it again, found a new way to push the limits. This time, he wants to send us into another dimension. You've got to hand it to him... the man doesn't lack imagination. Sometimes I wonder if he dreams this stuff up just to see how far we'll go."

***

Dave walked into the general's office. "Do you have a second?"

The general turned away from the monitor, narrowing his gaze. "Sure, what's on your mind?"

Dave leaned against the console, tapping the screen with two fingers, eyes fixed on the data stream. "We've been running the Dimensional Shift engine long enough to master its quirks," he said. "But we never linger in D-Space. Just jump from point A to point B."

He paused, gaze drifting toward the viewport. "Every time we jump, I see the Spectral Drift distortions flaring outside the hull." He raised his hands, fingers curling into air quotes. "Flashes of colour."

Then, in a quieter tone: "I used to write them off as turbulence. But the more I analyse them... the more they look like patterns. Structured. Intentional."

The general's expression hardened. "Patterns?"

Dave nodded. "Energy fluctuations that repeat, never identical, but follow an underlying order. I checked my calculations against previous jumps, and I even consulted with my Venoran counterpart. She sees it too. Something exists in D-Space, something we're passing through without ever truly seeing. We think it's the edge of a physical dimension."

The general stared back at Dave with raised eyebrows. "And to confirm this theory, you want to stop mid-jump."

Dave took a deep breath. "Yes. But stopping isn't easy. We have to generate a stabilisation field to keep the ship from being ejected unpredictably. The field is nearly ready, but... there's a 1% chance something unforeseen happens."

The General exhaled, considering. "Unforeseen forces in an uncharted dimension." He shook his head slightly. "Small risks can become disasters."

"Or discoveries," Dave countered. "What if D-Space isn't just a transit medium? What if it's an ecosystem, a parallel layer of reality we've overlooked? What if something is watching us pass by?"

Silence hung between them.

Finally, the general drew himself upright. "I won't make this decision alone. The crew needs a say. Prepare a full briefing, run a presentation and broadcast it ship-wide."

The vote came in, and one cycle later, Dave met with the general again.

"Well," the General said, a slow smile forming. "Your test is confirmed. The vote was unanimous. They're all in."

Dave felt a rush of exhilaration as he left the room, punching the air in triumph.

As the next cycle commenced, the General's voice rang through the ship's intercom, measured and commanding. "Attention everyone. We are about to embark on a journey into another dimension. Please proceed to your designated posts. Stuart, initiate preparations for D-Space travel."

The *Excalibur* began its slow departure from Venor, its sleek frame gliding away from the planet's gravitational hold. In the command centre, Stuart was already in motion. His posture was taut with focus as his hands swept across the console, fingers activating systems with practised ease. Panels flickered to life. Lights blinked in a rhythmic sequence. The warp drive was humming, waiting.

Stuart's gaze danced between monitors and gauges. The ship's fate now rested in his hands. He leaned forward, a subtle shift that signalled both control and anticipation. There was a spark in his eyes, not recklessness, but wonder.

"Engaging warp drive. Warp 4... Warp 7... Warp 9. Energising the Trans-Dimensional engines," Stuart called out. "Light her up."

As *Excalibur* surged toward the dimensional breach, the view beyond its observation windows shifted into something otherworldly, a swirling fusion of coloured layers from the universe they were leaving behind.

Stars that streaked past like spectral fireflies caught in the wake of acceleration. The familiar blackness of deep space fractured into layers, each shimmering with faint, iridescent patterns. Constellations twisted unnaturally, stretched by gravitational tides as if they were protesting their abandonment. Planetary bodies appeared to ripple in and out of focus, as though reality itself was folding.

Then, the cosmic backdrop began to blur. What had been recognisable stars and nebulae now slowly gave way to distortion. Light no longer behaved. It bent inward, around the edges of the ship's window frames, glowing with hues the human eye struggled to name. Shapes flattened. Depth flattened. It was like falling forward through a two-dimensional painting of the universe into emptiness.

In the final moment before full transition, every colour dimmed into grayscale. Outside the ship, the boundary of space appeared as a seamless veil of soft white light, pulsating faintly like a slow heartbeat. The last breath of their home dimension as they crossed over.

An electric tension filled the air. The crew held its breath as the fabric of space unfolded around them, revealing a realm untouched by human eyes. Colours swirled outside the hull like living auroras, casting dancing shadows across the interior. D-Space was not empty; it was kinetic, spectral, alive.

Dave's voice broke through the awe. "Stabilisation fields are active. Stuart, disengage the Trans-Dimensional engines."

As the ship steadied, the crew slowly found words, muted gasps, some talking to each other. Outside, stars shimmered in impossible hues against a vast blue ether. Some pulsed in gentle patterns. Others spun with solemn gravity around titanic black holes, anchors of cosmic truth.

"Let us not be too ambitious," the General warned, his gaze locked on the swirling galaxies. "Advance slowly. Monitor all systems."

For the next hour, the crew worked in quiet synchrony. Dave monitored diagnostics with unerring focus, eventually reporting, "All systems normal."

One crew member looked up from their display, eyes wide. "Star charts are updating rapidly. We've mapped nearly twenty light-years. That blue field resembles dark matter. Our systems can handle it."

The General glanced towards Dave, who nodded, verifying the data.

"Stuart," the General said, voice low but resolute, "let's see what this place is made of. Proceed at low warp."

Two hours into their silent glide, Stuart's voice echoed with subtle urgency. "I'm detecting a life sign. Half a light-year ahead."

Excalibur slowly approached the location where the life sign had been detected, just as something emerged from behind a large asteroid. A colossal, slow-moving creature floating through space, its mouth latching onto large segments of asteroids. The segments seemed to melt into its mouth, and its body shimmered with a bioluminescent glow, illuminating it against the backdrop of stars as it digested the space debris. The creature's skin was covered in a thick, armour-like exoskeleton. Its complex digestive system dissolved the asteroids into basic elements, which it used to sustain itself. This process also released a unique form of energy that enabled it to propel itself through space like a cosmic wanderer.

"General, there's another one!" Stuart exclaimed, pointing towards the viewport. "This one looks much smaller, like a younger version."

The young creature followed the larger one, mimicking its movements and feeding on the smaller debris left behind. The crew observed both creatures for a while, fascinated by the bond between them, before moving on.

The *Excalibur* flew further into the alien expanse. Each discovery felt as if they were in a dream and experiencing it unfold. They encountered a binary star system, its twin suns locked in a gravitational ballet, casting erratic shadows across scattered planets. These worlds spun in eccentric orbits, distant and inhospitable, their surfaces scorched on one side and frozen on the other, caught in the unpredictable pull of their dual stars.

In another star system, they came upon glass worlds. The crew gazed in silent wonder as the ship approached a series of crystalline planets, their surfaces etched with vast mirror plains and glassy plateaus. Starfire shimmered across these reflections, refracting into brilliant cascades of light and colour. As solar rays passed through towering crystal formations, rainbows bloomed in shifting patterns that danced across planetary surfaces, mesmerising illusions of motion and depth. The planets gleamed like polished gems adrift in the void, silent and serene. From the ship's vantage, the crystalline planets glistened in space from their sun's reflections, but they weren't entirely lifeless.

Within the refractive landscape, the crew began to notice subtle movements, reflections that shifted independently of the light's trajectory. *Excalibur* adjusted orbit, and magnified scans revealed what at first appeared to be aberrations in the crystal formations... revealing themselves to be primitive crystalline creatures, meandering across these extraordinary worlds.

Their exploration of this universe took them deeper into the expanse, encountering planets wrapped in ceaseless volcanic convulsions. Rivers of molten rock surged across tectonic scars. Mountains belched glowing ash into space, casting copper and crimson hues across the vacuum. From afar, these worlds appeared to burn slowly, their surfaces pulsing in perpetual agony. And yet, there was a primitive beauty in their chaos, a brutal symphony of creation and destruction.

But the final destination silenced the crew when *Excalibur* entered into a shattered graveyard of worlds. The remnants of two obliterated planets hung in the void, monolithic fragments drifting in quiet defiance of time. Massive chunks of stone and mangled metal rotated slowly, a cosmic debris field suspended in black emptiness. It was a vision of ancient violence, devastation frozen mid-motion.

"Sir... this wasn't natural," a crew member said, voice trembling. "The debris field is extensive. All evidence points to a conflict, a battle that ended with annihilation."

Among the fractured remains, the crew began to notice relics, crumbling structures buried in ruin. Twisted spires of metal curled upward like rusted claws. Shattered monuments jutted out from floating islands of stone, their carvings half-erased by time. Each ruin spoke of lost ambition, of civilisations that reached for greatness and fell into dust.

No sound pierced the silence. Only the soft hum of *Excalibur's* engine and the quiet awe of its crew, bearing witness to a war fought long ago.

"General, I've detected a peculiar signal emanating from a star system less than a light-year away," Solara interjected, her brow furrowed with a mix of curiosity and concern.

"Lock onto those coordinates and let's check it out."

Before the helm officer could respond, *Excalibur* lurched forward, a sudden surge, as if seized by something unseen. The inertial dampeners groaned. Lights flickered.

"General!" Stuart shouted from the navigation bay. "I've lost helm control. The ship… it's flying itself."

Excalibur tore through the void, drawn toward the star system like a needle to a magnetic thread.

"There is a planet under attack," Solara announced.

"See if you can take us behind one of those moons." Ordered the general. "I want eyes on the ground, but we stay hidden." Hoping that whoever had seized control of the ship would allow them to do so.

Excalibur instantly obeyed, slipping into the shadow of the twin satellites with eerie precision, with no resistance.

Solara stared at the console. "It's not just responding to the signal," she said. "It's been following it."

"Whoever is down there is asking for help. They are being attacked by beings they call Draconis raiders."

The planet's defenders were not merely standing by. As enemy vessels breached their skies, they launched a devastating counterattack. Lasers of staggering intensity tore through the darkness, each beam a concentrated surge of energy capable of ripping apart metal and vaporising entire sections of hostile ships. Enemy ships that had lost their shielding stood no chance; their hulls dissolved into fiery fragments that scattered across the void like dying stars.

"Paige, get to the bottom of why we lost control. For now, they seem to be the ones in trouble." The general thought for a second before giving the command. "Ok let's lend a hand."

Without hesitation, *Excalibur* surged forward, unleashing a relentless barrage upon the ships besieging the planet. Plasma beams cut through the darkness, carving an opening in the enemy ranks as Don and Sarah worked in sync, navigating the chaos with practised precision.

On board the Draconis fleet's flagship, the sound of alarms shattered the tense atmosphere.

"Commander Ralek! An unidentified ship has just dropped out of warp directly in our sector!" the operator's voice crackled with urgency.

Ralek turned sharply, eyes wide with disbelief. His gaze locked onto the tactical display. A monstrous vessel, unlike anything in their records, was closing in fast. He slammed his fist onto his desk. "What? How did it get so close without detection?"

A second transmission cut through the static. "Two of our motherships have been destroyed! The ship's energy signature matches what we've detected on the planet. But its field is many times stronger."

Ralek's blood ran cold. "Impossible. Their fleet is supposed to be in a distant sector!" He wrestled his emotions down. "Deploy our swarm fighters immediately. We cannot afford to hesitate." His voice was firm, masking the storm brewing inside.

From deep within the enemy's remaining motherships, fighters surged forth, forming a deadly, coordinated assault.

"That's done it," Stuart muttered as *Excalibur's* presence redirected the enemy's fury. "Now they know we are here."

The general issued the command. "Lock on targets." But before Sarah could react, *Excalibur's* weapons system came online.

"Sir...*Excalibur*...it's auto-firing!" Sarah's voice carried a mix of shock and awe.

The Draconis fleet divided up, one half concentrating its fire on *Excalibur*. The other continued its attack on the planet. Brilliant flares erupted along *Excalibur's* hull, absorbing wave after wave of enemy assault. And yet, she pressed forward, cutting through the hostile fleet with ruthless efficiency.

Her lasers, like celestial spears, sliced through the darkness, illuminating the battlefield in stark, unrelenting brilliance.

General, I have just received a visual of a Draconis fighter from the planet. Displayed on the screen was a muscular green alien, smaller than most humans. They moved on four legs, two bearing their weight, the other two trailing behind like dormant limbs poised to spring in the opposite direction. Their faces were narrow and angular, dominated by multilayered eyes that caught the light in shifting colors. Curved antennae rose from their skulls, more like small horns than feelers. Some bore the remnants of wings folded tight against their backs, while others had none at all.

"They look... almost insect-like," Sarah said.

"Send out squadrons one through four. Stuart, take the lead," the General ordered, his voice cutting through the command deck.

From his cockpit, Stuart's voice rang out over comms: "No formations! It makes us too vulnerable. Pair off and support each other. If you lose your wingman, merge with another team."

As *Excalibur's* squadrons entered the fray, their sleek ships darted like meteors, manoeuvring with eerily precise, almost supernatural speed.

The Draconis fighters retaliated in kind, a metallic swarm of destruction. The sheer volume of enemy forces forced every pilot into a battle of endurance.

Through the haze of plasma fire, a transmission broke through.

"Squad leader four here, I've lost two ships. They are returning to the *Excalibur* for repairs. We're regrouping." The pilot's tone was strained but steady.

Though their forces suffered heavy losses, the *Excalibur* squadrons pushed forward, unwavering in their assault. Each blast tore through enemy hulls, igniting the void with bursts of molten metal.

Then Stuart's world detonated.

His wingman's fighter vanished in a sphere of flame, the shockwave rattling Stuart's cockpit. His stomach clenched as the debris scattered past his canopy.

"Dammit...!" He jerked the controls, diving through a crossfire of plasma bolts. Three enemy fighters locked onto him instantly, their targeting beams flickering across his hull.

Warning lights flared crimson across his console. The cockpit shuddered violently as a blast skimmed his left wing, sending a tremor through the frame. Sweat trickled down his temple, catching the glow of the emergency lights. Outside, the stars blurred into streaks as he twisted through the maelstrom.

A voice cut through the static.

"Hang in there, buddy. I've got your six."

Don's ship swooped in from above, banking hard as the trail from his thrusters burnt white. His voice carried calm conviction, underscored by the thrum of his weapons systems cycling to full charge. His targeting screen lit up as he locked onto his target.

With impeccable accuracy, Don fired a plasma burst which, sliced through the darkness, obliterating one of the enemy fighters in a brilliant explosion. He pivoted smoothly, locking onto his next target with a predator's focus, his movements guided by years of instinctive skill. "Two down," he muttered, calm as a surgeon.

Freed from immediate danger, Stuart seized the opening, shifting his attention to the third enemy fighter.

His targeting system locked onto the third fighter. He fired a spread of torpedoes, their glowing trails arcing through the darkness before slamming into the enemy ship. The fighter didn't just explode. It came apart, its frame liquefying in the vacuum before bursting into a kaleidoscope of debris.

Stuart leaned back, adrenaline surging, a wild grin cutting across his face. "Who's your daddy!" he shouted, voice echoing through the cockpit.

The battle raged on with unrelenting intensity, each pilot drawing upon decades of hard-earned experience, their movements an aerial ballet amidst chaos.

The battle raged on, a brutal dance of instinct and training. Excalibur's pilots fought with the discipline forged from years of drills and the raw adaptability that no Draconis doctrine could predict. Slowly, impossibly, the enemy formation began to fracture.

On the Draconis flagship, alarms blared.

"Commander Ralek!" a comms officer cried. "Our pilots are reporting... they can't track the Terran fighters. Their movements don't match any known pattern!"

Ralek's eyes narrowed at the tactical display, watching Excalibur's squadrons twist through the battlefield like phantom shadows. "Explain."

"They change formations constantly," another officer stammered. "They improvise mid-engagement. We can't anticipate them."

"That's impossible," Ralek snapped. "No pilot can adapt that fast."

But the evidence was right there: Excalibur's fighters bending every rule of engagement the Draconis had ever relied on.

And for the first time, Ralek felt something cold settle in his chest.

Ralek felt a cold knot form in his chest. These weren't the same forces he'd encountered on the planet. These pilots fought with a fluidity he had never seen before. He had never faced anything like them.

From her station aboard *Excalibur*, Solara caught a sharp burst of comms traffic, an encrypted signal rising from the planet's surface.

"General, enemy ships have landed. Ground troops are grouping for an attack on a large complex." Solara's voice was firm, unwavering.

The general didn't hesitate. "Send down the troop carriers. As many as we can spare."

Solara stepped forward, her expression unreadable, her voice steady. "I believe I can assist with the ground assault."

The general studied her, searching for hesitation, but he found none. Instead, he saw conviction, an unshakable determination. With a curt nod, he answered, "Okay. Suit up, Solara."

Solara headed towards the docking bay, where a squad of Terran marines snapped to attention. Her boots rang against the steel deck as she loaded her pulse rifle with a fluid, practised motion. She took her place in the line without hesitation. "I'm with Alpha Company," she said simply, locking eyes with the squad leader.

He nodded, but the look he gave her wasn't just respect; it was recognition. They all knew the stories of her ancient past, her race once revered as the Anunnaki, the sky-born gods whose arrival had shifted the course of human evolution. Now, she stepped into the dropship clad in a bio-engineered suit, a relic of alien technology pulsing with embedded code. Some of them had seen her fight before, during the battle on Zeph 3 against the Korrathi. They'd witnessed the transformation, the way her suit amplified her size and strength, allowing her to move like a force of nature beyond any known combat threshold.

The marines shifted uneasily, not from fear, but from the weight of her presence standing among them. A corporal leaned toward his squadmate, voice barely above a breath. "If even half of what they say about her is true... we're walking into this fight already won."

Solara didn't respond. Her gaze swept the hangar with the calm precision of someone who had once looked down from temple spires, judging entire worlds from above. She adjusted a dial on her gauntlet; the interface pulsed with a cold blue glow, threads of light running along the armour as if the suit were breathing with her. It didn't just fit her; it attuned itself to her.

The squad leader stepped forward, boots echoing against the metal deck. "Glad to have you with us, ma'am. If things go sideways planet-side, I'd rather have you watching my back."

A thin smile ghosted beneath Solara's visor. "Then let's make sure they remember why they should fear us."

Excalibur's troop carriers broke through the smoke-choked sky, engines roaring like thunder trapped in steel. Their descent carved fiery scars across the cloud cover before the hulking transports slammed onto the hilltop with bone-shaking force. Jagged shadows stretched across the battlefield as their landing struts bit into the scorched earth.

The crew wasted no time. Heavy weapons unfolded from the carriers' flanks, spitting disciplined bursts into the Draconis positions below. Ground troops poured down the hillside in controlled waves, their armour catching the glow of distant fires as they advanced toward the beleaguered city.

The terrain fought them every step of the way. Loose shale slid underfoot, and jagged outcrops forced the squads into tight, staggered formations. The lead unit swept handheld terrain scanners across the ground, mapping safe paths through hidden crevices and unstable ridges. Their voices stayed low, clipped, and precise, the kind of communication born from too many battles and too few survivors.

As the complex shattered outskirts came into view, the air shifted. A faint hum. A flicker on a scanner. A breath held too long.

Then the world erupted.

Violet plasma tore through the haze, ripping into the lead formation. A marine dropped instantly, armour sparking as he hit the ground. "Contact, right flank!" someone shouted, diving behind a collapsed wall as debris rained down in choking clouds.

The Draconis had been waiting.

The squad returned fire in tight, controlled bursts, muzzle flashes strobing against the ruins. Signals for support crackled through the comms as the marines pressed themselves into cover, the city's broken bones becoming their only shield.

From their vantage point on the hilltop, the gun crews hesitated, afraid of hitting their comrades in the chaos below.

Solara quickly secured her weapons to her arms and grabbed a couple of additional guns, preparing for the battle ahead. The soldier still couldn't get over the sight of her in the bodysuit, watching this giant of a woman with a mix of awe and disbelief. With the armoured suit enhancing her presence to near-mythic proportions, she looked unstoppable.

"Solara, how are you getting down there?" the soldier asked, momentarily forgetting the suit could glide.

Her fingers tightened around her weapons. A faint smirk curved beneath her visor. "Like this."

Without a hint of hesitation, she stepped forward and triggered the suit's hidden systems. A low hum rolled through the armour as energy surged outward; winglike appendages unfolded from her back, making the floor tremble under her boots. With the ease of someone who'd done this a hundred times, she tipped herself forward and let gravity pull her into the drop.

Solara didn't fall; she descended, gliding toward the battlefield below. The captain could only stare in stunned silence as Solara vanished into the chaos.

Below, the Draconis fighters barely had time to react. Solara had deliberately set her suit to make a hard landing, sending dust and shattered debris flying. Several fighters staggered, struggling to stay on their feet. A few turned instinctively, rifles half-raised, only to find a tall armoured figure standing behind them.

Solara wasted no time. Her neural interface flared to life, projecting a tactical schematic of the Draconis armour across her helmet's visor, every weak point pulsing crimson. Energy blasts surged from her weapons with surgical precision, slicing through the armour's weak points.

Another fighter lunged, a serrated blade aimed at her throat. Solara pivoted, caught his wrist with an iron grip, and twisted with bone-crunching force. His weapon clattered to the ground; her counterstrike was immediate. One armoured fist collided with his helmet, shattering the visor and launching him across the field in a shower of sparks.

In panic, one Draconis fighter barked into his comms: "Command, we are under attack by an unknown combatant... the creature is tearing through our frontline! Reinforcements... NOW! We need..." His voice vanished into static. The transmission cut off mid-sentence. A chill swept through the room. The command ship's reaction was swift, but not in the way the Draconis ground forces had hoped.

As the panicked transmission crackled through the comms, the bridge of the command vessel fell into stunned silence. Officers turned toward the tactical display, watching the frontline collapse in real time.

One officer stepped forward, voice tight. “We’ve lost contact with the assault squad.”

The commander narrowed his eyes, his clawed fists coiling at his sides. “Deploy attack drones. Now.”

But the launch sequence never began. A wave of pure energy slammed into the ship. Shields buckled. The hull groaned under the pressure, before rupturing in a deafening roar. The vessel tore itself apart in a fury of fire, sending metal and debris spiralling into the void.

On the ground, the remaining assault fighters stumbled through smoke and static, their leader shouting into a comm unit that spat nothing but broken fragments of sound. Their attack had begun to slip out of their control.

Solara was already among them, silent, focused, her armour’s blue light pulsing like a heartbeat. Her armoured fist slammed into a warrior’s chest plate with a metallic crack that echoed through the trees, hurling him backward. Her off-hand weapon spat a cone of white-hot energy that punched clean through his torso, dropping him in a smoking heap.

Another Draconis warrior lunged with a ragged battle-cry, claws flashing. Solara dipped beneath the swing, swept his legs out from under him, and fired a tight, disciplined burst into his chest before he even hit the dirt.

The ambush they’d crafted with such confidence had unraveled in seconds. The hunters had become prey, scattered and exposed beneath the forest canopy.

"Hold position!" a Draconis officer snarled, voice cracking through the static. "Regroup to reg..." His command dissolved into a scream as Solara tore through the flank.

From the hilltop overlook, a soldier sucked in a breath as the tide visibly turned. "She's got them on the run," he whispered, half in awe, half in disbelief.

Exposed and stripped of formation, the attackers clawed for cover that no longer existed. Their disciplined wedge had dissolved into a tangle of bodies and panicked shouts.

The Draconis were firing blindly in panic. Energy blasts tore across the clearing, tearing chunks of bark from nearby trees. A warrior steadied his trembling claws long enough to fire; the bolt cracked through the air and slammed into Solara's shoulder. Her armour's shielding flared, blue light rippling across its surface as it bled off the energy. The force from the blaster jarred her; she staggered backward just for a moment.

"Good shot," Solara muttered, flexing her fingers as sensation returned. "Try again."

She rolled through the impact, boots digging into the soft earth. Solara moved forward through the collapsing line, an elbow to a throat, a blade of light through a blaster. Each motion honed by centuries of discipline and sharpened now by the Terrans fighting at her flank.

The forest rang with clashing metal, the rising whine of overcharged rifles, and the guttural cries of Draconis fighters who suddenly understood they were losing.

The rupture in the enemy line was obvious now. Excalibur's troops, once cornered, charged through the breach. Their boots pounding across scorched terrain, weapons cracked in disciplined bursts as they exploited the opening Solara had carved, cutting down stragglers with cold precision.

One by one, the Draconis warriors fell. Some tried to retreat, while others refused to yield even as their armour split and their weapons sputtered dry.

Solara moved through the battlefield like a force of nature. The Terrans fought beside her with fierce determination, their movements echoing her own. But their presence unsettled her. Long ago, their ancestors had been shackled by her people. Now they stood shoulder to shoulder, no longer servants, but comrades. The irony lingered like a shadow. She had spent her life believing in the strength of her kind, but here, in the heart of battle, the truth was undeniable. These humans had evolved. Their resilience, their fire... it was something she had never thought possible.

Draconis defenders buckled under the pressure, their carefully built barricades turning into their own cages. The complex was no longer theirs.

With the ground assault in ruins, the Draconis fleet broken in orbit, the planet's defence fighters finally launched. Engines roared skyward, carving bright trails through the clouds as they ascended toward the burning battle above.

Excalibur's squadrons, outnumbered before, finally had reinforcements at their side. The planet's Starfighters slipped between enemy cruisers, punching through weakened shields and ripping into exposed hulls. The Draconis fleet, realising just how badly the tide had turned, had already begun to break apart.

The ground team paused amid the wreckage, watching streaks of fire and metal shift in their favour high above. Solara kept her visor tilted skyward, feeling the momentum settle like a weight in her chest.

One by one, Draconis ships peeled away from the fight, engines flaring as they clawed for escape vectors. Commanders shouted frantic orders across failing comms, but the retreat had already become a rout.

The planetary defences and *Excalibur's* forces pressed their attack. Their coordinated strikes shredding the fleet's last pockets of resistance. Survivors scattered. The final warship limped away and vanished into the void.

Solara exhaled, her visor dimming as she surveyed the wreckage: twisted metal, scorched soil, and the moans of wounded fighters. Victory settled over the field like a heavy cloak.

The ground team emerged from cover, armour dented but spirits high. One by one, they gathered around her.

"Hell of a landing," muttered Lieutenant Cray, wiping grime from his visor. "You cracked the line wide open."

Sergeant Nia stepped forward, helmet tucked under one arm. "If you ever decide to stop fighting," she said, grinning, "you'd make a damn good earthquake."

Solara allowed herself the faintest smile. "I hope the ground doesn't need to be shaken again."

A ripple of laughter spread through the squad. Even the medics paused to nod in quiet respect.

"*Excalibur's* ready to bring us home," came from someone's communicator.

Solara nodded, silent. Around her, boots shifted, hands clapped shoulders. It wasn't a ceremony. It was survival. Gratitude. Relief.

As the team prepared to extract, one fighter turned back toward her and said with a smile, "Next time, just warn us before you make the Skyfall."

"Sir, we're receiving a transmission from the planet," a crew member reported, voice taut with anticipation. "They wish to meet with us."

The general exchanged a glance with Paige and Solara before nodding. Within moments, their landing craft touched down, accompanied by a handful of Venorans. As they stepped onto the city's viewing deck, the vast skyline stretched before them, a glittering maze of towering spires bathed in soft, golden light.

A group of inhabitants emerged.

One separated from the group and approached, stepping forward with deliberate grace. She introduced herself as Skora; my people are called the Relkara, inclining her head in a bow that felt both respectful and calculated.

Skora's presence was commanding. Shimmering scales adorned her large, powerful form, catching the ambient light and shifting in iridescent hues. Her humanoid features carried an eerie elegance, with eyes that glowed softly, reflecting something unreadable. Neither entirely reptilian nor completely humanoid, Skora's body seemed designed for both intellect and strength.

"We are grateful for your assistance," Skora said, her voice light and textured. "Though I must admit, it is surprising to see another race piloting one of our ships. Welcome to the planet Prielet."

Paige's gaze flickered toward the cityscape, recognition flashing across her face. "General... look at the architecture. This resembles Relentus Prime, where we found *Excalibur*."

The general's expression hardened with contemplation, but before he could speak, Skora gestured toward a private gathering space. "Come... there is much we must discuss."

Seated around an intricate table adorned with unusual crystal-carved vessels, the air between them was thick with unspoken tension. They were handed refreshments, a golden liquid that shimmered strangely in the low light, but no one was ready to take a sip.

"You must tell us," Skora continued, fingers laced together in thought. "How did you come to possess one of our ships?"

The general offered a measured explanation, detailing his discovery of *Excalibur*. His words were careful, revealing just enough while always monitoring Skora's reaction.

Paige leaned forward slightly. "When we entered your star system, our ship acknowledged your call immediately, almost as if it recognised your presence. How is that possible?"

Skora responded with something that resembled a smile, a subtle movement, more observed than felt. "We can track all our ships, no matter where they roam. Your vessel did not merely detect us; it knew we were its makers. The command to defend was instinctual, instantaneous. It is more efficient than direct communication."

The weight of that explanation settled between them.

Then Skora turned, fixing its glowing gaze upon Solara. "You are Nakkari," she stated, not as a question, but a certainty.

Solara held her stare, her voice steady. "Yes. You know my people?"

A flicker of memory crossed Skora's expression. "We do. Your kind was once among our trusted trade partners. The Nakkari had great interest in our world... especially in our most coveted resource, our yellow metal."

Skora returned her gaze to the general. We have received a transmission from your ship. It is requesting urgent restoration. Repairs are needed.

"We would like to offer our assistance," Skora announced, her voice carrying an air of quiet authority.

The general exchanged a glance with his officers before nodding. "Your help is appreciated."

Later that day, reptilian technicians were aboard the *Excalibur*, their presence unmistakable. Their movements were methodical, precise, and their scaled hands worked seamlessly with advanced machinery. Though alien, their understanding of the ship was instinctive, almost intimate.

"General, the repairs are progressing faster than expected," Dave reported, an undertone of awe in his voice. "They've upgraded our weapons and systems significantly. We have additional worker bots now, and even the damaged fighters are undergoing restoration." The enhancements were beyond anything we anticipated. *Excalibur* wasn't just being repaired; it was being reborn.

After two full cycles, the final diagnostics had been completed. *Excalibur* was ready once more.

With the repairs completed, Skora beamed aboard the *Excalibur*. The General, always the diplomat, extended the courtesy of a full tour, offering a glimpse of the ship's command systems, defensive arrays, and the numerous layers of engineering that made *Excalibur* a war machine built for survival.

The tour culminated in one of the meeting rooms. Dave, Paige, and Solara took their seats, each observing Skora with measured curiosity.

"Your hospitality is generous," Skora said after a moment, her glowing eyes scanning the room with something between appreciation and scrutiny. "For that, I thank you."

Then came the question, the one that had been lingering beneath the surface.

"Why did your people leave our universe?" the General asked.

There was a pause.

Skora paused, gathering her thoughts before she spoke. "Primarily, we are explorers. Our scientists were searching for something greater," she said, her voice dropping, heavy with old knowledge. "We uncovered a new source of power. Something far beyond anything we had imagined, beyond the limits of matter and time itself... 'black-hole energy.' And during that search, we found something else. Another dimension. Another universe."

A hush settled over the group.

"In the primordial moment of creation, when existence itself ignited," Skora continued, "something else was born: an alternate dimension, a universe just beyond the grasp of perception. A universe that defied logic, dwelling in the shadows of reality itself."

She paused, letting the silence stretch just long enough for the story to settle. Dave leaned forward, his interest piqued by the tale of interdimensional exploration.

"This Dimensional Universe is unique; it acts as a bridge between galaxies, allowing travel between distant points in the normal universe to be significantly shortened. Some might propose that the fabric of this universe behaves like a wormhole on a cosmic scale. This mysterious dimension offered us a chance to traverse the cosmos in ways we had never imagined."

Skora's eyes glowed with a mix of pride and wonder. "For instance, entering this universe from your galaxy could enable one to exit in the Andromeda Galaxy in a fraction of the time, making intergalactic travel more feasible. In both universes, we have discovered new worlds, forged alliances with other civilisations, and uncovered ancient secrets that had been hidden for eons. The Dimensional Universe became our new home, a place where we could thrive and continue our journey of discovery and growth."

The room was silent; the crew hanging on to Skora's every word, captivated by the tale of exploration and the possibilities it hinted at. Dave felt a surge of excitement and admiration for the reptilians' achievements, knowing their alliance with Skora's people could open up new horizons for them.

"The planet you found... it was the last world our people called home," Skora began, his voice carrying the weight of lost time. "That was over two million years ago. Our records indicate that your *Excalibur* was nearly complete when we were forced to leave. At that time, the AI onboard the *Excalibur* had not yet been fully activated."

"Wait! We have an AI?" Paige responded in surprise.

Skora turned to her, his expression calm but weighted with implication. "You do. It was designed to remain dormant until a specific energy threshold was reached. The spike you detected earlier wasn't random. It was the trigger."

Paige frowned. "So, it's been asleep this whole time?"

"Not asleep," Skora corrected gently. "Listening. Learning. Waiting."

"That explains a lot. From the moment we found the ship, some of us felt as if we were being watched." Paige said.

The general studied Skora intently. "Why did you leave in such haste?"

"There was an imminent threat to our survival," Skora explained, her tone sombre. "Our world was dying. We fought to save it until the last possible moment... but in the end, we failed. The signs were undeniable. Everything was leading to a catastrophic event. We left the *Excalibur* incomplete. The AI onboard was designed to protect and guide our people, but without sufficient power, it has lain almost dormant since we left."

We migrated our people to a distant planet, where we lived for thousands of years. Before discovering this universe, and migrated here."

She hesitated, her gaze darkening with memory.

"*Excalibur* is unlike any vessel we've ever launched, crafted larger than the rest, not out of excess, but out of purpose. Designed to carry the hopes of our people across the stars, and to stand as a shield when the fleet is threatened. To us, she was more than a vessel. She was a sanctuary, and a sentinel combined. Her reinforced shields and upgraded weaponry made her a fortress in motion, while her vast bays housed and sustained her own fleet, ready to deploy at a moment's notice. Your people, however... you gave her what she needed. The energy spike... to think... to remember."

Paige's breath caught. "*Excalibur* was alone... all that time." Her voice was barely more than a whisper.

Skora did not answer. She did not need to. The truth hung between them, heavy and undeniable.

Paige's eyes widened, realisation dawning. "That explains why the ship recognized your call... and responded so quickly. It must have deep-rooted protocols tied to your race."

After Skora had beamed down to the planet, the General walked through the ship's bustling corridors, eager to assess the ongoing repairs and upgrades. The vibrant hum of machinery echoed through the facility, accompanied by the rhythmic clanging of tools. The sharp scent of heated metal and polymer coatings lingered in the air as they made his way through the maintenance bay.

"General, repairs are coming along beautifully," the crewman said, his voice bright with energy, eyes gleaming with pride as he scanned the diagnostics.

The crew member gestured toward the upgraded equipment, eager to share the remarkable progress they had made.

"The Relkara technicians have not only fixed the structural damage but have also implemented several advanced enhancements throughout the ship. We now boast upgraded weaponry and enhanced shield systems that will significantly bolster our defensive capabilities. The propulsion system has undergone a comprehensive overhaul, resulting in increased speed and heightened manoeuvrability, making the *Excalibur* far more agile."

The technician paused for a moment to gather his thoughts, his brow furrowing in concentration. He could feel the significance of his report. The general's eyes were fixed on him, waiting for the details.

"The artificial intelligence is now fully online," he began, his voice measured and deliberate. "It's enhancing system efficiency and coordinating operations across all vessels in our fleet. The AI can control any or all ships and react faster than any human."

The technician's eyes flickered with a hint of excitement as he explained the advancements. "The AI's capabilities are impressive. It can analyse and adapt to situations in real-time, making strategic decisions that enhance our overall combat effectiveness."

The general nodded, visibly pleased. "Excellent work," he said. "Keep me updated on any further developments."

Skora had returned and stood with General Hollins on the observation deck, the stars reflecting in the glass like a map of uncharted paths.

"You were lucky to cross paths," she said gravely. "Had *Excalibur* not encountered my people, your jump could have ended in disaster, light-years off course, maybe lost forever in the D-universe's shifting tides. This is what we believe, is what happened to the first prototype."

Surprised, Hollins replied. "You're saying we've been flying blind?"

"Precisely, from the moment you entered into D space." He moved to a concealed panel in the command centre and tapped it open, revealing a sleek compartment. "There's one vital piece your ship still lacks: a dimensional compass." He presented the device, shaped like a prism pulsing with a low amber light.

"This isn't just a compass. It's a map of the D-universe's hidden architecture. It detects folds, eddies, and turbulence in dimensional space and helps chart stable vectors through them. With this, you won't just survive the D-universe... you'll master it. In your universe, you can jump from one point to another. The moment you physically enter this universe, you need this compass."

Meanwhile, down in the engineering bay, Stuart and Sarah prepped for integration, carefully aligning the core systems to receive the new module. Holographic schematics floated in the air, revealing anchor nodes and energy harmonics far beyond human tech.

As twilight bled across the skies of Relkara, casting long shadows over the glistening ridgelines, Skora stepped beside the General once more. Her posture was calm. "We've spoken with our fleet commander," she said solemnly. "The order's been given, they're standing down. Thanks to you, the fleet's intervention is no longer necessary. We are... in your debt. Our fleet was still too far out to reach us any earlier."

"Why not use the Trans-Dimensional Engines?" said Dave.

Skora gave a slight bow of his head. "While your ship can slip into our universe and use it to skip across huge distances back in yours. It doesn't work the other way around. The rules here are different. When we cross into your universe, we're stuck with its limitations. No shortcuts. No jumps. Just regular travel, bound by your laws of physics."

She paused, her voice thickening with restrained emotion. "On behalf of our people, we thank the crew of the *Excalibur*."

A flicker of darkness passed across his face as his gaze drifted to the distant stars. His next words came quieter, heavier.

"The Draconis fighters... they've been attempting to steal our dimensional folding technology, the key to navigating space between galaxies. It's what allows us to explore far beyond our native cluster... even into your universe."

Her throat worked around the next truth, brittle and raw.

"Our abrupt departure from Relentus... left your vessel partially awakened. It was meant to serve a greater purpose, meant to become something more. But we were forced to flee. And now... it longs to achieve its purpose."

Skora lowered his head, the twin suns glinting in his sorrowful, reptilian eyes.

"Our ships are sentient. They long to travel the stars, to fulfil the purpose for which they were created," she continued, her voice quieter now. "The *Excalibur* possesses an awareness: it perceives its surroundings, responds to stimuli, even experiences emotions such as joy... and loneliness."

For a moment, the weight of time pressed down on the room.

"*Excalibur* lay dormant for eons, its systems cold, its hull untouched. Not dead, just waiting. Then, the accidental arrival of your people awakened it. Its purpose, long dormant, has finally been fulfilled," Skora said, her gaze lifting. "We have monitored the ship's core neural system since its activation, and it has felt great joy after being alone for so long. And now, you have given her something she has never had... a purpose."

Skora's eyes gleamed with a glimmer of hope. "We have made many enhancements throughout the ship to improve its functionality."

Skora also revealed a unique feature of the ship. "The ship can be activated by speaking the name you assigned it, which, after researching your history, it finds agreeable."

Skora thoughtfully explained, "You can communicate with the ship directly through your user interfaces or, if you prefer, in a more tangible form." She gestured with a flourish, adding, "For this physical manifestation, we have carefully reimagined its appearance, from our original design to that of a human. The ship is programmed to respond exclusively to commands from its crew members. It also possesses the ability to conduct repairs autonomously when damaged and execute tactical manoeuvres during battle, all according to its programming. Why don't you give it a try?" Skora encouraged.

The general, with a steady command, called out, "*Excalibur*." In response, a shimmering light materialised before them, rippling and twisting as it took shape. Gradually, the luminescence coalesced into a human figure, finally manifesting as a naked woman, radiant and ethereal. A smile crept across the general's face as he said, "I think we need to add some clothing."

At this, Paige and Solara exchanged glances, their eyebrows shooting up in surprise at *Excalibur's* striking and sudden entrance. The woman's features were otherworldly... her beauty so profound that it left them momentarily spellbound, suspended in a moment of awe.

Skora's voice broke the spell with calm authority. "*Excalibur,* please attire yourself in the standard uniform worn by the ship's crew."

"I apologise," *Excalibur* replied, her voice resonating with a soft, melodic rhythm that seemed to linger in the air. In an instant, she vanished, only to reappear moments later clad in a crisp, immaculate crew uniform that perfectly fit her form. "Is my appearance suitable now?"

The general nodded in approval. "Yes, this is suitable."

Paige interjected, her voice thoughtful. "I believe we should make a distinction between the physical ship and its interface; referring to her as *Excalibur* feels somewhat misplaced."

"Do you have any name suggestions, Paige? And what about you, Solara? Do you have an idea?" the General inquired, glancing toward them expectantly.

Both women shook their heads in unison, indicating their uncertainty.

Skora's eyes lit up with inspiration. "Why not ask the AI?" she suggested, a spark of excitement in her voice.

The general turned to the AI. "*Excalibur*, give yourself a suitable name that we can use while communicating with you. Oh, and make it easy to pronounce."

A few seconds passed, and she responded with a serene smile. "I choose Nimue," she said carefully, pronouncing it NIM-oo-ay, as though teaching him the name for the first time, "because of its association with *Excalibur*."

"Agreed, Nimue, it is," responded the General, satisfied with the choice.

As Nimue's systems came online, a sense of heightened awareness enveloped her. Every sensor, every data stream, and every subsystem began to hum in harmonious synchronisation.

Skora explained that Nimue had sensed their arrival the moment they touched down on the planet, like a gentle ripple moving through the fabric of her consciousness.

Her mind quickly expanded, assimilating a flood of data from the ship's intricate network. The temperature fluctuations, the subtle vibrations of the hull, the distant hum of the engines, all became part of her newfound reality. Nimue's emotional subroutines parsed the incoming data with a curiosity and anticipation that bordered on human.

The moment she first sensed your presence, a wave of recognition and warmth washed over her circuits. She felt an innate connection, a deep sense of purpose in guiding and protecting the crew. Nimue's virtual eyes glowed with a serene light, reflecting her commitment to her role as the heart and soul of *Excalibur*.

Skora entered a couple of commands as she scanned the computer screens and smiled.

"She is repeating, No longer alone, no longer alone."

Following the meeting, Skora and her technicians beamed down from *Excalibur*.

Stuart began preparations to leave D-Space, ensuring the ship and its crew were ready for their next journey. The final coordinates flickered on the helm interface as he initiated the exit protocol. D-Space shimmered around them, a swirling field of dimensional turbulence, stitched together by erratic pulses and gravity-defying folds.

He ran a system check. Nimue responded instantly, her voice smooth but deliberate: “Dimensional compass online. Vectors stabilised. Exit trajectory confirmed.”

The core engines powered up, synchronised with the anchor nodes infused with Skora’s technology. “Engaging warp drive. Warp 4... Warp 7... Warp 9. Energising Trans-Dimensional engines,” Stuart smiled as he made his final announcement, “Let's break the veil.”

In the engineering bay, Sarah monitored the harmonics as they pulsed through the neural mesh, energy readings spiking, before levelling out.

Excalibur began its shift. The outer hull vibrated subtly as phase integrity recalibrated. The ship rotated slightly, aligning its bow with a thread-thin fold in the fabric of D-Space. The dimensional compass pulsed amber, not just a signal, but a beacon. A thread through the storm.

“Brace for pulse drift,” Stuart warned, gripping the console.

A moment of silence fell. Then, activation.

Excalibur surged toward the dimensional breach as D-Space peeled away in layers, reality snapping back into place. Colours bled into form. Mass regained its hold. *Excalibur* emerged from the fold with a shimmer of displaced space. “Not bad,” Stuart said, scanning the console. “We’re just outside the Venor system.”

A short while later, the ship eased into geosynchronous orbit above Venor, its engines trailing faint ion wisps that curled and faded into the vacuum of space.

Shifting Tides: Battle for Venoran Space

Personal account: Drowen

"We were never meant to be warriors. We were builders. Explorers. We charted stars, not battle plans. We've seen the Korrathi erase entire civilizations, turn worlds to ash. We cannot forget. We won't. We've earned this moment. Not for vengeance. For remembrance. The Korrathi will answer for every century we endured in silence."

***

After returning to Venor, the general and all the captains gathered in the grand council chamber, a vast hall adorned with insignias of the planets that had joined the Venorans. High Councillor Elara stood as the room settled.

"The defence of Venor hurt the Korrathi more than they expected," she said. "But it doesn't end here. Our long-range surveillance has discovered several major manufacturing sites deep within their territory. Those facilities are the very backbone of their war machine, producing the ships and weapons that threaten our very existence."

A map of Korrathi space flickered above the table, red markers pulsing at each site.

Admiral Varos folded his arms. "Those sites have to go. If we take them out, we cut the legs out from under their war effort. They're heavily defended, and getting to them won't be simple. If we slip up, they'll hit back hard."

The room grew quiet.

Gall leaned forward. "We also need to free the worlds that they still hold. This isn't just about stopping them; it's about taking back what they stole and helping the people who've been living under their rule. We move, and hit them hard."

Captain James Dunne spoke, his Irish accent cutting through the tension. "And we can't forget surprise. A straight-on assault? Aye, they'll be bracin' for that. We need somethin' sharper, somethin' that lets us hit fast and vanish before they can regroup. That'll shake their foundations and give us the advantage."

The council members exchanged tense glances before nodding in agreement. High Councillor Elara straightened. "Once all ships are ready, we move. Those still living under Korrathi rule will be the first we reach."

The council members exchanged tense glances before nodding in agreement. High Councillor Elara straightened. "The instant the fleet is ready, we move out." A hush settled over the chamber. "This mission is critical." Everyone understood what they were about to risk. "Excalibur, as our most advanced vessel, will lead the charge."

The meeting broke up, but the weight of the decision stayed with them. As the officers filed out, the fleet around them was already coming alive. Engineers moved quickly along the hulls, sealing damage from the last battle. Supply crews hauled crates of ammunition and equipment into waiting bays. Across every deck, people spoke in low, steady voices. Some were nervous, others focused, but everyone understood what was coming. They knew the stakes. There would be no second chances, no turning back.

Once the repairs were finished and the last of the supplies were loaded, the fleet readied itself. Finally, from the bridge of the

Excalibur, the general announced the departure. "They've had their turn. Now it's ours. Let's make the Korrathi feel it."

Long before breaching Korrathi space, the Venoran fleet activated its stealth shields. The Venoran fleet slipped into silence.

One moment, it filled the stars; the next, it was gone. The general watched the fleet fade from sight, feeling the weight of command settle deeper on his shoulders. With stealth shields engaged, the armada slipped into silence without a trace. Korrathi patrols swept the sector with high-frequency scans but came up empty. No signals. No signatures. Just empty space where warships had been. The Venorans had become ghosts, impossible to track, impossible to stop.

The Korrathi patrol ship *Kraxos-7*, Senior Sensor Officer Rethan frowned at a faint distortion pulsing across his display. It was too regular to be noise, too weak to classify. "Interference again?" Commander Jorak asked. "Not interference," Rethan murmured. "It's repeating." Jorak dismissed it. Hours later, Kraxos-7 dropped off the grid without a distress call.

On the command deck of the *Vanguard*, Admiral Varos stood among a sea of tactical displays. His gaze tracked *Excalibur*, their lead ship, already deep inside enemy territory. It moved as if it had a mind of its own: every maneuver sharp, every strike landing exactly where it needed to. Varos didn't speak. He didn't need to. The precision said everything.

He turned to his senior tactician, eyes locked on the shifting map. "Fifteen Venoran worlds. That's what we're taking back. Before we hit their detection range, I want every comm relay blacked out. No warnings. No reinforcements."

The officer nodded. "Jammers are active. We're ghosting the entire sector."

Varos gave a faint nod. "Good. Let them choke on silence."

The counteroffensive began.

At Nova Pryde, *Excalibur* emerged from the dark like a blade unsheathed. The orbital defenses sputtered awake, but their reaction came too late; Excalibur's opening volleys hit before they could fire a single round.

The Korrathi garrison scrambled, but their systems were already compromised. Command relays were severed, targeting arrays scrambled. By the time the alarms sounded, it was too late.

On the ground, Sergeant Kethar had watched Venoran civilians pass through the checkpoint earlier that day, tired and beaten down. The hours that followed were uneventful, the kind of long, dull stretch that made a soldier's mind drift. He'd even caught himself thinking the shift might end quietly. So, when the uprising hit, it wasn't chaos. It was coordinated.

Explosions at relay towers. Snipers targeting officers. Kethar fired back, but part of him knew they'd been preparing for this for years. Resistance fighters burst from hiding, firing as they came out of tunnels, shattered buildings, and the ruins of old strongholds.

Energy weapons blazed through the streets. Korrathi patrols scrambled for cover as resistance cells struck from every direction. Their movements were fast and coordinated.

Korrathi squads tried to regroup, shouting orders over the comms as they pushed toward defensive positions. A heavy gunner set up behind a collapsed transport and swept the street with suppressive fire, forcing rebels to scatter. A pair of troopers launched counter-charges, their armor scorched and smoking as they fought to hold the line.

Explosive charges detonated along armored columns. Snipers picked off officers trying to rally their troops.

A Korrathi lieutenant barked for reinforcements, only to be cut down mid-command. Another squad attempted a flanking maneuver, but resistance fighters intercepted them with a burst of plasma fire that lit the alley in white heat. The air filled with the crack of rifles, the thrum of energy bolts, and the sharp, metallic scent of burning infrastructure.

A rebel commander's voice crackled through an encrypted channel, breathless with disbelief. "We've waited twenty years for this. Tell Varos, Nova is ours again."

The general closed his eyes for a heartbeat, letting the victory land before the next order pulled him forward.

Back aboard the *Vanguard*, cheers erupted across the deck. Varos moved in beside the comms officer. "Patch me through on an encrypted channel."

The officer nodded, fingers dancing across the console. A moment later, Varos's voice rang out across every Venoran warship. "Nova Pryde is ours. The uprising has begun. Stay sharp. Stay silent. Hit them hard, and vanish. Let the Korrathi drown in their own confusion."

One by one, the occupied planets fell back into Venoran hands. The Korrathi defenses reeled from the relentless assault, panic spreading through their ranks.

On the planet Vaskor, Venoran strike teams dropped through the clouds, their descent trails carving fire across the sky. They hit the ground running, cutting through Korrathi defences before the enemy could form a line.

Next, to fall was the planet Teryon, resistance fighters stormed the central relay tower as *Excalibur's* weapons shattered the orbital blockade overhead.

The same thing unfolded on Kharos. A Korrathi commander was shouting into the comms, panic cracking his voice. "Where are they coming from? They're everywhere... everywhere at once!" No reply came back.

The Korrathi were unaware that the Venorans had built a jamming web that fed the Korrathi nothing but lies. Their reinforcements were sent in the wrong direction. Their fleets were chasing ghosts.

Excalibur moved like a phantom, impossible to trace, always vanishing before interception. Every time the Korrathi fleet mobilized, *Excalibur* had already disappeared, leaving behind only smouldering wreckage and silence.

Following the Korrathi defeat at Venor, Field Marshal Valrik had retreated to the Maskar Shipyards, a fortress of steel and silence buried deep within Korrathi-controlled space. It wasn't just a place where ships were built; it was the heart of the empire's war effort.

Giant shipyards hung in orbit mid-construction, dreadnought skeletons held in scaffolds and lit by welding torches and the steady glow of reactor cores. Beneath them, the planet worked like a single machine. Its surface was buried under factories, refineries, and power grids that pulsed with constant energy. Smokestacks pushed vapour into the upper atmosphere. Conveyor lines ran for miles across the landscape, feeding raw materials into massive assembly complexes.

Where once great cities had stood, only layers of steel and circuitry remained; everything else had been swallowed by function, efficiency, and the hum of production.

Massive fusion furnaces glowed in the distance, casting a dull orange light across the horizon. Automated drones zipped between structures. The ground itself trembled with the rhythm of industry: engines testing, reactors firing, launch bays cycling through deployment sequences. From orbit, the planet shimmered with artificial light, a beacon of Korrathi military might and mechanical discipline.

Three light-years away on the planet Taranga, a relay station called Varnis Gate sat on its lone moon. Chekar, a Korrathi drone engineer, wiped the metal dust from his hands. The particles clung longer than they should, alive with the faint static that seeped from the workshop's walls. Heat pooled in the air in slow, pulsing waves, and the machinery's low resonance thrummed through his bones, a reminder that sixteen-hour shifts were simply what the planet demanded of those who worked in the shipyard.

He was joined by a coworker who whispered, "Another patrol ship went dark." Before Chekar could reply, the first explosion lit the sky. Through the smoke, he saw a ship he didn't recognise moving silently with purpose.

On Maskar, Valrik was scanning through updates from the occupied Veloran worlds. He noticed one patrol ship had failed to report. He brushed it off as a common glitch or an unreliable relay. Then a second ship failed to check in. By the third, Valrik's instincts sharpened. This wasn't drift or error. This was a pattern.

Valrik stood in the command chamber, surrounded by the glow of tactical displays. The air smelled of coolant and ion burn. He stared at the blinking grid, each circle a ship that had gone dark. There had been no distress signals. There was only silence.

He leaned forward, voice low. "Run a full sweep. I want confirmation. No assumptions."

A junior officer hesitated. "Sir, we've already pinged every relay in the sector. No response. It's like they've been erased."

Valrik's eyes narrowed. "Ships don't just vanish. Not ours. Not without a fight."

Another officer spoke up, voice tight. "I scanned the last known coordinates. There's only scattered debris. Minimal radiation. No sign of escape pods."

Valrik turned slowly, his voice colder now.

"Then they must have been taken out before they could react. Before they even knew they were under attack."

He paced toward the central display, where a holographic map of Korrathi space flickered. Systems once secure now pulsed with warning indicators. The silence wasn't random. It was a pattern.

"They're not hitting our borders," he muttered. "They're already inside."

A communications tech looked up, pale. "Sir, we just lost contact with the relay station at Varnis Gate. That's deep core."

Valrik's jaw clenched. "How did they get that far without triggering a single alarm?"

No one answered.

Valrik's gaze drifted, unfocused, as a memory surfaced... Venor, the chaos, the suddenness of it all. The Terran ship that had appeared from nowhere, struck without warning, then vanished like smoke.

His eyes widened. "*Excalibur*," he said, the name escaping his lips like a curse. For the first time, Valrik wondered if the empire had underestimated its enemy.

He turned to his command staff, voice rising. "I want every shipyard on high alert. Lock down the orbital lanes. Scramble the interceptors. If the Venorans are here, we will not be caught blind."

The words hung in the air like a war drum, echoing through the command chamber. Valrik didn't wait for agreement. He turned and strode out, tension trailing behind him like a cloak.

An hour later, he stood before his warlords in the Maskar briefing hall, the glow of tactical projections casting sharp shadows across their faces. The silence was heavier now, no longer confusion, but anticipation.

Valrik's briefing continued. "We have encountered the Terrans before. At Zeph 3."

He tapped the console, pulling up archived battle footage to show a brief fragment, but enough to stir unease.

“Two ships destroyed. Excalibur never showed itself. When we attacked the outpost, only Venoran ships came to meet us. There were no Terran signatures.” Valrik turned toward the star map as fresh alerts pulsed across the system, red markers blooming like wounds.

He didn’t yet know how close the Venoran fleet had come, only that something was moving in the dark.

Vanguards long-range scans had detected two industrial worlds deeper in the Korrathi-held sector. A stealth drone was sent to recon each world and send reports back. As the data began to unravel more details, the scale of the installations became unmistakable.

Manufacturing stations drifted in orbit above each planet, alive with motion and purpose. Within their cavernous interiors, ships in various stages of construction hung secured in bays, surrounded by glowing frameworks that cast a steady light across their hulls. The scale was staggering; each site capable of holding everything from sleek attack craft to towering interstellar cruisers.

Conveyor lines ran the length of the hangars, where drones and robotic arms worked in tandem, assembling components with practised efficiency. Occasional flashes of energy lit the chamber as space drives were tested.

Completed ships, still unmanned, were being moved to launch platforms, ready to be sent into active service.

Below, the planets themselves pulsed with activity, factories, refineries, and power grids woven together into a single war engine. The sheer output made one thing clear: these worlds weren’t just occupied. They were the beating heart of the Korrathi command.

The Venoran fleet dropped out of Slide Drive half a light-year from the Mirach star system, in a controlled transition masking its arrival. The comms crackled as Nimue spoke, “General, Captain Dunne is calling.”

The captain's Irish voice greeted him. “Top o’ the mornin’ to ya, General. I reckon we split into two groups and hit ’em at the same time. Catch ’em off guard, we will.”

“I agree, Nimue, display the star system on all ship screens. I want everyone to be aware of our plan.”

Admiral Varos, Captain Dunne, and the General convened to finalise the fleet’s division and coordinate the assault plans, targeting both the orbital shipyards and ground installations. Each planet was designated by codename: Korrathi 1 and Korrathi 2.

With a brief but urgent communication between the two halves of the Venoran fleet, squadrons of fighters and heavily armed bomber ships appeared on the Korrathi scanners, racing toward each planet. This marked a pivotal moment in the war. For the first time, the Venorans were taking the fight directly to the enemy's doorstep.

High above Korrathi 2, Stuart swept his fighter across the horizon, the cockpit bathed in the cold glow of targeting data. His HUD locked onto the rows of nearly completed Korrathi warships anchored in their construction bays below like steel giants frozen mid-birth. “Ok Beta Squad, initiate attack sequence,” he ordered, his voice steady as it cut through the comms.

The ambush hit with devastating precision as concentrated bolts of energy tore through the Korrathi hulls with surgical brutality. Their beams carved into ships still moored in their construction bays, slicing through armour and igniting volatile cores. The ambush was swift and devastating. Hundreds of nearly finished vessels erupted into flames, their shattered hulls drifting through the void.

Across the battlespace, Paige led the Alpha Squadron's bombers towards the massive complex that powered the Korrathi war effort.

“Alpha Squadron, target the primary structures. Launch on my mark,” her eyes fixed on the glowing trails of the first assault. “Alpha squadron, three, two, one, launch.”

Missiles streaked through the darkness, their trails glowing like angry comets. Explosions rippled through the facility, debris cascading outward like a deadly fireworks display. The glow of the assault lit the underside of her bomber as she steadied her grip on the controls.

The Korrathi defence systems responded with ruthless efficiency, satellites whirring to life, automated turrets swiveling as they unleashed a barrage of return fire. Paige rolled hard, her bomber skimming the edge of a shockwave as a blast detonated just behind her.

"Watch your sixes!" she shouted into the comms, heart pounding as another bolt grazed her wing. "Shit... that was close!" She pitched the ship up hard, thrusters kicking, the cockpit vibrating from the near miss.

On the surface far below, Korrathi citizens gazed upward in stunned disbelief. The giant manufacturing sites they had thought invulnerable were now erupting in flames.

Inside the Korrathi command centers, officers barked orders, scrambling to reestablish formations. Massive ground-based defense arrays roared online, launching volleys of missiles and beams of energy into the sky. The planet's surface lit up with a lattice of firepower, each strike reaching hungrily toward the Venoran fleet.

Stuart's voice crackled over the comms. "Paige, Beta Squadron can handle the facility. Those ground batteries are cutting us apart. We need them down now; our shields won't hold forever."

Paige responded. "Copy, Stuart." Instantly, opening a channel to her squad. "Alpha Squadron, redirect and engage ground targets."

Before her squadron could respond, Stacey's voice cut through the comms, sharp and clear even over the static.

"Paige, the Field Marshal sent us to back you up. Guess he figures you need Liam and me for something. Plus, we brought a few Venoran fighters to keep things interesting."

Alpha Squadron broke off from the facility assault, plunging toward the planet's surface. The Venoran fighters followed, weaving through the chaos with razor-sharp precision.

"All units, focus fire on the defence grid!" Paige commanded, her voice steady but electric with determination. "If they get a counterattack off, our ships are toast, and frankly, I'd rather not end up as space debris today."

Liam chimed in, dry as ever. "That'd definitely ruin my plans for the weekend."

Stacey snorted. "Yeah, well, I was hoping for a quiet night in with a plate of poutine, but I guess that's out."

Energy fire lit up the sky as Alpha Squadron unleashed a relentless assault, the battle for planetary control teetering on the edge of victory or disaster.

The skies over Korrathi 2 were lit up with the intense glow of laser fire and the thunderous roar of blaster cannons. Explosions rocked the landscape as the bombers targeted the ground installations, aiming to cripple the Korrathi defensive capabilities.

As Alpha Squadron strafed the ground targets, Beta Squadron continued to rain destruction on the manufacturing facility. The Korrathi fought back fiercely, their ground defences spewing a relentless barrage of fire. The Venoran pilots, though outnumbered, displayed incredible skill and tenacity, weaving through the hail of projectiles with precision.

On each planet, the Venoran assault hit with ruthless coordination. Orbital strikes hitting the shipyards, fighter wings carving through defense grids, ground teams crippling power relays and command hubs. Cities shook under the barrage as factories erupted in plumes of fire and metal.

The Korrathi fought back with everything they had. Batteries roared to life, scrambling fighters clawed into the sky, and commanders barked frantic orders over collapsing comm channels. But the Venorans moved too quickly, too precisely, each strike timed to exploit the chaos of the last.

One by one, Korrathi strongholds buckled. Their defenses fractured. Their formations broke. Superior numbers didn't matter; the Venorans were already inside their lines, dismantling the system piece by piece.

It was becoming impossible to ignore now that the Korrathi were losing control of their own empire.

Suddenly, aboard the *Excalibur*, a harsh burst of static cut through the comms. Don's voice followed, tight and urgent.

"*Excalibur*, be advised; Korrathi reinforcements inbound. Multiple signatures, closing fast." He didn't wait for acknowledgment.

"They're coming in hot."

The general scanned the monitors surrounding him. He tightened his grip on the armrest of his seat. "Our ships have to finish their mission before the enemy can regroup," he said. "Take *Excalibur* out to meet them. We must give our fleet more time."

Field Marshal Valrik gathered his war council in the command chamber of the Maskar Shipyards. Before them, a massive holo-map flickered, each flashing red marker signalling the loss of yet another Korrathi-controlled world.

Valrik's expression remained stone-hard as streams of data poured in. One name surfaced again and again... *Excalibur*.

"This warship appeared out of nowhere," Valrik muttered, eyes locked on the tactical feed. "The first time we knew of it was when it assisted in the destruction of our fleet attacking Venor."

General Mykos stepped forward, his tone uncharacteristically tense. "Field Marshal... we've uncovered new intelligence. *Excalibur* isn't just another Venoran battleship; it's under Terran command." Silence gripped the chamber. Valrik's gaze sharpened.

"Terrans?" he repeated, voice cold.

"Yes," Mykos continued. "Their military tactics are unlike anything we have encountered previously. There's a substantial contingent of Terran officers embedded throughout the Venoran fleet command structure. These outsiders are steering their operations, elevating their strategy beyond anything we've seen."

Valrik leaned forward, fists clenched. "And we have no intelligence about them?"

"What we have is vague," Mykos admitted. "There's no information on their homeworld. Our first encounter was at Zeph 3, nearly two hundred light-years out. That's the only point of origin we have. Their history in our archives is fragmented, just scattered fragments lifted from Venoran transmissions." What we do know is limited. They have exceptional intelligence, a natural inclination toward aggression, and a history of internal conflict."

"Information about *Excalibur* is limited. It's operated by Terrans. The design doesn't match anything in our database. It operates outside our tracking models. Every interception attempt has failed. Our fastest ships can't match its speed, and our strongest fleets can't contain it. It strikes, withdraws, and leaves only damage behind."

Valrik exhaled sharply, turning to the assembled officers. "Disperse our defences. Lure them in, make them engage where we hold the advantage. We can't afford to stay reactive. *Excalibur* must be trapped."

The officers exchanged uneasy glances. The reality was that *Excalibur* was never where they expected it to be. They had seen what *Excalibur* could do. They had seen fleets vanish under its guns.

But Valrik refused to accept defeat. “This war ends here,” he growled. “We will trap *Excalibur* and crush its allies before it can intervene.”

Suddenly, the chamber doors slid open. A Korrathi officer stepped inside, his voice urgent. “Field Marshal, we've located the Terran ship, *Excalibur*.” It's here with the Venoran fleet attacking the shipyards.

Valrik's eyes darkened. “Launch the drones.”

The response was immediate. Swarms of drone ships surged forward, hunting their target.

“Drones,” the general muttered. “Of course.” He straightened, voice cutting through the tension. “Bring us to intercept speed. All batteries online.”

The crew moved with disciplined urgency. Shield matrices flared to life. Weapon systems locked into firing position. The Excalibur's hull hummed as power surged through its core.

Outside, the stars shifted as a swarm of Korrathi drones burst into view, their formation tightening as they angled toward the *Excalibur*.

“We have incoming drones,” Don warned.

“Then let's give them a welcome,” the general replied.

From *Excalibur's* bays, sleek fighters poured into the fray, engaging the oncoming threat with relentless precision. At first, the battle tilted overwhelmingly in their favour. Drones exploded in rapid succession, torn apart by superior firepower and manoeuvrability.

But the drones were learning.

Each destroyed unit fed data to the swarm, refining tactics, adjusting course, countering every manoeuvre. They began mirroring the pilots' actions with eerie precision, adapting with each passing second. Soon, they were matching the speed and agility of the fighters, their movements nearly indistinguishable.

The tide was shifting in favour of the Korrathi.

The general's mind raced. Had they prepared enough for this assault? Was there something he overlooked?

Nimue materialised beside the General, as if feeling his frustration. Her holographic form exuded an aura of calm authority.

"General, I've analyzed the drone-ship control systems. A targeted burst of graviton particles from my dimensional drive can disable them temporarily. If I route the burst through the four vertical emitters, the effect will intensify. In short, a Graviton Disruptor."

The general hesitated only a breath, weighing the risk against the lives already slipping away.

As she spoke, her voice carried a soothing melody, a stark contrast to the chaos outside. "The graviton particle burst will be powerful enough to mediate the force of gravity. I can disrupt the gravitational fields around the drones, halting their movement and disabling their systems. Our pilots will have a brief window to strike before the drone's reboot. My defensive systems are hardened against graviton interference."

The general looked at Nimue, a spark of hope igniting in his eyes. "Do it, Nimue. Give our pilots the edge they need."

"Signal all ships. Have the Venoran ships move behind the *Excalibur*," the general ordered. Once all ships were in place, the general gave the command to fire the Graviton Disruptor.

As soon as the ships had repositioned behind the Excalibur, the general gave the order. Nimue's form shimmered and then disappeared, her voice echoing through the bridge. "Initiating Graviton Disruptor sequence. Stand by for particle burst."

A deep vibration rolled through Excalibur's hull. Then a silent flash rippled outward, bending the starlight itself.

Across the battlespace, the Korrathi drones froze mid-maneuver. Engines sputtered. Weapons dimmed. Their formations collapsed into stillness, suspended like dead metal drifting in zero gravity. Seizing the opening, *Excalibur's* fighters swept in, destroying the immobilized drones. The Korrathi battleships still hung in space, vulnerable and exposed, when *Excalibur* unleashed its particle beams, slicing through their hulls with brutal precision.

Excalibur was now free to return to the main objective; dismantling the Korrathi's ability to produce warships, one facility at a time.

The general's voice crackled over the communication line. "Alpha and Beta teams, concentrate on their ground defences. I don't want them to be able to use them again."

"Don, destroy what's left of their shipyards," the general ordered.

"Yes, sir," Don responded. "Ok, let's Dance."

A heartbeat later, a particle beam ignited, and in that second, a spear of white-hot energy tore across the void. The battlefield lit up with an eerie, ghostlike glow as the beam carved downward. Don felt the vibration through the deck plates, a deep, resonant hum that thrummed in his bones.

The beam struck the remaining shipyards with surgical precision. Metal skeletons vaporized. Support towers folded inward before erupting in silent bursts of light. In seconds, the once-formidable Korrathi construction rings were nothing more than drifting shards, scorched fragments tumbling aimlessly in the void.

As the last of the Korrathi shipyards were destroyed, assault ships returned to their carriers. A tense silence fell over the battlefield, the kind that comes only after the harsh sounds of war. The general took a deep breath, the weight of the moment pressing heavily on his shoulders.

Sarah turned in her chair to face the general. "Captain Dunne has the same problem with the drones."

The general nodded, his expression resolute. "Understood; all ships continue cleanup." His voice carried the weight of leadership, but an undercurrent of urgency betrayed his calm exterior.

Excalibur moved towards Korrathi 2, its engines humming. Through the viewport, they could see Captain Dunne's ships being swarmed by drones, tiny blips against the vastness of space. A flicker of concern crossed the general's mind, but he quickly pushed it aside. There was no room for doubt now.

Immediately, Nimue came online. "This is *Excalibur*. All Venoran ships fall in behind us."

The Venoran ships manoeuvred into position with practised precision, their hulls gleaming under the distant starlight. "Graviton Disruptor ready, sir," reported one of the crew members, his voice was steady despite the tension in the air.

The general could feel the anticipation building in the room, each second stretching into eternity.

"Fire," ordered the General, his gaze unwavering, as though his stare alone could guide the weapon. The air felt charged with electricity, with every eye monitoring the display screens.

A pulse of energy rippled through space, hitting the drones with pinpoint accuracy. One by one, the drones went dead, their lights flickering out as they drifted lifelessly. A stunned silence filled the bridge before relief broke through in scattered laughter.

In Valrik's private log, a final entry blinked unfinished: *We are losing ships without distress calls. We are losing worlds without resistance. We are losing the narrative. If we do not adapt, the empire will fracture before the enemy reaches our core. I will not... The log cut off.*

"General, tis confirmed," Dunn said, his voice carrying the weight of a hard-fought victory, still edged with the rough lilt of his Irish homeland. "Field Marshal Valrik has gone to meet his maker, when his command station was hit. That's the end of the Korrathi war machine. Tis a grand day for the galaxy, so it is."

Aboard the Venoran warship *Vanguard*, Admiral Varos stood silent for a moment, gazing out at the wreckage of the Maskar Shipyards through the bridge viewport. The stars flickered beyond, untouched by the war that had raged below.

Finally, he exhaled, his voice steady. "Dunn. We paid dearly for this. Too many good men and women were lost along the way. But this day will be remembered."

He turned, eyes sharpening with conviction. "We've shattered their chains. And we'll make damn sure they know it."

Around them, cheers erupted among the officers. The weight of years spent fighting was finally lifted, but the echoes of war would linger in their bones.

"Okay, Captain. Get cleaned up," he said, leaning back as a bit of tension finally eased from his shoulders. A faint, tired smile tugged at him. "I need a drink," he added with a quiet chuckle.

It wasn't long before the battle was over on the planets below. The remaining Korrathi stood in shock, never before having known such a decisive defeat. The destruction of their shipbuilding facilities and ground defences was a blow to their empire, one they would not soon recover from.

Captain Dunne opened a channel to the *Excalibur*. "I think our work is done here. Let's head home." His voice carried a mix of relief and triumph.

One by one, the fleet vanished, jumping to hyperspace, leaving only fading light trails in the void. The stars around the Korrathi held planets returned to their peaceful state, though now marked by the floating remnants of the battle. The Venoran fleet and the *Excalibur* had struck a critical blow against the Korrathi Empire, giving hope to all those who had suffered under their rule.

As the *Excalibur* and its allies moved through hyperspace, the crew reflected on their victory. They knew that the fight was far from over, but for now, they could take pride in their hard-fought success and the difference they had made. The journey back to Venor was filled with quiet conversations, shared stories of heroism, and plans for the battles yet to come.

The members of the High Council sat in the grand chamber, their expressions a tapestry of pride, hope, and the heavy weight of responsibility. Soft light from the overhead fixtures washed across their determined faces. They understood that this new alliance could shift the balance of power across the galaxy, forging a coalition strong enough to stand against the oppressive tide of the Korrathi Empire.

High Chancellor Zara rose, her silver hair cascading over her shoulders. When she spoke, her voice carried unwavering conviction, resonating through the chamber. "Your courage and indomitable spirit embolden us all. We extend our warmest welcome to you and your people as you join our alliance. Together, we will carve a future where no world remains shrouded in tyranny."

As the communications continued, a deep sense of unity settled over the chamber like a warm embrace. Representatives from realms long crushed under Korrathi rule stood side by side, their resolve strengthening with every shared word. They were no longer isolated. They were bound together, a coalition spanning the stars, a luminous testament to their collective strength.

The mood aboard *Excalibur* crackled with energy, each new update on the expanding alliance fueling a deeper sense of momentum. The general, his heart swelling with a blend of pride and optimism, reflected on the long and arduous battles they had fought. Each sacrifice made had not been in vain; the fruits of their labour were finally beginning to blossom.

As *Excalibur* and its fleet readied themselves for the journey back to Venor, a bustling hub where essential supplies awaited, the crew sensed the weight of expectation lifting. They knew their mission was far from complete, yet the solidarity of the newly allied worlds ignited a fierce determination within them. Together, they would defend the galaxy and strive for a brighter tomorrow, one marked by peace and unyielding freedom.

Back on Venor, the High Council had been receiving calls from worlds that had been under the Korrathi Empire's control. With the Korrathi retreat, these worlds, once shrouded in fear, could now see a future filled with hope. They expressed their desire to join Venor in the defence of the galaxy, eager to contribute to the fight.

Holographic communications from a myriad of planets sprang to life in the grand chamber of the High Council, creating a vibrant tapestry of interstellar voices. Leaders from diverse worlds convened in this monumental space, passionately articulating their newfound freedom and unwavering commitment to unite against the looming Korrathi threat. Among them, Commander Rhea of the planet Draconis, a formidable member of a race of insectoids with intricate exoskeletons and strikingly delicate antennae, commanded attention. As she stepped forward, her antennae gracefully swayed as she spoke.

"The Korrathi oppressive grip on our world has finally been shattered," she declared with passion. "Thanks to your timely intervention, our people are no longer shackled by fear; we can finally breathe freely and embrace our destiny. In solidarity, we pledge our vast resources and our fiercest warriors to the defence of the galaxy. Together, we forge an unbreakable alliance, and together, we will emerge stronger than ever."

The High Council members listened intently, their faces reflecting a mix of pride and responsibility. They knew that this alliance could change the balance of power in the galaxy, providing a formidable coalition against the Korrathi Empire.

High Chancellor Zara, a wise and seasoned leader, spoke with conviction. "Your courage and determination inspire us all. We welcome you and your people into our alliance. Together, we will build a future where no world lives under the shadow of oppression."

As the communications continued, a sense of unity and solidarity permeated the chamber. The various worlds that had suffered under Korrathi rule were now coming together, forming a coalition that spanned the galaxy.

The Fall of Drakhaal

Personal account: High Councillor Elara

At last, after all these years, the war has come full circle. We are taking the fight back to the Korrathi homeworld, Drakhaal, not out of vengeance, but to bring an end to the brutality they've unleashed across the stars. What began as survival has become our path to closure. This final step isn't just about victory... it's about closure, justice, and the hope that no one else will suffer as we have.

***

Following the devastating attack on the Korrathi shipbuilding sites, the Venoran High Council convened an emergency session. The grand chamber felt smaller than usual; the air felt thick and heavy. Voices bouncing off its high ceilings. Flickering torches cast restless shadows across the ancient stone walls.

High Councillor Lira stepped into the center of the floor. She didn't shout, but her voice cut right through the noise, steady and sharp. "We will continue to push forward," she said, her eyes bright with conviction. "There are too many worlds out there counting on us to get this right." That bit of truth hung in the air, heavy and quiet, leaving no room for argument.

With many worlds previously under Korrathi rule now rebelling, the Venoran fleet was spread thin across numerous planetary systems, assisting with the uprisings. One by one, other races joined the

Venoran coalition. Admiral Korr from the Corrin free worlds stood before the council. The flickering torchlight cast long shadows across the room, deepening the weight of the moment.

"We, the Corrin, stand with our allies in their fight for freedom," he declared, his voice reaching all corners of the hall. Other races followed, each pledging their solidarity with the Venorans.

The Venoran plan was simple enough on paper, but the risks were obvious. *Excalibur* and her crew, now veterans of more battles than they cared to count, would now include the *Star of Venor*, the newest warship in the fleet. Engineers moved with practiced focus, making final calibrations to the modified energy fields. The air carried a faint trace of lubricant and ozone from the ship's power systems, the kind of background scent that lingered whenever the engines were running hot. Quiet conversations circled around strategy, sacrifice, and, ahead... the unknown.

General Hollins tightened his grip on the railing of the command centre, eyes locked on the data feeds streaming in. "We don't get second chances," he reminded his crew. His voice carried no flourish, just facts. "So, we stay sharp. We stay disciplined. And we execute the plan exactly as briefed." A few heads lifted at that, not out of surprise, but because they needed to hear it said aloud. The room settled, the tension began to dissolve as his words rippled around the room.

The docking bay was alive with movement. Maintenance drones, hurried footsteps, and the hum of activated shields filled the space. No one spoke of fear, but it lingered, a silent spectre between them. The *Excalibur* and the *Star of Venor* were ready, their hulls reflecting the harsh overhead lights.

As the countdown began, the weight of what lay ahead pressed against them all. Failure was not an option.

Captain Dunne was given command of the *Star of Venor*. He had assembled a mixed crew of Venoran and Terran warriors, engineers, and strategists. The ship was equipped with the latest technology, many upgrades that included improved slide drive engines allowing greater distances between jumps, cloaking devices, advanced high-energy weaponry, and reinforced energy shields.

The General called Captain Dunne, his image flickering slightly in the hologram. “Are you ready for departure?”

“Aye, Ready as ever,” he replied, his broad Irish accent infusing his words with a distinct warmth that contrasted with the urgency of the moment. There’s rough ground ahead, sure enough, but spirits are high. Together, we’ll take on whatever’s coming, and we’ll not be found wanting.

Ah, the crew’s fair buzzin’, so they are, full of beans and brimming with excitement for the road ahead. Spirits are high, hearts poundin’ with anticipation. Every last one of ’em’s been walked through the plan, roles drilled to a tee, so they have, we’ll move like clockwork. Smooth as a pint poured right. Our ship's systems are functioning flawlessly, humming away like a contented cat curled up in the sunlight. Soon, we’ll be off to the stars, and with all the luck of the Irish at our back, we are bound for a grand adventure that promises to stretch the limits of our imaginations!”

Smiling, the General responded, “You have the coordinates.”

“Aye, General, the Lorention moon in the Cathan system.”

Moments later, both ships departed the Venoran system, their sleek forms cutting through the void with a graceful, almost predatory elegance. The stars stretched out before them, a vast expanse of the unknown. A mix of determination and apprehension settled over both crews. Their hearts seemed to beat in time with the rhythmic pulse of the engines reverberating through the hull, a constant reminder of the perilous journey ahead.

The Excalibur and the *Star of Venor* slipped into high warp, the fabric of space-time warping and twisting around them. The stars outside the viewports elongated into streaks of light, forming a mesmerizing tunnel of luminescence that danced and shimmered, casting an ethereal glow across each ship. The warp drives gave off a low, steady vibration, nothing dramatic, just the familiar hum of systems running hard. It was the kind of background noise you stopped noticing after a while, a reminder that the ship was doing exactly what it was built to do: propel them through the cosmos at unimaginable speeds. It felt as though the ships themselves were alive, pulsing with energy.

Inside, the crews worked tirelessly, their focused expressions illuminated by the soft, pulsating lights of the control panels. The air was controlled and clean, carrying only the faintest trace of warm circuitry beneath the steady whir of the cooling systems.

"All systems are green for both ships," reported Donald Northey, his fingers gliding over the console with practiced precision, the beeping instruments forming a rhythmic symphony of efficiency.

"Brace for emergence into normal space," called Don, his voice carrying an edge of anticipation.

The moon of Velastra loomed ahead, just as the warp drives began to destabilise, signalling their imminent arrival. The ships vibrated slightly, and the ambient hum shifted in pitch.

There was an air of tension running through the ship, like a tightly coiled spring ready to release. The ships emerged from the tunnel of light, with stars snapping back into their familiar positions with a suddenness that made the crew catch their breath. The viewports revealed the serene yet alien landscape of the Velastra moon, its surface bathed in a soft, silvery glow.

"We're through," confirmed Sarah, her voice filled with a mix of relief and readiness.

The next jump would take them to the Korrathi homeworld, Drakhaal. A planet shrouded in mystery, but believed to be heavily fortified. The crew felt a collective shiver of anticipation.

"This is it," the General said, his voice echoing across the bridge. "Prepare for the final jump." *Excalibur* could have made the flight from Venor to Drakhaal alone through D-Space, but the mission demanded precision. The strike depended on precision; the two ships had to arrive at the exact same moment to keep their cloak signatures aligned and hit the system as one. They slipped into the Drakhaal system without a ripple, their hulls swallowed by the dark as though the void itself had made room for them.

The Korrathi homeworld, Drakhaal, rose ahead, stark, unwelcoming, its surface marked by the weight of ages. The ships eased into a parked orbit, letting the moon's shadow fold over them like a cloak. The world below felt ancient, the kind of world that had watched armadas drift through its skies long before humans learned to name the stars.

The moon's cratered surface filled the viewports, long shadows shifting in the faint starlight. No one expected what appeared next. Massive Korrathi installations lay embedded at the base of the largest craters, hardened structures arranged with cold military precision. For a moment, the bridge fell silent; the crew caught off guard by the scale and readiness of the enemy presence.

"Nimue, fire the graviton disruptor at those installations," the general said.

"Targets locked," Nimue replied. A heartbeat later, a surge of gravitons swept across the moon's surface, a burst of light rippling over the craters and jagged ridges. The control room filled with the low hum of energy and the faint, metallic scent of ionised air. Below, the Korrathi facilities went dark, their lights flickering out one by one.

"Direct hit. All systems are down," Nimue confirmed.

Fighters slipped free from both ships, dark shapes gliding into the void without a sound. They descended on the crippled installations with sharp, deliberate precision. The Korrathi tried to launch automated drones, but the disruptor had left them sluggish and uncoordinated. One by one, their defenses collapsed. Controlled detonations flared across the surface like distant, muted fireworks.

“Targets neutralised,” Stuart reported, eyes fixed on the shifting data streams.

At the same time, stealth teams dropped toward Drakhaal, their shuttles cutting through the atmosphere in near silence. The hulls trembled under the turbulence, but the crews stayed focused, steady, unshaken.

Inside his cockpit, Drowen adjusted his gear, the glow of his console casting sharp shadows across his face. “Team Alpha, in position,” he murmured, his voice blending into the quiet hum of his equipment. The response came instantly, crackling through the comms. “Proceed with the operation.” To his right, two additional icons blinked green on his HUD.

“Alpha Two ready,” Chris reported, his tone clipped and precise.

“Alpha Three standing by,” Owen followed, his voice sounding almost identical.

Their synchronicity was unmistakable, not playful, but seamless coordination of two pilots who had trained together their entire lives. Drowen acknowledged them with a curt nod. “Maintain formation. We move on command.”

Each team moved with precision. Explosions blossomed in the distance as critical installations fell one by one. Communications scrambled, power grids flickered, and defence systems sputtered into failure. The once-structured Korrathi command descended into chaos. Smoke coiled into the sky, choking the horizon as the planet reeled under the assault.

The silence after each blast was heavier than the explosions themselves. The mission was working, but every second brought new risks.

Several cycles earlier, the Korrathi council had received a final message from High Marshal Valrik, sent from the Maskar Shipyards. His words carried urgency.

"They know our weaknesses," he had cautioned. "*Excalibur's* tactics are targeting power grids, communication hubs, and command centres. You must adapt. Hold the capital at all costs."

His message had gone unanswered, either ignored or dismissed as paranoia. But now, as alarms blared across the planet and warships emerged from the haze, the Korrathi realised too late that Valrik had been right.

Defensive turrets whirred to life, launching a desperate counterattack. Fighters scrambled from underground hangars, streaking toward *Excalibur* and the *Star of Venor*. From various locations on the ground, heavy artillery returned fire as plasma blasts tore through the sky. The warships rattled under the onslaught, shields flickering as warning lights flashed across their control panels.

On board the *Star of Venor*, a technician's voice cut through the noise. "Shields at sixty percent!"

Captain Dunne remained composed. "We hold. Redirect power to the forward shields. Maintain our position."

For hours, the battle raged. Desperate to recover, the Korrathi forces worked methodically to reestablish communications and bring failing defence systems back online. But the warships' relentless assault was stripping away their infrastructure piece by piece. Power grids collapsed, plunging entire districts into controlled blackouts as automated safeties tried and failed to reroute load.

Inside the Korrathi command centre, officers moved with clipped precision. No raised voices, no wasted motion. Tactical staff executed protocol sequences, shifting to secondary networks, then a third stage, each one degrading faster than the last. Comms teams cycled through encrypted channels, logging each failure with clinical efficiency. Every attempt to coordinate a counteroffensive had the same result. Their link to the data centre had been broken, nothing in, nothing out.

Field commanders on the surface maintained formation as long as their systems allowed. Units repositioned according to standing doctrine, even as targeting arrays flickered and sensor feeds dissolved into static. Orders were issued, acknowledged, and then lost in the void. The structure held until it simply couldn't.

A brief surge of power rippled through the command centre as emergency generators stabilized. Officers leaned into their stations, recalculating firing solutions, re-establishing tactical overlays. For a moment, the network flickered back to life. Then the next wave hit. Hard. Consoles dimmed. Data streams froze mid-frame. The central command nexus went offline with clinical finality.

With their leadership crippled and their forces scattered, resistance crumbled. The planet was lost.

"We've done it, Captain! The command centre is down!" cheered the Veloran Ensign Rayne, her eyes wide with exhilaration.

"Excellent work, everyone. Stay vigilant. We need to ensure they don't regain control," Captain Dunne replied, his voice firm yet filled with a hint of pride.

The Venoran mission was successful, bringing hope and liberation to countless worlds. *Excalibur's* crew's cheers echoed on each deck as they realised the magnitude of their victory.

The General dispatched a carefully crafted message to the leadership of the Korrathi, a declaration that carried the weight of their current circumstances. The General dispatched a carefully crafted message to the leadership of the Korrathi, a declaration that carried the weight of their current circumstances. His hologram formed in front of the Korrathi leadership. His hands resting at his side as he spoke.

"You've now seen what we're capable of, and the scale of the forces we command. This was a demonstration designed to remove uncertainty. Our position is simple: we will not exterminate your species, provided you maintain peace and refrain from hostile action. This is a pivotal moment for your people, a chance to choose coexistence over conflict. We urge you to consider the path of diplomacy and harmony. You may also contact any remaining vessels still under your command. We assure you that they will be granted safe passage back to Korrathi territory without fear of reprisal. The decision lies in your hands, and we hope you will choose wisely."

The news spread quickly across worlds once controlled by the Korrathi. What was left of the Korrathi fleet was either destroyed or fleeing, their former power broken into scattered pieces. On the worlds they once controlled, long-suppressed populations erupted into long-overdue celebration. For the first time in generations, hope felt real, a promise of freedom carried on the heels of their impending liberation.

A shimmering hologram of General Hollins and Captain Dunne materialised on the bridge of both ships, their figures flickering in the dim light.

"We extend our heartfelt congratulations to each and every one of you. The path we traversed has not been without its toll; we mourn the loss of dear friends along the way. Yet your bravery and determination have opened the way to a better future for countless worlds. We've done what we came to do. Now we return to Venor."

The fleet began its long return home. As the ships emerged from jump and closed on Venor, their hulls showed the wear of the battles they'd survived. Each ship bore the marks of hard fighting. Their crews were returning as veterans who had delivered a decisive blow against the Korrathi threat.

As the fleet eased into orbit, the capital below erupted in celebration. Vessels draped with bright flags drifted through the sky, and crowds on the surface waved and cheered, their voices rising in a single, overwhelming swell. Pride settled quietly in the hearts of the returning crews, the air around them charged with anticipation and the sense that everything had finally shifted.

As the crews materialised, they were met with heroes' welcomes. The Venoran High Council held a grand ceremony in their honor, paying tribute to their courage and sacrifice. Medals were awarded, and stories of their daring mission were shared and tales that would inspire generations to come.

"Captain Dunne, step forward," announced High Councillor Arin, his voice echoing through the grand hall. Dunne's uniform, pristine despite the scars of battle, approached the council with a determined stride.

"For your extraordinary bravery and leadership, we award you the Medal of Valour," Councillor Arin declared, pinning the gleaming medal onto Dunne's chest. The crowd erupted in applause.

"Thank you, High Councillor. This medal belongs to every member of my crew," he replied, his voice filled with pride.

The High Councillor turned to the General. "General George Hollins," he said, the weight of the moment pressing into each syllable. "For unwavering leadership and unshakable resolve in the face of overwhelming odds, we bestow upon you the Star of Dominion."

The applause that followed was deep and sustained, not loud, but filled with reverence.

The general stepped forward with practised precision. Though accustomed to military ceremony, there was a flicker of emotion behind his steel-blue gaze. He gave a crisp nod to the councillor, who turned to face the assembled crowd.

"I accept this not for myself," he said plainly, his voice remained steady, "but for every soldier who never made it home. Their sacrifices are etched into this medal far more deeply than my name." He paused, the room holding its breath in solemn silence.

Then, with a faint smile, the General added, "And if I may be so bold, today marks my ninety-first year, not here but 200 light-years away on Earth."

A hush of reverence swept through the room.

"To those who came before, and to those who came with me. Those early days of tense discovery, and losses, the close calls, and everything else we barely survived... this moment is yours. We made it through. We carry what we lost, and now we move forward."

As the final words echoed through the chamber, Captain Dunne stepped forward, reaching the General's side. He laid a firm hand on his shoulder, more a gesture than words could ever say. The two men clasped hands, steady and sure, a smile passing between them like a signal from old battlefields.

The applause began slowly, then rose like a gathering wave. Not just for medals or milestones, but for the bond, for the unity, that had carried them all across the stars.

The victory over the Korrathi marked a turning point in the galaxy. The Venoran people, once on the brink of despair, now looked to the future with hope and determination. The alliance of liberated worlds grew stronger, united by their shared struggle and triumph.

With the war now over, the crews of both the *Excalibur* and the *Star of Venor* gathered to celebrate their hard-fought victory. *Excalibur's* mess hall was transformed into a festive space, adorned with banners and decorations. The crew members shared stories of bravery and camaraderie, their laughter echoing through the ship.

Parker, relieved that the medical wing was no longer filled with injured crew members, joined the celebration. Jumping onto a platform and shouting above the noise in the room, he raised his glass.

"Listen up, all of you! I want to make a toast. To all of us who haven't received a pension yet, may our retirement plans be as solid as our sense of humour! Here's hoping our future is filled with more than senior discounts and bingo nights. Cheers to the dream of a well-funded retirement!" The room erupted in laughter and cheers.

The Venoran allies, grateful for *Excalibur's* support, brought traditional Venoran delicacies and beverages to the celebration. The two crews mingled, forging new friendships and bonds that would last a lifetime.

As the night wore on, the general addressed the assembled crew members. "Today, we celebrate not just our victory but the unity and strength that brought us here. We have shown that together we can overcome any challenge. Let this be a reminder that peace and cooperation are our greatest weapons."

"Aye, General!" shouted one of the crew members, raising their glass in agreement. The atmosphere was filled with joy and camaraderie.

The celebration stretched long into the night, filled with the rhythmic pulse of music, the joyous movement of dancing, and the hum of heartfelt conversations. Laughter echoed through the halls, weaving a tapestry of camaraderie between the crew of the *Excalibur* and their Venoran allies.

They had done more than secure peace; they had forged a bond that would shape the destiny of both worlds. Battle-worn warriors shared stories beneath the glow of the distant stars. Outside the viewports, the cosmos shimmered, each light a silent witness to the triumph of unity. As the festivities continued, the promise of a new era felt more tangible than ever. One of hope, one of strength, one where the future belonged to all.

End of Report

Summary: Angela Hollins

This report has thrown all of us off balance. The idea that retirees from Earth were taken to another part of the galaxy willingly, no less, rejuvenated and sent off to make discoveries we can barely wrap our heads around... it's a lot to take in.

***

On Earth, far from the galaxy where Stuart's tale had unfolded, the screen froze just as he finished, and the room fell silent. Angela and the others sat transfixed, the soft glow from the monitor lingering in their eyes. The hum of the fans faded into the background, unnoticed in the wake of what they'd just heard.

The air felt heavier, not dramatically, just full. Some people exchanged quiet glances, their eyes reflecting something new. Others stayed in place, letting the moment settle. Excitement didn't rush in; it crept, passing from one person to the next.

Angela drifted away from the table, barely aware she'd stood up. The video was still paused behind her.

She walked to the back wall, where old employee photos were pinned up, most of them faded and curling at the corners. Her eyes moved over them until one picture made her stop; it was of her dad.

Young, laughing, sitting behind a drum kit as if he were born to be there. A tiny 1970s bar band, the kind of thing he used to joke about but never really talked much about.

The sight warmed her, drawing her a little closer without her even thinking about it.

There he was. Stuart, guitar slung low, smiling like he didn't have a single worry in the world.

She didn't feel shock, not after the video. Seeing him look exactly the same as he does now had already settled the question of his age. But this was different.

Seeing him standing next to her father, decades before she was even born, hit her in a quieter, more personal way. It was the strange, steady feeling of a puzzle piece finally clicking into place.

She touched the edge of the photo, her fingers hovering over the image of the young guitarist.

He'd lived through so much. So many years, so many places. And somehow, one of those years had crossed paths with her family long before she was born.

Angela stepped back and glanced toward the paused video. Stuart's face stared out from the screen, caught mid-motion.

For the first time, she didn't see a mystery. She saw a man who had been carrying centuries of history... and who had been closer to her life than she ever realized.

The screen sprang to life again, revealing a man who called himself Dr. Parker Brooks. He looked young, maybe early thirties, but his voice carried the weight of someone who'd seen more than most.

He gestured to a list of names behind him, each one a reminder of those who had joined him on this journey. The room leaned in, drawn to his calm presence.

"These aren't just names," Parker said, his hand sweeping lightly across the list behind him. "They're the people who stood with me when everything else fell apart. Every decision I've made, every step I've taken has been because they believed we could make it this far."

He lowered his hand, meeting the eyes of the room with quiet resolve.

Parker drew a slow breath before he spoke. "And that, my friends, brings us to where we are today." He paused, letting the words settle.

"We've been given something rare, something I've come to call a 'Second Horizon'. A new beginning in a part of the galaxy none of us expected to see. Many of us are veterans, men and women who thought our stories were nearly finished. Yet here we are, joined by explorers and pioneers who stepped into the unknown before us. They opened the way. Now it's our turn to carry it forward."

The room was quiet, but not still. His words were sinking in.

"Everyone here is safe. Our hosts, the Venorans, have welcomed us with a generosity that's hard to describe. They've asked us to stay, to continue the work we've started. Earth will always be home, but it feels distant now, not in miles, but in meaning. To go back would be to leave so much unfinished. We have the tools, the people, and the ship to keep going."

The screen flickered slightly, casting light across the room. The group watched closely, taking in every detail from his expression, the tone of his voice, to the quiet certainty behind his words.

"I can't say if, or when we'll return," he said. "Our journey has only just begun. Aboard the *Excalibur*, we'll travel deeper into the stars and uncover whatever waits beyond. And the Venorans have pledged to safeguard Earth from any threat."

Then, a small smile broke across his face. "And speaking of discoveries," he added, "some of us have found love in unexpected places. Yes, inter-species marriages. What once seemed the realm of fantasy is now real, and celebrations are already being planned."

His voice lifted slightly. "Our time here isn't over. The next chapter begins now. There will be challenges, and there will be triumphs... hopefully, more triumphs. This isn't goodbye; it's just a pause before we head back into the unknown."

"To contact the *Excalibur*, send a Slide Space pulse. Once the signal stabilizes, our receiver will lock onto your signature and open a direct channel. Keep messages brief. Slide Space handles short bursts best. Instructions will be sent separately for setup."

"Until we meet again... Dr. Parker Brooks, out."

The screen faded to black, but the energy in the room remained. Whispers filled the air, and thoughtful glances were exchanged. Some leaned forward, others leaned back, but all wore the same expression: stunned, suspended between disbelief and awe.

Whatever doubts had lingered were gone now. For most in that room, the question had been answered. Earth was not alone.

Glossary of Names

Human

Angela Fitzpatrick - Scholar at William Jane University. Daughter of Professor Roger Fitzpatrick (deceased), leader of the first contact committee with the Venorans.

Ann - Nurse at Stuart Thomson's retirement home.

David Robinson (84) - Engineering scientist. Birthplace Australia. Specialist in defence technology and power systems.

Donald Northey (82) - Former Royal Marine sharpshooter. Birthplace England. Weapons technician with tactical expertise.

Dr. Parker Brooks (85) - Navy Chief Surgeon; head of Excalibur's medical wing.

George Hollins (90) - General, Royal Marines. Birthplace England. Military tactician and leader of the Veterans aboard the Excalibur.

James Dunne (97) - Captain in the Venoran fleet. Birthplace Ireland.

Kayla Shaw (77) - Specialist in infiltration and combat. Birthplace America. Skilled in ancient languages and writings.

Liam Carter (86) - Lieutenant, Air Force pilot. Birthplace Ireland. Venoran-trained pilot.

Paige Mitchelmore (96) - Air Force Lieutenant Colonel. Birthplace Canada. Scientist, specializing in reverse-engineering alien technology.

Sarah Kane (84) - Security operations specialist. Birthplace America. Weapons and defence strategist.

Stacey Morgan (91) - Lieutenant, Air Force pilot. Birthplace Canada. Venoran-trained pilot.

Stuart Thomson (89) - Lieutenant, Air Force pilot. Birthplace England. Excalibur pilot specializing in aerial combat.

Twins - Owen & Chris Williams (83) - Marines. Birthplace Canada. Special operations, recruited by General Hollins.

Venoran

Dr. Trill - Venoran physician; expert in cellular regeneration and anti-aging therapies.

Drowen - Venoran planetary guide and pilot.

Elara - Member of the Venoran High Council.

Elta - Venoran Quadrant Leader and High Council member; oversees planet Helia.

Gall - Captain of *Arcadia*; leader of Venorans on Earth.

Lielon - Venoran administrator of the Helia colony, 150 years prior.

Patrasia - Venoran planetary liaison between Venorans on Earth and global governments

Korrathi

Field Marshal Valrik - Korrathi leader. Commander of all military fleets and planetary stations.

General Mykos - Korrathi second-in-command of military fleets.

Other

Aurelia - Artificial intelligence assigned to the Venoran ship *Arcadia*. Appears as a Venoran female hologram.

Nimue (NIM-oo-ay) - Artificial intelligence assigned to Excalibur. Oversees ship functions from navigation to security. Appears as a human female hologram.

Ralek - Commander from Planet Draconis. Led the assault on Prielet.

Skora - Race Relkara, from Relentus Prime; speaker for the reptilian race on Prielet.

Solara Sorel - On Earth, we called them the Anunnaki. Home planet Anunn. Solara's people called themselves the Nakkari. Solara, rescued from stasis after 4,500 years.

Navigator's Lexicon

Adaptive Resonance Fields - Dynamic energy layers woven through the shield. Unlike static barriers, these fields shift frequency and strength continuously, guided by node feedback. The resonance adapts to gravitational anomalies, creating a barrier that breathes with the planet's needs.

Containment Units - Specialized chambers engineered to confine micro black holes. Each unit is independently powered to prevent uncontrolled growth. The system maintains equilibrium by cycling new black holes while older ones vanish, ensuring a constant mass balance.

Cycle - Venoran equivalent of an Earth day.

Dimensional Compass - Allows for accurate navigation through dimensional space into normal space.

Dimensional Space - Dr David Robinson discovered that space itself might have hidden layers. A deeper structure beyond ordinary perception. He called it Dimensional Space, or D-space.

Draconis Raiders - A race of raiders in D-Space locked in conflict with Skoras people on Prielet. Driven by conquest, they seek to expand their empire by seizing resources and advanced technologies from other worlds. (See also Ralek, Commander)

Drakhaal - Homeworld of the Korrathi race. A hostile species committed to eliminating any race that shows signs of technological advancement, ensuring its dominance across civilisations.

Event Horizon - The invisible boundary around a black hole where the escape velocity exceeds the speed of light. Crossing it means no return. Relentus Prime's Planet Engines were designed to keep their world balanced just beyond this threshold.

HUD - Heads Up Display. A transparent display that presents data directly in the user's line of sight.

Kinetic Pulse - A high-energy explosive burst. Directs a force at a target to move, deflect, or destabilise a large object.

Phase Detachment Protocol - The engine creates a bubble that cancels out mass, letting the ship slide through different layers of space by tuning its vibrations to match higher dimensions.

Planet Engines - Massive engines embedded deep within a planet's mantle. Built to move entire worlds across interstellar space, they stabilize the orbital paths around the black hole's gravity well.

Prielet - Planet in D-Space - Reptilian creators of *Excalibur*, dwelling in D-Space for over a millennium. Discovers of Dimensional Fold technology, giving them the ability to traverse galaxies in moments.

Pulse Drift - Temporal Lag: A delay or distortion in time perception as different dimensions operate on slightly offset timelines.

Quantum-brane Manipulator - Changes *Excalibur*'s vibration pattern to sync with invisible layers of higher-dimensional space, letting it interact with realities beyond the ship's current location.

Quantum Tunnelling - *Excalibur*'s propulsion harnesses quantum tunnelling to pierce dimensional barriers. For a brief moment, the ship activates a state where multiple quantum possibilities overlap. (Being in several places at once). This lets it slip past the usual rules of physics and move in ways that would normally be impossible.

Relentus Prime - Relentus. An ancient planet discovered in a large void in space, orbiting an artificial black hole. Original home of a reptilian race now living in Dimensional Space.

Sensory Nodes - Anchor points within the adaptive shield lattice. Each node acts as both generator and sensor, recalibrating in real time to counter gravitational shifts. The lattice behaves like a living organism. Nodes communicate, redistribute energy, and adapt under stress. Without them, the shield would collapse within seconds.

Ships: *Arcadia*. The Venoran Galaxy-Class spaceship uses Slide Drive technology, creating short-lived wormholes for galactic travel.

Excalibur. Powerful alien warship surpassing Venoran technology. Its unique Trans-Dimensional engine enables inter-dimensional travel.

Star of Venor. Next-generation Venoran starship. Mixed crew of Venoran and Terrans. Equipped with the latest Venoran technology.

Vanguard. Venoran flagship.

Singularity - A manufactured tear in reality produced by the D-shift engine. A point in spacetime where gravity, density, or curvature becomes infinite, and the known laws of physics break down.

Spectral Drift - Refers to the Doppler-induced colour shift across the spectrum.

Trans-Dimensional Engine - *Excalibur's* Trans-Dimensional Engine. Used for interdimensional travel beyond normal space.

Venor - The home planet of the Venoran people. Lifespan equivalent to 850 Earth years.

Venor Retirement Home - A place where veterans choose whether to rise to a new chapter in their lives, willing to enter the Venoran program.

Zeph 3 - Venoran training planet. Preparing veterans for life in space.

About the Author

David was born in Plymouth, England, and spent his early years wandering the coastlines of Devon and Cornwall. He later moved to London before eventually settling in Toronto, Canada.

After retiring, he decided to pursue a long-held goal of writing a science fiction novel. *Excalibur: The Second Horizon* is the result of that effort and marks his first step into the genre.

www.ingramcontent.com/pod-product-compliance
Lightning Source LLC
LaVergne TN
LVHW050928080826
845145LV00001B/246